CLIMBING PATRICK'S MOUNTAIN

CLIMBING PATRICK'S MOUNTAIN

Des Kennedy

To Terri,

with memories of Ireland,

Des K

Library and Archives Canada Cataloguing in Publication
Kennedy, Des
Climbing Patrick's mountain : a novel / Des Kennedy.

ISBN 978-1-897142-39-4

I. Title.

PS8571.E6274C65 2009   C813'.54   C2009-902908-1

Cover image: iconogenic, istockphoto.com
Author photo: Richard Porter
Copyeditor: Heather Sangster, Strong Finish

 Canadian Heritage Patrimoine canadien   BRITISH COLUMBIA ARTS COUNCIL   Canada Council for the Arts Conseil des Arts du Canada

Brindle & Glass is pleased to acknowledge the financial support for its publishing program from the Government of Canada through the Book Publishing Industry Development Program (BPIDP), Canada Council for the Arts, and the province of British Columbia through the British Columbia Arts Council and the Book Publishing Tax Credit.

Mixed Sources
Cert no. SW-COC-001271
© 1996 FSC
FSC

The interior pages of this book have been printed on 100% post-consumer recycled paper, processed chlorine free, and printed with vegetable-based inks.

Brindle & Glass Publishing
www.brindleandglass.com

1 2 3 4 5 12 11 10 09

PRINTED AND BOUND IN CANADA

Only in a house where one has learnt to be lonely does one have this solicitude for things. One's relation to them, the daily seeing or touching, begins to become love, and to lay one open to pain.

▨ Elizabeth Bowen

Most of them trying to sell you some rubbish you didn't need or want. Charities on the beg. Opinion surveys. Bugger them all.

"Ah, well, we, of course, have most certainly heard of you."

"Have you now?" Something in Gallagher roused like an awakening old guard dog.

"Indeed. Well, of course, your work with roses is widely recognized."

"You're a rose fancier then, are you?" Gallagher was never above reacting to a bit of flattery. He gazed out through the kitchen window at the perfectly blue summer sky.

"Only at a distance, I'm afraid. Too busy with the business of business most of the time, you know how it is."

"Oh sure." Anxious to get back to his hybridizing, Gallagher shuffled his feet and prepared to cut the conversation short.

"But we do know of your work. Your introductions." There was a kind of smirking, gelatinous self-satisfaction in how this fellow said things.

"You do."

"Certainly. Most ingenious. And the names, Mr. Gal Panties' and all the rest, how outrageously *pour rire*." The caller chuckled as though the two of them were old pals sharing a familiar joke. Gallagher didn't say anything, partly because he didn't know what the French term meant. There was a moment's awkward silence. "Yes, I saw it all mentioned in your dossier," Berenice continued. "Very droll, Mr. Gallagher, extremely droll."

"My dossier?" Who the hell had compiled a dossier on him? Gallagher watched a sowbug emerge from under his dirty breakfast dishes and crawl methodically across the Formica kitchen countertop. As it drew close, it paused, a miniature armadillo, its tiny antennae flicking the air for information.

"Only what's in the public record, I assure you, sir. Nothing confidential, no unseemly prying." Apparently determined to ingratiate himself, Berenice plowed forward single-mindedly. All Gallagher wanted was to get rid of him. "Your introductions. Your Rose Society awards. That recent profile in *Knowing Growing* magazine."

Gallagher felt a stab of resentment at being reminded of the idiotic story that had appeared recently in a leading gardening magazine.

The young writer the magazine had sent out to interview him had been pleasingly deferential in her manner, and Gallagher had been less guarded in his comments than he should have been. When it finally appeared, along with gorgeous photos of his roses, the piece had depicted him as a horticultural idiot savant and had made repeated smirking criticisms of the names he gave his roses. He watched the sowbug retreating towards the sugar bowl, reached out with his forefinger and firmly squashed it. "Well, the less said about that pack of rubbish the better," he muttered. "I tell you, the horseshit that finds its way into print these days, it's enough to make you gag."

"Indeed it is." Berenice cleared his throat to indicate that the preliminaries were at an end. "Mr. Gallagher, I have a proposition I should like to place before you . . ."

"A proposition? Sorry, squire, I'm holdin' out for Pamela."

"Ha. Ha. Very funny." Berenice's laugh had no laughter in it. "I like that—a quick wit, a clever quip. Does wonders in our business. But no, sir, I certainly wouldn't want to come between you and Ms. Anderson. Rather, I'm speaking of a business proposition and one I think you'll find most attractive."

"Not interested," Gallagher said abruptly. "Goodbye." He had no nose for business and distrusted those who did. Liars and thieves, most of them. But, oh, they could talk, couldn't they? Charm the pants off you with their sincerity, the whole time scheming how to get their hands on your money.

"Hold on, Mr. Gallagher." The intruder snagged him before he could hang up. "Believe me, I'm not attempting to sell you anything whatsoever."

"Oh, no, of course not."

"Mr. Gallagher," Berenice continued, obviously not to be shaken off by sarcasm, "I would like you to go to Ireland."

"What the hell would I want with goin' to Ireland? I'm happy enough where I am. More than happy." And a damned sight happier than I'd be getting within a hundred miles of dirty old Ireland, he thought to himself. By now he'd had enough of this fool intrusion. "Goodbye, sir, and best of luck." Gallagher replaced the receiver on the wall, shaking his head at the dimwits on the loose out there. He flicked

4

the remains of the sowbug into his palm and then into a compost bucket under his sink. "I would like you to go to Ireland," he mimicked Berenice's fruity tone as he pushed open the door and re-entered the greenhouse. "Feckin' Ireland, of all places."

He'd no sooner got back to his workbench than the phone rang again. "Oh, bugger it," he muttered, suspecting it was the same cracker back again, and it was.

"Now, look here," he growled, prepared to be rude if rudeness was called for.

"Mr. Gallagher, let me explain, *please*. I run a travel company . . ."

"Aye, you said that already."

"Part of our business—a significant part of our business—involves organizing group tours of gardens overseas. France, England, Ireland."

"Squire, you're boring the living shite outta me here, all right?"

"Hold on, Mr. Gallagher! I'm not trying to *sell* you on a tour. I'm inviting you to *lead* one!"

"To what?"

"To lead the tour. Be the tour director."

"You must be daft." Gallagher caught sight of himself in a little mirror hanging on the kitchen wall. He made a poncey face at himself, a mockery of the perfect, tidy tour director.

"Far from it, Mr. Gallagher, far from it. We have an upcoming tour all set. A number of important clients are included. We shall be visiting some of Ireland's most distinguished gardens, both public and private, meeting and talking with the gardeners, several of them quite eminent, much like yourself. All that is lacking at the moment is a qualified tour director."

"And you're mistaking me for a qualified tour director?"

"You must admit that you are acclaimed within the Canadian gardening community." Berenice's voice dripped with honeyed reasonableness. Gallagher shifted the receiver to his other ear and leaned against the wall. Out through the living room window he noticed the first tiny hints of white beginning to show on the massive Kifsgate rose he'd trained up over a dead maple tree.

"I don't know bugger all about tour groups, and I don't want to."

"Of course you don't. And that's the beauty of the thing, don't

5

you see? Nothing stale and ordinary with you. None of the same old, same old. A fresh perspective. An original voice. Something entirely new, different, exciting. Perhaps just the least bit abrasive. And as to authenticity—well! The clients will love it, I'm convinced of that, Mr. Gallagher."

"I'm pleased you are, because I'm not. Goodbye, Mr. er . . ." Again Gallagher went to hang up.

"There's money in it for you!"

"Money?" Gallagher's magic word. With scarcely a penny to his name, he had no skill with money at all; the closest he came to a business plan was to buy a lottery ticket every week and dream of some day hitting the jackpot. So Berenice's siren song snagged Gallagher easy as jigging for rock cod.

"Yes indeed. A generous honorarium plus all expenses paid."

"And what am I expected to do for this generous honorarium?" He reached inside the neck of his shirt and scratched an itchy spot.

"That's the beauty of it, Mr. Gallagher, the true beauty of it. You scarcely have to lift a finger. Everything's already arranged—the hotel, meals, the coach, and there's a local tour guide who looks after all the details. You just go along on the tour, chat up the clients every once in a while. Be a bit of a presence, you know."

"A presence?" Again he mugged to himself in the mirror.

"Your expertise with roses. Your Irish background."

"You know about that too?"

"Only that you were born and raised in Ireland. County Cork, if I'm not mistaken."

"And left the poxy place twenty years ago and never went back and have no desire to go back, with or without a tour group in tow." He was wondering just how much this fellow really did know about his background, how thick was his dossier. You couldn't be too careful nowadays, with dark forces at work everywhere, spies forever prying into private places. One thing was clear: money or no, Gallagher wasn't getting into any Ireland game. "Sorry, squire, you'd best find someone else."

"Mr. Gallagher, let me be completely frank with you." Gallagher's gaze wandered out through the kitchen window to the gardens beyond, where sunlight was playing green and gold hopscotch in the glossy foliage. "I confess I find myself in something of a tight spot at the moment. We've promoted this tour for several months and the response has been excellent, even though the cost is considerable. We've booked fifteen clients, which was our objective. Intimacy, you know; intimacy's everything in this sort of excursion."

"Intimacy." Ireland and intimacy both. Sweet Jesus. He'd just as soon have pestilence and famine. He had no intimacy in his life, nor did he desire any, beyond affection for his home and his roses, and idle fantasies about the celebrated beauties after whom he named them.

"The tour begins in less than two weeks' time, but our tour director has backed out at the last moment."

"And you can't find a replacement?"

"Not for Stephen Aubrey. He's a very hard man to replace."

"Aubrey?" This caught Gallagher's attention for sure.

"Yes, we sold the tour on the strength of his name. The women came flocking in, of course—the chance to spend a week strolling through fine Irish gardens with the great man himself. It was perfect!"

"But?"

"He called me yesterday. A family crisis is all he would say."

Family crisis, my arse, thought Gallagher. Old Aubrey must be in the middle of another messy break-up with his latest teenage lover.

"We have no contract with him," Berenice said. "I can't force him to go against his will. But neither can I just replace him with some Joe Schmoe. The clients would riot. Or, worse still, cancel. There's a lot of money already tied up in airfare and hotels and everything else. I desperately need a VIP, Mr. Gallagher, and your name is the one that keeps coming up."

"After you'd tried everyone else, I'll bet."

"My dear sir . . ." Gallagher had hit the nail smack on the head.

"Spare the blarney, squire. I'm no Stephen Aubrey."

"Well, who is? No, with all due respect, we can't hope to duplicate his sophisticated charm, his charisma, his star power. It was an absolute coup that we booked him in the first place and a bitter disappointment that he's now unable to fulfill his obligations, I'll be perfectly honest about that. But all is not lost. I'm convinced some good can still come of this because you, sir, can bring something else entirely to the table."

"Yeah, a couple of pints of Guinness, after which I'd be tellin' your precious clients to go take a piss in the Grand Canal."

"Ha Ha." Again the mirthless laugh. "No, I don't believe that for a minute, Mr. Gallagher. It's true you have a certain . . . what? . . . edginess about you."

"Edginess, you call it?" Gallagher was noticing how many scratches and stains there were on his countertop. The whole thing should be ripped out and replaced, but where would you stop? The whole bloody kitchen should be ripped out and replaced. "No, I just don't like people very much, plain and simple."

"Mr. Gallagher, from everything I've read and everything I've been told . . ."

"Told by who?"

"Well, by Stephen Aubrey, among others."

"Aubrey? What did he have to say?" Gallagher had never seen eye to eye with that old queen, but he knew full well the high regard in which *maestro* Aubrey was held.

"He recommended you."

"Aubrey recommended me?" Gallagher watched as an enormous jetliner ascended into the blue sky and banked westwards, bound out across the Pacific.

"Unequivocally. Said he could think of no finer replacement."

"He was pullin' your wanker, squire."

"I don't believe so. Mr. Aubrey is as committed to the success of this tour as everyone else here at Berenice Travel."

"What exactly did he say?" Fool, Gallagher thought to himself, fool to even care what Lord Aubrey All-Sorts had to say about him.

"He said—let me recall his precise words—that Mr. Gallagher possesses an authenticity perfectly attuned to the Irish experience."

"That's what he said?"

"Word for word."

Gallagher heard the clop! clop! of horses' hooves on the roadway and remembered he should be getting a load of fresh manure delivered this week. "Nah, he was really putting one over on you. Authenticity, hah!" But he was secretly gratified to hear of old Aubrey singing his praises.

"How much?" Gallagher asked bluntly.

"I beg your pardon?"

"How much are you offering for my authentic services?" Gallagher couldn't believe that he was even asking, as though he might actually agree to this nonsense if the price was right. Somebody else, not himself, seemed to be taking over the negotiations, some quick-thinking agent accustomed to cutting deals and putting packages together.

"Suppose we were to say, oh, three hundred a day times seven days, that would come out to a very tidy twenty-one hundred dollars."

"Three hundred a day." Gallagher sounded as though he'd been insulted by so paltry a sum although he'd never earned anything close to three hundred a day in his life. "Twenty-one hundred. For a week's work."

"Hardly work, Mr. Gallagher. Almost a vacation."

"Oh, aye. Plus a long flight there and a long flight home."

"All expenses paid."

"That's nine days altogether. Jet lag. Customs officers. Lost luggage. Maybe catching some crapulous disease on the plane. For a measly three hundred a day." Gallagher smacked his lips, the shrewd negotiator at work. "Really now, you'd have to admit it's a bit of a pittance for chaperoning a bunch of old ladies around day after day. The responsibility and all."

"Ah, but hold on there, Mr. Gallagher," Berenice hopped in deftly. "We're not talking a group of old ladies, far from it." There was a smirch of lewdness in his tone.

"What then?"

"A mixed group. Several seniors, naturally. But some younger folks as well."

"Is that so?"

"Oh, yes. Several young ladies. And, if you'll excuse my being just the tiniest bit indiscreet, several very attractive young ladies." Cognizant of Gallagher's penchant for naming his roses after famously beautiful women, Berenice obviously had calculated where resistance might most easily be breached.

"You're spinnin' a yarn here, aren't you?"

"Not in the least. Unless I'm very much mistaken, this is a group you'll greatly enjoy being a part of."

"Aye, maybe so." Gallagher had not enjoyed being part of any group anywhere ever. "Still and all . . ." The money fluttered through his imagination like a flock of brilliant cockatoos. Two thousand bucks would come in handy right enough. Fix the old place up a bit, maybe buy a few new tools for the garden. But Ireland. Bloody Ireland. No, not in a million years. "You wouldn't have another tour you need a hand with would you?"

"What do you mean?"

"Oh, like say Spain or Italy or one of them sort of places. I could maybe see my way clear to leading a group in that direction, like." Sunlight was pouring into the kitchen now, lighting up dusty cobwebs in every corner. A litter of leaf bits and other scraps lay across the worn linoleum floor.

"No, no. Ireland's the issue here. And unless I'm very much mistaken, you're the man for Ireland."

"But still and all, it's a tremendous lot of aggravation for a couple of hundred a day. Nah, all things considered, I think not."

"A four-star Dublin hotel." For the first time there was a note of impatience, almost irritability, in Berenice's tone. "All meals included."

"And drinks?"

"No, I'm afraid not."

"Ah, best forget it then."

"Mr. Gallagher, you must understand there are certain budgetary constraints within which I'm obliged to operate."

He couldn't tell if Berenice was implying he was a chronic boozer. But it was near enough to an insult to get him standing on his dignity. "Well, I'll tell you a little something," he announced, puffing himself up like the lord of the manor. "I'm not a feller's easily bought, see? I've got my principles and I've got my responsibilities, and I'm not prepared to sacrifice them for any amount of money, no matter what Stephen Aubrey or anyone else may have told you."

"But . . ."

"Goodbye, sir, and best of luck to you." Gallagher peremptorily returned the receiver to its cradle on the wall. Ireland. Jesus. For just the briefest moment he'd been tempted by the lure of easy money, he couldn't deny it. And, God knows, he could have put the cash to good use, limping along as he was on next to nothing. Berenice's flattery. Aubrey's praise. For a minute or two he'd almost been fool enough to take the proposition seriously. Now he was amazed at his own credulity, however fleeting. Nothing good awaited him in Ireland and no amount of money could in a rational moment bribe him into returning there. He had left unfinished business in the Old Country, unpaid debts and outstanding obligations. Betrayals too, and among those he had betrayed were people for whom revenge was a way of life. He'd spent twenty years eluding the shadows of his past and was not about to face them now. Why should he? His current situation offered him all he required: a little house on a generous piece of land in the semi-rural enclave of Southlands in Vancouver, close by the Fraser River. This was one of the original Southlands properties, dating back to the 1940s, when land was cheap and the city far away. It was the family home of an elderly gentleman who'd grown up here, then gone on to become one of Vancouver's wealthiest men. He was more benefactor than landlord, and Gallagher was afforded all the time in the world to devote to his one true passion, the propagation of plants that brought new and extraordinary forms of beauty into the world. Perfectly satisfied with where he was and what he did, why the hell would he want to go traipsing off to Ireland, or anywhere else for that matter?

Shaking his head at the folly of humankind, he stepped from his kitchen back into the greenhouse, cursing the battered door that scraped along the floor every time it was opened. The greenhouse was as airy and expansive as the attached house was pokey, and the rows of carefully labelled and arranged pots bore witness to far greater attention to detail than did the domestic slovenliness indoors. Large containers of potting soil, sand, and starter mix squatted under the lengthy plank bench, and an array of polished pruning tools hung from hooks above it. He approached the bench and picked up the little rose bush with its head still in its bag. "Some wanker on the phone," he said to it, "wanting me to leave you all alone. It's nothing but money these days, and every grubby little pisser pushing to the front to see who can grab the most of it." Having resisted temptation, he could now indulge in a bit of righteousness at the venality of others. He replaced the rose on the bench. It was one he'd developed several years previously and named

Michelle's Mischief, after Michelle Pfeiffer, one of his favourites. "Don't you worry, my beauty, I'll not leave you in the lurch. Tomorrow will be your grand day. We'll make love, you and me, when the sun shines down on us tomorrow."

■ TWO ■

BACK AT his workbench the following afternoon, Gallagher removed the polythene hood from the naked rose. He examined the head closely, observing how its protruding stigmas showed a gleaming stickiness that had not been there the day before. If a plant could be said to manifest sexual craving, surely these protuberant stigmas were doing so. They demanded caressing, brazenly exposed themselves for hot, sticky rubbing. Gallagher licked his puckered lips in anticipation. "Oh, I'd say you're receptive enough all right, aren't you, Michelle, my beauty? Now let me go find you a partner as will give you satisfaction." Tenderly he replaced the bag to prevent any insects from slipping in with fragments of rogue pollen while his back was turned, took a pair of secateurs from their hook on the wall, and stepped out of the glass house into his garden.

He paused for a moment on the rough stone patio, with the house and greenhouse behind him and the main garden spreading slightly downhill to the south and west, bordered by a line of young conifers beyond which lay an exclusive golf and country club. As he stood there, a cascade of floral beauty surged forward and broke over him in aromatic waves. An outrageous spectacle of massed blooming roses—ramblers and climbers, hybrid perpetuals, floribundas and polyantha pompons, centifolias, damasks, Bourbons and Portlands, cumulus upwellings of roses of every colour and complexion. There was no discernible plan to their placement by virtue of either size or colour; hulking ramblers loomed above petite shrubs, pillars and miniatures squeezed together as though in a crowded elevator. Brassy magentas blared alongside dainty pinks, blazing scarlets contrasted with luminous yellows. Nor was any other species to be seen—no grey-leafed mulleins nor Stachys nor lavenders stood as foil to the profligacy of roses, no dark green yews lent the strength of their sobriety to the roseate wantonness. Gallagher stood before them as though conducting a thunderous symphony of scent and colour. "My beauties!" he cried aloud, his arms spread wide, an ecstatic smile lighting up his face. Wagging his head from the unconditional splendour of it all, and reflecting how the eminent Stephen Aubrey had never come remotely close to producing so magnificent a show, he made his way over to a rose shrub that was massed with rich blooms of sullen velvet petals.

"Well, Nicole," he said, cupping one of the sumptuous flowers in his hand, "I've come for you at last." It was another of his own hybrids, introduced a few years previous and named Nicole's Knickers for Nicole Kidman. His penchant for naming his introductions after various body parts and items of underwear belonging to glamorous women, while peculiar, was not entirely singular amid the curious subculture of plant breeders. Others, for example, had produced variegated hostas named Teeny Weeny Bikini, Striptease, and Hanky Panky, a dahlia called Boy Joy, the floribunda rose Sexy Rexy, and the classic daylily Crotchless Panties. All of these reflected an aesthetic not dissimilar to his own. Over the years there'd been sundry attempts by nursery people and suppliers to convince him to change his names. They were an impediment to sales, the retailers claimed, frequently an embarrassment. How many rose fanciers of sophisticated taste would desire in their gardens something, no matter how lovely, called Nicole's Knickers? If the industry hotshots were to have their way, they'd slap on some innocuous name and replicate his roses by the thousands for mass distribution through big-box stores. But they would not have their way. Not with Gallagher. He was impervious to persuasion. They were his roses and he'd name them what he damn well pleased. He would not, could not, see that the names might be offensive to some. Above all, he was fiercely independent, readily offended by those who criticized his work, and tenacious in the holding of grudges. Never forget; never forgive. The Irishman's credo. In this regard he had been perfectly honest with that fool of a travel agent. His knack for insulting and offending people would make him the worst imaginable choice for leading a tour group. It's why he saw as little of people as possible, being perfectly content to live alone, as he had all his adult life.

Still, the rose he now held in his hand was truly outstanding. Its perfume was sublime and its period of flowering protracted. After blooming, its spent blossoms would drop cleanly and its hips in autumn were attractively large and a bright coppery red. He'd made a penny or two all right from the lovely Nicole's Knickers. A cross between it and the equally appealing Michelle's Mischief might well produce another winner. He snipped the stem beneath the bloom in his hand and hurried back to the greenhouse. At the bench he uncovered the stripped seed parent and then he pulled the petals of Nicole's Knickers back, as the actor herself might draw her long hair behind her head, and pinched them against the stem with thumb and forefinger so that her anthers were pushed prominently forward. "You'll be the pollen parent, sure," he murmured to her. "And now, my sweethearts, let's make love." With utmost delicacy he touched Nicole's exposed anthers with the tip of his little finger and then ever-so-gently rubbed the fingertip against Michelle's sticky stigmas. "Ah," he sighed breathily at the sensuous touch that marked the moment of pollen transference. "Ah! Ah!" as though he himself was achieving orgasm. He paused, eyes closed. A sudden shudder raced down his spine like a spider. And then it was done.

His part in the process was over, at least for the present. With luck, the pollen grains would germinate and pollen tubes would grow down into the hidden depths of the receptacle to fertilize an ovum and create an embryo. Ripening and after-ripening of the seed pod would last for several months; then he would sow the seeds; their germination might take up to a year. Finally, with luck and luck alone, for the odds were long against it and the opportunities for imperfection immense, perhaps a successful seedling, a choice new variety of rose might be brought into the world, then named—perhaps Jennifer's Jewels, as he had Jennifer Connelly in mind for his next success—and propagated for distribution. The ritual from start to finish was to Gallagher an act of love both selfless and sublime.

It was the only act of love he knew. Although gregarious, he had few friends, and no family at all. He looked mostly to his roses for companionship, beauty, trustworthiness. They were his life, providing him with a meagre livelihood and whatever enjoyment he experienced. His introductions were highly regarded in rose society, but he himself occupied an equivocal position. He was perfectly aware that streaks of idiosyncrasy and cantankerousness in his personality repeatedly undermined the respect and affection his accomplishments might otherwise

15

have inspired. That, if anything, he was disliked all the more because of his success. The horticultural who's who earnestly desired a charming and sophisticated person in his place. Such a one would be their David Austen, his glory theirs to share. But Gallagher, for all his gifts, was not their man. He was nobody's man.

A familiar mood of melancholy crept over him as it invariably did after the moment of consummation. He felt spent. Empty. As always, he took to remembering a long-ago lover, a girl whom he'd loved and lost as a young man and whose like he'd never met again. Forgetting that he was trying to forget. He had other cross-pollinations awaiting him, but he could not perform them straightaway. It would be a type of promiscuity to leap too suddenly to another. In this moment of wistful repose he suddenly recalled he had dreamt of old Ireland last night, his childhood among tumbled stones and sculpted saints. That poxy phone call yesterday had triggered it, stirring up a troubling dream whose details were now lost but not the mood of gloom it had lain upon his restless sleep.

Suddenly he was roused from his musings by the sounds of a car crunching over the gravel driveway out front. Now who the hell could that be? After a brief delay, a car door slammed. He re-entered the house to a soft but firm rapping on his front door.

When he swung open the wooden door, its hinges screaking for want of lubrication, he looked straight into the anthracite eyes of a small dark woman standing on his front step. Young and polished, she was dressed in a stylish black business suit of expensive cut and carrying an attaché case. Her raven hair was pulled severely back to the nape, reminding him of Nicole's petals drawn back to the stem. Behind her a brilliantly vermillion sports car shone in the midday sun, low and forward-leaning, like a panther crouched to pounce.

"Good afternoon, Mr. Gallagher?" It was a half-question asked by someone who already knew the answer.

"Aye." He was slightly off balance, as though he'd been rapped on the head by this unexpected apparition.

"Hello. I'm very pleased to meet you." She extended her right hand, which was tiny but surprisingly firm as Gallagher shook it. "My name is Wendy Trang. I'm an attorney at Levins, Levins, and Yaspur here in Vancouver. I have some important business I need to discuss with you. I apologize for not having phoned, but my cell was dead and I happened to be nearby and thought I'd risk just dropping in. Is this a convenient time?"

"What sort of business?" To Gallagher, any lawyer represented only two things: trouble and expense.

"It concerns your home here," she said, smiling, with an almost imperceptible nod to indicate his house. "We represent the estate of Mr. Fanslau."

"Fanslau. Estate." He was receiving the words in disparate chunks, like concrete blocks lifted from a pallet to be laid up for a wall. Mr. Fanslau was his landlord. He lived not far away, just up in West Point Grey. What the hell was this about estates?

"You did know that Mr. Fanslau passed away some time ago?" The woman's efficient precision seemed to make demands of him that he was incapable of fulfilling.

"Passed away? You mean to tell me Mr. Fanslau's dead?" Shocked, he looked away, over her shoulder, seeing again the predatory car crouched in his driveway.

"I think it would be best if I came in," the woman said. "Or if you prefer, we could make an appointment to meet at my office at a time that's more convenient for you." There was a chilling neutrality about her manner of speaking that wholly disconcerted Gallagher. He was instinctively intimidated by most women, and this highly polished specimen seemed to him particularly formidable.

"No, no, that's all right," he mumbled, recovering himself, "Come in if you will." He held the door wide and she stepped past him into his tiny hallway. She smelled, he thought, of someplace exotic, the Spice Islands maybe. His house, on the other hand, smelled of boiled cabbage and mould. He wished he'd cleaned the place up a bit, and wished that he was wearing something a little more presentable than his tattered old work clothes, but she'd arrived unannounced and would have to take him as she found him. "Please, sit down," he indicated his best chair, an enormous fake leather recliner parked in front of the television.

"I have some papers," Wendy Trang said, slightly raising her attaché case, "perhaps the kitchen table . . . ?"

17

"Sure, sure." He motioned towards the arched doorway that led through into his cramped kitchen. Two wooden chairs faced each other across the Formica-topped table. Gallantly Gallagher pulled one back for the woman, the way he'd seen waiters do in classic movies.

"Thank you," she said, seating herself. He swept some toast crumbs from this morning's breakfast into his hand and threw them into the sink. Old Fanslau dead. Jesus. The lawyer placed her attaché case on the table, released its latches with a snap and withdrew a manilla file folder and pen, snapped the latches shut, and placed the case on the floor alongside her chair. Her fingernails were outlandishly long and polished a brilliant crimson.

"What happened to Mr. Fanslau?" he asked, sitting down opposite her. "I had no idea."

"A heart attack, I'm afraid, very sudden. Completely unexpected."

"Musta been. He was here not all that long ago," he said, "looked fit as a fiddle to me."

"One of those inexplicable occurrences," Wendy Trang said. "The mystery of death. So inevitable, so commonplace, and yet so repeatedly inexplicable." The arbitrariness of death stole through the kitchen like a cold draft along the linoleum floor, leaving the two of them frozen for a moment within their thoughts.

Gallagher said nothing. What could he possibly say of sense to this elegant stranger arriving on his doorstep with news of death? He knew enough to know that every death has its resonances. He and Fanslau had enjoyed a peculiar but enduring relationship. True, it was devoid of any overt intimacy or even spoken acknowledgement, but it had been a strong and lasting bond nevertheless. Old enough to be his father, Fanslau was more his patron than friend. They lived in entirely different worlds, for Fanslau was a businessman, and an astute one at that, having amassed a sizeable fortune in the hospitality industry. He was frequently overseas on business matters, and several months might go by during which Gallagher saw or heard nothing of Fanslau, but then he'd reappear and perhaps visit Gallagher two or three times in a week. So it had been nothing out of the ordinary that Gallagher hadn't seen the old gent for a while.

Wendy Trang was rattling on in her clipped, efficient manner about the estate and inheritance taxes and capital gains and outstanding receivables, all of which sailed entirely over Gallagher's head. None of it meant anything to him. While doing his best to appear attentive, he was mesmerized by how light seemed to play among the raven-black strands of his visitor's hair. She was entirely incongruous sitting in his shabby little kitchen with its peeling wallpaper and sagging cabinets, like a bird of brilliant plumage confined to a rusty cage.

But then gradually an unseemly line of thought began to wriggle its way into his mind. The estate. Inheritance. The spoils of death. He tried to brush these venal whisperings away and focus more on the sadness of the moment, but without success. He found himself unable to resist a growing and exhilarating intuition that perhaps old Fanslau had made him a beneficiary in the will. That must be why this young lawyer was going on in such detail about the finances, that it was necessary that he understand the facts and figures of the case. Perhaps, Gallagher dared now to conceive the wild dream, perhaps old Fanslau had bequeathed everything to him, made him an instant millionaire! Snapshot images flashed before him of yachts and five-star hotels and of himself reclining poolside on a chaise longue, margarita in hand, while lovely young women in revealing swimsuits paraded past him.

"There are only two beneficiaries to his will," Wendy Trang said, as though she'd read his thoughts, and paused dramatically. His hopes momentarily dipped but then leapt again, this time more realistically, for he knew old Fanslau had a sister of whom he'd been fond, but nobody else that he knew of. Maybe half the estate would be his, and half of Fanslau's considerable fortune was a damn sight better than nothing.

"He used to talk about his sister up in Summerland," Gallagher said, feeling a glow of benevolence towards his co-beneficiary, "married to an orchardist, if I remember right." They'd have something in common then, the love of growing, as they divvied up the spoils. This would help get beyond any resentment the sister might feel over having to share the inheritance with himself.

"That is correct. As well he had a son. Those are the only two surviving relatives."

"A son?" Gallagher took the blow like a man and tried to hide his disappointment. "He never said anything about a son."

"Now living in Calgary. An oil man."

"Funny Mr. Fanslau never mentioned him."

"I believe they had been estranged for many years." Wendy Trang held his gaze, her dark liquid eyes unblinking.

"Ah." Again he had nothing to say. But estrangement, yes. He knew all about estrangement, for wasn't he himself the most estranged of sons? Some ruptures can be irrevocable, their finality absolute. Perhaps this Calgary man, like Gallagher himself, was one of those. Room for hope still.

"Mr. Fanslau and yourself went back a long way, I understand," the lawyer said, tilting her head attentively.

"Oh, aye. He hired me on as his gardener when first I came to Canada. That's twenty years or more now. He got me on my feet over here and I'll never forget him for it."

"Now, Mr. Gallagher, your arrangement with Mr. Fanslau concerning this house and property was informal and rather—how shall I put it?—irregular? Wouldn't you say?"

"Suppose it was," he allowed. "We were friends, like."

"Indeed. I understand that he was a great admirer of your roses."

"Aye, Mr. Fanslau knew his roses right enough."

"And I take it that it was this mutual—what shall we call it? Passion?—that led to your unconventional arrangement." The woman had the damnedest way of asking questions that weren't really questions, as though she were enticing a child down a pathway by leaving candies strewn along it.

Gallagher didn't care for the drift things were taking and decided to firm up his position. "If it's my tenancy here you're questioning, Mr. Fanslau said I could have the place for as long as I wanted it in order to carry on with my work."

"Indeed. And would you pay him a regular rent, Mr. Gallagher?"

"Ah, not really, no." He hesitated, sensing a trap. It was hard to explain exactly, how old Fanslau had insisted that he didn't need or want rent, that he had so much money already he didn't know what to do with it all, that money was more of a damned nuisance than anything else, always making demands on you. It was the kind of thing millionaires tended to say to poor people, but Gallagher hadn't minded it so much coming from Fanslau. And the old guy did love his roses, no doubt about it. Whenever he had a few spare moments, Fanslau would come over and just sit in the garden. They wouldn't talk much. Maybe have a cup of coffee together or a sip of whiskey, depending. But mostly Fanslau wanted just to sit quietly by himself with the flowers. He'd often say that all the money in the world couldn't buy him half so much peace.

"I see." Wendy Trang pencilled a note. "Did you have any kind of..." Just then the telephone shrilled in the little kitchen, startling them both. Gallagher always kept the ringer at full volume, so that he could hear it in the greenhouse, even though nobody of consequence ever called.

"Excuse me a moment," he said, scraping back his chair, "I'm expecting an important call." This was nonsense, but useful in getting a leg up on Wendy Trang. The call was from a man with an impenetrable accent apparently wanting to enrol him for a triple platinum credit card. Gallagher leaned against the wall, gazing out the window, and played the call for all it was worth. "Hmm . . . Yes . . . Certainly . . . I understand . . . Yes, most interesting . . . All right, get back to me, won't you?" He hung up and returned to the table with the air of someone who'd just completed a master stroke.

"As I was saying," Wendy Trang continued, "did you have a signed agreement with him? A lease agreement or anything of that nature?" Back she was to the business, like a dog that can't stop chewing a stick.

"No, nothing of the sort. We had a gentlemen's arrangement. On the shake of a hand. As good as gold."

"Of course." She looked at him directly with her impossibly dark eyes.

"Is there a problem, then?" He already sensed there was. Otherwise this chic creature would not be perched at his kitchen table probing into unpaid rents. Obviously he was no more a beneficiary of the will than he was a Balinese Buddhist.

"The difficulty we have is this." Wendy Trang took up some papers from her file folder. "In his last will and testament, Mr. Fanslau instructed that his considerable estate be divided equally between his sister and his son."

"I see." No fortune for Gallagher then, but trouble coming sure as stones.

"He did in addition stipulate in an appended codicil that it was his wish that the informal arrangement that you and he enjoyed with respect to this property should be continued for as long as you wished."

"Well, that's a wonderful thing." Gallagher felt a gentle breeze of relief blowing through him. "He always told me not to worry myself about being left in the lurch. So he came true, as he always did, a gentleman to the end." Gallagher's apprehensions concerning his visitor, he realized, had sprung from an intuition that she possessed the power—or was aligned with those who possessed the power—to have him thrown out onto the street. If that were to happen, he'd be a ruined man, for he'd never find another place like this, not one he could even dream of affording. And to have to abandon his hundreds of roses out there, his life's work—no, it was unthinkable. But he'd been spared that eventuality at least, and now felt the relief people feel when disaster bears down on them but strikes them only a glancing blow on its headlong rush to someplace else. The tornado had passed.

"However, I must tell you, that certain complications have arisen," Wendy Trang said, snatching away what she'd only moments ago bestowed.

"Complications? What sort of complications?"

"Well, as I told you, Mr. Fanslau expressed in the codicil to his will a wish that your situation be maintained."

"Aye." Gallagher was distracted by seeing another sowbug making its way across the Formica tabletop towards the lawyer's papers. Damned little fuckers were all through the house now. They loved the damp and the darkness and chewing on rotting wood. They'd have the whole place down in a heap sooner or later if he didn't do something. But what was he to do about this one? He could hardly squash it in front of the lawyer. But if she spotted it, perfectly trim and immaculate as she was, perhaps she'd have an attack of hysteria. Women were like that, he knew.

"But a wish is just that, a wish," Wendy Trang continued. "It contains no directive for normalizing the situation."

22

"I don't get your meaning." He wondered if he should calmly scoop the intruding bug up and toss it outdoors.

"Well, had Mr. Fanslau stipulated, for example, that ownership of this property should be transferred to yourself, that would be simple and clear to all concerned."

"I don't need to own the place so long as I can live here."

"Yes, but that's where the problem arises, you see. Mr. Fanslau's son, Peter, is of the opinion that his father's expressed wish has no substantive legal standing."

"Tell me he's wrong." Gallagher was just about to rise when Wendy Trang took a file folder and deftly swept the sowbug off the table, but in such a way that he wasn't certain she'd done it by accident or design. The sowbug landed in a far corner where it lay on its back on the linoleum, its multiple little legs thrashing frantically in the air.

"As I say, it's extremely difficult. Frankly the will should never have included so nebulous a clause."

"Why did it then?" A vicious little panic was crawling into his consciousness.

"It was drawn up, under Mr. Fanslau's instruction, by the senior Mr. Levin at a point in that gentleman's distinguished career when his lawyerly acumen was no longer what it once had been."

"Some old lawyer screwed it up, is what you're tellin' me?"

"I wouldn't put it quite that way," Wendy Trang said, leaving unsaid but understood that she wouldn't put anything quite the way Gallagher put things.

The apprehension that he might be forced from his home crept over him and settled like toxic fog. Everything else became obscure and indistinguishable in the murk of this unforeseen threat. It was not just a house, nor just a garden, that he might be forced to abandon. His whole life, his passion, the substrate of his being, was localized in this cottage and acreage. He was inconceivable to himself anywhere else. He could not, must not, allow them to force him out. "But if Mr. Fanslau said I should remain here, I don't see how they can go against his wishes."

"You'll notice I didn't say *they*," she corrected him. "Mr. Peter Fanslau is certainly of the opinion that the courts would not uphold this requirement. But Mrs. Kettrick, the deceased's sister, feels that her brother's wishes should be honoured and that you should be allowed continued residency here. So we have a fundamental difference of opinion on the matter between the two beneficiaries."

"What's to be done then?" His gloom had lifted off ever so slightly.

"Neither beneficiary wants the issue to become the subject of a long and costly legal wrangle. There have been ongoing discussions as to how the matter might best be resolved. Nothing as yet has been decided and those discussions continue. One avenue that's currently being explored—and this is in part the reason for my visit with you today—is the possibility of making the property available to you for purchase." She casually laid her forearm along the table edge spreading her fingers with their magnificently lacquered nails.

"For me to buy the place?"

"Correct."

"That's not what Mr. Fanslau said should happen."

"No it isn't. But it may represent the best available compromise between the disparate views of the beneficiaries."

"I can't afford to buy this place."

"Mrs. Kettrick has indicated that if this course is decided upon, the terms of purchase must be favourable to you."

"How favourable would that be?" Gallagher was sinking.

"The property is currently evaluated by the Assessment Authority at, let me see . . ." she searched for and retrieved a copy of the most recent assessment notice. "The house and outbuildings are essentially worthless—they're listed at a token $20,000." This was perhaps being generous. Gallagher's little tumbledown cottage was smaller than most of the neighbours' garages. "The real value, of course, is in the land—$978,000." Gallagher gulped. It might as well have been a billion. "Mr. Peter Fanslau believes the land is undervalued, that if it were to be developed into townhouses, for example, its value would be substantially higher."

"But it's farmland," Gallagher objected. "It can't be developed."

"Quite correct," Wendy Trang agreed. "The land is currently a part of the Agricultural Land Reserve and as such is not available for subdivision or residential development. However, Mr. Peter Fanslau believes that there's a good likelihood that he could have the property withdrawn from the land reserve and rezoned to allow a higher density development in which case the property would be worth several million dollars."

"Jesus," Gallagher muttered. How could a grand old gent like Fanslau have fathered such a greedy little prick? Small wonder they were estranged; Fanslau probably couldn't stand the arsehole. "Well I can't afford hundreds of thousands of dollars, much less millions. What the hell am I to do?" He threw himself on the mercy of Wendy Trang.

"Nothing for the moment, I would suggest. No decisions have been made, but I believe it's extremely unlikely that you'll be able to continue living here as you have. I think it's fair to say that purchase of the property may represent the only realistic possibility for your remaining on it. Some outlay of money to satisfy Mr. Peter Fanslau in particular will almost certainly be required. On the upside"—she suddenly smiled at him for the first and only time, a smile of great charm touched with compassion—"given Mrs. Kettrick's stand on the matter, you may be able to pick the place up for considerably less than its full market value." She returned the documents to the file folder, placed it in her attaché case, snapped the case shut, and stood up. "I'm sorry to have been the bearer of such unwelcome news," she said. "I hope that things can be worked out in a way that is satisfactory to you. Here's my card." She produced a business card by apparent sleight of hand, the way a magician pulls a playing card from thin air, and handed it to him. "I shall be in touch just as soon as there are any new developments. Goodbye, Mr. Gallagher." She perfunctorily shook his hand with her silken steel grip.

"Goodbye," said Gallagher and watched in stunned disbelief as she briskly left his house and climbed into her phantom car, which sprang to life with a purr, then glided smoothly down the driveway.

◙ THREE ◙

GALLAGHER SAT slumped in an old Adirondack chair in his back garden, wearing his shabby work clothes still. His wiry hair was dishevelled, and his face looked drawn and weary. He'd been there for hours, sipping Jameson's and brooding over loss. The roses that surrounded him whispered among themselves, but he was oblivious to them, just as he was unaware of the big jetliners rumbling in and out of the airport across the river and of the distant wail of sirens in the city. A bitter history of confiscations and evictions gnawed at him. Ghostly figures of dispossession, gaunt with hunger, some carrying babes in arms and with small children trailing behind them, wandered through the shadowy half-world of his musings. Exile and tragedy, the familiar old tale. He remembered his mother's stories, passed on from her own mother who had lived through the great famine and had seen the starving families wandering the byways, surviving on grass and weeds. She'd seen the landlords' men tearing the roofs off cottages, putting places to the torch. How could he have been such a fool? To trust, because he had for so long been safely hidden here, in a little enclave on Canada's West Coast, that he would remain safe forever. Had he known no better than that? After all he'd seen of evil and misfortune, how could he have sequestered himself on these couple of acres and succumbed to the delusion that evil and misfortune would not eventually track him down and pillage the little he had? This had been the way of things for centuries; why would anything change merely because the pillagers no longer swooped down on their victims riding great warhorses and wielding long swords?

Although the lawyer had cautioned him that nothing was settled as yet, Gallagher knew in his blood and bones that he was to be driven from his home. And then what would he do? Sure he might be able to find a rundown shack on a scrap of swampland someplace up the valley where real estate prices hadn't yet gone completely beserk the way they had in the city. But he'd never be able to transplant his collection of mature roses out there, his glasshouse, his propagation chambers.

Although only in his forties, he felt certain he wouldn't have the heart for starting from scratch again. He preferred to picture himself in some squalid walk-up apartment downtown, surviving on dog-food sandwiches and waiting for death's eventual rapping on his door. Pathos swamped him. But to lose his roses! To think of them bulldozed and burned to make way for a row of trendy townhouses. It was insufferable, unbearable. Long he sat as evening slowly drenched the rosary in the colours of pale blood. Ancestral memories of forfeiture and bereavement intermingled with his own impending dispossession, trailing like vapours through the twilight.

Wallowing in morbid gloom—there was a perverse comfort in its pain—his thoughts drifted aimlessly over the landscape of loss. Fanslau's death touched him now more pointedly than it had during Wendy Trang's unsettling visit. He still could hardly believe that the old gent was gone. Few people populated Gallagher's world, and he now felt the loss of a good and gentle soul whom he had, in his own way, loved. Fanslau had used his influence at the outset to secure landed immigrant status for Gallagher and had given him work to get his feet on the ground. He'd been a father figure of sorts to him, the kind of father you'd want, wise and accepting, a mentor, a bedrock. Certainly a wholesome alternative to Gallagher's real father, that crapulous little Irishman with his temper and intolerance. Gallagher could picture him still, smell him still, strutting around his little pigsty of a farm out in the wilds of West Cork as though he were lord of the manor. From the earliest he could remember, Gallagher had lived in fear of him, of his sudden, flashing anger that erupted for no reason. Nothing was right, nothing was good enough for Mr. Donagh Gallagher. He treated the boys, Patrick and his little brother, Bosco, as though they were nuisances he'd just as soon not have. They learned from early childhood to stay out of his way, and to avoid him entirely whenever he was in his cups.

How his mother put up with the skinty bastard, how she tolerated him at all, Gallagher never understood. If anything, she was treated worse than the boys were. On Saturday nights she'd shoo them off to bed early, so they'd be fresh for Sunday Mass early next morning, or so she'd say. But her real reason was that they'd be out of harm's way by the time himself got home from the pub reeking of liquor and tobacco and bile. Lying awake in the loft of the little stone farmhouse, they'd hear him come in, the clatter and banging of him, hear the sneering contempt with which he addressed his wife, how he'd accuse her of frigidity, taunt her over her stupidity. "You're as thick as them feckin' brats of yours," he'd jeer at her, and young Patrick, hearing him, would seethe with shame and rage.

But his mother would say nothing in reply to the drunken abuse. "There, now, Donagh." She'd make soothing noises. "Sit down and I'll bring you a bite to eat." She'd fuss and scurry about, providing whatever comforts the lout demanded.

Next morning they would walk to church in the village, Patrick and Bosco and their mother, leaving Lord Pisspot snoring in his bed. They'd say nothing about the night before, as though it had not occurred at all. But throughout the Mass, even at the moment of receiving Holy Communion, when the body of Christ Himself was placed on Patrick's tongue, his mind would be roiling with hatred of his father. Patrick loved his mother as fiercely as he despised his father, and it was his father's treatment of her that rankled him most. The occasional blows and abuse he suffered himself meant little compared with the pain of seeing her misused so badly. It was so fucking unfair, so profoundly wrong that she of all people should be debased and berated by him. She loved her sons—my bonny lads, she called them—and deftly manoeuvred to protect them from his brutality. She laboured like an unpaid servant to keep the household running, endlessly preparing meals, doing laundry, mending, cleaning, and all the rest. Even as a youngster Patrick could see the days wearing her down, making her old long before her time. But never a word of thanks from his lordship; nothing but complaint and criticism. Jesus, Gallagher could shriek with fury at the unfairness of it.

And the stinking hypocrisy of him! Anyone outside the family who exercised the least authority, the old man treated with abject deference. The priest, the doctor, even the feckin' postmaster—he'd bow and fawn over them with disgusting obsequiousness. "You're a credit to the parish, truly you are, Donagh, you and your fine family both," the addle-headed priest would repeat on his annual visit to the house.

And the old man would nod and smile, gratefully servile, the humble and honest workingman he was to all the world. Fuck!

Patrick had sworn to God he would kill him someday. "I'll kill you, you fucker!" he'd screamed at his father a hundred times, but always far out of earshot, down where the surf was heaving and thundering from off the wild Atlantic or up on a windswept hilltop where only the startled sheep could hear. He would imagine himself grown tall and strong, coming upon his father abusing his mother and thrashing the old tyrant to within an inch of his life. Just picturing it, he could feel the strength in his arms, the power in his fists as he battered the old bastard senseless. He'd dreamed of taking his mother away someday. Of making a success—he wasn't sure just how—that enabled him to get her out of that hellhole, away from *him*, to some place where she could live in the comfort and contentment she deserved. Patrick would look after her, make things better for her, make everything good.

Instead, in the end, he'd done precisely the opposite. He'd stolen their life savings and fled the farm, then fled the country and never went back. Christ only knows what additional misery his mother suffered because of his treachery. He'd made everything worse, especially for her, and he couldn't bear thinking of it now. Twenty years he'd spent not thinking of that sin. In the end, he'd proven himself no better than the landlords and their goons, no better than his bloody father, just another shifty Mick grabbing what he could and getting the hell away. But he hadn't got far enough away, had he, for here was the landlord's lawyer rapping on his door, here was the notice of eviction, thank you very much, here was his chance to lose everything he loved. Hah hah. The joke's on you, Mr. Patrick Gallagher, and what do you think you're going to do about it, eh?

▣ FOUR ▣

IT WAS the arrival of the surveyors that finally forced Gallagher into action. Wendy Trang had called him to arrange a suitable time for a survey team to clearly establish the corner posts and property lines preparatory to any possible future transactions. Yes, she admitted, that might include subdivision and development, should the land be successfully removed from the Agricultural Land Reserve. Again she assured him that nothing was imminent, nothing as yet decided, but that if he was considering an option to purchase he might wish to proceed sooner rather than later, while Mrs. Kettrick's generous resolve towards him remained firm. The sight of the surveyors in his yard several days later with their tripods and lenses and shouted directions back and forth stirred in Gallagher a dark ancestral hatred of the invader, the despoiler against whom he was powerless. After the survey team had left he discovered along the back property line that they'd carelessly hacked their way through a large rose he'd named Raunchy Rachel, a sport of Rambling Rector. A rage boiled up in him seeing the mutilation, and he again envisioned his roses uprooted and put to the torch. It was himself they would be tearing from the earth, his own flesh and bones and blood hurling into the flames. He must resist them, he must fight for this scrap of land in whatever way he could or else he was entirely lost.

But what was he to do? He owned nothing of value; his meagre savings were a pittance compared with the vast sums being suggested as a purchase price. Whenever he entered his rosary now, he felt close to tears from the dreadful sense of impending loss. As he lay awake at night, fretting and tossing, he was menaced by feral snarls of panic and despair. Try as he might, he could think of no solution. He increased his outlay for lottery tickets, but even as he handed over the cash to a sulky cashier at the nearby convenience store, he knew himself to be a fool, throwing good money after bad. In his calmer moments he realized that what he really needed was another Fanslau, someone blessed with abundant capital and a philanthropic streak. A benefactor. But how the hell do you go about finding such a person? The new people piling into his neighbourhood, tearing out the old homes and replacing them with multimillion-dollar monstrosities, wouldn't be of any use, being up to their eyeballs in mortgages.

Then one bright morning, when he had no heart for propagation or much of anything else, sitting idly at his kitchen table nursing a cup of tepid tea, he found himself re-examining the conversation he'd had with that damn fool travel agent, the invitation to lead a group of distinguished gardeners through Ireland's finest gardens. Having scarcely thought about it since, he now turned the proposition over in his mind with a reflectiveness he'd not applied to it at the time. His thought was not that the stipend he'd been offered would be of much use, a mere two thousand whereas he needed five hundred times that much, but rather that the tour might—and it was a very slender might, but he was now grasping at whatever slender straw he could—yes, it just might provide a means for his meeting a benefactor. It would, after all, be a well-heeled group he'd be chaperoning. And they'd be visiting some very high-end gardens owned by extremely wealthy people. All he needed was one of them, just one, with some extra cash on hand looking for a good long-term investment. A large piece of land in Vancouver's sizzling real estate market, to be picked up for considerably less than full market value—yes, indeed, this might prove a very tempting proposition to a shrewd investor. And of course he'd work up the gardening angle, his world-class rose collection, and the acclaim accruing to anyone who assisted in its preservation. Perhaps, too, he'd allude to the possibility that his new patron might be immortalized by having a new rose named after her.

The longer he thought about it, the more this course of action developed from idle fantasy into what seemed to him a realistic stratagem. He imagined the group might visit a grand Dublin garden whose owner, bloated with the overnight wealth of the Celtic Tiger, would take a shine to him and be perfectly happy to assist. More realistically, he conjured up the image of a wealthy heiress, a lover of beauty, perhaps living in a swanky district of Toronto, secretly ashamed that her inherited wealth had come from exploitation of poor people in some far-off place, determined to make amends by using the money now for noble purposes, and finding in his plight a perfect opportunity. Such a one might easily be on the tour. He imagined she'd have a distinguished name like Gwyneth Mandeville-Hampton, in which case he might call the rose he developed for her Lady Gwyneth. He had met such people over the years, members of rose societies and the like, but had never cultivated their attention because he'd felt no need of them. However, his confidence grew that, given the right circumstances, he could trade upon his reputation as distinguished rosarian and authentic Irish character, to charm this good lady into becoming his patron. Elaborating further, he considered that she might wish to abandon the brutal winters of Toronto entirely and build a new home on his property—there was sufficient acreage for this—where she could enjoy first-hand the long growing season and the splendour of his roses. He could picture her clearly in his mind's eye, the stylishness of her attire, the warm smile with which she'd greet him when they happened to meet in the rosary on a splendid spring morning. The more he imagined, the more convinced he became that great possibilities awaited, if only he could summon the courage to seize them.

Even so, was it worth the risk? Realistically what would his chances be of getting into Ireland unnoticed and out again unscathed? Sure the tourists could go for a golfing holiday in Kildare or fish for salmon along the Shannon or go bicycling the Ring of Kerry and believe themselves on the Emerald Isle, in the land of saints and scholars. But Gallagher knew better. He'd seen first-hand more than enough of the hard men and bitter women, tyrannical priests, and unscrupulous plotters of that treacherous place to last him a lifetime. The people he'd betrayed twenty years ago were all down in the West country, and that for sure would be out of bounds for him, but would any place be safe?

And there was something else too, harder to put your finger on but equally sinister: the hauntings of old Ireland. Gallagher had learned of it as a child, listening to his mother's tales of fairies and ghosts. Sitting by the hearth on winter evenings, while the dark Atlantic wind moaned around the stones and slates of the farmhouse, he would listen in fear and wonder to his mother's recounting of how long lines of dead people wandered down the lanes after dark. They were, she said in a voice almost a whisper, the souls of peasants who'd been starved and driven from the land, now returned as the undead, restlessly roaming the old places they'd known in life. She spoke of apparitions that she herself, or those she knew, had experienced—ghosts sometimes glimpsed flitting through the lower garden. One time she took Patrick to a tumbledown cottage hidden away in a copse of briars and hazel. Twin holes where windows once had been stared at him like hollow eye sockets. A family had lived here once, she told him, but the mother had gone mad and killed all her children, slitting their throats while they slept. "If you came at night," she told him, "which you must never do, you could see them here, the dream children. But they are evil beings who would do you great harm. You can only keep them off by brandishing a crucifix at them." She believed unquestioningly in an unseen world, inhabited by ghouls and fairies, malignant spirits intent upon working their mischief among the unwary. They especially loved to prey upon children and carry them off to their world. After an evening of her stories, Patrick and Bosco would creep to their bed and listen in terror to the voices of ghosts keening in the gale.

Gallagher no longer believed such superstitious rubbish, any more than he believed in the supernaturalism of priests or fortune tellers. But there remained within him, deeper than conscious thought, a residual instinct that unseen dark forces were at work in the world, and nowhere more so than amid the inscrutable mysteries of old Ireland.

His choice boiled down to this: returning to the real or imagined perils of Ireland, or succumbing to the entirely real financial peril he faced here at home. Resist as he might, try as he might, he could come up with no possible alternative to embarking on the tour. It was madness. Pure madness. But it was that or nothing, find himself a patron or face utter ruin.

GALLAGHER leaned against his kitchen wall, staring at the chair where Wendy Trang had perched during her fateful visit. He held the receiver of the phone idly in his hand. He had resolved to call John Berenice, then decided against it, then waffled again and made the call. He'd been put on hold for an interminable time during which he was forced to endure several of the greatest hits of Julio Inglesias. He dangled the receiver well away from his ear and hummed a lewd ditty he remembered from his youth to hold Iglesias at bay and studied the ivy-twined Grecian urns on his faded kitchen wallpaper.

At last the travel agent came on the line. "Well, I must say you're the last person I expected to hear from," Berenice said with an unmistakable frostiness.

"I was thinking over your proposition," Gallagher replied, trying to sound like someone who never took a step in any direction without first giving the matter scrupulous consideration.

"I greatly appreciate your calling, Mr. Gallagher," Berenice cut in peremptorily, "but I'm afraid our Gardens of the Emerald Isle tour has been cancelled."

"Cancelled?" Gallagher was caught completely sideways. "Why's that then?"

"A number of the clients have simply refused to participate if Stephen Aubrey isn't accompanying the group."

"Oh, for God's sakes!"

"I'd informed all the clients straightaway that we were endeavouring to secure your services at extremely short notice, but several of them were unconvinced. They would not consider going without Aubrey."

"How many?"

"Five were absolutely adamant. No room for compromise whatsoever. Some of the others were less unreasonable and I managed to bring them around. But not enough of them. In the meantime, of course, you declined our offer, even with the additional perks we discussed, and I have been unable to secure the services of anyone else."

Gallagher thought for a moment. "How many was willing to go if it was with me?"

"Only ten, I'm sorry to say."

"And that's not enough?" From out the window Gallagher watched a dark line of brooding cloud advancing from the west.

"We'd need eleven as a bare minimum. Just to break even. That's our cut-off point. It's clear that Stephen Aubrey's presence was a *sine qua non* among a certain element. Without him the tour is simply a non-starter."

"I see." Gallagher had assumed the tour would be his for the asking.

This unexpected twist had him stumped. "So there's no way around it then?"

"Am I to take it," Berenice asked with a ring of condescension in his tone, "that you've had a change of heart about our proposition?"

"Well, the more I thought it over, the more I considered it was an ungenerous act on my part to leave you in such a difficult position, not to mention denying your clients the opportunity to see Ireland."

"Very magnanimous of you, Mr. Gallagher." It was hard to tell if Berenice was being ironical or not. "Unfortunately it's now a moot point."

"That's a pity." Gallagher was evenly split between relief and consternation. "And there's no way at all the tour can still go ahead?" A breeze had kicked up outdoors ahead of the advancing clouds and the rose canes were rattling irritably in the wind.

"Well, we haven't yet notified the clients of the cancellation nor returned their deposits, only because I was still hoping against hope that something could still be worked out. It would certainly be our preference that the tour proceed. Without question. People have made arrangements and so forth. Cancellations are very difficult and do nothing to help consolidate our client base." He paused for a moment and then added in a voice that implied considerable large-heartedness on his part, "I tell you what: I might be able to salvage the tour without our having to absorb too great a loss if you were amenable to coverage of all expenses plus a stipend that was fifty per cent of what we previously discussed."

"Half?" Cripes, he'd lost a thousand bucks overnight, but he wasn't going to take it lying down. "Perhaps seventy-five per cent of what we discussed would be about right."

"No, I'm sorry, I can manage sixty per cent but that's absolutely the very best I can do."

Gallagher hesitated, trying to weigh the pros and cons again. He pictured Gwyneth Mandeville-Hampton somewhere along the Bridle Path, a string of pearls around her neck and a chequebook in her hand. He imagined the alternative: bulldozers and ruination.

"Mr. Gallagher?"

"Yeah, yeah. Okay. All right." He was in. For good or ill, he was in.

TWO days later he presented himself at the travel company's office on West Broadway. It was one large room splashed liberally with vivid travel posters showing happy tourists cavorting at Cancun, Honolulu, Machu Picchu, London, and innumerable other destinations. Phones were shrilling incessantly and the room vibrated with a strange frenzy that entirely belied the carefree enjoyment depicted on the posters. Gallagher asked a frazzled young woman near the front for John Berenice and was told rather curtly to take a seat and wait. There were four other people already waiting. None of them looked very happy. The posters laughed down from the walls.

Eventually a short man, balding, wearing a business suit, and shaped like an Anjou pear emerged from a glass-walled office in a back corner of the room and approached Gallagher. John Berenice looked just like he sounded on the phone. The pale hand he extended was soft and spongy as a mushroom, his smile so inauthentic it might have been wrapped in cellophane. Though Gallagher had worn his best suit with a smart little diamond-pattern cardigan under his jacket, a new tie with bold tangerine and fuchsia stripes and a pair of brown Oxfords he'd spent half an hour polishing beforehand, he suspected his appearance was not the least bit reassuring to Berenice. The agent led Gallagher back to his office, closed the door, and bid Gallagher sit down. "You must excuse us this morning, Mr. Gallagher," Berenice said, straightening his jacket and tie as though he'd just been using the toilet. "We've got an extraordinary crisis on our hands at the moment."

"I wondered," Gallagher said, but tactfully said no more.

"An Alaska cruise ship packed with . . ." he began to explain, but was interrupted by a ringing phone. "Yes?" he answered it testily. "Yes, all right. No, we will not. Absolutely not . . . Fine. Fine. Call me back when she's decided." He hung up. "Jesus Christ," he muttered, as though Gallagher wasn't there at all. "Ah, yes, Mr. Gallagher," he snapped back again. Berenice gave the impression of a man whose brain was divided into cubicles, like the outer room, and that his awareness would flit from one to the other as each moment demanded. "So sorry. A wholesale outbreak of food poisoning on board."

"What?" Gallagher was beginning to think Berenice was seriously unhinged.

"The Alaska cruise. Eighteen hundred passengers, and over half of them come down with food poisoning just as they're returning to port. Vomit and diarrhea in every direction. It's an unmitigated disaster. We've got over sixty…" Again the phone intruded and Berenice almost shrieked into the receiver. "What?… Oh, for Christ's sakes! All right. All right, I'll be down straightaway." He slammed the receiver down and stared wildly at Gallagher as though mistaking him for a suicide bomber. "They're crying for blood, Mr. Gallagher. Sixty-three of our clients, at least forty-seven of them violently ill. Outraged family and friends. Emergency medical services overwhelmed. We'll have perfectly decent people lying in the gutters of Gastown choking on their own vomit before much longer."

We already do, mused Gallagher, but thought better of saying it.

"I do apologize, Mr. Gallagher, but I've got to get down to the terminal straightaway. They're baying for blood and it's mine they'll have before the day is out. But never mind, I'm going to pass you to my assistant Ms. Jeffries. She'll provide you with everything you require." Berenice was on his feet rifling through documents scattered on his desk and stuffing certain ones into a bulging satchel. Gallagher stood up as well, wondering if he should bolt from the place and never come back. A poster on the wall behind Berenice caught his eye. Beneath gleaming-white hillside buildings overlooking a turquoise sea, it said "Greece—once you've visited, you'll forever long to return."

Berenice opened the office door and led Gallagher to a nearby cubicle where a young woman sat staring intensely at her screen. "Ms. Jeffries," Berenice said formally, "allow me to introduce Mr. Patrick Gallagher, our celebrity host for the Gardens of the Emerald Isle tour." Ms. Jeffries smiled dutifully at Gallagher. She had a mop of wiry hair not unlike his own and wore a pair of enormous spectacles. Her jaw seemed set, as though wired shut following an accident. "Ms. Jeffries will look after everything," Berenice said while withdrawing from the cubicle. "Thank you once again, Mr. Gallagher. Best of luck. I'm sure you'll do splendidly." He pumped Gallagher's hand, slapped him convivially on the shoulder, and scuttled towards the door.

Gallagher sat down alongside her desk, and Ms. Jeffries produced a canvas travel bag bearing the Berenice Travel logo and containing an information packet with plane tickets, flight itinerary, toll-free numbers, cancellation insurance, a pre-trip checklist about his passport—yes, Gallagher assured her, he did have a valid passport—travel documents, medications, traveller's cheques, and other valuables. On and on Ms. Jeffries droned in a voice as flat as Saskatchewan, tapping her pen tip at point after point on the interminable checklist. Gallagher's brain felt like a stuffed butterball turkey. The whole expedition was so laced with precautions and preventative measures you'd think they were going on foot across Antarctica.

She gave him a list of the clients on the tour, all of whom would be flying independently from Canada and would meet at their Dublin hotel. The clients' safety and enjoyment throughout the tour, she emphasized, were his responsibility and primary concern. Gallagher nodded in solemn agreement, though he didn't like the sound of this responsibility. There was something onerous about it, something insinuating the potential for criminal negligence on his part. There was an itinerary for all the gardens they'd be visiting, garden entrance fees and gratuities for their local guide and driver, and a float for incidentals as required, three hundred and fifty euros.

"I was wondering about my fee, like," Gallagher finally said in a voice that might have been Oliver Twist asking for more gruel.

"Yes, of course." Ms. Jeffries extracted an envelope from her top drawer. "Here is a cheque covering a fifty per cent advance on your fee, the balance to be paid upon successful completion of the tour." Aha. So Berenice had held back half the cash in order to keep him on a short leash, had he, the crafty bugger. Ms. Jeffries placed the itemized materials in the bag and handed it to Gallagher. "Best of luck," she said to him with a lockjaw smile, as though luck and luck alone stood between him and an immense tragedy. It was a presentiment Gallagher, bag in hand, shared with her completely.

That nagging sense of impending misadventure followed him home on the bus, and he had to keep reminding himself that he had no choice, that he was risking possible misfortune in order to forestall certain tragedy. The sense of foreboding followed him up his driveway and out into his garden. He'd be leaving for Dublin within a week and already his roses, sensitive to his imminent departure, were beginning to pout and dwindle. Diseases seemed to be besetting every bush. Leaves were yellowing and curling and canes turning brown as though fire blight had scorched them. Cancerous-looking galls were swelling on the canes and tubercular black spots blighted leaves. Gallagher could not shake off the dreadful apprehension that his darlings would be grievously weakened in his absence and the most delicate of them might not survive at all. A beautiful little double pink-flowering shrub he'd developed only two years previous and named Shania's Thighs was languishing dreadfully. Her chances of enduring a sustained period without him were dismal at best. The entire rosary seemed beset by sorrowful mysteries.

"It breaks my heart to think of leaving you, my darlings," Gallagher addressed the assemblage with his arms extended wide, like the Good Shepherd, wishing to embrace them all. He was in the habit of regularly talking to his roses, although usually in a more intimate, one-to-one way. Under present circumstances, a grand peroration seemed in order. "But you must understand that I'm setting off on this journey for all our sakes. Were I not to go, were I to stay here with you, as my heart longs more than anything in the world to do, it would mean the ruination of us all. I must leave you in order to save you, because a great evil is approaching. If we cannot find the means to repulse it—and this is what I must leave you to seek—we are lost, all of us, altogether lost."

He let his arms collapse against his sides and his head bow forward. Although he could see no alternative, neither could he escape the dreadful presentiment that he was making an incalculable mistake. He was at a turning point in his life, as he'd known from the moment Wendy Trang had stepped into his kitchen. The great wheel of destiny would turn by its own devices, indifferent to whether he acted or not. But could he perhaps alter, by however minute a degree, the course of its inexorable turning? Love now impelled him to risk everything on a course that was uncertain in outcome and imponderable in possibility.

⊞ FIVE ⊞

THAT EVENING Gallagher collapsed into his recliner and turned on the TV to distract himself while he ate his supper of baked beans and Italian hot sausages with toast. There was a documentary in progress about a young guy who'd gone hiking in a remote desert canyon in the American Southwest. Somehow the fellow had managed to get his arm irretrievably trapped between the canyon wall and an enormous boulder. Gallagher couldn't figure out how anyone could do something so dumb, but this was a true story. The guy tries everything he can think of to get himself free, but nothing works. He sits for days and days waiting for somebody to happen along, but nobody does. Finally, convinced he'll die if he doesn't take action, he decides to amputate his trapped arm with a blunt pocketknife in order to get free. So that's what he does, and not only lives to tell the tale but also gets to be in a TV show about it.

Completely absorbed by the story, Gallagher forgot all about eating his baked beans and toast before they grew cold. Though not normally given to metaphorical brainwork, he'd seen in the hapless hiker a version of himself. For hadn't he long ago performed a similar amputation, escaping his old homeland by leaving behind bloodied pieces of himself that he'd crudely cut away. Now he must risk returning to that place of entrapment. He shuddered to think of finding those severed pieces of himself as though still twitching on the ground where he'd left them.

There was the problem with his parents to begin with. Although it was twenty years ago now, he could vividly recall every detail of the day he betrayed and abandoned them. They'd gone into Ballydehob for the market on Saturday morning and his brother, Bosco, with them. He had the house to himself, as he'd planned, for he was about to execute a well-considered heist. He knew from overheard conversations that whatever money his parents possessed they kept hidden somewhere in the house, because his father held a great distrust of bankers. Young Patrick reasoned the hiding place must be in his parents' bedroom, a sanctum to which he and Bosco were forbidden entry. But enter it now he did, a crowded little room with a wooden dresser and double bed covered with an ancient patchwork quilt. A picture of the Sacred Heart hung above the bed and a votive candle guttered before a statuette of the Blessed Virgin Mary on a corner shelf. Careful not to disturb anything, he searched the room. With stone walls and wide plank floor, it offered few opportunities for concealment, and he soon found what he was looking for: under the bed, a loose piece of planking, easily removed, and, hidden beneath, a small black metal strongbox. Locked, of course. He searched with rising frustration, but there was no key to be found in the room, or anywhere else in the house. The old man must keep it on him. Patrick was at a juncture: he could replace the box where he'd found it and nobody would be any the wiser, or he could take a step beyond which there would be no turning back.

He was nineteen years old at the time, and although a dutiful son who'd avoided ever getting into serious trouble, he was now in more trouble than he knew what to do with. He needed money and he needed to get out of Cork, and the strongbox he held in his hands contained his best chance of doing so. He carried it out to the barnyard and placed it on the big oak chopping block where his mother would decapitate unwanted roosters, then fetched a heavy pickaxe from the tool shed. A cold wind was rattling around the barnyard, kicking up bits of straw and leaves and scattering them across the wet cobblestones. The stone cottage and outbuildings huddled like little grey outposts of shame at what he was about to do. Planting his feet apart, he raised the pick high above his head and brought it down with a smash against the box. The point of the pick barely dented the metal top, but enough that he was now beyond any chance of stopping. He smashed at it again. And again. In the hefting and swinging and smashing he felt his rage towards his father driving him on, for he was set upon revenge as much as theft. "You fucking bastard!" he cried, walloping the box. Eventually the battered coffer split entirely open. He threw down the pick and plucked from the crumpled metal a wad of rolled bank notes, more money than he had ever seen before. He felt a surge of exhilaration at what he had done. But then, in sudden panic, convinced that his father was returning home early and would catch him in the act, he grabbed his jacket and a little rucksack he'd packed and fled his home forever.

Gallagher shook his head now, remembering that overwrought scene of two decades ago. The ignorance and impetuosity of youth. He'd neither seen nor heard of his parents since and had no idea whether or not they were still alive. Nor did he know what had become of his brother. Through that one desperate, foolish act he'd lost his family forever. Now he wondered whether there'd be any police record of that theft, any outstanding charges. He doubted it, not after all these years. But he wasn't quite as sanguine about a twin bit of pilfering he'd done at the same time, when he'd lifted a few hundred punt from the local battalion of the bold IRA. Might the lads there—even in a half-assed little backwater brigade like the one he'd been briefly mixed up with— not have a slightly longer memory when it came to betrayal by one of their own? Of course, from the bit he'd learned on the news, conditions had changed dramatically, and in the newfound prosperity the old antipathies were supposedly a thing of the past. Gallagher thought he'd believe it when he saw it.

In the meantime he'd be giving the West Cork brigade, as well as his old parents, as wide a berth as possible. The tour itinerary, he'd confirmed, was confined to the greater Dublin area, so they'd be many miles away from his childhood haunts. He certainly wouldn't be advertising his presence to anyone, and he considered it extremely unlikely that he'd be bumping into any of his old acquaintances in the posh gardens of the capital. Still it nagged at him, the remote possibility that he'd be spotted by someone who'd connect him with the minor crimes of a foolish youth long ago. He switched off the television and placed his dinner tray on the coffee table alongside his recliner, then lay back, gazing absently at the yellowed plaster ceiling above him.

IT was Francie O'Sullivan who'd driven him to thievery and flight. Who'd damn near driven him to madness. She was the beauty of West Cork, at least their little corner of it. Her delicate features and cream-smooth skin, her flowing hair and flashing eyes, the way she moved, the statuesque languor of her long, slim body—every boy in school was mad for her, and half the married men in the district, if only they'd dared acknowledge it. But Gallagher had the advantage over all of them, for Francie lived just two farms down from him and they had known each other all their lives. A year older, Patrick had escorted Francie to school in the village on her very first day, and most days after that. They fell naturally into the sweetly innocent intimacy of childhood. The ruins of an old abbey on his family's farm was one of their first and favourite haunts. They'd make up fantastic stories about the people who'd lived there, and the ghosts that still roamed on dark nights down the tumbled corridors of the cloister. Together they explored shingle beaches and wild hills of blooming heather, poked through the ruins of ancient forts and abbeys, examined tottering gravestones in time-worn cemeteries gone to moss and nettles. Friendship with Francie brought magic into his childhood, and he loved her from the first as he loved nobody else.

On one of their rambling expeditions, down along the seashore, when he was eleven years old and she ten, the two of them got caught in a sudden squall and sought shelter in a small sea cave hidden among huge boulders at the base of a high cliff. The briny scent of fish and seaweed filled the place and the sounds of the heaving sea made the cave space pulse like the chamber of a heart. Huddled together, aroused by the intimacy of the enclosure and its secretive removal from the staring world beyond the cave's small opening, they'd daringly removed their clothes and stared in wonder at each other's naked bodies. Excitement banished all embarrassment or shame.

"Let's lie down," Francie had said, her voice made husky by the resonances of the cave. They lay down together awkwardly on the sea-smoothed pebbles, pressing their cold young bodies together, clinging to each other with thin and tender arms.

"Do you want to marry me when we grow up?" Francie whispered, her face pressed to his neck and shoulder.

"Oh, yes," he said fervently, "more than anything."

"Shall we promise to?" Her pale face was gleaming in the sealight of the cave.

"Now, you mean?"

"Yes."

"And we'll be bound by the promise?"

"Yes, of course." She laid her hand gently against the side of his face. And at that moment, it was what he wanted more than anything in the world.

"All right then. I promise."

"No, you have to say it right, with your name and my name and everything."

"All right. I, Patrick Gallagher, promise to marry you, Francie O'Sullivan."

"So help me God—go on, say it."

"So help me God."

"Say, I swear to God Almighty."

"I swear to God Almighty."

"Good." She raised her head and looked him directly in the eyes, a shy smile on her pretty child's face. "And I, Frances O'Sullivan, swear to God Almighty that I'll marry you, Patrick Gallagher, so help me God." They looked at each other shyly, thrilled and terrified by what they had done. "Now we must kiss, to seal the oath," Francie said. They had not kissed until then. They had held hands and hugged, but now as they lay naked in each other's arms in the dripping cave, they brought their lips together and kissed with a deep and startling tenderness.

Afterwards they walked down the beach hand in hand. The squall had blown over and the sky was jubilant with sunshine and skimming clouds, the pebble beach glistening with foam froth and precious stones. They were both shy and exhilarated over what had happened. "Does this mean we're engaged, do you think?" he asked.

"Of course it does, silly." Francie laughed, nudging him towards the tideline. "So I'd better not ever catch you looking at another girl."

"I never will," he promised.

"Me neither. At a boy, I mean."

Betrothed as they considered themselves to be, both remained true to that childhood pledge. Even when Gallagher prematurely stopped growing, and his childhood impishness faded into homely adolescence and young manhood, while Francie blossomed into extraordinary beauty, their bond of affection held. Boys and men alike flirted with Francie and tried whatever they could to attract her interest. She'd dance gaily with them at parish dances and laugh at their jokes or stories at social gatherings. She was never aloof, but at her heart she was inaccessible to any of them. She had pledged herself to Patrick and would never renege on that pledge. She loved him to the core, loved everything about him—his stories, his uncanny knack for discovering beauty in things that to her had seemed commonplace until he spoke of them in words that rang like poetry. Her *Seannacai*, she called him, her storyteller. He might not look like a movie star, but she knew his heart was true and that he was devoted completely to her. And so he was. The more she grew in loveliness and grace, the more he marvelled at his astonishing good fortune, that he of all people should have become so intimately bonded with this beauty.

Observing them walking out on the lanes together of an evening, hand in hand—Francie by now the taller of the two—neighbours shook their heads in bemusement. Beauty and the Beast, he knew they called them. Short and ugly, long and lovely. Could it possibly last, they wondered. His peers did not know what to make of Patrick at all, how he had pulled off such a coup. "Is it the size of your feller has got her mesmerized?" they teased him. "Or is it that tongue of yours that's grown so mighty after all yer talking?" Gallagher let them natter, aware of their envy, immune to their taunts.

Only his mother troubled him about Francie. "You have to be careful of girls," she'd cautioned him throughout his adolescence. "They can get a young feller like you into a lot of trouble." Sex was what she was warning him against and the wiles of women in using sex to entrap a guileless boy. The more apparent it became to her that Patrick and Francie were inseparable, the more she fretted that her son would lose his head over that young beauty only to have his heart broken, or worse, once the girl fully realized that her looks could win her a far grander prize than Patrick.

Talking solemnly together one evening, after they'd kissed and kissed for hours in a lonely spot far from prying eyes, where wild fuchsias bloomed in scarlet profusion, the lovers decided they should wait until they were married before they consummated their union. This was a precaution that had been hammered at them relentlessly from the pulpit for as long as they could remember. Neither had spoken to their parents about marriage. Francie's mother had died some years previous and her father, an ambitious man (some called it cunning) whose ambition had yet to bear fruit, saw in his daughter a great opportunity for advancement. It hadn't escaped his notice that among the males who circled her longingly were several sons of leading families in the county. With a bit of judicious arranging, Francie's future might well be brokered into something quite handsome for himself. Like Patrick's mother, he was concerned about the peculiar bond between the two young people, but was likewise convinced that his daughter would soon drop Patrick and widen her horizons in search of a husband worthy of her.

Conscious of the obstacles they faced, the impossibility of marrying without a livelihood, the lovers waited, and in the waiting their hunger for each other swelled to the breaking point. Then eventually it burst one mad evening at the Harvest Festival at Ballydehob, the annual merrymaking that marked a successful harvest and the end of summer. Half the town would be gathered along the sidewalks of the main street. Kids running everywhere. Old ones standing at their doorways having a look at the goings-on, pretending to think it was all tomfoolery but wanting to see it nevertheless. Geezers spilling out of the pubs, pints in hand, so's not to miss anything. The crazy turnip race up the hill, with everyone cheering and laughing from the doorways. Music in the streets all night. Among the highlights was the wheelbarrow race that involved one guy pushing a wheelbarrow, in which his partner sat, up the hilly main street of town, with designated stops along the route at which bottles of beer had to be drank. On the evening in question, Patrick and his pal Doonan were competing as a team. Being smaller and lighter than most, Patrick got to sit in the barrow and guzzle the beer while Doonan did the pushing. It was all craziness and done in good fun and no one much cared who won or lost.

Although they'd won the previous year, Patrick and Doonan didn't win that night, Doonan having lost his shoe halfway up the hill and tumbled into a gutter. But when they crossed the finish line a respectable third, there was Francie standing slightly apart from the crowd, waiting for him. She was wearing tight blue jeans and a pink camisole that left her arms and shoulders bare and the smooth soft top of her chest exposed. Patrick was unusually jolly from having swilled too much beer so fast and the night was warm with a sensuous closeness. The carnival atmosphere of the festival seemed to encourage abandonment, the lifting of strictures for this one night at least as summer drew to a close. Francie and Patrick walked arm in arm away from the crowd, down a darkened street of large brick homes and past an abandoned mill derelict with age and neglect. Beyond the mill they came to a field that was overgrown with wild grasses and, without any words, they wandered together into it. Ripe with seed heads bleached golden by the late summer sun, the tall grasses whispered at their passing. From back in town the music of fiddles and pipes danced in the mild evening air.

It began with a kiss that sent shivers of excitement down through the two of them. In no time at all they were thrashing together in the grass, fondling and wrestling, sweating and panting. Resistance collapsed, all their fine intentions and firm resolve swept away in a maelstrom of passionate longing from which there could be only one release. For all their inexperience, fumbling and clumsy, virgins both— oh, the sinful, lustful, mad rapture of that night!

Afterwards, they lay tangled together blissfully, staring up into the dark velvet dome of the summer sky, silent with a million shining stars. Her head rested on his arm, her long hair spreading across his chest, an unconscious duplication of how they'd lain eight years before as betrothed innocents in the sea cave.

That one night of rapture marked the beginning of the end for them. Soon afterwards the filthy Irish winter moved in, with lowered skies and drifting mists. Colour fled the landscape and the dark little cottages hunkered down in grey gloom. Then the devastating news, predictable as death: Francie was with child. Her pregnancy tore everything apart. "What can we do?" she wailed after she'd told him. They spent long hours discussing the possibility of an abortion in England, but Francie didn't think that her conscience would let her go through with it. They considered eloping, but where would they go? How could they survive? Fear and anxiety overran them, goading him to anger and her to petulance. They quarrelled bitterly, each blaming the other. Then the worst of all outcomes: Francie in her torment and confusion took her troubles to the confessional and revealed her situation to the parish priest.

"You told Feeney?" Patrick was incredulous when she reported what she'd done. "Oh, Jesus!" The dripping stone walls along either side of the boreen down that they were walking seemed to move in on them, thick with tree roots and mosses, squeezing them into a trap.

"It was in the confessional, Patrick. He won't tell anyone; he's forbidden to." Dark oak trees above them rattled arthritic limbs in the wind.

He couldn't believe her gullibility. He knew straightaway that he and Francie must flee as soon as they could, and to do that they'd need money, whether for an abortion or just to get away. Without a word to her, he set a plan in motion. First he connived to get Jimmy Sloane, the dimwitted treasurer of their little IRA cell, to advance him three hundred punt with an elaborate tale of their helping finance an upcoming action in the North. The following day he stole his parents' savings. He was racing down the road from his house to Francie's with the roll of banknotes in his pocket, the sky above him boiling with huge bruise-coloured clouds and the wind tearing at old bracken in the fields, when he saw her older sister, Mary, running towards him. "Patrick," she panted, her loose coat flapping in the wind, a wildness in her face and manner, "our dad knows."

"How? Did Francie . . ."

"Father Feeney was just up. I overheard him tell Da. He said something about the sanctity of life outweighing the sanctity of the confessional." She held her coat to her chest against the tearing wind.

"Shite!" A terrifying uncertainty seized him. Mary's thin hair blew about her face and the grasses of the fields writhed in panic.

"He's locked her in the cellar and he's fetching his gun. You'd better run, Patrick, run for your feckin' life!"

And run he had, out of Cork to Dublin first and then clear out of the country to Canada. And never gone back.

GALLAGHER shifted uneasily in his recliner, still gazing upward at the ceiling, as though those scenes of childhood had just played out on its rough plaster surface. Far sharper than the guilt of petty thievery, he felt a renewed wash of shame over his abandonment of Francie. What had become of her, he wondered. Was she happily married to some unsuspecting husband, plump and happy now with a houseful of kids. He imagined so, hoped so. Hell, she might be living in New

Zealand or South Africa now for all he knew. But of all the old ghosts he must avoid in the coming week, he recognized that the ghost of wronged Francie was the one he could least afford to encounter. Then, chiding himself that all of this was lost in the distant past, and that likely nobody remembered any of it other than himself, he climbed out of the recliner and slowly made his way to bed.

SIX

THE FIRST glimpse he had of Ireland was looking down into a mass of curdling clouds with only a small archipelago of dark mountaintops breaking through the soggy shroud. Maybe the Mountains of Mourne, Gallagher thought. He was squeezed in at the window seat alongside a bulky Russian and his wife, neither of whom spoke any English. He was altogether fed up with being confined in so small a place for so long. Unaccustomed to flying—he'd crossed the Atlantic that first time working aboard a tramp steamer—for him this trip had been a horror, over nine hours in the air, and jet lag was coating his brain like slime. He felt a pressing need to take a piss, but the Fasten Seat Belt signs were on already in preparation for landing. He stared out again at the smothering cloudbank beneath them. "Sheep shit and showers, that's your Ireland for you," he half-muttered to the uncomprehending Russian as the big plane tipped its wings and plunged suicidally down into the mist.

When they emerged from under the clouds, startlingly, they were almost on the ground. Through beaded streams of moisture on the window he peered into the depths of a watery world. Green fields and trees wept openly in the wind. Gallagher felt a wave of panic assail him, though whether it sprang from the plane's sudden plunge or from uneasiness at returning to the country of his birth, he couldn't tell. Touching down with a bounce, the jet screamed along the runway. Tall grasses alongside the tarmac swayed in the wind like seaweed. Vastnesses of sodden green swam up against grey sky.

Disgorged from the plane, he and his fellow passengers tramped into Dublin airport, numbly following the signs for luggage. Far larger than he'd expected, the airport roared with voices and machines. He ducked into a toilet and relieved himself with not a moment left to spare. Drearily the passengers waited at the luggage carousel for their bags to appear. Finally a warning horn blared and the carousel shuddered into motion, its articulated metal sheets moving like the underbelly scales of a snake, and luggage began tumbling out of a chute. He retrieved his bag—a brand-new rolling duffle from the Gypsy Rover Travel Shop on Kingsway—and was directed by coloured stripes on the walls into the customs area for non-EU travellers. After queuing for a few minutes, he pulled his bag up to the customs counter.

"Passport please," said the officer, a big florid fellow with his cap on askew who looked to Gallagher like he was just fresh in off the farm. He searched through several zippered pockets in the nylon pants a persuasive salesman at the travel shop had talked him into buying for the trip—like a magician's coat, they were wonderful for the wealth of pockets they contained—found his passport, and slapped it on the counter. The officer glanced through it indifferently. Gallagher had never been anywhere really, but he'd got the passport because he liked to go down to Reno every once in a while for a bit of a toot— the package tour bus prices were great—and the Yanks had become so paranoid and snarky at the border crossing recently you needed a passport to get through. The customs man glanced at Gallagher and then at the passport photograph. He swiped the passport on some kind of computer thing and stared at the monitor impassively. "One moment please, sir," he said and disappeared through a door behind his booth. Another officer farther along smiled companionably at Gallagher, managing through the simple twisting of a few facial muscles to both apologize for the inconvenience and warn him to remain exactly where he was.

"Would you mind stepping this way please, sir?" the florid officer said from the doorway. Gallagher went in through the door pulling his rolling duffle behind him. The officer left the room, closing the door.

"Good morning, sir," said another officer who was standing behind a long table and holding Gallagher's passport in his hand. He was a trim young man with eyes like watery skim milk. The blank walls of the room were an insipid green and there were no windows. A stink of disinfectant filled the room. "Mr. Gallagher, is it?"

"That's right." He knew straight off that this was an interrogation room like they had on *Law & Order*.

"Born in County Cork, I see."

"Correct."

"Beautiful country that though, isn't it?"

"Nice enough all right." Gallagher was standing awkwardly in the middle of the room.

"The seascapes. The agriculture. Old Ireland at its finest. Good craig down that way, eh?"

"Suppose so. Haven't seen it in twenty years."

"Have y'not? Y've not been home in twenty years?" The fellow tipped his cap back, as though in amazement.

"Something like that. Canada's my home now."

"Ah, yes, of course. Wonderful country from all I've heard."

"It's all right." Gallagher was fingering the handle of his bag, wanting to get on.

"Mountains. Prairie. Tundra." The officer gestured grandly towards imagined landscapes. "I'd love to see it myself."

Gallagher didn't respond. He distrusted customs men and cops on principle and was perfectly aware that this wanker was up to something. Perhaps stalling for time. Perhaps trying to soften him up. Gallagher had watched enough TV shows to know all the games cops like to play.

"So you've been in Canada twenty years now, have you?"

"Near on."

"And how do y'find it, then?"

"Look," Gallagher snapped, losing patience, "I been flyin' all night, I've got important work to get on with, and I ain't got the time to stand around here nubbin' with you about life in the Great White North, all right?"

The officer was unperturbed by this outburst. "What brings you to Ireland now?"

"I'm leading a garden tour."

"A garden tour?"

"That's it. Where a bunch of people tour a bunch of gardens." Sarcasm was beginning to rise like bile in Gallagher's esophagus. "I'm in the employ of an internationally recognized travel company," he added for good measure.

"You're a gardener, are you?"

"No, I'm a feckin' trapeze artist that does garden tours as a sideline. What's all this about, anyway?"

Just at that moment there came a discreet tapping at the door.

"Excuse me for a moment, will you?" the officer said and slipped out through the door. Gallagher could hear a low murmuring of voices on the other side. Then the door swung open and the customs man re-entered followed by a woman in police uniform. "Mr. Gallagher," the customs man said, "this is Sergeant Leary from the Gardai."

"Hello," the woman said briskly. She seated herself at the table and snapped her briefcase open. Gallagher realized it was a laptop computer. She clicked on it several times, waited, clicked again, then nodded to the machine as though thanking a helpful colleague. Gallagher could see right away that she was of the grey-haired-granny-made-of-granite type. She looked him up and down.

"Now, Mr. Gallagher," she said in a voice that he instantly recognized from the nuns who'd taught him in school, "how long do you plan to be in Ireland?"

"Twelve days," Gallagher said. He had decided to stay on for several days after the tour in case his quest for a benefactor required a bit of extra time.

"And where do you plan on going over the course of those twelve days?"

"Dublin mostly. Why, what's it to you?"

Leary looked at him as if considering whether or not to give him the strap. "Mr. Gallagher, we're quite aware of who you are, you know."

"My introductions, you mean? I wouldn't have thought word had spread this far."

"I refer to your past criminal associations and behaviour."

His brain felt a sudden lurch and snap, as at the drop of a hang-man's trap. Jesus Christ, he was thinking, I'm not out of the feckin' airport yet and already the fukkers are on to me. Composing himself, he decided to bluff his way through. "What? Gettin' a bit merry on a Saturday night a time or two with my pals. You're callin' that criminal behaviour." He was holding his ground, chin up, with an aspect of fear-lessness like that of a matador in full control of his bull.

"No, sir, I mean your past association with extremist elements of the Republican movement."

"Hah! You think I'm with the feckin' Provos? That's a laugh. No, you've got your inputs spannered there, missus; I was never one of the lads. Never." But how much did they really know about his past activities, he wondered.

"You mean you were never caught?"

"Never had grounds for bein' caught. Never did anything meritin' catching." His bravado held true, building like a wind from the west.

"Lack of a criminal record is not necessarily the same thing as absence of criminal intent or conduct." She could have been a Mother Superior, this one. "As I'm sure you well know, a number of your less fortunate associates did indeed spend time in prison. Several are still incarcerated for what can only be described as heinous crimes."

"What associates would them be then?" Gallagher's demeanour of confidence remained masterful.

"Dermot Finucane, for one."

"Never met the feller."

"Or Bobby Storey?"

"Nope."

"Or Bernard Shannon?"

"Not him neither."

"And of course you didn't participate in planning the cowardly ambush of a security patrol on Rosnareen Flats in 1981?"

"No I did not!" The accusations were really starting to stick in Gallagher's craw. Okay, he may have put a bit of an oar in here and there for the Cause back in the old days, but he'd be damned if he'd stand still against an accusation of cowardly ambush. Who did this silly cow think she was?

"And you didn't attend the funeral of Colm McGirr, a known member of the IRA, in 1983 at Coalisland?"

"No I didn't!"

"Isn't that interesting," Leary said, looking as though she'd just tricked him into confessing his crimes. She clicked again at her laptop. "I wonder how it is then that we have a photograph of you attending that very funeral."

"You can't have. I wasn't there. Simple as that." Gallagher sounded as though he was still on firm ground, but he didn't dare glance down.

"Take a look." She spun the laptop around on the table. "There you are, Mr. Gallagher, as plain as day, all dressed up in your Sunday best." Gallagher stepped forward and looked. An arrow on the screen pointed to a face in a huge throng of mourners.

"That's not me!" He wanted to add "you silly bint," but didn't. The photo was entirely inconclusive, wildly speculative at best.

"No? Why don't we take a closer look." Oh, she was full of herself this one. She clicked a couple of times and the monitor zoomed in on one small cluster of the crowd. The arrow pointed to a face that Gallagher might have sworn was his own. "Still maintain you weren't there Mr. Gallagher, do you?"

"I was not!" But surety was slipping like a greased piglet from his grasp. "The resemblance is uncanny, I'll grant you that. But that tosser isn't me. I never was in Coalisland in my life and I never attended no IRA funeral." Resemblance, hell, it's me all right, he was thinking, must have been on a batter and forgotten all about it. Too late now; he'd have to sham his way through.

"Nor any IRA assassination raid?"

"Not on your life! They're a bunch of murderin' thugs who I had no earthly use for then or now." This was overstating things a bit, but with this harridan menacing him, he considered a touch of overstatement to be not entirely out of order.

"Is this the only luggage you've brought with you?" She pointed to his rolling duffle as though it might contain a grenade launcher.

"It is."

"May we examine its contents?"

"I can hardly prevent you, if that's what you want t'do, now can I?"

Leary nodded to the customs man who'd been standing attentively in the background. He came forward and hefted the bag onto the table. The zippers were locked with laughable little padlocks you could crush with a nutcracker. "May I have the key please, sir?" the customs man said.

Gallagher dug around in his pockets again and found the miniature key on a ring with Saint Christopher. The officer unlocked the zippers and returned the key to Gallagher. He unzipped the various pouches in the bag and began pulling out their contents: rain jacket, umbrella, a plastic bread bag stuffed with underwear, another full of socks, more nylon shirts and trousers like the ones Gallagher was wearing. He handed across to Leary the large manilla envelope from Berenice Travel, containing the itinerary and vouchers and petty cash float for the tour. She went through the whole package page by page.

Once all the bag's contents were spread on the table, the customs man meticulously searched the bag for anything that might be hidden in secret compartments. Putting it down finally, he shook his head at Leary.

"Your backpack too please, sir," Leary said, not looking at him as she thumbed through his documents. "And empty all your pockets."

Jays, thought Gallagher to himself, they'll be groping up me arsehole before they're done. He took the little backpack from his back and passed it over, then emptied all his pockets onto the table. The bottle of Jameson's whiskey that he'd purchased at the duty-free was placed on the table. Leary glanced at it as though it were further evidence of corruption. But there was nothing the least bit incriminating in any of his stuff.

"Fine," Leary said at last, snapping her laptop closed. "Mr. Gallagher," she said in a stern voice, fixing him with a stare that would have frozen boiling fat in a chipper, "we know who you are, we know where you're staying, and we know what you're supposed to be doing here in Ireland. I would strongly advise you to do just that and nothing more. Any contact with persons of interest to us from a national security point of view will not go unobserved. Do I make myself perfectly clear?"

"Y'do, yeah," said Gallagher, feeling his already-tenuous position additionally compromised by having his underwear and socks spread on the table between himself and the woman. He was wishing he'd included new socks and especially underwear in his purchases.

"Were it not for our desire to avoid any unpleasantness between ourselves and the government of Canada," she said severely, "we should be inclined to deny you access to the Republic of Ireland. We will not take that extreme measure, because of the legitimate business you appear to have at hand. But you'd be well advised to confine your activities and your contacts to that legitimate business and that legitimate business alone."

"That's exactly my intention," Gallagher said with his chin thrust out.

"I'm delighted to hear it," Leary said, not looking the least bit delighted. "My advice to you, sir, is to step very carefully. Step very carefully indeed."

And my advice to you, thought Gallagher, is to go step in dog shite all afternoon. But he held his tongue. This formidable policewoman, like the nuns of old, had succeeded in bringing him to heel.

He repacked all his stuff and shuffled his way out through the crowded terminal. The place was swarming with a planeload of passengers returning from a pilgrimage to Lourdes. Many were in wheelchairs or on crutches or had other visible infirmities. They were being met by crowds of family and friends, with tears and embracing. Miracles were expected to have occurred. Maybe had occurred. Gallagher could hardly navigate through all the commotion around him, he was that thrown off by Leary's interrogation. The photograph especially had knocked him out of kilter. It was plain that the authorities knew at least that much about him that he hadn't known, or hadn't remembered, himself. Caught in the crush of crippled pilgrims, he wondered for a wild moment what else they knew about him. In the bedlam of the terminal, Gallagher thought he could hear strange cries and laughter, as though the Fates had just flown in themselves in jubilant mood to claim him.

⊞ SEVEN ⊞

AFTER STARING at a bewildering map of serpentine bus routes on the terminal wall, he decided to catch an air coach from the airport into the city. He bought a round trip for ten euros ("bloody robbery," he muttered under his breath), then stood on the sidewalk waiting for the coach and looking up blankly into the sprinkling sky. His nerves were shredded badly from the interview. He felt as though he'd had his head pushed through a wall into another dimension, one he'd never visited before but which was nevertheless disturbingly familiar to him. Had that really been him in the funeral throng at Coalisland? It was a mystery to him, and he realized anew it was part of what he hated about this feckin' country: it was forever crawling with mysteries. Secrecies and labyrinths that had a way of getting you by the throat and sucking the lifeblood out of you like some stinking bog-drain. He'd been here barely an hour and already he could feel the clammy hands of secrecy fumbling at his flesh.

Seated on the coach, he was viscerally aware of Leary's warning that he'd be under observation throughout his visit. He'd been flushed from his home to begin with, and now he was out in the open, fair game for Christ only knows what predators might be prowling about. The couple in the seat right behind him on the coach, for starters. Their ostentatious demonstrating that they were from Australia—a few too many "fair dinkums" and "good on yers" to be quite credible—had him wondering if they were tailing him. For one thing, they were decked out exactly the way informers would dress if they were pretending to be tourists, in poncey travel gear, Tilley hats and all. Several times he caught the coach driver—a smartass little yob with shaved head and earring—observing him in the rear-view mirror. Oh, yes, he was being watched all right.

The coach was soon mired in a traffic jam caused by construction work on the M1 motorway leading into Dublin City. Gallagher gazed out the window morosely. Grey clouds were scudding eastwards overhead. Ragged gobs of rain splattered like spittle in the construction mud. For all the elaborate detours and consequent delays, not a lot of actual road building was evident in the churned earth. Why the hell had he come to this godforsaken place anyway? And what of his roses, pining for him back home? Were their lovely petals cascading to the ground, their long canes prostrate for want of him? He'd left a university student from down the road in charge of them, an enthusiastic girl who appeared to be majoring in volleyball, but he doubted she'd be up to the task. I'm a feckin' idiot, Gallagher told himself, to make a stupid choice like this. How was he ever going to save his home by wandering about in a country now grown entirely alien to him? They plunged forward through the mud.

Eventually, closer to town, as the coach shouldered its way through the teeming streets of Whitehall and Glasnevin, he saw swelling crowds of football fans gathered at corners and pouring out of pubs. Some carried banners or flags, almost all were dressed in club colours. They seemed impervious to the dripping conditions. Gallagher roused himself at last, recognizing that many were dressed in the red and white of Cork, his old club colours. It did his heart good to see signs of Fightin' Cork, whose star players had been his boyhood heroes. For the first time since his bruising encounter with Leary, Gallagher felt his spirits rising. Other fans, dressed in orange and white, he guessed were from Armagh. It must be an all-Ireland match, he thought, over at Croke Park, though whether it was Gaelic football or hurling he had no idea. "Hey, driver!" he called forward, "what time's that game scheduled for startin'?"

"Dunno," the yob mumbled back.

"What is it, then? An All-Ireland final or what?" Gallagher called. The driver caught his eye in the big overhead mirror. He pointed to a sign beside the mirror warning passengers to stay behind the white line while the coach was in motion and not to distract the driver. Gallagher made a face of frustrated disgust and threw his hands in the air. "Bollocks!" he said loud enough for the driver to hear. But aroused from his despondency by the fighting colours of Cork, like a child whose mood can swing dramatically in an instant with each new stimulus, forgetting the mix-up with Leary and her troubling photograph and the thought of his loved ones languishing at home, Gallagher took to waving out the coach window and giving the thumbs-up to the milling

Cork supporters, none of whom were paying the least bit of attention to either him or the coach.

Soon they were in the heart of the city, inching towards the O'Connell Street Bridge. Gallagher craned his neck looking for Madigan's, an old pub on O'Connell Street he remembered. And the Oval just around the corner, and Sean O'Casey's only another block up. He'd lived in Dublin only for a short while after fleeing Cork and arranging passage to Canada, but he was reminiscing to himself as though he'd spent years in the city. He stared out at the gridlocked traffic and the shoals of pedestrians, their clustered umbrellas moving like a plague of shiny black beetles through the dreary streets. The coach crawled past the General Post Office, where Pearse and Collins and the rest had started the Easter Uprising, and where bullet holes were still visible in the pillars out front.

Having reached the O'Connell Street Bridge, the coach bogged down in the middle. Gallagher peered down at the River Liffey. The tide was out and the sad little stream was sunken to a scummy runnel. Garbage and dreck littered its exposed banks. He'd forgotten how small it was, and in his imagination had developed a more exalted notion of Dublin's fabled river than what in reality it now appeared to be. Compared with the mighty Fraser, one arm of which emptied into the Salish Sea not far from his home, the Liffey, for all the blather about Anna Livia, was little more than an urban ditch. But looking upstream, he saw the Ha'penny Bridge and, even in the gloom, with the Liffey at its lowest, the graceful ironwork arch of the footbridge and its reflection in the river gave the illusion of an enormous watery eye with the smaller arches of the Gratton Bridge forming its pupil. In the pearl-grey light the composition tinged the slimy Liffey with a lingering tint of Joycean magic.

Above the city skyline enormous building cranes loomed like preying insects.

Nudging through the maelstrom again, they swung around Trinity College and stopped at Nassau Street. "That's my stop!" exclaimed Gallagher, jumping up. He clambered out of the coach and retrieved his bag from the driver at the back. "How do I find Molesworth Street from here?" he asked the driver. The yob tilted his head towards

Grafton Street without a word and returned to the coach. Rude little pisser, thought Gallagher.

Another passenger, who'd also disembarked and claimed his bag, now said to Gallagher, "Excuse me, I couldn't help but overhear. I know Molesworth Street and am going that way myself. It's a bit of a zigzag from here, shall I show you the way?" The fellow spoke with the flat tones of a Canadian, and Gallagher had to suppress a small annoyance at being directed in the city by an outsider.

"I'm headed for Stanton's Hotel," he said to the stranger.

"Indeed? That's precisely where I'm bound for too. You wouldn't by any chance be part of the garden tour, would you?"

"I would," said Gallagher, surprised, "Happens I'm the tour director."

"You're Mister Gallagher? Well, I'll be damned! What a happy coincidence. I'm Michael Wickerson." He thrust out his hand and shook Gallagher's warmly. "How are you? I'm one of your tour-goers."

"Are you now?" Gallagher said, looking him over. Thirty-something probably. Smartly but casually dressed. A pleasing face with fine features, clear and honest-looking eyes, and silky, flaxen-coloured hair. An air of sophisticated informality. "That's grand."

"Shall we go then?" Wickerson gestured across to where tourists were surging like spermatozoa up onto Grafton Street. The rain had retreated again into drizzling mist and the wind had dropped away entirely.

They crossed at the corner and were swept into Grafton Street by the crowd. Tacking this way and that, they dragged their bags through shoals of shopping tourists, past buskers, musicians, mimes, landscape painters, photographers, beggars, and assorted street-life forms all suckling like piglets on the swollen teats of Grafton Street pedestrian mall. There was even a McDonald's partway up the block. "Look at that," said Wickerson, pointing to it with distaste. "This used to be a real neighbourhood—people still remember the glory days when the poet Patrick Kavanagh would emerge from the Eblana Bookshop, clapping on his big hat and striding off down Grafton Street with his hands clasped behind his back, muttering poems that only he could hear. And now it's reduced to this: Yankee burger joints and trashy kitsch. Could you find a more vulgar final insult shouted through what's left of the Celtic Twilight?"

Gallagher, who'd been having a hard time manoeuvring his rolling duffle through the crush while listening to his new acquaintance, several times rolling right over some gawker's feet, struggled to keep up with Wickerson, who walked with an easy, long-legged stride. "Worse than Robson Street on Friday night," Gallagher grouched as they detoured left and into a back eddy of relative calm on the way over towards Dawson Street.

"You're from Vancouver, are you?" Wickerson asked him, as though surprised at the news.

"Aye. Been there twenty years since leaving here."

"It's my home too."

"Is it?"

"Yes, I teach at UBC."

"Ah, not far from where I live then." A brief pang pricked Gallagher as he thought again of his home and its peril.

"Where's that?"

"Down Southlands."

"Very nice. A bit of the countryside right in the city. I envy you."

"Yourself then?"

"Kitsilano at the moment. A tiny house that the bank and I own, now suddenly worth a fortune."

"Tell me about it. How is it you know Dublin then?" They had to squeeze their way around a pod of motorcycles parked all over the sidewalk. A couple of muscular bikers were sharing a joint and laughing.

"I teach English literature and specialize in Irish authors. So I'm over here off and on, for conferences and that sort of thing."

"I see. Why would you be bothering with this little tour then?"

"Well, you know, I needed a break for personal reasons; I'm on sabbatical now. And, as often as I've been here, I've never paid any attention to the gardens, although of course they are an important element in much of the writing. Think of Seamus Heaney's spade sinking into gravely ground, or Yeats' daughter living like some green laurel." He pointed casually to a trough of pelargoniums blooming jaunty red outside a small boutique. "So I thought, here's my chance to fill that void and be shown around some pleasurable places with absolutely no effort on my part." Wickerson smiled impishly, as though he were the class best boy caught doing something slightly naughty.

"Right you are. Very wise." Gallagher had taken a quick liking to Wickerson, which was not something he did readily with strangers. Suspicion of others was his default mode. But he liked this fellow's easygoing manner and apparent lack of pretence. They walked on past small shops and offices until they emerged onto Dawson Street, where Wickerson stopped suddenly and pointed to a bronze plaque embedded in the sidewalk. "Now look at this, Mr. Gallagher." The plaque bore a quote from *Ulysses*: "'You're in Dawson Street,' Mr. Bloom said. 'Molesworth Street is opposite. Do you want to cross?'" Gallagher couldn't make heads nor tails of it.

"It's Mr. Leopold Bloom speaking to a blind man on the street," Wickerson explained casually. "It's one of the things I love best about Dublin, how it drips with literary history. You'll turn a corner and there'll be a sculpture of Oscar Wilde or GBS smiling down at you. I find that absolutely wonderful."

"Aye."

Gallagher had never thought of it before, and of course he hadn't known Dublin all that well to begin with. Wickerson's familiarity with it underscored how superficially Gallagher was connected with the place.

"Well, we've come to Molesworth Street." Wickerson swept his arm forward, as though for royalty. "Shall we cross over?" And across they went into the little street that, notwithstanding Ulyssean immortality, was only one block long. Their hotel, Stanton's, was at the far end, just down from Kildare Street and the National Museum. The hotel consisted of several converted and conjoined Georgian townhouses.

"Not exactly the Ritz," Wickerson said, standing in the modest lobby with his bag, "but I suppose it will do handsomely enough for us, don't you think, Mr. Gallagher?"

"I guess." Gallagher was no familiar of luxury hotels, and the authenticity of this place appealed to him.

"Now, to my way of thinking, Mr. Gallagher," Wickerson said, "no matter how tired or jet lagged one feels from a long flight, the very worst thing to do is to surrender to the bed. You want to adjust to the new time zone straightaway, get your circadian clock ticking properly from the get-go. So you stay awake, stay active until it's time to sleep for the night. Don't you agree?"

"Right you are," Gallagher said, though he was longing for a good lie-down. He hadn't even known he had a circadian clock, but he could see some sense in what his new friend said.

"Suppose," Wickerson proposed, "we were to check in, unpack, freshen up, and then go find ourselves a drink?"

"Now you're talkin' my language."

The girl at reception—identified as Nuala by the name tag on her blazer—produced an envelope for Gallagher when they were checking in. He stuffed it into one of his pockets. The room they gave him was rather small and gloomy, but he didn't mind; he was accustomed to small and gloomy from his own little rat's nest back home. He unpacked, shaved and showered and brushed the fuzz off his teeth, then returned to the lobby refreshed to meet up with Wickerson, whose room was elsewhere in the rabbit warren.

"Would you mind telling me where a person might get a drop in these parts?" Gallagher asked Nuala at the counter. "Being as I'm unfamiliar with this section of the city."

"Certainly, sir." She had a lovely smile and a fine way about her, this Nuala did. "We've our own bar just around the corner here."

"Oh, aye."

"Or if you'd prefer," she added, "you could walk up here to Saint Stephen's Green"—she pointed off behind her—"then take a left on Merrion Row." The girl's voice had the lilting rise and fall of the Kerry Hills and it did Gallagher's spirits no end of good to hear it. "Just on there a bit you'll see O'Donoghue's on the far side, or a bit farther along on Baggot Street Lower you'll have Connell and Larkin's or Big Jack's Baggot Inn across the way."

"And which would you recommend, like?" He was admiring the way she brushed her long auburn hair back from her face with slender fingers.

"Depends what you're after," Nuala said. "Big Jack's is pretty heavy on the rock music nowadays."

"Oh, aye. Say, you must be from County Kerry yourself, are you, with a voice on you like that?"

"Yes, I am," Nuala said, smiling sweetly. "A little place called Kilcummin. I'm sure you've not heard of it at all."

"No, I've not," Gallagher said. He was finding himself becoming more Irish by the minute and more of a gallant than he'd been for a good long while. For all his misgivings about this returning, he was pleasantly surprised to find the spirit of old Ireland so much alive in him still. "I'm from West Cork meself."

"Are you?" She cocked her head sideways and let her lovely eyebrows camber fetchingly.

"Aye. Little place not far from Ballydehob."

"That's grand. You might prefer Toner's then; it's more like an old country pub."

"Ah, that would be lovely, wouldn't it?" He was leaning familiarly on the counter now.

"Mind you, I'm told Connell and Larkin's has some nice old snugs."

"Does it now?" He could have talked pubs with Nuala all night.

"They say it's where the journalists and politicians and all that sort go for their gossip." Oh, the lilt of that voice!

"Kinda private, like, then, is it?"

"They say so, yes."

"Y'don't go yourself, then?"

"No I don't. My husband doesn't care to drink and he hates the smoke in those places." She wrinkled her nose in distaste.

"Your husband?" We could have done without him, Gallagher was thinking.

"Yes."

"And y'don't go without him?"

"Oh, no. Truth to tell, I don't much care for them either." She smiled apologetically.

"No? Not a bit a fun on Saturday night, like?"

"No. I'd rather watch the television."

Gallagher's fantasies, barely aloft, tumbled to Earth just as Wickerson emerged into the lobby. "Well, thanks for the tips," he winked and cocked his head at Nuala in one quick motion.

"No problem," she said and went back to her paperwork.

The two men had barely turned the corner onto Kildare Street when three little red-headed kids, all holding hands, appeared in front of them. "You look funny," the oldest little girl said to Gallagher, and all three kids giggled.

"What?" said Gallagher, staring down at the freckled midgets.

"Damien! Mary! Justin! Get back here this minute!" shrilled a young woman nearby. She was grappling with a baby carriage and was hugely pregnant. The little kids ran back to her, giggling.

"Jays," Gallagher said under his breath, "still breedin' like feckin' rabbits over here I see."

"So it would appear," Wickerson agreed, then went over, with a gallant bow, to assist the woman get her carriage over the curb.

"Well, some things change and some things don't," Gallagher said, as he and Wickerson set off again up Kildare.

"Undoubtedly true," Wickerson agreed. He was glancing this way and that, apparently taking in the architecture of the street.

"'Course it is." Gallagher had to half-hop every few steps to keep up. "It's the priests put 'em up to it, y'know. Not the screwing, of course, that's the last thing the clergy would ever encourage. Still, priests or no priests, they manage to get up to it one way or another, even if they don't enjoy it all that much and feel guilty as sin the minute the jism's spilt and then they can't get to a confessional fast enough to tell the priest all about it."

Wickerson smiled at Gallagher's analysis.

"Not like your Eyetalians, for example." Gallagher was off and away on one of his favourite themes. "Eyetalians are every bit as industrious, but they don't necessarily keep their eyes closed the whole time they're humping away, as your Irish lover is inclined to do, nor neither do they feel it's imperative to produce a child after every tumble they way they do here. You follow my meanin'?"

"Indeed. Most intriguing." Wickerson seemed more interested in the National Museum building across the way, but Gallagher held to his thesis.

"It's the clergy here, y'realize, tell 'em they can't take preventative measures, even if they want to, which most of 'em don't. You're supposed to hold off until the right time of the month if you don't require any progeny just then. But either they feel in need of the extra mouths to feed or they simply haven't the patience to wait 'til the time is right because the kids keep popping out as regular as the sperm pops in." Gallagher made popping in and out gestures with his hand. "But what beats me is why the priests in Italy aren't on about the same thing. There's no one more Catholic than the Eyetalians, they get most of the popes and everythin', but you don't see them trailin' around with a dozen kids apiece. And you can't tell me the Eyetalians are exercisin' moderation, because they don't know the meanin' of the word. There's no one screws more enthusiastically than your Eyetalian. So they must be takin' measures, don't you agree?"

"I would think so." Wickerson gestured off to his left and they made the turn.

"But why the Eyetalian priests are allowing contraception and the Irish ones aren't is a mystery to me. Do you think it's maybe tied up with the sex scandals here? Y'know, they found one of the archbishops or something of that sort—I believe it may have been here in Dublin itself—was leading a double life. He was. Had a mistress or a wife, I don't remember which, and a house and kid, all neatly tucked away someplace so no one knew a thing about it. Remarkable that was."

"Are you familiar with the Triads of Ireland, Mr. Gallagher?" Wickerson asked out of the blue.

"I don't think so."

"Ninth century. One of them says something along the lines of 'Three ruins of a tribe: a lying chief, a false judge, a lustful priest.'"

"Aye, well, they've got the lustful priests here, no doubt about that, and probably the other two as well."

"Do you have children yourself, Mr. Gallagher?"

"Me? Oh, no. No, I'm not even married." He'd long ago ceased thinking of the child he'd fathered with Francie as his own. If it had ever even been born. But Wickerson's question, perhaps because of the jolt of being back in Dublin after all these years, caught him in a tender spot he hadn't known was there. A child, his child. He quickly brushed the idea aside, wishing that Wickerson had got into the spirit of kicking the clergy around. Then he wondered if maybe Wickerson was religious and had been offended by his remarks. They carried on to the pub without speaking further.

They found Connell and Larkin's main room was filling up and got themselves settled in a tiny snug. "Ah, that's better." Gallagher smacked his frothy lips after his first sip of Guinness. "None of that disgustin' Coors Light and Labatt Blue an' all that half-brewed alley-cat piss. A pint of the regular here makes you remember what real drinkin's about."

"I love it," Wickerson agreed, smiling amiably. "For all that drinking's a hopeless fetish in this culture, the experience itself is marvellous." He tilted his glass in acknowledgement of Gallagher. "And I like Dublin immensely. It's not what it was, of course, 'in the rare old times' as the song has it, but nevertheless there's still a certain something here I don't experience in other cities."

The laughter and humming energy of the crowd, and the comforting scents of several centuries of drink and smoke enveloped the two men. "You've travelled a lot have you?" Gallagher asked.

"Not really. I go here and there for conferences every so often," Wickerson said, waving a hand dismissively, "but at those events you spend most of your time sitting in a hotel or on a campus, either one of which could be anywhere. The dutiful hosts usually drag you around to a couple of tourist 'must-sees,' but you're seldom experiencing the real country or its people."

"Grafton Street again." Gallagher winked and sipped his pint.

"Right. That's what appealed to me about your tour, getting out and meeting some real people in their gardens, 'gardens where a soul's at ease,' as Yeats put it; that and . . ." He paused and a shadow briefly crossed his face. It was a handsome-enough face in which both gentleness and strength were present. A shock of long, fine hair fell across his forehead and he brushed it back reflexively. "Well, let's just say I'm happy to be here," he said, forcing a smile for Gallagher's benefit.

"Something the matter?"

"No. Well, yes actually. Everything."

Gallagher waited for him to go on. Suddenly a roar erupted from the pub crowd. A game must be underway on the television. "How do you mean?"

"This is difficult for me." Wickerson was plainly under some emotional duress. He stared at the tabletop for a minute, tracing a pattern on it with his forefinger. "But perhaps it's best I tell you." He looked up then, straight at Gallagher. "I lost my wife last year."

"Lost her how?"

"I mean she died, Mr. Gallagher."

"Ah, no." He didn't know what else to say.

"Of course I've been in the most dreadful funk ever since."

"Naturally you would."

"This may sound peculiar, but she was the gardener in the family, you see."

"Yes, it's mostly the women."

"And since she's gone, I've felt more drawn to gardening myself."

"You would, yes." Hopeless in matters of bereavement, Gallagher looked intently at a large stuffed salmon hanging on the wall across from him.

"So that's also partly why I'm here. To learn a bit about gardening. And I've . . . well, anyway, sorry to be a wet sock." Wickerson smiled weakly, pulling himself together.

"Not a bit of it."

"Perhaps," Wickerson added, "you'd do me the kindness of not mentioning any of this to anyone else in the group. I don't want to be singled out as an object of pity."

"Of course," Gallagher agreed. "Speakin' of the group, I'd better look at this letter here. May be somethin' important." He extracted the letter Nuala had given him, opened it carefully, and held it up to the faint light coming from a small and very dirty window behind them.

"What's it say?"

"It's from our guide. Bird named Ruth Wilburn." He was squinting to read the note. "Says she's arranged a meeting for everyone at the hotel before dinner."

"What time?"

"Let's see . . . six o'clock, it says. Dinner's at seven."

"Must be near to that already." Wickerson squinted at his watch. "Yes, it's ten after five already. We'll have to drink up and be on our way."

⊡ EIGHT ⊡

AS GALLAGHER entered the spacious but low-ceilinged meeting room below the hotel bar, he hesitated for a moment at the door. A dozen or so people stood in small groups of twos and threes, chatting with the nervous fidgetiness of strangers confined in an unfamiliar place. By their clothing they were unmistakably tourists, jaunty and informal and, well, touristy. An empty circle of chairs occupied the centre of the room, and he spotted Wickerson standing beyond the circle talking with a pair of young women. Every instinct in Gallagher urged him to flee. He was an imposter here, a counterfeit Stephen Aubrey. These people had each spent a considerable whack of money in the expectation that he would be providing them with invaluable insights in the elevated echelons of horticulture. But it was a sham, a fraud, a hoax. If he could he would have turned on his heel and fled.

But before anything could happen, he was approached by a thin brisk woman wearing a tartan skirt and carrying a clipboard. "Mr. Gallagher?" she greeted him enthusiastically.

"Yeah."

"Ruth Wilburn." She stuck out her right hand and Gallagher shook it. She had a grip like the Jaws of Life. "Delighted to meet you. A pleasant flight, I hope?"

"Was all right."

"Excellent!" She spoke with an English accent as unlikely in an Irish guide as her Scottish tartan. Forty-something, Gallagher guessed, one of those leathery birds with boundless energy; he could see her running a marathon in her seventies. "I tried to phone you earlier to see if we might have a bit of a preliminary get-together, make sure we're on the same page, you know, but the girl at the desk said you'd gone out."

"I'd a few things to attend to."

"Of course. I hope you don't mind my convening this little gathering?" She tilted her head in inquiry.

"Not a bit of it." He could faintly hear the roar of the game from a TV in the bar above.

"Don't want to be stepping on anyone's toes, you know." The woman had extremely thick eyebrows that lent her green eyes an unnerving intensity.

"No. Good idea this." Gallagher gestured towards the circle of chairs.

"Wonderful! So much better to get off on the right foot from the very beginning. Put everybody at their ease. Get the group bonding process underway. Establish some parameters. Don't you agree?"

"Yeah, I do." Insecure in his own position, Gallagher was feeling grateful to have this British bulldog on his team.

"Would you like to facilitate the meeting, or should I?"

"Eh? Oh," Gallagher said, "if you don't mind doin' it, I'd be very grateful. I'm still fightin' the jet lag, like." Not to mention the Guinness, which he didn't.

"Very good." She ran a hand through her close-cropped hair. "All right, everyone!" she called in a voice that was neither loud nor demanding but nevertheless brought instant attentiveness to the room. "Perhaps we might take our chairs and get on with our little soiree."

People shuffled to the circle of chairs and seated themselves. Wickerson, sitting opposite Gallagher, smiled encouragingly at him. Ruth Wilburn remained standing, clipboard angling out from her hip like a Hollywood gangster's Tommy gun. "First of all," she said with a practised professional smile, "let me welcome you all to Dublin. How many of you are visiting us for the first time?" Everyone raised a hand except Gallagher and Wickerson and one of the women he'd been talking to. "All but three new, that's wonderful!" There was a high-pitched chirpiness to her voice, like that of a slightly mad headmistress. "Let me introduce myself. I'm Ruth Wilburn and I'll be your official tour guide for the next week. You may be wondering why I don't sound very Irish and there's a perfectly good reason for that." She grinned again around the circle with her Tourist Board smile. Everyone was watching her with polite reserve. "I'm not very Irish. In fact, I'm not the least bit Irish at all!" She almost threw her clipboard to the heavens in acknowledgement of this outlandish state of affairs. "I'm from Surrey. But I did have the good fortune to marry an Irishman, so here I am and here I've been for a good many years."

Gallagher was scanning the group as she talked. Several nice young birds all right—Berenice hadn't fibbed about that after all. Only two men besides Wickerson. Several older ladies. Maybe not too bad then. Gallagher had something of a touch with older ladies once he turned his mind to it. He might just be able to finagle his way through here after all. As for finding a patron, well, he'd just have to wait and see.

"Now it's my very great pleasure," Ruth Wilburn continued, "to introduce to you our tour director, Mr. Patrick Gallagher." All eyes turned to him and everyone was smiling, so Gallagher gave his heartiest impish Irishman smile in return. Wilburn took a step and placed her hand familiarly on his shoulder. "Now, some of you may well be asking yourselves why on earth do we have a tour guide as well as a tour director? Surely one or the other would suffice." She scanned the circle with mock imperiousness while people tried their best to appear not to have, themselves, harboured such an impertinence. Legs were crossed and uncrossed. Several people coughed.

"I'll tell you why then, shall I?" Wilburn's smile erased all discomfiture. "As your *guide*, I shall make sure that you get safely and efficiently from A to B." She brandished her clipboard to indicate each point of transit. "Whereas Mr. Gallagher, as your *director*," she emphasized, patting him on the shoulder, "will at each of those points unlock for you their contents and deeper significance. I shall be your mover, and he your shaker, if you will." Again she smiled charmingly at them and everyone laughed appreciatively. "Here's my rule of thumb: I'm in charge while we're on the bus, and Mr. Gallagher is in charge when we're not." Removing her hand from his shoulder, she continued, "As many, if not all, of you are undoubtedly aware, Mr. Gallagher is highly esteemed in Canada for his work in hybridizing roses and I for one greatly look forward—as I'm sure you all do—to learning as much as we can from him on this tour about the real secrets of great gardening. Mr. Gallagher . . ."

There'd been a roar from the overhead television that Gallagher was sure had followed a score. "Eh?" he said, startled. All eyes in the circle were again turned on him. The Wilburn woman seated herself alongside him and now looked at him expectantly. "Oh, yeah. Well . . ." Gallagher began, wetting his lips and stalling for time. What with the long plane ride, the unsettling incident with the airport security people, and the glorious Guinness shortly ago, he didn't have much of a grip. Loquacity was never a problem for him in safe and familiar circumstances, but here he was swimming in waters whose currents and depths he didn't know. Nor was exposition his strong suit. He was a narrative man. Talking about himself in an honest and straightforward manner was something in which he had neither experience nor aptitude. He leaned forward in his chair and, to be on the safe side, struck a tone more solemn than his normal. "I'm delighted of course to be here with you all. Truly delighted. It's a particular pleasure, as you can well imagine, for me to be returning to my ancestral homeland for the first time after many years abroad." He paused, wondering what he could possibly say next. The gardens, he realized, he ought to say something about the gardens. "And I think we're all going to be delighted with the gardens we'll be seeing this week. Some of them of course will be magnificent and others more modest." He waved a hand to indicate how capricious the gardening life can be. As for the gardens themselves, he was largely making it up as he went along, because he had neglected to give the tour itinerary more than a superficial glance, figuring that he would study each day's featured gardens the evening before. "But I think we'll find each of the gardens will offer us something of interest. That is to say," he glanced around the group engagingly, but without making eye contact with anyone, "I'm sure we'll have a grand time of it altogether." Considering this more than sufficient for the moment, he smiled and nodded to Ruth Wilburn to indicate that his remarks had reached their logical conclusion and thus she might continue.

"Thank you, Mr. Gallagher," she said, not missing a beat. "Now before Mr. Gallagher and I outline for you the procedures and protocols of the tour," a deferential nod in his direction—she was a sly bint, this Wilburn, Gallagher realized—"we thought it might be beneficial that we go around the circle and each of us introduce ourselves and, if we're comfortable enough—and remember: we are among friends here—say a few words about where we're from, etcetera. Now, who'd like to start?"

Nobody wanted to start. A nervous shuffling beset the group, people shifting in their chairs and rustling discreetly.

"Very well, I'll go first," a woman sitting near Wickerson said. Somewhere in her forties, Gallagher guessed, around his own age, prim as a post with a keen, sharp face. Glasses. Blonde streaked hair styled to perfection. Expensive-looking outfit, linen or something. Matching earrings and brooch. Nice legs. Nobody's fool. Must have been a real looker once, and handsome enough still in that country club way of the wealthy. "My name is Elyse Frampton. I live in Vancouver. In Shaughnessy actually, where I have a small but—I flatter myself to think—rather unusual and interesting garden." The Shaughnessy address caught Gallagher's attention right off. Old money as often as not up there. Lots of it as often as not. Possibilities here, boyo, he was thinking, distinct possibilities. "My daughter, Amanda, and I," she continued, nodding slightly towards the girl seated on her left, "are travelling together. I'm very much looking forward to viewing fine gardens, perhaps with an eye to making some small improvements at home." She paused for a moment, as though considering whether or not she should say more, then continued. "I'd just like to say that I'd be less than honest if I didn't make clear at the outset how disappointed I was to learn that Stephen Aubrey wouldn't be accompanying us, as originally advertised. I don't know your work, Mr. Gallagher," she looked straight at him and Gallagher felt his sphincter spasm, "but I'm confident that we'll learn a great deal from you as well. That's all, I think." She inclined slightly towards her daughter beside her, indicating the girl should speak next. "Amanda."

The daughter was maybe twenty and seemed as ample as her mother was sparse. Tall and well structured, her big frame was softened by a layer of residual baby fat so that she resembled a Renaissance beauty, perhaps by Tintoretto. Her dark hair was clipped short and she wore a cream-coloured blouse and loose slacks that nicely showcased her youthful sensuousness. With her gaze fixed on the parquet floor in the centre of the circle she began nervously, saying, "I don't know much about gardening really." A pink flush bloomed ever so slightly on her neck and face, so that her high cheekbones shone. "But I adore all gorgeous things," she said, lifting her gaze and suddenly animated, "I really believe that if we spend our time in pursuit of beauty, true beauty, we become better and more beautiful people ourselves." It was a moment of startling ardour, almost a plea, but it subsided as quickly as it had arisen. "So I'm really looking forward to this week. And I hope that by the end of it we'll all feel like, and actually be, each in our own way, more beautiful people." She suppressed a nervous giggle as she finished, so it was difficult to tell if she really believed what she'd just said or not. The mother, Elyse, beside her, looked both proud and slightly displeased.

"I'm Robert Long," the man sitting next to Amanda said, "and this is my wife, Nicole." The woman looked at her husband with unabashed admiration. Though they were both of medium height, by tilting her head sideways she gave the impression of looking up to him, as though he were considerably taller. Of average appearance, they were without distinguishing characteristics, except for the fact that they resembled each other so closely. They might have been brother and sister. "We're from Edmonton, Alberta. We both love to garden. It's something we do together a lot. It helps keep us young, right, honey?" She beamed in affirmation. "And, er, it helps keep our relationship strong and vibrant." He finished, but then remembered to add, "Oh, and we have three kids, but they've all left home now. The youngest just flew the nest this spring. So we kinda thought we'd take this tour to reward ourselves for all them years of raising kids, right, Nicole?" She reached out a hand and laid it gently on his forearm, nodding demurely in agreement. Gallagher caught Wickerson's eye for a split second but was unsure of what he saw there. It might have been contempt, or envy, or who knows what. Then Gallagher remembered that Michael had recently lost his wife. So that was it, poor bugger. Anyway, the Longs wouldn't even make the long list of potential patrons.

Having been spoken for, Nicole didn't speak. Which wasn't lost on the next person in the circle, an older lady wearing a billowing dress that was almost a muumuu and patterned with vibrant peonies. "Loretta Stroude's my name, spelled like 'loud' but pronounced like 'rude,'" she said, smiling expansively, and everybody laughed. She's used that line more than once before, thought Gallagher, but it's a good one, so why not? "I'm from Abbotsford, BC. I've gardened all my life and loved every minute of it—well, maybe not quite every minute," she chortled good-naturedly so that her several chins wobbled like Jell-O, and the whole group chuckled too. "Like our esteemed leader here," she continued, gesturing with her hand towards Gallagher, several oversized bracelets clinking around her wrist, "I, too, have a particular passion for roses." Her mouth, with an overly generous application of very red lipstick, had a peculiar way of sliding sideways at the conclusion of each sentence, as though she considered what she had said to be terribly wry and clever. "I've probably been on nine or ten garden tours over the years and I've adored them all. Yes, they're each a bit different. But always *so* interesting. And you meet such *fascinating* people!" She beamed at them all, as if in eager anticipation of their fascinating aspects being revealed. "I'm just tickled pink to be here. And while I've enjoyed several remarkable tours with Stephen Aubrey, and was of course distressed to learn that he was unable to join us this time, I was delighted that Mr. Gallagher was selected as his replacement, because being something of a rosarian myself, I know that we rosarians hold one another in the highest regard, do we not, Mr. Gallagher?"

"Indeed we do," Gallagher said. This old Loretta was a sizeable bit of business, he thought, but didn't look like any kind of millionaire.

"And now," Loretta continued, "let me pass you to my very, very dear friend and fellow master gardener, might I add." She twinkled at Gallagher and his spirit sank as it always did when encountering the expertise of master gardeners. "Yes, we completed the course—what? Two years ago now, Suzy?"

"Yes, two years." Suzy was as small and contained as Loretta was voluminous.

"So: Suzy."

"Hello, everyone. Yes, I'm Suzy Fong and I'm not Irish either." Everybody laughed again at the charm of her Asian self-deprecation. "I'm from the Fraser Valley also. Clearbrook, to be exact. My family has farmed there for three generations, since coming from China." Grey-haired and tiny, Suzy spoke with perfect, measured diction. "I'm here because Loretta told me I had to be." Again nervous laughter tittered around the group.

"Only because my probation officer wouldn't let me go on my own," Loretta threw in. More laughter. Jesus, thought Gallagher, well at least these old birds will keep everyone lightened up. But a source of big money? Hardly. Again there was a roar from the TV overhead.

Suzy smiled sweetly and gestured with her hand for Michael Wickerson to take his turn.

"My name is Michael," he began, "Michael Wickerson." Sitting upright in his chair, his hands folded on his lap, he glanced around the group engagingly, with the practised ease of the professor accustomed to speaking in public. "I, too, live in Vancouver where I teach Irish literature at UBC—sorry, that's the University of British Columbia." Favourable reactions were registered around the group. "Well, you see, I know my Colm Toibin and my Austin Clarke well enough, but I'm afraid I'm a complete neophyte when it comes to gardening. So why am I here?" He looked around the circle again. People shuffled a bit, unsure whether the question had been rhetorical or now required a response. "I'll tell you why, although I hadn't intended to, as I informed Mr. Gallagher before this meeting." Gallagher was watching Wickerson intently, caught off guard by Michael's admission. "I suffered the great misfortune last year," Wickerson said, then paused, clenching his jaw as though to suppress an upwelling of emotion, "of having lost my wife." Everyone in the circle instantly registered reactions of shock and sympathy.

"Her name was Rose-Ann," Wickerson continued, briefly raising his gaze towards the ceiling as though to draw strength from her memory. "We'd been high school sweethearts, and attended the same university. We got married shortly after graduation. The happiest day of my life, bar none." He radiated for a moment a glimpse of that romantic happiness. "Then I went on to do post-graduate work while she supported us and ran the household. She planted a garden at our place and grew the most beautiful flowers that I have ever seen." Wickerson stared at his hands clasped in his lap as though they held a bouquet. But Gallagher was instinctively alerted by the difference in tone between how Michael had spoken with him about his loss and how he was now almost making a public performance out of it. Yes, that was it, thought Gallagher, this is almost a performance. But why? "Petunias, marigolds, chrysanthemums—they all bloomed splendidly for that dear girl," Michael carried on. "People on the street, passing strangers, would pause in front of our little place and simply look for a few moments at all the flowers blooming there, the bright colours, the butterflies flitting among them, and you could plainly see they simply felt better about themselves and each other and the world around them, for having spent those two or three minutes enjoying Rose-Ann's garden. I often thought at the time: how much greater a gift is that to give people—that vision of a better and more beautiful world—than all my pedagogical posturing." There was a ring of sincere humility in what he said, an acknowledgement that his professorship, however much social cachet it might attract, was paltry stuff compared with the high art of horticulture. It was a sentiment guaranteed to excite gratification in any group of gardeners. "For myself, I'd never known such happiness before and I realized even then that most people might spend a lifetime without ever knowing the bliss I experienced every day.

"Alas," Wickerson deftly switched the mood with just two syllables, "some part of me knew at the time it was too good to last. And, unhappily, I was right. It was destined to end. Rose-Ann fell ill the winter before last." Wickerson's lower lip trembled. "Of course I nursed her as best I could. The doctors did everything possible. But Rose-Ann's fate was in other hands than ours by then." He again raised his eyes to the ceiling momentarily. There was sniffling in the room. Nicole Long, holding her husband's hand, seemed to be trying valiantly not to sob.

"Sure enough, by the beginning of March she was fading away." Wickerson suddenly stood up and moved outside the circle, with a visible struggle to get his emotions under control. Everyone watched him intently. "I sat by her bed day and night." He began walking slowly around the perimeter of the circle, as though in a funeral cortege. "She took my hand one time near the end." He held out his hand, palm upward. "Her hand in mine felt lifeless already. 'Michael,' she said to me, her voice barely a whisper. 'Yes, my darling girl,' I replied. 'Keep the garden up, will you? To remind yourself of me.' It was the last thing she ever asked of me. She passed away that very evening, peacefully, in her sleep, for which I'm eternally grateful.

"So that's my story, friends, sad but true," Wickerson continued after a long pause, resuming his seat in the circle as he spoke. "I'm here to learn how to garden, in order to honour my promise to Rose-Ann and keep her legacy of beauty and my memories of her alive."

All the group sat unmoving, besieged by a profound melancholy. Even Ruth Wilburn seemed at a loss, so moving had been Wickerson's recounting. But something itched in Gallagher's brain, some sense that what he'd just heard did not ring entirely true. Wickerson had told him privately that he was interested in Irish gardens because of their importance in the literature he taught. But this rendition was all about his wife's dying wish. It almost sounded, he was surprised to realize, like a tale he might have told himself.

Just then a cell phone rang, playing the tinny notes of "I Love to Go A'Wandering." "Oops, sorry!" exclaimed Wilburn as she started digging in her bottomless bag. Finding the phone, she retreated to a corner of the room where she began a whispered but animated conversation. Gallagher thought he should do something with the group, but he didn't know what.

Eventually the man sitting beside Wickerson cleared his throat. "Shall I go, Mr. Gallagher, or wait until . . . ?" He gestured towards Wilburn.

Gallagher hesitated.

"Let's keep going, shall we?" said Loretta of the billowing muumuu.

"Right, carry on then, why don't you," Gallagher said.

"Very well. My name is Piet van Vliet," the man said with a pronounced Dutch accent. Small, lean, sixtyish, with closely cropped silver hair, he was wearing an expensive blue business suit and immaculately shining shoes. He sat stiffly in his chair, one hand laid formally on each thigh. "Also from British Columbia, South Surrey in fact. I have a degree in horticulture from Leipzig University." Oh, God, Gallagher thought, still somewhat disconcerted by Wickerson's tale, not another ringer. He was going to have to be on his guard the whole time with this bunch of experts. "I am most interested to know what species and varieties do best here in Ireland so that I might determine whether some of them will thrive also in our West Coast climate. Especially I am interested in alpines and hardy perennials." He spoke in a clipped and systematic monotone without any facial animation at all. "I, too, as the others have said, am anxious to take advantage of the expertise of Mr. Gallagher in learning about certain plants which are currently unknown to me."

Gallagher smiled weakly. From the very outset he'd doubted his ability to provide the type of expertise the tour required, but he'd lulled himself with an assumption that the tour-goers would be largely unsophisticated, at least as far as plants went, and that in the kingdom of the blind his one eye would suffice. Now he was finding himself surrounded by master gardeners and horticulturalists, none of whom, with the possible exception of glossy Elyse from Shaughnessy, appeared to have access to the level of wealth he was most interested in. Instead of wealthy know-nothings, he'd landed up with a bunch of impoverished know-it-alls. Jays.

"Hi, I'm Bonnie Raithby," chirped one of the young women Wickerson had been chatting up. "I come from Saskatoon. I graduated last year with a degree in landscape architecture." Jaysus, Gallagher moaned inwardly, another feckin' expert. No glamour-mag beauty queen, the girl nevertheless had a peculiar radiance that illuminated the room as she spoke. Her shoulder-length hair was cinnamon brown, like the skin of a polished chestnut. Her smile betrayed a hint of impertinence playing along its edges. But it was her eyes that most intrigued. Both were blue, but the colouring of one seemed deeper and more intense than the other. "My friend Carla and I," she said, gesturing to the girl beside her, "plan to start up a landscaping business in Saskatoon. We thought this tour would be a great way to experience some really interesting landscape concepts, things that we could maybe adapt in our work back at home, make what we do really distinctive, because we're both into the Celtic thing, like music and art." Her honeyed voice and amiable smile together curled around her listeners like a softly purring cat. She tossed her head, causing her hair to swirl like a Clairol commercial. "And Mr. Gallagher," she addressed him directly, looking at him with a gaze of mingled admiration and impudence and something else, "I really, *really* love your work." Gallagher gulped. "Your latest, Nicole's Knickers"—even the unique name sounded reasonable on those propitious lips—"I think is the most gorgeous rose I have ever seen in my entire life."

"Thank you," Gallagher said in a squeaky voice. An unfamiliar emotion suddenly welled up in him. Perhaps it was the long flight and the guards harassing him and the drink and Wickerson's tale that had together rendered him vulnerable, but this girl's words touched him in a tingling, unfamiliar recess.

"Of course we can't grow it in Saskatoon."

"A pity that," he managed to get out.

"Oh, I know!" She clasped her hands above her lovely bare knees. "But I saw it exhibited last year at our hort show and I just about cried when I came upon it. That rose is *soooo* beautiful. And to think I'm now sitting here with the genius who created it!" She extended both hands towards him in fond appreciation, then turned to address the group as a whole. "I think we are, like, brilliantly lucky to have got Mr. Gallagher for our guide. He may not be as widely recognized as some others, but he's truly a national treasure."

Though an eager recipient of flattery from almost any source, Gallagher was not a man easily overthrown by compliments. Life had taught him hard lessons about keeping the stones in place in your walls. Nevertheless, within moments Bonnie Raithby had effortlessly breached his customary defences. There was something peculiarly alluring about the woman, no question, and some intangible potency as well that he had no experience dealing with. Maybe he was losing his grip entirely, but, Jays, he was a puddle under her lovely gaze.

Ruth Wilburn, who'd slipped back into the circle during Bonnie's speech, was beaming approvingly at the progress that had been made during her absence.

"And I'm Carla, Carla Pridge," said Bonnie's sidekick. Heavier-set than her friend, she was comely enough in her own way too, but definitely a satellite alongside beaming Bonnie. Who wouldn't be? Carla's sandy-coloured hair was cropped boyishly short and she had the ruddy complexion of someone who worked outdoors in all weathers. "I'm just so thrilled to be here, I have to keep pinching myself. And I know we're going to have a fantastic week together."

So there it was, thought Gallagher, at best maybe one reasonable prospect to pursue, a solitary and rather sombre version of his imagined Gwyneth Mandeville-Hampton. And Bonnie Raithby, no patron obviously, but a person of interest nevertheless, and perhaps useful in persuading others, like Elyse Frampton, for instance, that he was indeed a national treasure.

"Very nice," Ruth Wilburn concluded the round. "Now I know how treacherous remembering names can be for some of us, so I've brought along name tags for you all." She fished in her oversized bag and drew out a manilla envelope containing the name tags—the kind with a little plastic envelope suspended by a thin string around your neck—and distributed one to each member of the group. Amazingly, she knew everyone's name already, only mixing up Bonnie and Carla. All dutifully put their tags on. Gallagher hated name tags as a rule, but he was dreadful with names and appreciated having this bunch tagged so he could attach names to the faces. Next Wilburn ran through what she called her modus operandi for the tour, essentially involving everyone being absolutely punctual for each departure of the coach.

Somewhere a clock struck seven, and Wilburn announced, "Meeting adjourned—it's time for dinner!" She took Gallagher loosely by the arm and together they climbed the stairs back up to the foyer, with the group following behind. "Well, that went very nicely, Mr. Gallagher, didn't you think?"

"Aye. Very good." Again Gallagher was glad to have this Girl Guide leader along.

"This way," she called out, leading them past some suspiciously fake-looking tropical plants in large pots and towards the dining room. The room had been done up in retro-Georgian style. There was a long table set out for the group. "Just take a seat wherever you like," Wilburn instructed, "no name cards this evening!" Gallagher, still besotted by the lovely afterglow of Bonnie Raithby's praise, had wanted to sit beside her in order to further their discussion of Nicole's Knickers, but Wilburn cut him off at the pass. "Do sit here beside me, Mr. Gallagher. Normally I wouldn't dine with the group, but I think it's important that you and I go over some of the nuts and bolts of the tour."

"Fine," Gallagher said, seating himself beside her. On the other side he had Loretta Stroude, rose specialist and master gardener in muumuu, who was keen to tell him about her own rose garden. "I've brought along some photos that I'd be pleased to show you later," she said, leaning towards him familiarly. Meanwhile, farther down the table, Wickerson was being consoled by Carla Pridge on one side and Nicole Long on the other.

AFTER the meal—a set menu of pork chops, carrots and peas, and several bowls of potatoes prepared in different ways—Gallagher slipped out of the hotel unnoticed and returned to Connell and Larkin's. He felt he needed air and space. Already these people were crowding in on him with their expectations and their claims. What he wouldn't give for a quiet hour or two alone in his garden right now. Perhaps the pub wasn't quite what he needed because the place was packed, forcing him to squeeze in along the bar. The air was thick with tobacco smoke and laughter. He ordered a pint and surveyed the scene.

"Say, gaffer, who won the game then?" he asked a portly gent beside him. The fellow was clinging to the bar as though to flotsam from a sunken ship. An ancient pungency arose from him.

"Eh?" Two tiny bloodshot pig eyes embedded deep in a roseate fleshy face searched for an answer. "Ah, t'Cork lads pulled it ou' in t'last coupla seconds, so."

"Ah, well, the day's not entirely lost then," Gallagher said, turning back to the room, glass in hand.

But, not to be so easily dismissed, the stranger tugged on his sleeve. "Ireland," he said aloud, his little pig eyes glowering aggressively, "best fukkin' country in the world! Bar none!" His glare dared Gallagher to contradict him.

"Aye," Gallagher agreed. "Cheers, man." He raised his glass in salute and sipped his Guinness. The fierce light in the drunk's eyes dimmed, and he seemed to retreat into his sty to await the next potential challenge to his homeland's supremacy among nations. Gallagher made his way over to a quieter corner where he could ponder his circumstances in peace.

Right off the top it was obvious that leading this garden tour was not going to be all beer and skittles, as Berenice had indicated it would. People plainly had high expectations of him, and if there was one thing in life for which he had little or no use it was other people's expectations. Things were only made worse by having master gardeners and landscape designers and trained horticulturalists in the mix. Gallagher was no scholar—his own education had concluded unceremoniously at the age of sixteen when he'd been told by his father to "get out and shift for yerself"—and he was intimidated by people who'd attained higher education. Not that he considered them necessarily more intelligent than himself, only that their privileged position gave them access to levers of power that were unavailable to him. He harboured elements of the workingman's contempt for educated elites, and was going to have to watch that none of it leaked out over the course of the week.

Gallagher had enjoyed his earlier chat with Michael Wickerson precisely because, even though the fellow was a university professor, he hadn't carried on as though the sun rose and set on his genius, the way some of them did. He'd seemed honest and sincere in his manner, without any of that academic loftiness that Gallagher found so contemptible. Nevertheless, there was something odd about Wickerson. How in private he'd given one version of his wife's death and asked that nothing be said of it to the group, as though he wanted it not known, but then proceeded to, himself, give a more emotionally charged version to the group. Gallagher couldn't quite put his finger on it, but he sensed a discordance that sounded, however distantly, an alarm bell in his instinctual self.

But what had truly unnerved him at the hotel was the upwelling of emotion he'd experienced under the bright gaze of Bonnie Raithby. Gallagher—notwithstanding his occasional boyish flirting with the likes of Nuala at the desk—was no womanizer. He'd loved one woman in his life and seemed destined never to love another. For a while, back at the beginning, he'd harboured dreams of contacting Francie and somehow getting her to Canada. But he'd had no way of reaching her. Every plan he devised collapsed underneath the shadow of her father blocking the way. If old O'Sullivan were to have discovered where Gallagher had fled to, and if he also knew that the Provos had an interest in Gallagher's whereabouts, his safety would have been compromised. And so he did nothing but pine for Francie and despair of ever seeing her again.

Eventually he tried his luck with another girl or two, but it was hopeless. One time a girl he'd been fond of invited him to her bed, but, once there, he froze up, unable to achieve an erection. Withdrawing in humiliation, he'd abandoned hope of ever meeting the love of his life. He'd already met her, and lost her. For years now his women were fantasy creatures, the movie queens and supermodels whom he incarnated in the blooms of the roses he named for them. They were companions of transcendental beauty and constancy, in a way that no flesh-and-blood woman, none after Francie at least, could ever be for him.

So how had it happened that he'd been so readily overthrown in a tumult of emotion by this Bonnie Raithby? Her love of roses, her praise of him, her elusive deliciousness had within moments conspired to breach his defences in a way no other woman had for decades. He went over the circumstances again—whether the long flight, the incident at the airport, the emotional impact of being back in his homeland after all this time, had together addled his head and rendered him susceptible to silliness. Whatever it was, he'd have to put a lid on it; he was here to find a benefactor, not a girlfriend.

And good luck with that, the benefactor angle. To say the least the group seemed sparsely populated with wealthy benevolence. On the surface, only the mother—what was her name again? Elyse—sounded as though she might have a few sheckles tucked away in her comfortable Shaughnessy digs. Lacking alternatives, he would set his sails in her direction to begin with and see if anything came of it.

As he was finishing up his pint, he became peripherally aware that someone off to his left was observing him. He looked casually away in the opposite direction for a moment and then glanced back quickly over his shoulder. The man who had been watching him instantly looked off and turned away. Gallagher was remembering Sergeant Leary's warning that his movements would not go unobserved. After a bit he looked furtively sideways and now there could be no mistaking it—the stranger was definitely spying on him. He was bald, with a moustache, and wearing a dark suit. Gallagher was considering going over and confronting him, but when he glanced over again, the watcher had disappeared.

◉ NINE ◉

GALLAGHER WAS halfway through his full Irish breakfast, savouring the lovely bacon and the eggs with golden yolks, when Ruth Wilburn came clattering up to his table, her big bag knocking against empty chairs as she approached. He'd chosen a secluded spot in a far corner of the hotel dining room in order to avoid having to talk to anyone, being a firm believer that breakfast and conversation do not belong together.

"Good morning, Mr. Gallagher!" Wilburn enthused. "You must have brought the good weather with you—we've got a gorgeous day to start the tour." She swung her arm energetically, as though to indicate that the vault of heaven itself was shining down on them.

"Um," Gallagher grunted as a lump of black pudding slithered down his gullet. It was his least favourite part of a full Irish, but he felt it should be eaten nevertheless, along with the sausages and bacon and toast and eggs and potatoes.

"Mind if I join you?" Wilburn was already pulling up a chair, undeterred by his secluded location and solitary disposition. She was wearing a brown, uniform-like suit that compounded the impression of her being one of those indefatigably enthusiastic types who elbows her way through life as though forever leading a pack of shrieking Girl Guides.

Gallagher motioned with his fork in tepid acquiescence.

"Thanks." Wilburn plopped down, waved over a waitress, and ordered tea and toast. "Oh, the busses were absolutely hopeless this morning," she launched in while settling her bag on an adjacent chair. "If there's one thing I miss from merry olde England it's dependable public transportation. Here you just never know. We're all the way out in Raheny, you see." She moved constantly as she spoke, looking this way and that around the room. "My husband takes the car, though he does drop the girls off at school every morning, God bless him, but for me, well, it's just simpler if I catch the bus. I wouldn't drive in the city anyway, it's such a madhouse and there's never parking to be had for love or money."

He dipped a corner of his toast into spreading egg yolk, resenting the distraction from what should be a rapturous moment.

"I mean to say, it ought to be simple, but seldom ever is," Wilburn carried on. "The bus is supposed to leave my stop at 7:35. I always get there ahead of time just to be sure, fool that I am. Because there's no being sure of anything when it comes to a Dublin bus. This morning I was there by twenty-five past at the latest, and when do you think the bus arrived?" She fished in her bag, retrieved a small compact, and examined her face in its mirror.

"Dunno," he mumbled just as a piece of greasy sausage pronged on his fork entered his mouth.

"Seven forty-three, that's when!" She snapped the compact closed. "A full eight minutes behind schedule. So, of course, I missed my connection—at least I believed I'd missed it, but miraculously a bus comes along soon enough, but whether it was my connection running late or the next one arriving early I'll never know. Still I caught it after all and here I am at last."

"Yeah," he said.

The surly waitress returned with her tea and toast on a tray. "Thank you," Wilburn said distractedly. "Honestly, I don't know why they go to the bother of printing schedules at all if no one's going to stick to them."

"Y'd wonder, wouldn't you?" His full Irish was well and truly ruined with all this rubbish about buses.

"Never you mind, Mr. Gallagher, we've got a fine day on our hands and two extremely interesting gardens to explore."

"That we do." Alarmed by the expertise of the group, he'd made a point of studying the itinerary last night, as Wilburn had suggested at dinner that he do, once it had become evident to her that his conception of the tour was sketchy at best.

"Oh, look! Here's Declan, our driver, let me introduce you." Wilburn was up and across the dining room, then back again in a minute with the coach driver in tow. "Declan, allow me to introduce Mr. Patrick Gallagher, our tour director, all the way from Canada."

"Mornin'," said Declan, a tall, thin man with a lined face and greying hair.

"Mornin'," Gallagher said.

Declan reached out to shake Gallagher's hand. Half-standing awkwardly over the loaded table, Gallagher hesitated. His right hand was greasier than a gearbox from handling his bacon because he'd lost his napkin under the table. He'd always been one for eating his bacon by hand anyway, which partly—along with the great pleasure he took in drinking his tea from a saucer—accounted for his love of solitude at breakfast. But he couldn't keep the driver standing there with his hand stuck out forever, so he gave it as quick a shake as he could, but he could tell Declan felt the smear of his grease. Wilburn sat back down to her tea and toast and Declan pulled over a chair as well, then he and Wilburn proceeded to swap stories from within the secret society of coach drivers and tour guides. Gallagher gulped his tea, sans saucer, excused himself, and fled back to his room.

As he brushed his teeth in the tiny bathroom a fresh moment of panic assailed him. There he was in the mirror: the great pretender. Did he really have the jam to go through a whole week of this? How long could he be expected to put up with a fuss-budget like Wilburn before he blew a fuse? Plus initiate his pursuit of Elyse Frampton; and, if not her, who? He felt a great weariness of soul—this when they hadn't even started yet—and was mightily tempted to crawl back into bed and forget the whole damn fool business.

THE group assembled at nine on the front steps of the hotel—not one among them so much as a moment late, thanks to Wilburn's admonitions the night previous—then, led by Wilburn, marched along Molesworth Street to Kildare Street and crossed over by the gates of the National Museum. It was indeed a lovely morning, the city scrubbed clean by yesterday's rain, the sky a pale eggshell blue and the soft air tingling with fresh vibrancy.

"You must make time to visit the National Museum here," Wilburn addressed them all on the pavement. "The collections of Bronze Age and Iron Age gold artifacts are magnificent. And the medieval pieces too, including the famous Tara Brooch." Wilburn was wearing a brooch of her own. Swans, it seemed to be. At a hand signal from her, Declan brought the big coach up from farther down Kildare. As the coach nudged up to the sidewalk, Wilburn shooed them on. "All right, now everyone on board. Quickly! Quickly!" The group members clambered aboard the enormous coach as smartly as they could and dispersed among its thirty-six seats. Everyone seemed in a more festive mood than Gallagher considered necessary for this hour of the morning. He had planned to sit with Elyse Frampton and begin sounding her out, subtly at first, as to her patronage potential, but he found she was already seated beside her daughter. Wickerson, sitting across the aisle from them, was talking about the wild swans at Coole. Gallagher ended up taking a seat behind everyone else, which suited him better anyway as he was in no mood for small talk.

The coach pulled away and Ruth Wilburn, sitting in a jump seat alongside the driver, addressed them all through a hand-held microphone. "Good morning, everybody!" she chirped.

"Good morning!" the group echoed, some more enthusiastically than others.

"Now could you have asked for a more beautiful day than this?" Wilburn effused rhetorically. "Now, as you all know from studying your itineraries (ahem!) we're off first thing to tour the National Botanic Gardens, which are out at the north end of town at Glasnevin. Since we'll be going right through the city, I'll just point out to you some of our more famous landmarks as we go, starting with Saint Stephen's Green up here on your left." Gallagher leaned his head onto the cushioned seatback and closed his eyes.

"How are you this morning, Mr. Gallagher?"

Startled, he looked to his right and found Bonnie Raithby sitting across the aisle from him. She was wearing a navy blue blazer and a pleated tartan skirt, like a Catholic schoolgirl's, which showcased her legs to marvellous advantage. With all his might Gallagher willed his unwilling eyes to lift from the honey-coloured skin just above her knees. "Might I sit with you?" she asked.

"Sure, sure," he muttered, disoriented, and moved to the window seat. The nylon pants he was wearing were coloured a kind of washed-out hospital green, his grey short-sleeved shirt was patterned with aquamarine seahorses, and his white runners were brand new and still unscuffed. Compared to her smart outfit, he knew, his get-up looked ridiculous.

"Thank you," she said and slid into the seat beside him. "I suppose this is all old hat to you, isn't it?" She was speaking in a husky low whisper under Wilburn's narration, a whisper that to Gallagher gave her voice a thrillingly erotic charge.

"What? Old Dublin?"

"Yes." They were passing the infamous sculpture of Molly Malone at the College Green end of Grafton Street, Wilburn explaining how Molly's magnificent bronze cleavage had quickly earned the piece the street moniker "the tart with the cart."

"Aye, I knew it well enough from the old days," he said.

"Has it changed much since then?" She was peering out at the passing street scene with eager curiosity.

"Well, I'll tell you," he said authoritatively, "on the one hand it's changed mightily in the intervening years. But that's the thing about old Ireland, no matter how much it changes, in some ways it remains the same as it's always been." His demeanour quickly became that of a philosopher pondering the *terra incognita* of the human condition.

"I suppose so." Bonnie's smile was incandescent. "I was here for a week myself a few years ago, with a girlfriend, right after graduation. We were doing the grand tour of Europe, you know."

"Ah, sure."

"I loved it instantly. Dublin, I mean."

"Did you now?" Although a born storyteller, and eloquence itself when it came to addressing his roses at home, Gallagher was unaccustomed to conversation with women like Bonnie Raithby. Though not what's thought of as conventionally pretty, she was peculiarly attractive nevertheless. Gallagher experienced again the sudden impact of her allure as he had on the previous evening. Disconcerted, to his horror he began to feel an insolent insurrection rising like Easter against his leg. It was surely draining blood from his brain. "Well, now . . ."

"Oh, yes! Merrion Square. Saint Patrick's Cathedral. Dublin Castle. The alleys down in Temple Bar—I thought it the most romantic place I'd ever been."

"Romantic. Aye."

"Excuse me, Mr. Gallagher!" Wickerson called to him from a few rows ahead, "Look!"

"What?" Gallagher wanted no interruption at the moment.

"Over here." Wickerson pointed out the window to his left. "Joyce's house! I thought you'd want to see it." They were creeping along a quay on the south side of the Liffey. An enormous banner, with James Joyce's portrait on it, was draped in front of one of the old houses. Wilburn was talking about the building's restoration.

"Ah, yes. Very good," Gallagher said, giving Wickerson a comradely thumbs-up. "Thanks, Michael."

"Oh, do you like Joyce?" Bonnie asked him.

"Well . . ." The little he knew about Joyce mainly involved yobs getting drunk on Bloomsday and making damn fools of themselves. He thought he could vaguely recall having thumbed through *Dubliners* years ago—or maybe he'd seen the movie, he couldn't remember.

"Oh, I just adore him. I did my thesis on *Ulysses*, you know?"

"Did you an' all? Well now, that's grand." He'd picked up a copy of the so-called greatest novel of the twentieth century at a thrift shop one time and ploughed through the first few incomprehensible pages before giving it up as ignorant.

"Yes, I majored in English literature—I only got into landscaping later—and I loved Yeats, but Joyce, I think, was always my favourite." She was peering out the window, almost like a child in her enthusiasm, Gallagher thought. "Part of me wishes I'd been Irish, like you, then I'm sure it would have been much easier to understand all the different levels the book functions on."

"It helps, that's true," he allowed.

"Oh it must!" She turned earnestly to him. "The internal echoes and allusions."

"Exactly."

"And the parodies of different literary styles! *So* brilliant."

"Priceless all right." His erection had mercifully subsided with the literary turn the conversation had taken, but this merely replaced one potential embarrassment with another. By now they'd crossed the Liffey, with Wilburn nattering on about the Guinness Brewery.

"You must identify strongly with the sense of exile in *Ulysses*, do you, Mr. Gallagher?"

Her mismatched blue eyes looked directly into his and the foundation of Gallagher's spirit trembled, as though in an aftershock.

"Eh?"

"Living so far from your home as you do."

"Oh, aye."

"Do you identify with Stephen or Bloom?" Had Bonnie twigged that he was no Joyce scholar? Was she leading him on, for a bit of fun?

"Well." He was free-falling like a skydiver with a tangled ripcord. "Bloom, I suppose, all things considered." He knew all about Bloomsday and the name felt closer to his roses than Stephen did, though he might have chosen that one too as a token of his eternal gratitude to Stephen Aubrey for having, however indirectly, secured for him this marvellous seat in this marvellous coach with this whispering young goddess by his side.

"Really? I'm surprised." She looked surprised. "Of course I don't know you at all, *yet*," she said, as though to imply this was something they'd soon rectify, "but knowing your roses at least a little bit, I'd have thought of you more as Stephen Daedalus, the artistic soul in quest of spiritual truth." If there was a whisper of irony in her tone, a probing of the comic possibilities that Gallagher inadvertently offered, it was lost on him.

"True enough." He wanted to say something clever and insightful but nothing sprang to mind. He was blank. Stupid and blank.

"I hope you don't think I'm being too personal?" She was misreading his confusion.

"Not a bit of it," he said, groping wildly for something, anything, to say, some branch or root in the cliff face of his ignorance to cling to, in order to break his fall. "I was just thinking of poor Mr. Wickerson up there, I suppose. Getting all excited about seeing Joyce's house back there on the quay, because we'd had a bit of a chat yesterday, about *Ulysses* actually."

"Poor man." Bonnie looked suddenly sad. "I can't imagine going through a loss like the one he's suffered."

Gallagher regretted having shifted the spotlight to Wickerson, but at least the diversion had got him out of the jam he'd been in. Cleverly he now steered the discussion away from Wickerson and from the treacherous shoals of literature onto the more solid ground of cultivating roses. The girl became instantly radiant. "I loved that piece about you in *Knowing Growing* magazine. It made me want to just go dash out and buy a rose, any rose, every rose I could. Unfortunately, I've got nowhere to plant them."

"Y've not a garden of your own then?"

"I'm afraid not. Not yet. Carla and I share an apartment. A couple of pots on a very tiny balcony is all we can manage at the moment."

"Ah, well, it's a start." In the best of all possible worlds, he considered, this charming woman would have been wealthy as well, and his quest for a patron a far more delightful prospect than wooing the formidable Elyse Frampton. But this, he'd long ago learned, was far from the best of all possible worlds. "In Saskatoon, is it?"

"Yes, close to the river. It's very nice."

"I'm sure it is."

"Mr. Gallagher!" Ruth Wilburn was summoning him through the speaker. "Would you like to say a few words about the National Botanic Gardens before we arrive?"

"What? No, no, that's all right," he called up to her, "you're doin' so brilliantly yourself, I'd not think t'try compete." Everybody laughed, including Wilburn. Bonnie smiled at him affectionately and he saw in her an innocence that suddenly made him want to weep. He felt a blush of shame that he'd betrayed her trust with his stupid dissimulations. He wanted to be what Bonnie imagined him, an artistic soul in quest of spiritual truth, not a deceitful fool slobbering over a pure-hearted girl like herself.

THE big gates of the botanic gardens were just opening as they arrived. After watching an introductory video about the gardens, they gathered outside the reception building in the sunshine where Wilburn introduced their guide to the gardens, a buoyant young woman named Mairi who led them off on a forced march through the lily house and the cacti and orchid collections. Carla Pridge, Loretta Stroude, and Suzy Fong clustered around the guide and were peppering her with questions.

"Fabulous glass houses, eh, Mr. Gallagher?" said Robert Long. Nicole was on his arm. They were standing outdoors in front of the enormous glass houses.

"Grand all right," Gallagher said. He was feeling some relief that

Mairi was handling the necessary explanations, leaving him free to look around for Elyse and perhaps spend some time with her now.

"Victorian, I take it?" Robert said, staring up at the elaborate glass roofs.

"Right you are."

"Built in 1884," van Vliet chimed in, having overheard them, "though the side wings belong to an earlier building. The central pavilion is earlier too, built by Richard Turner, the Dublin-born iron master, in 1848." This van Vliet could begin getting on your nerves pretty damn quick, thought Gallagher, who had no aptitude himself for recalling dates or names and very little patience for those who did.

Mairi led them into the aquatic house, and they clustered around its large circular central pool whose walls stood about three feet high. Steam hissed from ancient iron pipes overhead rendering the air densely moist and clammy. Most of the pool's surface was covered by the enormous round leaves of a gigantic Amazon water lily. It was not in flower. "Introduced here in the 1850s," Mairi told them, "and at the time considered one of the wonders of the age." To Gallagher the giant aquatic looked sinister and evil, seeming to brood in its dark pool like a malignant anaconda, perhaps feeding off the corpses of ancient resentments and enmities submerged in the murk among its massive roots. Across the other side of the pool, Suzy Fong was calling to him and gesturing with her arm, wanting him to move aside so she could take a photo of the monster without him in it.

It turned out Mairi was a lover of trees most of all, and she marched them ebulliently around the grounds, stopping to admire a grove of California redwoods here, a magnificent copper beech over there, a hugely spreading tulip tree, eucalyptus and eucryphia, a dove tree and monkey puzzle tree, pines and palms, and on and on and on.

"What a marvellous arboretum, Mr. Gallagher," Loretta Stroude exclaimed, "the size of everything!" She was wearing a short-sleeved pantsuit with brilliant splashes of red and blue, every bit as colourful as yesterday's muumuu. She'd painted her toenails, visible in her sandals, those of one foot vivid red, and of the other an equally vivid blue, to match the outfit. He noticed that, for such a large lady, how remarkably small her feet were.

"Very impressive altogether," he agreed, though he wasn't much for trees himself, seeing them mostly as nuisances to be cut down in order to let the light in for more important plants—a point of view he was scarcely going to champion in an arboretum. Wickerson, he noticed, was tramping along happily chatting up Carla and Bonnie. Mairi had galloped far ahead of them with Piet van Vliet and the Longs. Gallagher casually drifted over to attach himself to Elyse and Amanda, with Loretta tagging along as well. Both Elyse and her daughter wore elegantly muted summer outfits.

"What is this lovely palm over here?" Elyse asked him, pointing to a tree outside the curvilinear range.

"Eh?" Gallagher looked at the palm. "Just a common palm, I'd say." Already he was aware that Elyse was not his type at all, far too polished and aristocratic, but he was convinced that she alone of the group perhaps possessed what could be thought of as real money. He despised the position he was caught in, this having to manoeuvre and calculate, to in essence deceive for secret purposes. But he felt he had no choice. Perhaps that odious water lily had darkened his spirits.

"Oh, Mr. Gallagher, I can see palm trees aren't your speciality, are they?" chided Loretta Stroude. She actually shook her finger at him like a scolding schoolmarm so that her bracelets jangled and the dangling fat of her arm wobbled like a water-filled balloon. "That's the famous Chusan palm, *Trachycarpus fortunei*, and well over a hundred years old."

"Really?" said Elyse, turning to Loretta. "Fascinating. Now I recognize the *Cedrus Atlantica* 'Pendula' over there, but what's that other large tree, the densely branched one with the peeling bark?"

"I think that's the *Zelkova carpinifolia*, isn't it, Mr. Gallagher?" Did he scent a whiff of condescension in Loretta's asking him to second her opinion? She'd only been teasing him about the stupid palm, he knew, and she'd meant no harm, but he resented having to suffer even a minor humiliation in front of Elyse.

"Right you are," he said grudgingly.

"From the Caucasus, is it not?"

"Spot on." He was holding his own on botanical questions, though barely, through the simple expedient of agreeing with anyone who apparently knew what they were talking about. For all his expertise in roses, he was essentially illiterate in most other areas of horticulture, and he had a particular dislike for taxonomists who to his mind were meddling gits forever changing plant names for their own sadistic enjoyment. He realized that for some people, nomenclature was the be-all and end-all, and his vulnerability in this area required that he be light on his toes to keep from being caught out. More critically, it seemed that plant names were important to Elyse, and by constantly butting in, this confounded Loretta was short-circuiting his opportunities to impress Elyse. Loretta, he was reasonably sure, was not a serious candidate for patron, but was beginning to resemble a first-class pain in the arse. Amanda, meanwhile, the daughter, wandered dreamily nearby without reference to what anyone else was saying.

The group reconvened at what Mairi introduced as "one of the most popular features of the garden. Does anyone know what this rose is?"

Gallagher swam upward out of the Amazon depths of anxiety and calculation into the singular beauty of the rose bush they had gathered around. Here he was himself, at last, not squeaking along playing second fiddle to any. "That's your famous Last Rose of Summer," he stood forth and spoke authoritatively. "She's a cultivar of the China Rose, *Rosa chinensis*, 'Old Blush'."

"Very good," Mairi said, as though he were a schoolboy who'd got the right answer. She obviously had no idea who he was, and why should she? "And does anyone know it's particular significance here?"

"Happens I do," Gallagher replied again, happy to flex his rosarian muscles in order to both champion the expertise of his group to Mairi and re-establish his position of eminence within it. "This beauty was raised from a cutting taken from a rose at Jenkinstown House in County Kilkenny. Tradition has it that the parent plant was the very rose that inspired Thomas Moore to write his famous ballad."

Every eye in the group was fixed on him attentively. Glints of admiration darted among them. He observed Wickerson smile and nod approval over his erudite turn. Even Elyse seemed impressed, as she came forward a few steps in order to hear him more clearly. This is more like it, thought Gallagher, at last dealing from a position of strength. Bonnie Raithby, her head inclined charmingly to one side, was looking at him with a tenderness that made his heart do a little backflip in his chest. Suddenly something gave way within him, an unexpected welling up of feelings, part elation, part longing, part melancholy. Overcome by the emotion of the moment, he glanced around the group, stepped forward with utmost dignity, took one of the blushing pink blooms in his hand, cleared his throat and began to sing in a quavering Irish tenor:

> 'Tis the last Rose of summer
> Left blooming alone;
> All her lovely companions
> Are faded and gone;
> No flower of her kindred,
> No rosebud is nigh,
> To reflect back her blushes,
> To give sigh for sigh.

He had the words by heart from singing the song often to his roses at home. He would sing to them frequently and with great affection, but always alone. Mostly he inclined to sentimental ballads and laments, particularly ones that featured roses, and many's the time he'd finish an evening of tippling while singing to his beauties by sobbing softly to himself, about what he didn't know. But never before had he sung to a flower in public. The old songs themselves had acquired for him an evocative resonance and he now thought to stop singing lest he embarrass himself by blubbering in front of the group.

"Oh, do go on, please, Mr. Gallagher," Bonnie pleaded. She was the one to say what perhaps all were thinking. "It's so lovely."

He lowered his head shyly, cleared his throat a bit, and picked up the song:

> I'll not leave thee, thou lone one!
> To pine on the stem;
> Since the lovely are sleeping,
> Go sleep thou with them.

Thus kindly I scatter
Thy leaves o'er the bed,
Where thy mates of the garden
Lie scentless and dead.

He gazed fondly at the faded petals strewn upon the ground and softly placed a hand across his heart. He sang for the rose he held cupped in his hand, for all his beloved roses back home that he was already heartsore to see again and whose future was still far from certain, for the enchantment of Bonnie, who was looking at him with a rapt expression on her face, even for old Ireland, which he had never thought to see again, for the boy and young man he'd been here, and for the great Celtic themes of tragedy and exile. The melancholy lament poured out of him into the soft Irish sunshine.

Soon may I follow,
When friendships decay,
And from love's shining circle
The gems drop away.
The true heart lies withered
The fond ones are flown,
O! Who would inhabit
This bleak world alone.

As the last quavering notes floated across the gardens, the group burst into enthusiastic applause and Gallagher was lifted up, borne away on a rapturous exhilaration of commingled sadness and sweetness.

TEN

THEY STOPPED for lunch in an overpriced pub where the locals looked them over rudely. Gallagher made the mistake of ordering a panini, which arrived in the form of a greasy coagulation, as though they'd used it to scrape dirty plates before serving it up to him. Nevertheless, he was feeling better than he had for ages. The young women especially had been floored by his bravura with the rose. Surprisingly, Amanda Frampton, who'd been until then largely invisible and apparently indifferent to almost everything around her, had approached him as they made their way out of the botanical gardens, laid her fresh pink hand on his wrist, and told him in her own blushing way that that moment alone had made the whole trip worthwhile. He was genuinely touched by the girl's shy sincerity. Bonnie and Carla had joined in too, glorying him with praise.

"Finally, I've got me own groupies!" Gallagher joked with the three young women clustered around him, and they'd all laughed together. "The Last Rose of Summer," although a melancholy lament, had lifted his spirits immensely. He began to feel for the first time a sense of comraderie with the group, the warm radiance of which spread outwards into an unaccustomed affection for humankind in general. Also, for the very first time, there came a glimmering of optimism about his prospects for the future. Who in the group could fail to be charmed by him now?

After lunch they boarded the coach again and headed back towards the south side of town. Gallagher thought it a propitious moment to advance his cause with Elyse, and so made a point of sitting with her on the coach, Amanda having conveniently abandoned her normal position alongside her mother in favour of chatting with Bonnie and Carla. Elyse seemed slightly taken aback to have Gallagher plop down beside her.

"Well," he started in enthusiastically, "that was a marvellous beginning to the tour, wouldn't you say?" He was uncertain how he should address Elyse. "Mrs. Frampton" seemed a bit too formal, but a first-name basis implied a liberty that Elyse had not indicated could or should be taken.

"Most informative," Elyse agreed. It was remarkable how nothing ever seemed even the tiniest bit out of place with her. No loose strand of hair, no wrinkle in her smart linen suit, no smudge along the perfect line of her pale lipstick. "I must admit the collections were more impressive than I'd expected and, of course, young Mairi's enthusiasm was very refreshing." She paused a moment, then continued, "You've a lovely tenor voice, Mr. Gallagher, I had no idea."

"Ah, well." Here was an opening, but before he could decide how best to exploit it, Elyse continued, speaking more quietly.

"Just one small thing . . ." she said.

"Eh?"

"You'll forgive my mentioning it, but I wonder if your song might not have been a bit painful for Mr. Wickerson."

"Painful?" Gallagher tugged on an earlobe nervously.

"The substance of it." Elyse was very matter-of-fact. "The lying scentless and dead. He has recently lost his wife, after all."

Shite! It hadn't occurred to Gallagher; he'd related the song only to the dying of roses, not death itself, and certainly not to Wickerson's bereavement, but he could see straightaway what she meant. He had hoped his operatics might have been a key to opening Elyse's firmly closed entryway, but instead they'd made him appear insensitive in her eyes. Damn it to hell! It was essential that he win her confidence, demonstrate his worthiness, before he could proceed to delicate issues of finance. But he found her an altogether intimidating figure, even more so after this initial misstep, and every line of advance he thought to employ was quickly abandoned under fear of giving offence. She loomed before him like a fortress whose walls he had no idea how to breach. They ended up chatting indifferently about the giant water lily and the succulents they'd viewed in the glass houses.

THEIR next stop was a visit to Margaret Foley's renowned city garden, a place the Royal Horticultural Society described as "Ireland's most outstanding private garden." While this was an appellation others might, and indeed did, skepticize whenever possible, Margaret Foley was unquestionably the reigning *grande dame* of Irish horticulture. A plantswoman of international reputation, a celebrated garden designer noted for her exquisite deployment of striking colour combinations and textural depths, she had entered the rarefied air of public celebrity by virtue of her books, lectures, and television appearances. This was one of the advertised highlights of the tour—to meet the eminent lady herself and be escorted by her through her magnificent garden.

There was a great commotion going on in the courtyard as Declan wheeled the coach up in front of the imposing brick house. "Oh, it's the TV crew!" Ruth Wilburn exclaimed. "I understood they were supposed to be here yesterday." Everyone clambered out of the coach and clustered tentatively on the sidewalk while Wilburn forged forward to survey the lay of the land. She chatted briefly with an animated youngish woman who appeared to be in charge while three guys of the shabby blue jeans, sweatshirts, and sneakers variety shuffled about with cameras, tripods, lights, sound equipment, and miles of cable. "Mr. Gallagher!" Wilburn motioned for him to join them. Not caring for the looks of this at all, he approached them warily. "Mr. Gallagher," Wilburn said excitedly as he came up, "this is Fiona Kinehan, who's the producer of *In an Irish Garden*, which is an enormously popular gardening television show."

"Hello," he said, shaking the producer's hand.

"Pleased to meet you, Mr. Gallagher," she said distractedly. Skinny as a rake, she sported hair like Medusa, her lips were brilliant vermilion, and her eyes made enormous with liner and shadow. She wore a floppy blue sweater, a silver micro skirt over black tights, and tall suede boots. There was a jangly, frenzied air about her, as though she were falling behind herself and frantically trying to catch up. She closed one eye and squinted at him through an imaginary lens formed by her thumb and index finger. "How would you feel about just a wee bit of makeup?"

"Eh?"

"Nothing extreme, just a bit of highlighting. Bring your eyes up a bit." Her own eyes were already darting away to the next thing.

"My eyes don't need any bringing up."

"Well, if you'd rather not, that's fine, but it would help, take my word for it." She seemed too preoccupied to care much one way or the other. "John," she called to the cameraman, "go get some cutaways of roses, will you. Lots of juicy close-ups if you can." The cameraman gave her a thumbs-up. "And Liam," she said to the sound guy who was holding a tall boom mike like a jousting knight's lance, "maybe pick up a couple of minutes of ambience round back while we're getting sorted here." The two men headed off around the house, leaving the youngest of the three pulling additional equipment from the van.

"What's going on here?" Gallagher asked Wilburn.

"Seems you're going to be a TV star," the guide said, fluffed with satisfaction, as though she herself were executive producer.

"I don't understand." Gallagher was all muddled. "Nobody said anything to me about this."

"No, it's all a bit spur of the moment," Wilburn said, "straight out of the blue. But isn't that the way with things nowadays, a sudden turn of events and everything's topsy-turvy. Miss Kinehan," she said, turning to the producer, who was trying to locate a ringing cell phone somewhere on her person, "Mr. Gallagher's caught a bit off guard, you see."

"We're shooting Margaret's regular segment today," Kinehan explained, finally locating the cell and glaring at it without answering, "our schedule's all bollixed this week, but she knew you were coming and she thought it would be brilliant to have you on with her chatting about roses."

"Ah, no," Gallagher said, putting up his hands to ward off this encroachment, "no I'm not one for being on television at all."

"I thought we'd got this all arranged," Kinehan muttered to no one in particular. Then looking again at Gallagher, she said, "Margaret's decided that's what she'd like to do and if you believe otherwise, I'd say good luck to you, mate." Turning abruptly, she called to the boy unloading equipment, "Charlie, do be gentle with the monitors, will you, they're not bleedin' bales of hay."

Before Gallagher could get another word in, the imposing wooden front door of the house swung open on enormous brass hinges and Margaret Foley herself emerged from indoors. She was younger and more vivacious than Gallagher had expected, not quite the weighty matriarch her reputation suggested. Dressed and coiffed for television, she seemed more movie star than gardener. A presence. She descended the front steps like royalty. Wilburn scuttled over and introduced

Gallagher to her. "I'm *so* sorry not to have been here to welcome you personally," she said, approaching Gallagher and taking both his hands in hers, "you will forgive me, I hope."

"No problem," he said, "but . . ."

"Good afternoon!" she announced, swinging magisterially around to address the group, which was still huddled uncertainly alongside the coach, people clutching their cameras like talismans. There was something in Margaret Foley's expression that indicated how dreadfully Canadian they all appeared to be. "Do please make yourselves at home," she said warmly, waving her arm with a grand gesture, as though she spoke for all of Dublin. "Mr. Gallagher and I are going to do a bit of an interview together, which of course you're more than welcome to observe—quietly, of course." She laughed and the group laughed with her. "I do apologize for the inconvenience, but it was such a golden opportunity to take advantage of Mr. Gallagher's presence," she said, gesturing appreciatively in his direction, "we simply couldn't restrain ourselves, could we, Fiona?" The question momentarily summoned the producer out of agitated preoccupation. "Afterwards," Margaret readdressed the group, "we can all poke around the garden together for a bit—I do have a few small treasures I'd enjoy sharing with you—and then I think you're having tea with us, are you not?" She looked to Wilburn, who nodded in pleased agreement. "Excellent! Now, Mr. Gallagher, shall we?" She motioned towards the garden gate where Kinehan stood waiting.

Gallagher had been turned to stone by the realization that he was being cornered into appearing on national television. As imprudent as it may have been for him to return to Ireland at all, given his outstanding debts and obligations, that decision would at worst be a minor miscalculation compared with the monstrous stupidity it might be for him to appear on one of the country's most popular television programs. There was nothing to be gained from it but much to be lost. Were he to make a public exhibition of himself on television, alerting any interested parties that he was back in the country and might be reached in Dublin, the sleeping dogs of his past would surely rise and in no time at all be on his trail, determined to bring him down. He could not, must not, agree to this reckless exposure.

"Er, Miss Foley . . ." he began.

"Margaret, please!" she expostulated, then took his arm and began steering him towards the garden. A powerful perfume suffused the air around her. "Did you notice my *Jovellana violacea* over here?" She guided him like a mannequin. "So much like *Lavendula calceolaria*, isn't it?"

"Very similar," he agreed, though he had no idea what plants in the tumbled border she was referring to. The place seemed chock-a-block with exotic specimens, most of which he'd never laid eyes on before.

"Oh, and I've become simply mad for foxtail lilies recently, haven't you?" She indicated a cluster of stately spires in soft pink and peach.

"Er, I like them well enough, sure. But . . ."

"Such a marvellous vertical statement, don't you think?" She trailed her hand from ground to sky.

"With all due respect, er, Margaret, I can't be appearing on your television show."

"Why on earth *not*?" she exclaimed, feigning mock horror. "Not camera shy are we?" She tilted her head and eyed him inquiringly.

"Well, sort of." Gallagher was grubbing around in his mind for a plausible justification. He certainly didn't want to disappoint Herself, but he wasn't going in front of any bloody television camera, no matter what she might want. Then suddenly it occurred to him that perhaps the program wouldn't be aired for months and he'd be safely back in Canada before it could do him any mischief. "It's not a live broadcast, is it?" he asked.

"No, no, nothing of the sort," Margaret said, patting his arm reassuringly, "we can make all the gaffes and howlers we want and they'll be edited out before it's aired."

"Which will be when exactly?" He tried to make the question casual.

"You know, I'm not sure if they're using it this week or not. Fiona!" She summoned the producer by grandly throwing one arm in the air, like Boadicea with her Celtic sword. "Mr. Gallagher would like to know when the episode will air."

"Tomorrow evening," Kinehan replied, running an impatient hand through her wild hair. "That piece we did last week on aeoniums was supposed to go tomorrow, but somebody made a bollix of the audio and we've got to plug this segment in instead and try get the other sorted for next week."

"There you are, Mr. Gallagher." Margaret beamed on him like a floodlight. "We'll be on tomorrow night, so you and the whole group will be able to catch it."

Like hell we will, thought Gallagher. "No I don't think that's going to work at all," he told Foley. "I'm sorry but ..."

"Ah, but I've been *so* looking forward to it," Foley said, giving no hint of having been dissuaded, "ever since Stephen told me you'd be visiting."

"Stephen Aubrey, was it?"

"Such a lovely man. However, he did forewarn me to anticipate some reticence on your part. I do find modesty in men of accomplishment a particularly charming characteristic. And I *do* apologize for springing this upon you without warning." Margaret's smile was a convivial acknowledgement that celebrities such as himself and herself were accustomed to being importuned in this way and to responding with magnanimity. Gallagher felt himself moving in a daze, drifting like a skiff torn lose from its mooring. Out of nowhere he recalled being in a similar confused state long ago, in his parents' bedroom, it was. Yes, he remembered, he was searching for the money. Then, like now, his fate had hung in the balance. Then, like now, his instinctual self heard distant warning cries. He could hear them now, feel them drawing closer, bringing ruin in their wake. Or, he wondered, was he just being paranoid? Was there really any danger of avengers coming after him, either old man O'Sullivan or his former Republican cronies? Chances are that Francie's old dad was dead or demented from the gargle all these years later. And that half-assed little group of Provos had probably mouldered over time, abandoned its revolutionary zeal, its former members now fat and balding and exposed to no greater excitement than football matches on the telly. Really, Gallagher asked himself, was there even the remotest likelihood of his being hauled off to jail, or of catching a bullet in the back of his head, from those long-ago associations. Ireland had changed so much in the intervening years he barely recognized it. Margaret Foley was the face of the new Ireland, wealthy, sophisticated, urbane. The boogeymen he feared were bare-knuckle bog-hoppers who'd long ago faded into the mists of history. He really needed to get some perspective here.

But still, the guards at the airport, that confounded photo, the warnings that he'd be watched—weren't these signals enough that the old enmities still lived, at least in certain dark corners? He was floundering in a muddled panic of indecision.

Margaret Foley still had him by the arm as they were nearing the gate. Kinehan's impatience was simmering like a kettle on the boil. Wilburn had tactfully herded the rest of the group over to the alpine garden in front of the house. Gallagher could hear Loretta holding forth on the reliable loveliness of harebells. Try as he might, he hadn't the strength to resist the force of Foley. She was one of those charismatic dynamos who surges through life at her own pace and in her chosen direction, sweeping others along with her. Gallagher could no more deflect the force of her insistence than he could turn the tide surging into Dublin Bay. He would appear on television with her. He would be widely seen. But would the Furies be unleashed as a consequence? Would even worse havoc ensue? Or would it not matter a spit to anyone?

◙ ELEVEN ◙

"WELL, YOU'VE had quite a day for yourself, Mr. Gallagher, haven't you?" Smiling amiably, Michael Wickerson tilted his glass towards Gallagher. They were standing at the far end of the bar in Connell and Larkin's, the room dense with jostling drinkers. They'd arranged to come away for a pint after dinner, which Gallagher badly needed because he was that topsy-turvy from the intensity of the day. There was a roaring laughter in the room and tobacco smoke as thick as mist. "Certainly your rendering of "The Last Rose of Summer" was a triumph," Michael said as he leant an elbow on the gleaming bar.

"Did you think so?" Gallagher asked, remembering Elyse's comment about his insensitivity to Michael's recent bereavement. "I was wondering in hindsight if maybe it wasn't a bit hurtful for you to hear that song."

"Of course not!" Michael said but then seemed to catch himself. "That is, naturally it did cause me to revisit that painful episode."

"I'm sorry for that," Gallagher said, but he was thinking that Michael hadn't initially been upset by the song at all.

"Think nothing of it," Michael said. "And you have to admit that you more than held your own with Margaret Foley." In point of fact, the interview, for all the risks it ran, at least in Gallagher's imagination, had gone rather well. He and Foley had strolled among her roses and, once among them, he'd gradually forgotten everything else and given himself over to their delectation. "Now what do you think of Madame Gregoire Staechelin?" Foley had inquired as they paused on the path where the lanky climber bent her long arms down from a high brick wall to display dozens of sumptuous pink chalices. "Heaven!" Gallagher had beamed up at the beauty. "Pure heaven! And that fragrance. Just sublime." He and Margaret had smiled together affectionately while Kinehan made frantic silent gestures to John the cameraman to catch the magic of the moment. By that point, Gallagher had sufficiently regained his composure that he was calculating whether the obviously wealthy and well-connected Foley, who'd plainly taken a liking to him, might herself play some useful part in the matter of a benefactor.

Nevertheless, all things considered, the day had been far from an unqualified success. He'd hit a stone wall with Elyse Frampton, leaving him at a loss as to how he might make any headway there. He'd made a special point of introducing Elyse to Margaret Foley after the interview, and the two women had hit it off straightaway, but he wasn't sure the introduction had won him any points with Elyse. As for the television shoot, he was entirely uncertain whether he had in fact been reckless in exposing himself that way, or if in reality nobody would give a toss whether he was back in Ireland or not. He was losing his footing in all of this and realized that he needed some good advice. For the moment he stared at the shiny rows of bottles gleaming like fabulous ornaments behind the bar.

"Mr. Gallagher?" Michael drew him back from his musings.

"Ach, it's a long story, Michael, and hardly worth the telling," Gallagher said. "I shouldn't have gone on that TV show is all."

"Why on earth not? I thought you did extremely well, especially for having no forewarning."

"Maybe so. Or maybe I've stirred up some old coals that should have been left undisturbed." Gallagher pushed up the sleeves of a dark sweater he was wearing against the cool of the evening. "And by the way, Michael, call me Gallagher, will you? I'm not accustomed to the *Mister*."

Wickerson nodded. They both drank and said no more for a bit. The noise of the pub was beginning to subside as the number of drinkers thinned. "Would you describe yourself as a superstitious person?" Michael eventually asked him.

"Superstitious? How do you mean?" Gallagher assumed he was referring to the television business.

"Well, there's so much of it in Celtic literature, I'm just curious how much, if any, survives among people like yourself. Not now necessarily, since you've been away for so long, but say when you were growing up here—you were in a rural area, if I'm not mistaken?"

"West Cork."

"Aha—the real Ireland."

"Some think so, yeah."

"I take it you were raised a Catholic." Wickerson smoothed the fall of hair back from his forehead.

"Sure, everybody was in those parts."

"And was there much belief in spiritualism apart from the Catholic teachings—I mean the old beliefs that were here before Christianity?"

"Well my mother for certain was a great one for the old stories." Gallagher rubbed his chin, remembering. "She told them to us all the time, my brother and me."

"What kind of stories?" Michael leaned forward, plainly intrigued.

"Oh, ghosts and fairies and all that sort of thing." Gallagher gave a short laugh, as though to disown such foolishness. He was conscious of Michael's smooth sophistication.

"Aha. Did she believe them, do you think, or were they just stories?"

The publican came up to them across the bar, a thin, dark man with a dreadful small moustache. "You lads okay then?"

"Fine, thanks," Michael said with a nod.

"No, no, she believed them right enough," Gallagher said, placing his glass on the bar and becoming mysterious. "As did the neighbour ladies. You'd hear them whispering together sometimes, about hauntings and the evil eye, children paying for the sins of their fathers, all manner of stuff along that line. It's what they did for entertainment, that and gossip."

"What would she say about fairies?" Michael took a sip and put his glass down too.

"Not the silly shite you see in movies. Tinkerbell and all that sort of rubbish. No, to her they were troublemakers. She was always on about fairies carrying off kids and replacing them with changelings. There was no end of her telling us as little kids to be careful or we'd be carried off somewhere. And whenever she got vexed at you for getting into mischief, like, she'd say you were surely a changeling, not the lovely wee child she'd given birth to." Gallagher chuckled. "That sort of thing."

"And she meant it, you think? She was being serious?" It was plain that Michael hoped she was.

"Well, not about us being changelings, no. But the rest of it she meant all right."

"And you said ghosts too." Michael sipped, watching Gallagher over the rim of his glass.

"She talked a lot about the Banshee, *Ben-sidhe* as she'd say in Irish. It was like a spirit in the house, an old woman whose wailing would warn of bad things approaching. Sometimes when the wind would howl in the evening, she'd look at us in a peculiar way, and she'd ask: 'Can you hear the Banshee, boys?'" Gallagher imitated her country voice and stared into the void as she must have done. "'Can you hear her shrieking in that dreadful wind?' Scared the living piss out of me sometimes, and out of poor little Bosco especially, who was younger than me."

Michael smiled. "Say, did she by chance ever mention a Banshee known as The White Lady?"

Gallagher scratched the back of his neck and scrunched up one side of his face, trying to remember, but then shook his head. "Not that I recall, no. The White Lady. No, I don't think so. But she did say that when someone was nearing death, the Banshee would draw near and then carry the soul away to a home in the fairy world."

"Interesting. Most interesting. What about witchcraft?"

"Oh, don't get me started on her and her witches! There was . . ."

"Patsy! Patsy Gallagher, is it? Well, I'll be damned!" A rough-looking character of about fifty approached them through the gaggle of drinkers. "How are you, y'old sod?" The fellow slapped Gallagher heartily on the shoulder. He was wearing a slouch cloth cap and a suit jacket he might have been digging turnips in for thirty seasons, though his scuffed boots had no honest mud on them. Gallagher had absolutely no idea who the fellow was.

"Joe Sheehy, Patsy. Y'haven't forgot yer old pal Joe, surely not?" He threw his arms wide as though to display himself as entirely memorable. He was broadly built and his craggy face had the rough-and-tumble look of an old prizefighter. He hadn't shaved in several days and his crooked teeth showed several gaps.

Sheehy, Sheehy, Sheehy, Gallagher scrabbled in his memory like a rubbish pile but couldn't locate any Joe Sheehy in it. "Ah, Joe, sure enough I remember you. Who could forget them days, eh?" Gallagher figured he'd play along and pick up enough from what Sheehy said to place him sooner or later. "Joe Sheehy, meet Michael Wickerson." The two shook hands.

"What's become of you, Patsy? Must be twenty years if it's a day since last I laid eyes on you."

"At least, I'd say, Joe. Yeah, I went across the water."

"Y're not a Yank now, are you?" Sheehy cocked his head and looked concerned.

"Canada," said Gallagher.

"Oh, that's not so bad then. I'd hate t'think of you as a bleedin' Yank, Patsy."

"Wouldn't be one, Joe, not if they paid me." He sipped his drink to rinse away the thought.

"Well spoken, boyo. That's an empire wants taken down a peg or two." Sheehy had an odd manner of tilting his face away slightly but then looking back sideways at the person he was addressing, which gave what he said a kind of secretive importance.

Wickerson watched the two old friends, smiling to himself. He drained his glass with satisfaction and placed it on the bar. "If you'll excuse me, gentlemen, I think perhaps I'll make my way back to the hotel. I'll leave you fellows to catch up on old times. A pleasure to have met you, Joe." He shook Sheehy's hand again, nodded to Gallagher, and made his way out through the crowd.

"Pal a yours?" Joe asked, cocking his head in Wickerson's direction.

"Just met him yesterday." Gallagher was still trying to place Sheehy and was wishing that Michael hadn't left him alone with the fellow.

"So what're y'doin here, boyo? On holidays, like, is it?" There was a kind of roguish mockery in how Sheehy spoke to him.

"Nah, I'm after leadin' a garden tour."

"A garden tour?" Sheehy's bloodshot eyes grew wide. "Y're pullin' me pistol!"

"Straight goods," Gallagher said with a click of his teeth. "Michael there is one of the people taking it. Here for a week."

"Where y'stayin'?" The question sounded innocent enough, but Gallagher wasn't sure.

"Stanton's down on Molesworth there."

"Ah, yes. Very nice." Sheehy nodded appreciatively. He was leaning forward, elbows on the bar, so that he and Gallagher seemed of similar height. "Y'goin down to Cork after, like?"

"I hadn't thought of it." Gallagher was disliking all these questions, especially as he still hadn't placed who Sheehy was.

"Get away wit you!" Sheehy slapped the bar top, again with roguish mockery. "Y'mean y'mightn't go down t'Cork a'tall after bein' away all these years?"

"Might not and then again I might." Alarm bells were ringing now. This fellow wanted to know his every move, and just why? Gallagher noticed that the barman farther down, while busy polishing glasses with a cloth, was casually keeping an eye on himself and Sheehy.

"Do you good to see the old place again, Patsy." Sheehy leaned towards him familiarly and Gallagher could smell a kind of sour earthiness about him.

"Changed much, then?" He'd ask a few questions of his own and see what the fellow revealed.

"Oh, ay, lots a dosh now." Sheehy winked. "Everyone's got a car, even the young uns. Everyone dashin' this way an' that."

"Same everywhere now," Gallagher said, glancing around the room. The triflers had largely cleared off and the serious boozers were settling into chairs to make a night of it.

"So much feckin' traffic," Sheehy said, tapping the bartop with the horny nail of an index finger, "they even got to put up barricades for the turnip race and the wheelbarrow race, would you credit it?"

"Go on! They still doin' them crazy races?" So Sheehy was familiar with the harvest festival at Ballydehob.

"Sure they are. Old John's still runnin' the show, though he can hardly walk up the hill anymore."

"A fine old feller all right." Gallagher remembered Old John from Ballydehob vividly, but he still couldn't place this damn Sheehy.

"Y'remember that one time you and Doonan were in the wheelbarrow race?" Sheehy grinned like a well-practised rascal.

"Let's see now . . ." Gallagher scratched his neck.

"Patsy, y've not forgotten it?" Sheehy straightened himself up and Gallagher saw the size and raw strength of him, how his arms and shoulders bulged beneath the cheap suit jacket. "What're you drinkin' over there in Canada, boyo?"

"I'm just rememberin' now."

"Surely y've not forgot Francie O'Sullvan?" This was almost a challenge.

"Ah, no." Danger here. Might this pug be some relative of Francie's lining up a bit of retribution?

"Jays, Patsy, you were hot for her that night. I can picture her still; she was wearin' them nice tight blue jeans an' a little camisole thingy that showed her chest in all its glory. Y'remember?"

"Who could forget it, eh?" Gallagher himself never would, but what was it to Sheehy? Somehow the memory seemed dirtied by this rough customer sharing it.

"Jays, 'tis a sight I'll never forget. I coulda died an' gone straight to heaven on that chest of hers! Then you and Doonan finally get to the top—he was pushin', as I remember, and you sittin' in the barrow—but by the time you get to the top of the hill, drippin' with sweat an' tipsy as pigs, there she's standin' with them beautiful mammaries for all the world to admire. I thought y'd have her that night, Patsy, or die in the tryin', and that, if I'm not greatly mistaken, is the last time I ever laid eyes on you."

"Musta been." Gallagher's mind was roaring. That this bloody Sheehy would know about that. He must have been there. Gallagher couldn't place his accent, couldn't be sure it was even that of a west countryman, but he was certain that he'd never laid eyes on the fellow before. Now he was torn between wanting to get the hell out of there and wanting to find out who Sheehy really was and what he was up to.

"Say, Patsy," Sheehy said, cocking his head, "let me get you another and we'll find a wee snug for a bit."

"All full a regulars, I think." Gallagher would as soon be gone, but saw no way of escaping.

"We'll see." Sheehy winked knowingly.

With fresh pints in hand, they made their way towards the back The snugs were full, but when they came to one at the back, at a nod from Joe Sheehy, the cluster of young drinkers in it promptly rose and left. Gallagher and Joe sat down alone.

"That was a nice bit a work out there, Patsy."

"Eh?"

"Pretendin' not to remember me an' all. Do you not trust that Yank y've got with you?"

"Michael? No, he's no Yank."

"Looks like a Yank."

"No, he's a university professor."

"Still an' all, I can see y've lost none of yer touch."

"S'pose I've not."

"You can't be too careful these days, boyo. If it ain't the fukkin' peelers on the one hand, it's scumbucket spies and turncoats on t'other." Sheehy stared hard at Gallagher. There was an edge to him now that hadn't been evident at the bar.

"Yeah." Gallagher returned his stare, but inwardly he was quailing.

"We've had a couple of rough years, Patsy, we have."

"You have."

"Good Friday an' all that shite." Sheehy almost spat the words.

"Yeah." Gallagher nodded several times, as though dismayed at recent developments.

"Renouncing violence, fer Christ's sakes."

"I know." Things were starting to clarify now.

"Tough on the lads, I'll tell yeh." Sheehy pushed his craggy face forward as though he were leaning into a gale.

"Must be, right enough."

"Ah well, we seen tough times before, so."

"We have." Gallagher would have to just play along here and not say anything to antagonize this fellow.

"An' there'll be more to come before it's over." Sheehy slumped back in his seat, looking Gallagher over.

"Likely so." Gradually it began to dawn on Gallagher who Joe Sheehy was. He hadn't known him from the old days, not at all, hadn't even met him as best he could remember. But knew of him. Everybody did. Head of a Kerry brigade—whether the IRA or Provos he couldn't now recall—a man with a reputation for absolute ruthlessness. Kneecapping. Murder. You name it. Jays!

"No one ever said it were going to be a doddle." Sheehy had lowered his gravelly voice almost to a whisper.

"Don't believe they did, no."

"So no sense mewlin' over it."

"None a'tall." Gallagher watched the fellow's large, gnarled hands resting on the table like blackthorn cudgels.

There was a silence between them and they both drank deep. Sheehy wiped his lips with the back of his sleeve and, leaning forward, spoke in an even lower voice. "It's a marvellous stroke of luck runnin' into you by accident like this, Patsy, because I'm lookin' fer someone to do a wee favour for me."

"What favour's that then?" Every molecule in Gallagher tingled with the apprehension of danger.

"There's a parcel comin' in for me from overseas in a day or two, like, and I'm needing someone trustworthy to pick it up for me."

"I see." Gallagher paused for a moment, peering at the table between them, as though considering how he could accommodate this request, then shook his head regretfully. "Sure I'd help you in a second on that score, Joe, if I weren't tied up the whole time on this tour."

"I understand your obligations, Patsy." Sheehy's stare bore into him. "But I thought you might be able to find a couple of hours somewhere there, one way or another, to help out an old comrade, like."

"Nothing I'd love better, but I don't think it's possible, the schedule's that tight." Gallagher was absolutely clear that he wanted nothing to do with this hoodlum or his parcel.

Sheehy's eyes narrowed and Gallagher winced at the glint of hardness in them. "Can I be straight with you, Patsy?"

"Sure, Joe." Gallagher couldn't reach for his glass, though his lips and throat were dry from fear.

"Unless I'm greatly mistaken, you've an outstanding debt still owin' to the Cause—y'know what I'm talking about?"

"Not sure I do." Gallagher was without a strategy, just tentatively placing one foot in front of another. He could feel little beads of cold sweat trickling from his armpits down his ribs.

Sheehy's eyes were chips of glacial ice, and Gallagher knew this is a hard, hard man; this is not a guy you want to fuck around. "Well, that's got me spannered altogether, Patsy, I don't mind tellin' you. I was thinkin' I could remember the lads in West Cork telling me a tale concerning you and a certain amount of cash."

Cornered like a rat by a terrier, Gallagher made a flashpoint decision to deny the allegation. "No, someone's been spinning you a yarn there, Joe, likely to cover their own tracks. Not surprising either, as there was a few loose screws in that West Cork group, believe me."

"Is that right?"

"It is."

Sheehy stared hard at Gallagher for a moment more. "Hm. Well, I'll be after makin' some inquiries, so, see who's been slanderin' yer good name in yer absence, like. But in the meantime I'd still appreciate havin' that parcel picked up, and if I'm not greatly mistaken, you're the man for the job. Tell you what: I'll get back t'you on it, Patsy." He rose abruptly from his seat but paused before leaving. "Grand t'see you again, boyo. And don't fret yerself unduly, we'll get this sorted right enough."

THE minute the coast was clear, Gallagher bolted from the pub. The menace of Joe Sheehy had been unmistakable. What the hell was the feller up to? Is this what Leary had been warning him about at the airport—the danger of his meeting with persons of interest to the authorities from a national security point of view? Had he been watched the whole time? Was he being watched now? He looked around the street nervously to see if he was being followed. As he scuttled past the old Georgian houses and the closed shops along Merrion Row, Gallagher felt a cold tingle tap-dancing up and down his spine. A burst of laughter as he passed Galligan's Restaurant made him jump, then scurry on. His heart beat frantically when he spotted a couple of heavyweights loitering outside the Huguenot Cemetery. The bruisers looked at him suspiciously and one of them spat on the sidewalk contemptuously, but he passed them without incident and they made no move to follow him. Even the brilliant lights of the Shelbourne Hotel spilling out onto the sidewalk gave scant comfort as he rounded the corner onto Kildare. He almost sprinted the two blocks down to Molesworth and into the welcoming warm safety of the lobby at Stanton's.

He was badly shaken by the encounter and couldn't for the life of him figure how Sheehy had known he was here, much less how he had connected him with that petty theft of twenty years ago, and with Francie at the festival. The parcel pick-up made no sense, why Gallagher was needed to retrieve it. That little gambit was obviously part of something bigger, something Gallagher didn't understand. Was it some plan to suck him back into the movement, make him vulnerable to exploitation by the Provos or the Real IRA or whoever the hell it was? Or could it be that Sheehy was working for the guards, and setting him up for some sting operation they had planned? Any way you looked at it, the thing stank of danger and entrapment. Lying sleepless in his hotel bed, he listened to the night sounds of the city and tried his best not to hear in them the wails of *Ben-sidhe* approaching.

▫ TWELVE ▫

"WE'VE GOT a very long coach ride ahead of us today," Wilburn solemnly informed Gallagher at breakfast. She'd again sought him out, though he was tucked into an even more remote corner of the dining room, screened, he had thought, behind a tour group of extremely voluble Spaniards. She was wearing the same brown uniform suit as yesterday, but she'd added a jaunty yellow scarf.

"Aye," he grunted listlessly. He'd ordered a kipper for breakfast—you can't get a decent kipper in Canada for love nor money, as he'd often remarked, and he'd looked forward to the rare treat of a properly prepared Dublin kipper. But now he picked at it indifferently, his spirits blackened by recollections of the previous evening. He'd lain awake half the night turning it over and over in his mind. He didn't like the stench of it at all, especially after those warnings from the authorities at the airport. At the time he'd brushed them off as the bungling of officialdom, but here they were, made real in Joe Sheehy showing up like some long-lost pal. And another thing—Gallagher had remembered it only halfway through the night—his being watched by a stranger that first evening in the pub. It wasn't Sheehy who'd been observing him, he was certain of that much. Somebody else then, but who? And why? When the hour of the wolf was at long last spent he'd finally lapsed into troubled sleep, eviscerated by unanswerable questions and lurid imaginings.

"But these two stops are entirely worth the journey," Wilburn continued, smartly buttering the toast that the same sulky waitress had brought her.

"Good." He didn't give a toss.

"And the M1's such an improvement now, we'll be up north in no time."

"Grand." Gallagher fished a small kipper bone from between his teeth.

"Is everything all right, Mr. Gallagher?"

"Eh?"

"You seem a bit dispirited this morning, if you don't mind my saying so. Nothing wrong, I should hope?" Her sharp facial features were softened with concern.

"Didn't sleep so well last night, that's all. New bed, strange place and all that."

"Ah, yes, my husband's the same." She leaned back, apparently relieved. "Out like a light by 9:30 he is, never wants to go anywhere or do anything. Always too tired. Everything starts too late nowadays. He has to get to his bed. Then he's awake by midnight and spends the rest of the night rolling this way and rolling that way, and tossing and flopping around like a fish out of water so nobody else can sleep either." She waved her hand this way and that to illustrate the tossing. "Well, I finally said to him, you can carry on like that all you want, but I need my beauty sleep and I'm not getting it with you flailing around for hours on end. 'Wot you want me to do?' he says to me. I want you to set up your own bed in your study there and sleep in it, I told him. 'Wot, not sleep together?' he says. I don't mind sleeping together, I told him, but I don't at all fancy lying awake together all night, so off you go!" She raised her chin imperiously and her thick eyebrows lowered to enforce the edict. "And he did, bless him. And I've never slept better in my life before and—you know what?—neither has he!" She took a triumphant bite of toast.

"Mmm." The Spaniards were all getting up from their table, making a tremendous racket in the process. His breakfast ruined, Gallagher sourly pondered how Wilburn's well-ordered universe would fare if he informed her right now that a Republican fanatic was on his tail, wanting to involve him in illegal activities. Would she still be looking on the bright side of life if she had Joe Sheehy sharing her coach?

"Ah well, cheer up, Mr. Gallagher," she said, beaming at him, "we've got another lovely sunny day at least. Maybe you can catch forty winks on the coach."

"Aye."

WITH Declan again at the wheel, they slowly extricated themselves from the city and out onto the mighty M1 streaking north towards Belfast. Gallagher had again positioned himself behind the others. Everyone else was chattering happily, but he had no heart for socializing. He knew he should be renewing his pursuit of Elyse, but having made no headway even while feeling so buoyant yesterday, he would make even less being down in the dumps as he was today. That damned IRA stuff was like some bloody fungus in the soil that you can't drive off for love or money. And as for fetching parcels—that had got him remembering what had happened to that poor little bastard Willy Croom. He and Willy had been the junior members of the local brigade, little more than kids, playing Step 'n' Fetchit for the Cause. One time there was a parcel needed pickin' up at Kinsale and droppin' off at Bandon the same day. Willy Croom was all for taking on the assignment, he was that anxious to show himself a worthy footsoldier deserving of promotion. So off Willy goes with that silly grin of his, riding his little motorbike. He gets the parcel at Kinsale no problem and straps it on the back of his bike and heads up the road for Bandon. Nobody knew how it happened, but just this side of Inishannon the bloody parcel exploded, tearing off half of Willy's backside. The last Gallagher had seen of him, Willy was lying face down in his bed at home with his old mam nursing him as best she could. "Look at that!" the old lady had said to Gallagher accusingly. "You call that pathetic spectacle a free and united Ireland?" Gallagher had slunk away and never gone back.

The big coach glided smoothly north beyond Drogheda and Dundalk, Wilburn now chattering away through the microphone about the remarkable Stone Age passage tomb at Newgrange, Ireland's most visited site. Then she got on to the Battle of the Boyne, as they crossed that storied stream, the battleground lying just off to their left, and beyond that the monastic ruins at Melifont Abbey and the great Celtic crosses at Monasterboice. Gallagher dozed away, indifferent.

Eventually they ground to a halt in the clotted arteries of Newry. They'd crossed the border into Northern Ireland without even knowing it. Gallagher had expected checkpoints and army patrols in Saracens, razor wire, and squaddies with machine guns everywhere. He'd braced himself for a grilling like that one he'd had at the airport. Thinking yesterday about the possibilities, he'd wanted it in a perverse way, to be singled out by the Tommies and questioned closely. The heroic dimensions of it had appealed to him, less for their own sake than to impress the group. He had thought it might be just the kind of bold stroke that would raise his profile in Elyse Frampton's opinion, make him appear someone for whom she'd be privileged to be a benefactor. And, most particularly, he'd imagined that he'd gladly suffer a bit of rough handling by the Brits if it meant that Bonnie Raithby, Gallagher's ardent admirer from Saskatoon, would gaze at him with something of the awe reserved for heroes.

But that was yesterday, before Joe Sheehy's appearance. Today he wanted nothing to do with the Troubles. Instead of heroics, they crossed a border that didn't exist and got snarled in a traffic jam.

Just as they'd finally wriggled their way through dreary Newry and picked up the B8 heading east, Bonnie rose from her seat and came back along the aisle, smiling at the other group members as she passed. "Good morning, Mr. Gallagher," she greeted him pertly. "May I sit with you for a bit?" Hunkered down, lost in heroic imaginings and gloomy apprehensions somewhere between Michael Collins and Willy Croom, at the girl's greeting he opened like a snow crocus in late winter sunshine.

"Of course," he said, brightening for the first time all morning. He straightened himself and made room for her.

"Are you going to sing for us again today, Mr. Gallagher?" she asked him archly as she slid into the seat next to him. There was a shine on her this morning, the illuminating bloom that makes youth beautiful. Immediately she had him thinking of Shania's Thighs.

"Ah, no, I don't know what come over me there yesterday," he said bashfully. "I'm no singer at the best of times."

"I thought it was lovely," she told him again, as she had at the time. As dense as they were, Gallagher's preoccupations evaporated like morning mist under the warmth of her praise. My Christ, she's a girl and a half, this one, he thought. "What are these hills here?" she asked him, leaning forward so that her tumbling hair brushed across his arm. She pointed through the window to the smoothly rounded hills looming off to the right, their summits veiled in mist. He felt an overwhelming impulse to plunge his fingers into her spilling hair, as he would into the earth, fondle handsful of its silken beauty and press his face into it as into the cool trickling of a hillside brook.

"Them's the Mountains of Mourne," he said.

"They're lovely," Bonnie breathed softly.

Not half so lovely as yourself, thought Gallagher. Covertly he admired her full lips and marvellous high cheekbones, the tawny smoothness of her neck, how her sweater swelled across her breasts. "Aye," he said, "I remember them well from when I was a lad."

"You do?" Her blue eyes turned upon him might have seen right into his soul had he not glanced away, embarrassed.

"Sure, I do, so." He stared out the coach window with the wistful melancholy of a romantic poet. Yeats, perhaps, dreaming of fairies.

"Well?" she prompted, smiling.

"Eh?"

"Won't you tell me about it? I know you've got a story, haven't you?" Again the girl's voluptuousness washed over him and giddily he felt his little gentleman stiffen and begin to rise to the chase. Sheehy was gone; his troubled past and uncertain future were gone; everything was obliterated by this wildly pulsing, present moment.

"Aye, well, I tramped them very hills there long ago as a lad," he reiterated. Why he launched so readily into falsehood he couldn't have said. The girl's nearness excited a giddy recklessness in him, so that truthfulness was trampled as he ransacked his imagination for alluring details with which to entertain her. The intoxication of the moment forbade him to pause and consider what unintended consequences his mistruths might entail. Any risk was justified.

"I thought so," she said, enticing him on.

"Had a sweetheart too," he admitted, slyly shy.

"I thought you might. What was her name?" The girl's forthrightness gave him repeated small shocks. It's this new generation, he reasoned, their brassy confidence and straightforwardness.

"Her name," he said, pausing effectively while calculating whether or not he ought to offer the one name that instantly presented itself, considering how vile a sacrilege this might be, then jettisoning the consideration, "was Francie O'Sullivan. God, I haven't thought of her for years." Two lies, innocently laid down in service of the greater good.

"Go on." Bonnie just about snuggled down against him, as though she were a doting daughter whose dad was reading her a bedtime story. The softness of her, the warm ripe feminine fruitfulness of her, washed over him with an ardent glow. If stories are what will hold her, he thought, stories are what she'll get. He would sell his very soul for a story that might win her.

"We cycled up here from Carrickmacross for the weekend one time." He smiled out at the hills with fond reminiscence, though in truth he'd never before laid eyes on them.

"How romantic!"

"We had a grand two-seater I'd borrowed from a pal."

"Oh, I love this!" She clapped her hands together with delight.

"Lord, we could fly along on that bike." He shook his head, smiling wryly over the recollection. He was in fact remembering cycling with Francie down the boreens of West Cork all those years ago, and his genuine affection for the memory excused his cannibalizing it for his present purposes. "She up front steering, me in the back pushin' hard and keepin' an eye on them lovely long legs of hers as she pedalled and her lovely young bum on the seat—you'll excuse me speakin' this way, Bonnie, I was only a rough lad back then," he confessed, trying his best to look the wise older gentleman who'd never now leer at a woman's buttocks—"and the bend of her back as she leaned on the bars, with the wind tossing her hair."

"Oh, Mr. Gallagher, you're going to make me cry!" The scent of the girl was driving him to madness.

"I remember"—he chuckled again at the memory—"we stopped in one of these fields here somewheres along the way to have our picnic lunch. The field was full of wild strawbries free for the pickin'. Francie was sittin' on a blanket in the shade of a hawthorn tree by the wall and I'm out pickin' strawbries to bring back to her, Sir Galahad himself, y'know." He winked with one eye and cocked his head to the same side, with a small click of his tongue, as men do in County Down. He was Mr. Quicksilver Celt himself by now and Bonnie was gazing at him with what he recognized as unmistakable ardor.

"And what happened?" she asked.

"Hmm? Oh, aye! Well, I'm pickin' away at the strawbries—I've got the flask cup half filled by this time and I'm thinkin' meself a grand feller by any account—when suddenly BOOM!" He smacked his fist into his palm. "I'm tits over teakettle in the grass. Hah!"

"Oh, my God, what was it? What happened?"

"A ram. A great bloody big ram had butted me in the posterior, horns an' all!" Bonnie's laughter spilled like sunshine. "Francie was laughin' her head off—once she'd seen I wasn't really hurt."

"Just your pride."

"Aye, but pride's a mighty provoker, is it not, Bonnie? I musta chased that feckin' ram fer three miles around the meadow, tryin' t'kick him back in the arse!" The two of them laughed giddily, like sweethearts, Gallagher thought.

"What's so comical over there?" Loretta Stroude was turned towards them from across the aisle one row forward. Smiling broadly, her lips painted a vivid scarlet, she was wearing another extravagant pantsuit, this one with fuchsia patterning that matched the colour of her lipstick. Enormous gold earrings dangled from her ears.

"Ah, nothin' at all," Gallagher said to her, reluctantly peering out from the magical enclosure surrounding Bonnie and himself. "Just rememberin' a lark from the old days."

"Rather a long haul all the way up here, isn't it?" Loretta sounded vexed behind the smile.

"It is that," Gallagher agreed, "but the two stops we'll make are well worth it in the end, I should think." He nodded reassuringly to Loretta and turned back to Bonnie as though drawing a curtain around them.

"Well, I've heard so much about Mount Stewart, I am very anxious to see it," Loretta said, declining to be excluded.

"I think you'll be very impressed indeed," he told her, although he had only the vaguest notions about Mount Stewart.

"It's a National Trust property, is it not?" the woman persisted.

"I believe it is so," Gallagher declared with a tone of closure.

"Such a wonderful organization, don't you think?"

"I do." He'd think anything she bloody wanted, if only she'd shut up and let him get back to spinning stories for Bonnie.

"I've visited a number of their finest estates in England, you know."

"Have you now." Looking past Bonnie over to the intruding Loretta, he could sense the girl drifting away across the countryside beyond the coach window. It was all he could do to prevent himself from taking her hand in his.

"Oh, yes. Wisely Gardens in the springtime. Absolutely gorgeous! The narcissus alone were enough to take your breath away. Fields and fields of them in the spring sunshine—it made me feel so young again." Loretta's eyes brightened girlishly, but Gallagher was watching the jiggling of her multiple chins.

"Aye."

"That was on one of Stephen Aubrey's tours, you know." This confounded Loretta was like a bloody mongrel that had got the leg of your trousers in its teeth and wouldn't let go.

"Ah, yes."

"Such a wonderfully well-informed person to view a garden with." Loretta winked at him disconcertingly.

"I'm sure of it." Shut up, Gallagher was screaming inside. Go away. Die.

"How he remembers *so* many botanical names I'll never know." Loretta's tiny hands flowered open on her fat arms. She'd left her bracelets behind today.

"It's a marvel all right."

"We did Hampton Court with him too."

"Did you?" Gallagher was striving mightily to avoid letting his impatience boil over. Still gazing absently at the passing countryside, Bonnie was humming an air to herself, entirely removed from this moronic exchange between himself and Loretta.

"And I believe Sissinghurst was on that same tour too. Suzy!"— she called to her friend sitting just ahead—"was Sissinghurst on that Stephen Aubrey tour? The one with Wisely?"

"No, that was on the second tour with Stephen," Suzy told her definitively. "Wisely was the first one."

"Are you sure?" Loretta was doubtful.

"Positive," said Suzy in her positive way.

"I could have sworn they were on the same tour. Ah, well, that's memory for you, isn't it, Mr. Gallagher, a leaky vessel that gets leakier by the day." She grinned at him again, like a faithful companion in the tragic comedy of memory loss.

"True enough," he said, his spirits disintegrating as Bonnie rose, smiled fondly at him, and at Loretta, and returned to her seat beside

Carla. Shite! thought Gallagher, shite in a pile on a plate! Another story to tell Bonnie had occurred to him, but the opportunity was lost. Ah well, he'd catch up with her later and regale her then. And he could work up some other yarns in the interim. If it was old Celtic tales the girl doted on, then it was old Celtic tales Gallagher would be telling, you could bet your pampooties on that.

"We also did a couple of tours with Evan Pomfret, you know," Loretta continued. The odd mannerism she had of letting her mouth slide sideways at the end of a sentence was adding to Gallagher's annoyance.

"Ah, yes, the Brit."

"Very knowledgeable also. An eminent rosarian like yourself." Was this flattery or irony? Gallagher couldn't tell. He was perfectly aware that this group offered him a level of protection against whatever menace Joe Sheehy represented. Simply getting out of Dublin with them for the day provided a small measure of relief. And he certainly hadn't abandoned his plan of pursuing Elyse Frampton as an avenue of deliverance from his financial woes at home. So it was imperative that he keep his annoyance in check and not ruin everything, with intemperate remarks, as was his wont.

"Aye."

"He knew of your work, you know?" As she said it, Loretta rose from her seat and sat down familiarly beside Gallagher where Bonnie had just been.

"Did he?" Gallagher felt imposed upon by the woman's bulk.

"Oh, yes, very complimentary."

"That's nice to hear." The flattery was hardly enough to compensate for the loss of Bonnie's company, and Loretta's lavender fragrance seemed all the more cloying after Bonnie's provocatively natural scent.

"He did seem to have a bit of difficulty with the names, however." Loretta lowered her head and looked at him coyly.

"Couldn't remember them, eh?"

"Oh, no, he had no trouble at all remembering them." She chuckled. "It just embarrassed him having to say them."

"Ah." Gallagher knew what was coming next.

"I recall he got completely confounded having to say one of your names—what was it now? Oh, Suzy!" Again she called ahead to her friend, "What was that name, you know, the rose of Mr. Gallagher's that Evan Pomfret was too embarrassed to say?"

"Oh, let's see," said Suzy, staring at the roof of the coach. "I think, yes, Raquel's Rack, I think it may have been."

"I wonder was that it." Loretta turned back to him, unconvinced, her great earrings swinging. "Named for Raquel Welch, was it, Mr. Gallagher?"

"No, no!" Suzy cried, remembering, "It was Claudia's Cleavage, that was the one Evan had so much trouble with."

"Yes, of course!" Loretta clapped her little hands. "Suzy, you're a wonder." The two ladies exchanged an affectionate smile. Gallagher noticed that Elyse Frampton and her daughter, sitting across the aisle from Suzy, were listening in on the exchange. Easy does it here, he said to himself.

"Well, try as he might," Loretta said to Gallagher but loud enough for the others to hear, "poor Mr. Pomfret couldn't get it out. He had Claudia's Cleeps and Laudia's Luggage and I don't know what else. Do you remember, Suzy?"

"Oh, yes," laughed Suzy, "it was a riot. The poor man was so tongue-tied." The old birds were having a good laugh at his expense, but Gallagher was not amused. Claudia's Cleavage was one of his more spectacular creations, a large, semi-double bloom, fully cupped, with gorgeous burnt-orange petals. He'd named it for the German super-model Claudia Schiffer and didn't at all care to have her beauty the subject of this flippant badinage.

"But you *are* a bit naughty, aren't you, Mr. Gallagher?" Loretta leaned towards him, swathing him in her confidence as though in a thick blanket. Her perfume was overpowering.

"Naughty?" Had she spotted his flagpole rising for Bonnie?

"With the names. Tell me, do you do it just to shock people?" She chortled good-humouredly, as though she herself were a person beyond shock.

"Not a bit of it. I do it because I love my roses and I admire beauti-ful women, simple as that."

"Yes, of course," Loretta agreed but didn't.

"It's no different from somebody naming a rose Queen Elizabeth or The Duchess of Kent. Personally I prefer Claudia Schiffer or Shania Twain to either of them toffs."

"That I can understand perfectly well." Old Loretta was nothing if not progressive in her views. "But the body parts, Mr. Gallagher— the thighs and lips and cleavage and all the rest—do you not think that's just a tiny bit demeaning to the beautiful women you wish to immortalize through a rose?"

"Demeaning?"

"Yes, the emphasis on the purely physical. As though they were no more than a slab of meat in a butcher's shop." She gestured with an arm towards the imaginary slab, so that pouches of fleshy skin sagged beneath her upper arm.

"Get away out of there with you," he said indignantly. "That's a frightful narrow way of looking at the thing. Roses are beautiful and women are beautiful and there's a natural celebration of the two together."

"Yes, of course," she agreed, actually laying a hand upon his arm, "but why not say Shania's Song, for example? It's the girl's singing, not her thighs surely, that should be celebrated."

"I'd say it's both of them together." Gallagher was finding this drivel really annoying. The woman was not actually accusing him, but at the best of times his tolerance for any criticism of his work was almost nonexistent. To have lost the pleasure of Bonnie's company for this bitchy meddling only made matters worse.

Apparently oblivious to his mounting displeasure, or perhaps just determined to make her point whether he liked it or not, Loretta waded forward. "But as a woman, Mr. Gallagher, I must say to you that this fixation on sexualized body parts . . ."

"Sexualized?" He was shocked that she'd say such a thing.

"Well, yes," Loretta said, looking as though she feared she'd gone too far, "in the sense that . . ."

"I don't believe you should be bringin' sex into it at all." Gallagher glowered at her.

"I only meant to say . . ." She shrank back from him in her seat.

"Well, I'll tell you what," he interrupted her snappishly, "why don't you develop a rose yourself and call it Shania's Singing and see how well it does for you, eh?"

"Now, Mr. Gallagher, there's no cause for . . ."

But he cut her off again. "I happen to think that particular woman's thighs are a gift from the gods so poor wee sods like myself can believe there's still occurrences of beauty in this poxbottle world, okay?"

"Of course." Loretta backed off entirely, startled by his sudden vehemence. Heads were turning in the coach at his outburst. Suzy looked concerned. Elyse was staring at him quite sharply. Fortunately, they were just at that moment arriving at their destination, the little town of Castlewellan, which was enough to distract everyone and draw the tension from the coach. The town's wide main street was swarming with uniformed students from the Catholic school, the boys in blazers and slacks, the girls in sweaters and pleated skirts. The coach swung left and nudged through the imposing gateway into Castlewellan Forest Park.

THIRTEEN

"MY LORD, won't you just look at this!" exclaimed Robert Long. "Ain't that just something else!" Some version of this expostulation was Robert's enthusiastic response to each of the gardens they'd visited thus far. As usual, dull and dutiful Robert had his dull and dutiful lookalike wife, Nicole, at his side. Gallagher had yet to see one of them without the other; they might have been Siamese twins connected at the hip. The Longs, Piet van Vliet, and Gallagher were standing at the top end of the eucryphia walk inside the Annesley Garden, a walled enclosure within the forest park. There'd been no formal tour arranged for Castlewellan Park, but the whole group had first walked past the lake and across the expansive lawns to view the castle, a Scottish baronial pile with buttresses and round towers. Above the front door the original owner's crest bore the family motto: *Virtutis Amore*, which Piet had translated for them as "For the love of virtue." Gallagher had pondered the phrase, its old-fashioned nobility, its inapplicability to what he was making of himself.

The plan was for all to explore the grounds at their leisure and reconvene at the coach in an hour. Bonnie and Carla had gone off arm in arm laughing about something. Michael Wickerson had again attached himself to Elyse and her daughter. Still looking deeply offended, Loretta had disappeared with Suzy, no doubt to plot revenge. Jays, Gallagher thought, what a balls-up. He should never have snapped at Loretta like that. It was likely that Elyse had overheard him, setting back even further his need to convince her that he was worthy and deserving of her patronage. This trying to be a gracious Stephen Aubrey substitute was wearing him right down. His mood, having brightened temporarily in Bonnie's company, had soured again, bringing him full circle to the gloom in which he'd started the day.

With Piet and the Longs he'd wandered over to the walled garden that formed the centre of the National Arboretum, an outstanding collection of mature conifers and broadleafed trees and shrubs. The four of them now gazed down upon the gently sloping walk flanked by flowering trees, the grass beneath the trees iced with fallen white petals. Filtered sunlight threw scatter rugs of green gold across the lawns. Within the honeyed fragrance of the eucryphia blooms Gallagher could detect the subtle fragrances of Bonnie as she'd curled beside him on the coach. Part of him still lingered within the magical orb that had enclosed her and himself. He flashed upon the sea cave long ago where he and Francie had huddled together in a world beyond the known world. As had been the case then, his fascination with this girl now was, he knew, against his better judgement, luring him into a domain of mystery and danger.

"These are mostly *Eucryphia glutinosa*," Piet van Vliet was explaining to the Longs, "flanked by *Eucryphia cordifolia*. There, you see the difference?" He pointed down the avenue of trees. "The cordifolia is the taller of the two and evergreen. Its flowers will continue well into November." Piet's grey slacks were perfectly creased and his black leather shoes immaculately polished. Although the day was sunny and warm, he wore a blue blazer with matching tie.

"Could we grow them back in Edmonton?" Robert asked, as he'd ingenuously asked about almost every tender and half-hardy plant they'd encountered thus far.

"I think not," said Piet, shaking his head. "They'd be zone eight at best, I should think, wouldn't they, Mr. Gallagher?" Although thoroughly informed, Piet was never dogmatic, and invariably deferred to Gallagher.

"If you're lucky," Gallagher said authoritatively. He was coming to like old Piet, recognizing that what he'd thought was priggishness in the Dutchman was in fact meticulous precision. Even the Longs, as hopelessly conjoined in dullness as they were, seemed to him deserving of more respect than he'd accorded them. But he needed to be alone, and eventually he managed to detach himself from the other three and wandered for a while through the near-deserted arboretum. The wide gravel paths of the upper garden were flanked with herbaceous borders and enclosed by clipped yew hedges festooned with the brilliant red blooms of the Flame Flower vine. At the garden's centre, where its two main axis pathways intersect, he came upon the Heron Fountain. He sat on a wooden bench, watching the single spume of water spurting skywards from the great stone chalice of the fountain. Above the bulging greens and golds and coppers of the massed tree canopy, a sky of palest blue was washed with feathery high white cloud. The splash of the fountain soothed his jangled nerves. There was, he thought, a double axis of sorts in his own predicament. One was the axis of fear that had sprung out of his impending eviction, been continued with the guards at the airport and was now intensified further with the emergence of Sheehy. Deceit and treachery lined that axis, and it led to places of great danger. The other intersecting axis was the line of affection grounded in his love of roses that had inflated into a larger love as he sang to the Last Rose of Summer and was now bursting with tenderness towards Bonnie Raithby. This axis was bordered with beauty and truth, but it, like the other, led to danger. They intersected here and now where he sat by this fountain in pale sunshine. He could sit here forever, he thought, lost in hazy dreams and imaginings, safe from the dangers towards that both pathways led.

Suddenly he heard footsteps crunching along the gravel and looked behind to see Michael Wickerson striding towards him. "Ah, there you are, Gallagher. Not interrupting, I hope. May I join you?"

"Yeah, sure. Thought you were off with Elyse and the daughter."

"And so I was." Wickerson sat on the bench beside him, stretched his legs out languidly, and gazed with contentment at the fountain. "This is lovely, isn't it, just listening to the plash of that water, and the rustling of leaves in the breeze."

"Aye, it's peaceful here."

"There's a wonderful line from Lord Dunsany, perhaps it's familiar to you—'the infinite mystery of the hills is borne along the sound of distant sheep-bells.' The sounds in here are similar, don't you find? Carrying distant mysteries somehow."

"Hm." Gallagher was off on infinite mysteries of his own, but he liked this habit of Michael's, how he could throw in just the right literary allusion at the right time.

"From a story called "The Kith of the Elk Folk." Do you know it?"

"I probably read it once upon a time."

"About the Wild Things that live in the marshes but have no soul. I teach it as part of an introductory course. But it brings up a theme recurring in so many of the old stories, about the unseen beings, spiritual beings that were believed to reside here. I'm fascinated by the topic—that's why I was asking yesterday about your peoples' belief in the old stories. You were just starting to tell me about witches when we were interrupted by your friend."

"Yeah, that's right. Only that fellow was no friend of mine."

"Oh?" Wickerson looked surprised. "I thought you were old boyhood pals. That's why I left you with him."

"It's a long story," Gallagher grunted, not wanting to be reminded again of Sheehy.

"Stories are my business, Gallagher, in a second-hand sort of way." Wickerson smiled at him but said no more, apparently content to enjoy the beauty of the place and the moment. The water lilies in the pool undulated gently from the plash of the cascade. Gallagher hesitated. He wanted badly to unburden himself to someone, there was so much roiling around in his brain. He couldn't get a toehold on his own somehow, the ground was that slippery. Still, he had lingering suspicions about Wickerson, nothing tangible, nothing specific, but a generalized unease that there was more to this affable young professor than met the eye. That he was perhaps up to something. But he was as close to a friend as Gallagher had at the moment. As close to a friend as he had back at home too, for that matter. Habitually, his most intimate disclosures were invariably made to his roses. Now he was beginning to sound the true depths of his aloneness in life. The sudden, frightening forcefulness of his feelings for Bonnie had stirred this awareness, and so had his sense of vulnerability about Sheehy. He worried his situation back and forth in his mind for a bit and then decided impulsively to hell with it.

"I'm in a bit of a jam here, Michael, I don't mind telling you."

"How so? You don't mean that bit of a spat you had on the coach with Loretta? She'll get over that soon enough."

"No, that's the least of my troubles." Gallagher stared at the stone herons in the chalice of the fountain.

"What then?"

"I seem to be caught up in something I don't understand."

"Tell me." Michael shifted around on the bench to face Gallagher, all considered attentiveness.

"It started when I first arrived at the airport."

"What started?"

"They had me in for questioning."

"Who had you in?" There was a note of surprise, maybe even alarm, in Michael's voice.

"The customs and the guards."

"Why would they possibly want to question you?"

"Oh, they were on about old political stuff from years ago. I'd done a bit of muckin' around with the Provos, back when I was a lad and knew no better."

"And they had information on you?" Michael had a look of real concern.

"Even had an old photograph."

"Of you?"

"Yeah. Taken up north. Coalisland. At an IRA funeral. But I don't remember being there, not at all. I mean, I could have been all right, I had a bit of a wild streak in me back in them days, and of course we were all for giving John Bull a good kick in the arse whenever we could." Gallagher grimaced skywards at the absurdity of it. "So I might have had a glass or two and wound up at some feckin' funeral, but I'll be bollixed if I can recall it. I'd almost swear not, but that photo they had's got me all twisted."

"Was it real?"

"What d'you mean, real?"

"I mean a print. On photographic paper."

"Oh, I get you. No, no she had it on a computer."

"Well, there's your answer right there." Michael threw his hands in the air.

"What's that then?"

"The computer. They can do whatever they want with a photo on a computer nowadays. Take your head off and put somebody else's head on your body. Anything they fancy."

"You mean they took my photo from someplace else and put it on some other git in the crowd?"

"Could be. Anyone can do that now."

"I'll be fukked. Makes you wonder what's real and what isn't anymore." Michael's explanation, although distressing in one sense, was also strangely reassuring.

"So what did they do?"

"Nothin'. Said they'd be watchin' me, though. And if I was to meet with the wrong people, for example, there'd be trouble. Then out of the blue, as you saw, that feller Sheehy shows up at the pub."

"And you're sure he wasn't just some tosser out on a pub crawl?"

"No, no, I knew him from the old days all right," Gallagher said, shaking his head. "That is, I didn't know him; I knew *of* him. He was a big noise locally with the Provisionals."

"Interesting. The police warn you not to meet with anyone like that and, before you know it, that's exactly what you're doing." Michael pursed his lips, considering. "Seems like more than a coincidence to me."

"Me too. Feels like I'm being set up for something, but I can't determine what or why. But Sheehy's mixed up in it somehow. He's asked me to pick up a parcel for him."

"A parcel."

"Yeah." Part of Gallagher hated being reminded of the mess he'd got himself into, while another part was feeling relief over sharing the information with Michael.

"So are you going to?"

"I am not. But I was fool enough to tell him where we're staying, so there'll be no escaping him if he wants to find me."

"What about informing the police?" Michael stretched his arm across the back of the bench.

"I've thought of it, but they're no more to be trusted than he is. And after them fingering me at the airport like that, I'd be afraid of backing myself into some trap and not knowing who had set it and who was going to spring it. I can't even be certain that Sheehy and the guards aren't in on this together."

"I see what you mean," Michael said, nodding thoughtfully. Gallagher liked Michael's way of talking about a thing without rushing to judgement or conclusion, how he allowed Gallagher to put his predicament into words of his own.

"Treachery is what this place is fashioned of," Gallagher said, rapping his knuckles on the bench. "That much I do know."

"Still, you think?"

Gallagher snorted. "Treachery isn't a thing that comes and goes with the trends. It's in the blood."

"I wish there was something tangible I could do for you," Michael said earnestly, looking Gallagher straight in the eye. "I have the sense that it's not easy for you to share your burdens with others, or to ask for help." Michael spoke with a candour and forthrightness unfamiliar to Gallagher. "But, you know, I think it's really important that you're not isolated in this. I'd like to do whatever I can, and I want you to know that you can call on me if need be, anytime, okay?"

"Thank you, Michael," Gallagher said, looking away from the intensity of Michael's gaze, off to a purple-red Japanese maple beyond the pool. The younger man's offer of help was quite moving to him, its sincerity and generosity. Setting aside his earlier misgivings, he experienced a kind of concordance with Michael that was an unaccustomed sensation for him. And although nothing had been solved, Gallagher felt considerably lightened by having got some of this off his chest, diminishing its hold over him by speaking it aloud, making it existent outside his own mind. And, who knows?—perhaps it would all blow over, that he'd see no more of Sheehy. Perhaps.

They sat quietly again for a bit. Warmed by Michael's thoughtfulness, Gallagher was wondering whether he should ask Michael's advice on the other pressing problem he faced: how best to approach Elyse Frampton and broach the delicate subject of his financial peril. Notwithstanding everything else going on, Gallagher had not lost sight of why he'd come on this expedition, but his initial conviction that he could charm his way into the confidence of his chosen Gwyneth Mandeville-Hampton had foundered in the face of Elyse's icy reserve. His singing at the botanic gardens had not gone over well with her, and her overhearing the little tempest he'd had with Loretta could only have made matters worse. He was well and truly stumped by her. And he'd observed that Michael's sophisticated charm obviously appealed to Elyse. So there was a good case to be made for his asking Michael for help.

On the other hand, he had no way of knowing how Michael might react to the request. He might easily be appalled by it. He might judge Gallagher a scheming imposter, a deceitful little gold-digger no longer worthy of his friendship or his trust. Of course, Gallagher didn't see himself in these terms at all. What he was attempting was perfectly reasonable and entirely ethical. It was just that, improperly conveyed, the situation could create an impression of dishonesty and deceit, and that would be ruinous.

Having waffled back and forth in his mind for quite some time, Gallagher finally bit the bullet. Overcoming his misgivings, he proceeded to lay out in considerable detail the full circumstances of his impending eviction, and his eleventh-hour attempt to forestall it by securing a patron, and how he considered Elyse Frampton to be his best, perhaps only, chance at a solution. He nervously watched Michael's face throughout his narrative, observing how it went from an expression of concern over his plight to surprise over his intended solution and then to an unreadable neutrality. By the end, he had no more idea of how Michael felt about his story than he'd had at the beginning. "I hate to ask you," he said in conclusion, looking down at his hands in his lap, "but do you think you could give me a hand with this, Michael?"

Michael hesitated. "What sort of thing did you have in mind?"

"Well, I wondered if maybe you could talk to Elyse, you know, sound out her prospects, like, then perhaps gradually work in a few details about my situation and how there's maybe a promising investment opportunity for somebody like herself."

"Hm." Michael pondered the request for a while, staring at the fountain's spume. Right away Gallagher could see that Michael was uncomfortable, that he maybe thought there was something sleazy in what he was proposing.

"Y'know there's nothing shifty about it," Gallagher sought to reassure him. "It's a straight-up business deal."

"I suppose," Michael said unenthusiastically.

"Do you think you could do that?" Gallagher realized that he was pressing his friend hard, but he felt it necessary to do so. "I'm getting a wee bit desperate, and now with all this other trouble coming . . ."

Michael nodded several times, acknowledging Gallagher's compound problems, stared at the fountain a while longer, then finally smiled and laid a reassuring hand upon Gallagher's shoulder. "Of course I will," he said warmly. "I'll do whatever I can to help."

"That's grand!" Gallagher said, hugely relieved on several fronts, not least of them that at last things might be getting underway.

"As it happens," Michael said, relaxing back against the bench after the tension of the past few minutes, "I've had several interesting conversations with Elyse already. She's quite a remarkable woman. Extremely insightful. I'm quite certain that I can mention your situation without in any way giving offence."

"That would be lovely." Again Gallagher felt an unfamiliar sense of affection and gratitude towards Michael, much as he'd felt about his old patron Mr. Fanslau after hearing news of his passing.

"Of course, I guarantee nothing, other than giving it the old school try." Michael was back to his smiling, affable self.

Again the two of them sat for a while without speaking, content to bask in the sunshine and the sounds of the fountain.

"Now, about those witches," Michael finally said.

Feeling beholden, Gallagher wanted to repay Michael with a generous supply of the old stories he liked hearing. And here Gallagher needed no inventiveness, for his mother had been a storehouse of hoary yarns, and he was grateful to have them at his disposal now, though he'd given them scarcely a thought for twenty years or more. "Well, my mam used to talk about how a witch could tie a bunch of knots in a string and make some kind of incantation that would then put a curse on someone. The old ones were a great bunch for putting curses on one another."

"So I've read. What about hypnotism?"

"Yeah, that too. There was a traditional story she told about a warrior who was surrounded by enemies, but a witch hypnotized his attackers into believing that a cluster of stones nearby weren't stones at all, but armed companions of the warrior they'd surrounded, so off they all charge and attack the stones instead. Lots of silly stuff like that."

"Hmm. I think that's from McPherson's *Ossian*. But truths of a sort are buried in these time-honoured stories, I would think."

"Aye, perhaps so." As a younger man, Gallagher had dismissed the old tales as folklore foolishness, although he knew there was lots of interest in them again nowadays.

"And leprechauns?"

"I don't remember her talking about them. She may have. But

mermaids, yes, she liked her mermaids, maybe because we lived down on the coast. The *Moruogh* she called them, the sea-fairies. They had long green hair, like seaweed." Gallagher ran his flittering fingers down imaginary strands of seaweed hair. "I think she preferred them because they weren't mischievous the way the land fairies were. I remember as a little kid being down at the shore and imagining I could see them among the seaweed flowing this way and that in the tide." His hand showed the ebb and flow. "They weren't something to be frightened of, like the land fairies, or the evil spirits that lived underground in the mountains and would come out at night to do their mischief, steal milk from the cows, or tear down bits of churches that were being built."

"What about elf-shots?" Michael asked. "I know they were the stone arrowheads of the ancient Irish and were held in great reverence and used as amulets to deflect the venomous assaults of enemies. I've read that some people thought they were the arrowheads of fairies and viewed them with great suspicion. Did you ever hear of one in your old neighbourhood?"

"Happens I did," Gallagher said, clicking his teeth. "From my mam, of course. Said when she herself was a young girl there was an ancient crone in the village believed to have an elf-shot in her possession. She kept it wrapped in a cloth and hidden somewhere in the byre because it was bad luck to bring it into the house."

"In ancient times she would have been a pagan priestess," Michael said.

"Well, she was no priestess to hear Mam tell it." Gallagher laughed. "But she might well have been a pagan right enough. Apparently she'd bring the stone out on certain occasions and perform some ritual or other with it, the end result being that a passing ship would be lured into shore and smash up on the rocks, so the locals could run down and salvage whatever was to be found in the wreckage. Of course everyone knew it was her powers had drawn the ship in, and the men would bring her choice items from the wreck."

"And could she calm the sea too, did your mother say?" Michael was watching Gallagher intently, as he always did with these old stories.

"Right you are. When the village boats were set out for fishing, she'd do another kind of incantation and the waves would subside for them." Just then, as if on cue, a large raven came gliding through the glade and disappeared into the tree canopy off to their left. "Funny stuff, all these old tales," Gallagher said, grinning. "If you hear the fairy music, Mam used to say, the *Ceol-sidh*, take your Bible in one hand and your crucifix in the other, and no harm will come to you."

"I think I'd take an elf-shot too," Michael said, smiling.

Gallagher glanced at his watch, then suddenly clapped his hands. "Oh, Jays! I almost forgot: I promised Ruth Wilburn I'd get together with her, something about duplicate vouchers for Mount Stewart she wanted to discuss. I'd best go find her straightaway. You coming?" He stood up.

"No, I think I'll have a few more minutes here savouring the infinite mystery of the hills." Michael stretched languorously back on the bench. "I'll see you down there in a bit."

"Michael," Gallagher said tentatively, standing alongside.

"Hm?" Michael opened one eye to squint up at him.

"Thanks for listening to my rubbish."

"Not at all," Michael said, looking openly at Gallagher. "My pleasure entirely, believe me. And thank you for the old tales."

"Well, thanks. I'll see you at the coach." Gallagher set off briskly down the central path, and as he did so, he noticed Elyse Frampton, alone and looking uncharacteristically agitated, walking on a parallel path in the direction of the fountain.

⊞ FOURTEEN ⊞

THEY STOPPED for a late lunch in Downpatrick. The walls and fences of the town were smeared with graffiti screaming "Brits Out!" and "IRA Rules!" From the outset Gallagher had wondered what visiting the North would be like. Having been away so long, living in a place where violence is lionized in the name of freedom only when it occurs elsewhere, he'd almost forgotten how it is to deal with those cold-blooded enough to kill without compunction. It was Dominic Farrell over at Timoleague who'd first recruited him to the Cause. Gallagher was only seventeen, an impressionable lad whose head was easily filled with tales of heroism by death-defying patriots. A gentle man, full of dreams of Celtic grandeur, a student of Irish folklore and collector of old tunes, Dominic was head gardener at a big house where Gallagher got his first job. It was Dominic who first introduced him to serious gardening, as well as to Republicanism.

But Dominic was no killer. He held a woolly-headed notion that a republicanism of the spirit, born from a love of the old ways, could be mobilized to bring such unrelenting pressure on Britain that the North would be eventually set free and reunited with the Republic, as geography and history demanded. Unlettered and footloose, young Patrick was impressed by Farrell's passion and touched by the older man's kindness towards him. They worked clandestinely together as part of a ragtag Provisionals cell. The Troubles were brewing again in the North at that time and gradually Gallagher glimpsed a different side of the noble cause. Bombing of civilian targets, terrorizing innocent bystanders, bitter factionalism and internecine warfare, drug trafficking and alignment with odious foreign regimes. Dominic became increasingly disillusioned, an old poet caught in the maw of violence that no longer seemed to require a reason. Eventually Dominic quit the organization in disgust and subsequently fled the country in fear for his life, abandoning the place that had been the defining centre of all he loved. Gallagher wondered whatever became of his old mentor, who seemed unimaginable anywhere but in Ireland. Without his leadership and passion, the cell had drifted into irrelevance, and when the crisis over Francie's pregnancy erupted, Gallagher had felt no compunction about duping its dimwitted treasurer and fleeing with the cash. There was an acrid taste in his mouth now as he scanned the graffiti-smeared walls. He thought again of the hardness in Joe Sheehy's eyes when he'd declined to help with the parcel.

The café where they took their lunch looked out upon an enormous police station that loomed across the street. It looked to him like a malevolent fortress squatting there—a full block long, black concrete and steel walls fifteen or twenty feet high, topped with coiled razor wire. At the corner, rising above the fence, a turret of bulletproof glass and steel bars bristled with video cameras pointing in all directions. Behind the glass, two heavily armed officers kept watch over the town. The whole place reeked of tragedy and unending sorrow.

As Ruth Wilburn joined him at his table, he pulled his gaze away from the fortress. She had a devilled egg sandwich, a piece of Day-Glo pie and a cup of watery coffee on her tray. He had no appetite at all. "Well, here we are, Mr. Gallagher, in the ancient town of Downpatrick. Feeling a bit more chipper now, are we?"

"Aye."

"I'm sure you know better than I do that your saintly namesake's buried here, though there's another tradition claims the holy man was buried at Glastonbury Abbey. All things considered, I believe Downpatrick's a likelier site, don't you?"

"I do sure." Gallagher was miles away.

She munched enthusiastically on her sandwich, small globules of egg and lettuce falling onto her plate. "By the way," she said, "I think perhaps it would be best if we stuck together as a group at Mount Stewart. We have a private tour of the house arranged, which I'm sure you'll all enjoy. But we're on our own in the garden, and sticking together will help get us moved along. We've really got too far to go and too much to see for one day. I told them that when I first saw the itinerary. People will be dead on their feet after all that long haul, I told them. Much better to stay up in Belfast for the night, not go all the way back to Dublin. But do you suppose anyone listened to what I had to say?"

"Imagine not."

"Right you are. And it's true that would have meant everyone packing up and unpacking again for just one night, which wouldn't have made much sense at all."

"No," he agreed.

"Mind you, we could then have carried on up the Antrim Coast and seen the Giant's Causeway and that really would have been a highlight for everyone, don't you think? Ah, Suzy! Loretta!" She hailed the two ladies. "Won't you come join us?" The older women put their trays on the table. Suzy sat down beside Gallagher. Loretta excused herself for a moment and walked over towards the toilets.

"Mr. Gallagher," Suzy said, leaning over to him confidentially and speaking in hushed tones, "forgive my brashness, but do you think perhaps you might want to make things up a bit with poor Loretta?"

"Make things up? What things?" Gallagher was whispering too. Wilburn finished off her sandwich discreetly, not missing a syllable.

"What you said to her on the coach."

"About my roses, you mean?"

"Well, yes. Telling her she should go name her own rose, etcetera. I do think you rather hurt her feelings. It's none of my business, of course, but I've always maintained that in such circumstances a timely apology can work wonders. Makes things so much less difficult down the road."

"I'm sure you're right." These people have no idea what real difficulties look like, Gallagher thought, but he decided to do as Suzy suggested.

"She's a sensitive lady, Mr. Gallagher, extremely sensitive, and, as you know, quite a respected rosarian in her own right. Oh, here she comes now." Suzy busied herself with a soggy-looking tuna sandwich.

"There!" Loretta betrayed no hint of bruised feelings as she took her seat beside Wilburn.

Gallagher watched the video cameras on the armed turret opposite. "Er, Mrs. Stroude," he started clumsily. She arched an eyebrow and looked at him but said nothing. Gallagher was seeing the curtains of purplish skin that hung like threadbare lace beneath her chin. "Er, I was just thinking . . ." Still she stayed silent. "That, er, mebbe I spoke a bit outta turn to you back there on the coach."

"Yes, you were rather—how shall I put it?—pugnacious in your comments." Loretta held her sandwich without taking a bite.

Pugnacious. Shite. I could show her pugnacious if she wanted. "So, er, I'm sorry if I offended you in any way. Y'know, hurt your feelings, like."

"I was more surprised than offended," Loretta said haughtily. "Not the sort of thing I'm accustomed to, believe me. Stephen Aubrey was never anything short of absolute graciousness on our tours with him, was he, Suzy?"

"Never," said Suzy, perusing her road map to peace.

"However, I do accept your apology, Mr. Gallagher, and thank you for tendering it."

"Right," he said. "All right. Good. Thanks yourself." A flimsy peace accord had been established, here in a region synonymous with shaky peace accords and the consequences of their breakage. He gazed out at the steel and razor-wire fortress across the street and brooded on the petty battles he found himself fighting today with this lot, compared with the patriots and zealots and thugs out there waging a real war of life and death.

BACK on the coach his spirits rebounded considerably when Bonnie once again joined him for the last bit north through County Down. There was nothing the least bit flirtatious in her approach, but rather an easygoing familiarity that appealed to him immensely. This girl really had got a bit of a hook into his heart, and it seemed that whenever he was sinking she'd appear at just the right moment to give him renewed buoyancy. "Did you know this part of the country when you lived here, Mr. Gallagher?" she asked him.

"Oh, aye, like the back of me hand, girl. We lived just a bit down the road beyond, not a stone's throw from Carrickmacross." Why he'd start off this way with an unnecessary fib he didn't know; he just heard himself jauntily making it up in order to impress the girl.

"It must have been lovely," she said dreamily, "the old Ireland."

"Aye, t'was lovely enough in its own way all right." Playing to her fascination with Celtic days of yore, Gallagher continued refining his role as authentic aul Irishman.

"Do you remember much about those days?"

"Like yesterday! Just like yesterday!" Mostly he remembered chicken shit on the kitchen floor and a cold wind blowing up his arse out in the bogs, but he knew this wasn't what she wanted to hear.

"Tell me the rest about Francie, then."

"Ah, no, the rest of that particular story's a sad bit of business, sure 'tis. Best leave it for another day."

"What about where you lived then, your home in Carrickmacross?"

"Well, we weren't in the town exactly. We were out on a farm, like."

"A farm? How lovely! I wish we'd had time to go see it. Tell me what it was like."

"'Twasn't much of a place a'tall, come to think of it."

"Oh, but there must have been interesting things going on," she said, smiling at him, "grist for the mill for a born storyteller like you." She dimpled so winningly he would have stormed the gates of hell itself to obtain a story he might tell her.

"Well," he said, scratching his chin, "let's see then. There was one time with the tractor, for example, I remember that well enough."

"What happened?"

"Well, it involved me brother Martin Michael. A dreadful feller he was for gettin' into the mischief." Bonnie again snuggled down in the seat beside him, awaiting the story. "One time the aul feller's away someplace, probly down at the pub, an' the aul lady sees the tractor's been left out up on hilltop. That machine must've been the first tractor ever seen in Ulster, it was that ancient. I think himself had won it playin' cards, or somethin' of the sort, and he no more needed a tractor around the place than a ditchdigger needs a didgeridoo, but there the tractor was nevertheless. The aul feller would run it up the boreen and muck about in our little scrap of field, pretendin' he was a gentleman farmer, like. But the bloody tractor would stall more than it would run. O'course the aul boy knew machines about as well as he knew brain surgery. Every time she stalled, first he'd flood her tryin' to get her started again. Then he'd stare at her like it was a wee Neddy wouldn't budge . . ."

"What's a wee Neddy?"

"That's a donkey, darlin'." He slipped the term of endearment in as smoothly as a key into a well-oiled lock.

145

"Ah."

"Next he'd kick the big rear tire so hard he'd hurt his toe and then let loose with a blue streak that would terrify a Hottentot. After which he'd say to hell with it and go find himself a drink."

Bonnie's smile was sunrise over a field of ripening barley. She snuggled closer to him in the seat, giving the impression that in the person of Gallagher she had won a rare and wonderful glimpse into the heart of an Ireland that had long ago disappeared. For his part, Gallagher was finding it increasingly difficult to concentrate properly on his story because of the lovely smooth fleshliness of her and the scent of woman coming off her. All his worries were forgotten in the intoxicating embrace of the girl's attentiveness.

"So Mam sees the tractor sittin' up hilltop and she hates the thought of it bein' up there with night comin' on and who knows what might befall it what with thievin' gypsies and travellers and God knows who else wanderin' around. So she says to Martin Michael, 'D'ye by any chance know how to operate that tractor, son?'

"Martin Michael looks up and doesn't miss a beat. 'Course I do, Mam.' Which is a bald-faced lie, because the aul feller never let anyone lay a finger on that tractor but himself, which Mam knew as well as we did, but I think mebbe she wanted to teach him a lesson for always buggerin' off for a drink.

"'Do y'think y'could mebbe fetch that tractor downhill all together?' Mam asks.

"'Sure I could drive that tractor up and down the Hill of Tara all Tuesday afternoon,' he tells her, so off she sends him.

"Martin Michael goes up the hill and me taggin' along behind him. 'Martin Michael,' I says, 'what're y'going to do? You don't know how to run that tractor no more than I do.' 'Pipe down, gossoon,' he says to me, 'a tractor's like a woman—you touch it in the right places and it'll do whatever you tell her.' Hah! That's Martin Michael for you!" Gallagher chuckled and shook his head, excusing himself to Bonnie for the indelicate talk on the grounds that it was only Martin Michael's very words he was repeating, not his own, and necessary for a full appreciation of the story.

Bonnie sat entranced.

"So Martin Michael climbs up onto the bloody tractor and pulls the choke out and gets me to turn the crank up front, which just about tears me feckin' arm off. But sure enough, she coughs and bangs and rattles and there's smoke pourin' outta her so thick I can hardly see anythin' a'tall. But Martin Michael throws her into gear and she rises up on her big back wheels like the Lone Ranger's horse—Silver, was it? Or Trigger or one of them—and off she plunges down the hill with Martin Michael hangin' on for dear life."

Here Gallagher became Martin Michael, riding the runaway tractor, his hands gripping the imaginary steering wheel and his eyes bulging wildly as he re-enacted the breakneck plunge downhill. "Halfway down she's goin' like the hound of hell and Martin Michael tries to slow her down by hittin' the brakes, but the track's all slick with mud from the previous evenin's rain and she starts slidin' sideways, so's I'm sure she's gonna go ass over tits and kill Martin Michael in the process. I'm runnin' behind her as fast as I can screamin' whatever I can think of, which isn't much. Down below Mam's out in the yard hangin' her wash on the line and I see her glance up an' the look on her face woulda made the pope piss his cassock, she's that stupefied. And the tractor with Martin Michael still on board comes roarin' down the hill and right through the yard and Mam's wash goes flyin' in all directions an' the chickens too an' the dog's barkin' and runnin' mad as a hatter and the tractor carries right on out the other side of the yard 'til it finally stalls in the middle of the aul feller's turnip patch, with its little poultry-wire fence wrapped around her like a scarf. Me and Mam come runnin' over to see if Martin Michael's mebbe dead or mortal wounded. But he's sittin' there on the tractor seat as tranquil as treacle. 'Mam,' he says as we come pantin' up, 'I got her down right enough, but I forgot to ask you where you wanted her parked!'"

Gallagher slapped his knee and roared with laughter and Bonnie laughed with him, as a sweetheart might. "Can you mind it?" He was near to tears. "Where she wanted her parked!"

JUST by the village of Greyabbey on the picturesque Ards Peninsula, they entered the grand Mount Stewart estate. They were led in a group around the house by a self-important fellow with a toothbrush moustache and baggy suit whom Wilburn seemed to know. While the guide nattered on about a Greek pentellic marble tombstone in the Hall, Gallagher noticed Michael Wickerson standing alongside Elyse and Amanda. They certainly seemed to have formed a bond, those three, as people do on tours, and Gallagher pondered whether Michael was already laying the groundwork with Elyse that he'd promised to do back at Castlewellan.

"Such a gorgeous house!" enthused Suzy Fong to Gallagher as they made their way into the drawing room.

"Aye," he replied with a wink, "we could settle in here comfortably enough, couldn't we?" Heartened by his storytelling success with Bonnie, as well as by Michael's interceding on his behalf with Elyse, and having got the spat with Loretta smoothed over, he was prepared to be gracious to all he encountered.

"Thank you for making things up with Loretta," Suzy whispered, squeezing his arm.

"No problem," he said gallantly and winked again.

Once they'd finished the house tour and were gathered under the portico at the grand front entrance, Gallagher addressed the group. "Well then, we've seen the house, and a fine house it is, I think you'll all agree, so next we may as well take a turn around the gardens. I'll lead you along and if there's any questions, just fire away and I'll do my best to answer them. All right." Now at last he was blossoming into the role of celebrity host in a way calculated to impress both Bonnie and Elyse. He marched off to his left with the group in tow. He'd been given a pamphlet containing a map and description of the gardens, which might have helped if only he'd had a spare moment to go over it. "Here we are then," he announced, pausing on a flagstone terrace on the west side of the house while the group gathered around him.

"What do we have here?" Robert Long asked, pointing down a flight of stone steps flanked with large topiary shrubs to a wide and straight stone path that led away from the house.

"Well, you've got your trees and a lawn down there," Gallagher gestured with his arm.

"Ah, yes," Robert said, as though this explained everything. "Can we photograph out here, Mr. Gallagher?" There'd been no photos permitted in the house.

"I can't see why not," he said looking over his shoulder as though someone might be watching them. And indeed someone was watching. A short distance down the terrace a man, by himself, conveniently just within earshot, was gazing across the garden. A suspicious-looking character, Gallagher thought.

"Yes, photography is permitted in the garden," Ruth Wilburn chipped in helpfully from the perimeter of the group.

"Good then, let's move on, so," Gallagher said.

"What's this topiary, Mr. Gallagher?" asked Carla Pridge. She'd taken out her video camera and was shooting across the terraces.

"Eh?"

"What are these clipped shrubs? Nothing that grows in Saskatoon I know."

"Them's, er . . . let's see now . . ." The shrubs looked vaguely familiar to him, but he couldn't be sure what they were and didn't want to make too obvious a mistake. He snapped his middle finger and thumb three times to help summon the name, without success.

"Bay trees, I believe," prompted Piet van Vliet quietly.

"Of course," said Gallagher, clapping his hands, "bay trees. It was on the tip of my tongue. Ah, well, that's memory for you, isn't it," and here he smiled especially at Loretta, since he was quoting her from the coach, "a leaky vessel that gets leakier by the day."

Loretta inclined her head ever so slightly in acknowledgement of his peace offering.

"Could I have you standing beside one of the bays for a minute, please, Mr. Gallagher," Carla said. She was dressed in pale blue designer coveralls and a Saskatoon Tigers baseball cap, on backwards.

"Sure." He stood beside a meticulously sheared tree.

"And Bonnie too," said Carla, smiling at her friend.

Bonnie took her place right beside him. She was wearing black tights under a tiny denim skirt, a dark jersey, and a jaunty maroon beret. Carla aimed her video camera at them, moving this way and that, and some of the others took photos as well. Gallagher put his arm tentatively around Bonnie's waist and grinned crookedly; his chest swelled with pride as he imagined himself a groom being photographed with his radiant bride alongside. The man who'd been eavesdropping came up and took a photo too. Dressed in a dark suit, he was a tall, cadaverous-looking character with a beaked nose and furtive air. Gallagher resented the fellow's intrusion into this private moment.

"Can you tell us about the sunken garden here, Mr. Gallagher?" Elyse Frampton posed the question once the photo op was done.

"Indeed. You can see how it's sunk all through here," he said, reluctantly withdrawing his arm from Bonnie's waist, "and surrounded by an arbor that supports a range of climbing and rambling roses, which we should go have a look at." The roses were well past blooming and badly blighted by black spot. Nevertheless, Gallagher felt an opening with Elyse.

"May I add a comment?" Loretta asked, huge in her fuchsia pant-suit. He nodded acquiescence. "The Sunken Garden is really quite intriguing because it was designed partly from a plan sent to Lady Londonderry by the renowned English garden designer Gertrude Jekyll. As you can see, the dominant colour here is blue, but in the springtime the flame-coloured azaleas are the central feature." She's been reading books about the place, thought Gallagher. Now she's trying to show me up, even though I've been bending over backwards to make things up with her. "And if you look straight down the central path," Loretta continued, "you can see the Shamrock Garden at the far end."

"Aye, we'll get there in due course," said Gallagher, reasserting his authority, "but let's go around to the south side here first." They shuffled around to the front of the house and into the Italian garden.

"I believe the formal beds were inspired by those at Dunrobin in Sutherland," Elyse Frampton said, "is that not correct, Mr. Gallagher?"

"Is that so?" he said. "Most interesting. I didn't know, but thank you for pointing it out." He smiled as winningly as he could at Elyse, delighted to be engaging with her in this way, as it marked the first real sign of connection between them. However his enthusiasm was dampened when he noticed that the wanker from the terrace was with them still, though pretending not to be. There was something sly and shifty about how the fellow was skulking along at the back end of the group.

"And you will observe the carefully designed colour schemes of the formal beds," said Loretta Stroude, addressing the group as a whole,

"the pinks, mauves, ruby reds, yellows, and blues here to the west"—
she swept her fleshy arm westwards—"while on the eastern side you
have blues and whites with maroon, scarlet and orange."

"Aye, I was just getting to that," Gallagher said with the slightest
touch of testiness. In point of fact, he hadn't thought to mention the
colour scheme, distracted as he was by the need to impress Elyse as well
as by the sneaking stranger. How was he supposed to continue being as
gracious as Stephen Aubrey while putting up with a pompous old bag
like Loretta who was plainly attempting to hijack his tour. The challenge he faced was to put her firmly in her place and keep her there
but in a way that would not offend those in the group whom he was
determined not to offend. By the time they'd made their way around
the Dodo Terrace and moved down to the Spanish Garden with its
magnificent arched cypresses, rounded pool, and curvilinear steps, it
was incontestable that the stranger was spying on them, going so far as
to take notes as various group members spoke. Gallagher thought to
shake him off with a quick trek over to the Shamrock Garden.

Once there they entered the space enclosed by sheared yew hedges.
"You'll notice the hunting party in topiary," Loretta said, pointing to
the clipped figures of people and animals emerging from the top of the
high yew hedge, "and, of course, the magnificent topiary Irish harp."
Oh, magnificent my arse, thought Gallagher. He had no patience for
topiary, all that brainless snipping and clipping to try fashion some
silly fox and hounds leaping out of the top of a hedge. Just the kind of
rubbish Loretta'd get herself all excited about.

"Is that Irish yew, Mr. Gallagher?" Robert Long asked in his
ingenuous way. He and Nicole were wearing matching sporty outfits
in teal.

"Indeed it is," he said, "a beautiful tree for clippin' so."

"Excuse me, Mr. Gallagher," said Suzy, who'd just been whispering
with her friend Loretta, "I believe this is English yew."

"What? A Celtic harp in English yew? Surely not!" he said indignantly. He strode over to the sculpted harp, took a frond of its needles
in his hand, and examined them closely. "Well, I'll be beggared," he
said to the whole group, like a man who'd been deliberately deceived
by scoundrels. "Suzy's right. It's an English yew, pretending to be Irish.

What a travesty." It was an easy mistake to have made, but Gallagher felt himself exposed as a poseur for having made it, the kind of slip he'd been largely successful in avoiding thus far. And it was doubly galling that it was Loretta, using her friend Suzy, who'd caught him out.

"Lady Londonderry, the owner, was a great supporter of the Celtic revival apparently," said Elyse in a tone that seemed to Gallagher warmly supportive of him in his predicament. Alongside her mother, Amanda in a wispy silk shift, had a wistful, dreamy look entirely appropriate to the Celtic revival. Close by, Michael Wickerson nodded in comradely solidarity.

"Aye, she was that," Gallagher agreed, giving Elyse what he thought to be an intimate smile. "So it's all the more surprising she'd have English yew in her Shamrock Garden."

The stranger had trailed after them, taking photos this way and that and repeatedly writing in his small notebook. By now he'd as good as attached himself to the group. Gallagher decided that he'd had enough. "Excuse me, squire," he said, approaching the man, "is there something we can be doing for you?" Ruth Wilburn, standing not far from the interloper, looked concerned.

"Oh, I'm dreadfully sorry," the man said in a toff Oxford accent, "I hope you don't mind. I'm afraid I'm here on my own and I'm not terribly well informed about horticulture, so I thought I'd just tag along behind your group and try to glean from you a bit about the genius of the place, you see. I certainly didn't mean to intrude."

"Well, you have, whether you meant to or not," said Gallagher, put off by the fellow's plummy tone. "This is a private party touring the estate under my direction, and if you wanted to join us, you might have approached me and asked, not just invited yourself along."

"I see. Yes, well, I'm sure that's quite right. I'm afraid I'm not really privy to the etiquette of these things. As I say, I didn't mean to intrude and I'm very sorry if I've offended. I'll be off then." He turned to go but Gallagher reached out and caught him by the sleeve.

"Just one moment, then."

"What?" The man looked down haughtily at Gallagher's arm on his sleeve.

"Let's have a peek at them notes you been takin'." If the fellow was just interested in learning a bit about horticulture, the notes would plainly show it. If he was up to something else, the notes would show that too.

"I beg your pardon?"

"The notes you been scribblin', let's have a look at 'em."

The whole group was watching tensely. Ruth Wilburn edged closer. "Er, Mr. Gallagher," she ventured.

But he ignored her. "C'mon, squire, we ain't got all day." He held his other hand out for the notes. Why Gallagher was making this provocative demand he wasn't fully aware. But he'd already been pressured by the guards, and by Sheehy, and he'd had more than enough of arseholes taking liberties. He didn't trust this sneaking interloper, suspecting that the fellow was far more interested in the group than in plants. He was quite sure the notes would confirm as much, and he could take it from there. He realized he was risking a scene in front of the group, but it was a scene from which he would almost certainly emerge triumphant, having exposed and deflected an external threat.

"I don't believe that's your prerogative, actually," the man said. "I'm sorry to have intruded. I meant no harm. Good day." Again Gallagher prevented him from leaving.

"Mr. Gallagher . . ." Ruth Wilburn leaned towards the two men.

"Leave this to me, will you!" he snapped at her. Irrational anger was electrifying him. Now there could be no backing down, no honourable exit.

"But . . ." said Wilburn.

"Squire," Gallagher said warningly, "I'll give you one more opportunity to pass them notes over and if you don't I may be after losin' my temper." Black blood was rising in him, hot and urgent, blinding.

"Now look here!" the man huffed indignantly. He was much taller than Gallagher, but weedy and delicate-looking. Gallagher took him for a poofter.

"The notes!" he demanded, his right hand extended almost into the fellow's face. He was beyond all reason.

"Mr. Gallagher . . ." Ruth Wilburn was practically pleading.

"All right, gentlemen," Michael Wickerson spoke reasonably, stepping forward, his arms extended in the gesture of a peacemaker.

"Stay outta this, Michael!" Gallagher barked. By now he was too far in to get out without losing face. And this he would not do, not in front of the group, not in front of Bonnie. "If you don't gimme them notes right now, I'm takin' 'em off you!"

"I'm dreadfully sorry, old man, but you really are most frightfully rude," said the man.

"I'll give you rude!" cried Gallagher, lunging for the notebook in the fellow's jacket pocket.

"Hai!" shouted the man so that everyone jumped in fright, and leaping sideways, he whacked Gallagher on the neck with a lightning-flash chop of his hand. Gallagher felt the sudden blow as though he'd been hit with an axe. Dark blood exploded in his brain and he blacked out, crumpling like a straw man onto the gravel path.

⊞ FIFTEEN ⊞

ALL DOWN the long and winding road back to Newry, Gallagher was only hazily aware of his whereabouts. He seemed for a while to be wandering alone on barren hillsides, searching for something. His home. He was trying to find his way home. But his house was gone, whether it was his parents' home or his own he couldn't tell. There were only scattered stones everywhere and rivulets of cold water trickling among them. Gradually he became more and more aware of the lovely comfort of a woman close beside him. She seemed at first to be his mother comforting him over the hurts of childhood. But no, it was Bonnie, of course it was Bonnie. He drifted in and out of semi-consciousness, dreaming he and she were on their honeymoon, standing beside a clipped bay tree on a terrace. Somewhere in Italy, he thought.

"Are you feeling better then, Mr. Gallagher?" she cooed, her soft healing hand on his forehead.

"Grand," he said, moistening his lips. Her warm body beside him recalled the peat fire embers of childhood. How he would lose himself in the solace of their gentle warmth. For years now he had had no warmth from within. Like a cold-blooded creature, he must get his warmth from outside himself.

"What an awful thing to have happen," she said.

"I've had worse," he whispered stoically.

"But that dreadful man." She placed a cool cloth on his neck where he'd been struck. "Is that all right?"

"Lovely."

"How's Mr. Gallagher, Bonnie?" Carla had come back from a few seats up and whispered to her friend.

"He's doing nicely," Bonnie told her.

"So should we stop at the hospital or not?"

"What do you think, Mr. Gallagher?" Bonnie put it to him, "Should we stop at a hospital in Newry and have you checked over?"

"The hospital? Nah, not a bit of it. I'll be right as rain shortly."

"You're sure?"

"Positive, girl. I've suffered enough severe blows in my time to know when one isn't."

"I do have my industrial first aid," Bonnie said, gently stroking his shoulder.

"Do you?"

"Yes, that's why I'm looking after you. Carla has hers too, so you're in good hands with us." The two women smiled down at him consolingly.

"I knew it all along," he said, managing a deathbed smile while contemplating the pleasures of an extended convalescence under Bonnie's care.

"I think we'll be fine just heading back to Dublin, as planned," Bonnie told Carla. "Perhaps you could tell Declan and Ruth."

"Okay." Carla went forward to advise the driver and Wilburn.

"Do you have any idea what all that was about?" Bonnie asked him.

"I've got me suspicions," he said. The rest of the coach was morbidly silent. The Mountains of Mourne off to their left brooded under a sullen shroud of mist.

"You don't think it was what he said, that he was just someone interested in the garden and wanting to learn more about it from you?" Bonnie posed the question innocently enough that Gallagher realized this was likely what she believed. At the time he'd thought the fellow an obnoxious trespasser who needed to be taught his manners. Nobody official, just a pain in the arse. He'd been upset, especially by that confounded Loretta trying to usurp him, and the wanker with the camera had intruded at just the wrong moment. Gallagher had sought to re-establish his position as group leader by dealing firmly with the interloper. Unfortunate that the thing had got out of hand and Gallagher had paid a heavy price. But he was not prepared to appear a fool for his mistake.

"Yer average gardener doesn't have no feckin' black belt in karate though, does he?" he asked, staring meaningfully at Bonnie.

"I suppose not." It had been truly startling, the merciless quick chop with which Gallagher had been felled.

"Plus him being a Brit. The North's crawling with them." Gallagher scratched the side of his head, as though it were infested with British lice. "And the notebook where he's scribbling down whatever anybody said. And taking snaps of the group. Nah, that feller weren't yer average fuchsia fancier, not by a long shot."

"But I don't understand. Was it political in some way, do you think?" The commingling of intensity and tenderness in Bonnie's expression made him weak.

"In Ulster everything's political." Reviving now, he was beginning to put the pieces in place whereby this little debacle could be turned to his advantage.

"But what could he possibly want with us? I mean, we're just a harmless little group of Canadians."

"Some might imagine so," he said, shifting slightly in his seat, pointedly enigmatic. Conspiracy and betrayal whispered furtively beneath his words.

"What do you mean?" she murmured, drawing herself closer to share in whatever the secret might be. She loved her secrets, this one, he realized, especially secrecy spiced with a pinch of danger.

"Yer man back there," he whispered.

"Yes?" she whispered too, drawing closer still.

"I'd reckon he was Special Branch, that feller."

"Special Branch? Do you really think so?"

"I do." She seemed not entirely convinced. "But listen: don't mention it to any of the others, okay? No sense gettin' innocent bystanders alarmed."

"Of course. I won't breathe a word of it. But why do you think Special Branch would be watching us?" Her fascination with the possibilities of intrigue suggested a storyline that became brilliantly, thrillingly clear.

He wiggled a tiny bit closer. "I'll tell you something really explosive if you promise to keep it an absolute secret, all right?"

"Okay."

"Just between you and me, like."

"Of course." They were both whispering closely. In the seat ahead of them Robert and Nicole Long were staring wistfully out the window and trying mightily not to overhear.

"Never a word to a soul."

"Absolutely."

Bonnie was in such tantalizing proximity, her miraculous chest mere millimetres from his face, Gallagher forgot his pain and humiliation entirely. He wanted nothing more from life than to press his face into Bonnie's mystical bodice and never withdraw it again. If a tall tale could keep him close against that sacred shrine, a tall tale he'd tell. "I'm being watched," he whispered.

"Watched? My God!" Credulity bloomed in the girl's blue eyes.

"The security forces were on to me at the airport as I come in and I been shadowed by them ever since."

"Why?" She breathed the word like a sacrament.

"Let's just say I'm a person of interest to the authorities." He glanced around the coach, as though to ensure they weren't under surveillance even here.

"Really?"

He took the girl's credulity at face value. He couldn't imagine him that she might be playing a game of her own, just as he played his. Realistically, even after the airport interrogation, he couldn't imagine that the authorities had any serious interest in him; the minor peccadilloes of his past might be something an arsehole like Sheehy would want to exploit, but the guards surely had bigger and fresher fish to fry. But never mind, the episode had provided him with grist for the tale-telling mill. "Those who love aul Ireland, truly love her, are never far from danger." He winced and touched his neck gingerly as though there might still be shrapnel fragments embedded in it.

"My God, Mr. Gallagher, I had no idea! Are you telling me you're in the IRA or something?"

"That's something's never said," he told her, doing his best to look extremely stern. Again the image of Sheehy's leering grin danced before him, and the peril he represented, but Gallagher banished it.

"I'm sorry. Of course. I just wondered . . ."

"Let's just say I'm one of the lads who's not let his country down in her hour of need and leave it at that."

"I see. Yes. Oh, my God, I can hardly believe this." She seemed genuinely awestruck. Oh, he'd hit the right note with her now, he knew it completely.

"I'd best be after havin' a rest now." He whispered the words like a dying Patrick Pearse.

"Yes, of course. Is there anything else I can do for you? Anything at all?"

"Mebbe . . ." he paused, considering.

"Yes?"

"I was just thinkin' mebbe . . . Ah, I dunno . . ."

"What?"

"Whether I should mebbe tell you the whole story, private like, y'know what I mean?"

"Oh!" Bonnie seemed unsure. He'd gone too far, maybe, put her on her guard.

"But only if you like. Perhaps not. No, best not. Not with the danger and . . ."

Suddenly the coach lurched to the left and braked hard. Declan leaned on the horn and everyone craned to see what was going on. "Sorry, folks," Declan said over the loudspeaker, as he shifted down and got the coach rolling again. "Some idjit on a bicycle trying to get himself killed."

"But if you think it might help . . ." Bonnie said.

"It would, I've no doubt." He paused, considering. "That's the hardest part of it, y'know."

"What's that?"

"The loneliness, like. Not havin' a soul to disclose anything to."

"You've no one?"

"Not a one. It's best not. The fewer know the better." He felt he was playing her like a maestro, if there can be such a thing as a maestro of fibbing and flirting. Was this his best self at work here? No, certainly not. But was it getting him where he wanted to be, in the brilliant embrace of this woman's affections? Oh, absolutely.

"I suppose so. But, how sad! How isolating!"

"That's it exactly. Isolatin'. You feel all alone in the world." He folded his arms across his chest as though to ward off the chill.

"I'd like to help if I can." The blue of her eyes was a cobalt sky into which he could swoop and glide, ecstatic as a swallow.

"Ah, you're a grand girl, Bonnie, no mistake." He patted her arm gently. "But, no, it's askin' more of you than's right."

"I don't mind. Really."

"Ah, no, all the same."

"Please!" My Christ, he'd got her beggin' now!

"Now don't go making it hard on me, girl." Which was exactly what she was doing. Not just the way her wee denim skirt was riding up on her lovely long thighs sheathed in black. No, more that, she was prying open the fortifications within which he lived. She was slipping inside, drawing close to his heart, and this posed a deliciously greater danger than all the spies and thugs in Ireland.

"Mr. Gallagher."

"All right, I can fill you in a bit if you insist. But not now. Not here."

"Of course not."

Another pause. Then, slyly. "I was thinkin' I might skip the group dinner altogether tonight."

"But why?"

"The events of the day. I'm thinkin' mebbe the group would be happier without me tonight."

"But if they only knew what was really going on back there . . ."

"Aye, then mebbe they'd understand right enough. But there's that isolation I was mentionin' just now, y'see? They can't know. Can never know. As far as they're concerned I'm just some little tomcock got his comeuppance."

"I'm sure nobody thinks that!" She cocked her head sideways like a chiding older sister.

"You're too kind t'me, Bonnie, by half, y'know that?"

"But you have to eat tonight. It's really important you get some nourishment after that trauma."

"Ay, I thought I'd slip away someplace quiet, private like . . ." He left it dangling and looked away.

"Would you like me to go with you?" Like a rabbit into the snare she came, simple and unsuspecting. He felt a little twinge of guilt at the ease with which he could manipulate her, as though he was betraying the true nobility of his feelings towards her.

"Only if y'd want, of course."

"Yes, I'd love to!"

"Really? You're not coddin' me?"

"No, of course not." She tossed her lovely chestnut hair with a gracefulness incompatible with codding.

"Good girl." He almost patted her approvingly on her maddening thigh, but restrained himself.

"Tonight then?" she whispered like Juliet.

"Grand. Now I better have a wee kip and gather me strength."

"Okay." She started to rise.

"And, Bonnie . . ." he stared up at her from the muddy trench of a battlefield.

"Yes?"

"Thanks for the nursin'. I feel ever so much better."

"You're welcome, kind sir." She gave him a cheeky smile and left him to sleep.

◻ SIXTEEN ◻

"THERE WE are, Bonnie," said Gallagher returning to their table carrying two pints. They were at Michael Quinn's on Anne Street South, well away from Baggott Street and the odious Joe Sheehy. Though the place was packed with Grafton Street flotsam, they'd secured a small corner table that was private enough. Bonnie was still wearing her black and denim outfit. As Gallagher well knew, there wasn't a youngblood in the place not conscious of her presence.

"Thank you," she said pertly and then sipped tentatively—Oh, those lips! As sweetly pink as the petals of Shania's Thighs herself!—and made a little face with wrinkled nose. "Tastes burnt or something," she said.

"That's yer roasted barley makin' a statement," he said with an authentic click of his teeth. "You'll get on to it after a couple a sips." He quaffed his own. Ah!

"Are you feeling better then?" Bonnie asked.

"I'm over the worst of it," he allowed, though wincing slightly from lingering pain. Too rapid a recovery could mean prematurely losing his nurse. "But a blow like that, y'know, can have serious repercussions for a good long while."

"Yes, I'd take it easy for a bit if I were you."

A ceilidh band was starting up at the far end of the pub and Bonnie turned with delight towards the musicians. A quartet of old duffers with faces like last year's potatoes, along with a couple of kids on fiddles. "I just love that music!" she glowed.

"Aye, that's 'Some Say the Devil's Dead,'" he said, nodding his head to the rhythm, "a grand old tune all right."

She listened in rapt attention for a few moments, tapping her slender fingers on the tabletop. The crowd was turned away from them, towards the band, and they were perfectly alone within the crowded room. She turned back to him and drew her chair close. "So what did you want to tell me? About ... you know ... the Troubles," she murmured. Their heads were almost touching.

"Aye, well," Gallagher stared into the bogbrown depths of his pint for inspiration. "You start off young, y'know. Too young really. I was barely a lad myself." He had no real sense of where, if anywhere, she stood on Irish politics, and chose his words so as not to be boxed in by them one way or another. "You begin by runnin' errands for the local brigade like, fetchin' stuff or transferrin' stuff from one drop to another, that sort of thing." This much had been true of himself as a lad, but everything beyond would require the storyteller's creativity. "Anyways, after I'd knocked about doin' such fer a couple of years, eventually I got the call to go off t'war."

"To war?"

He thought he could detect a wisp of disbelief in the girl's expression. "No other word for it, Bonnie. For 'tis war. The war of the Irish nation for what's rightfully ours." Notwithstanding his cleverness on the coach ride earlier, an apprehension was gnawing at him that perhaps he was losing himself to her more surely than he was winning her to himself. Everything now seemed to hinge upon how masterful a telling of the tale he could muster, for properly told it would surely have her in his thrall. He knew the outline of the story well, not as his own, but as one that his old mentor Dominic Farrell had told him years ago. He saw no good reason not to adopt it as his own in the present circumstances, with all due deference and respect to old Dominic, for who's to say where the bounds of truth lie in any story, or the rights of ownership either.

"So you took up arms?" she asked. Far off the band had leapt into the reel "Newly Mown Meadow," led by one of the geezers playing a mean accordion.

"My brother Martin Michael and me was called to an action, sure. A bold plan too, it was." He sipped his pint with an air of grim determination.

"I can hardly believe you're telling me this!" Her blue eyes widened, bluer than blue. "It seems like another world or something."

"It was exactly that, as you'd know full well if you'd been there. I was all of eighteen at the time and itchin' t'fight, as young fools are. We were livin' at home with the aul ones still. I can picture me old mam that mornin' like it were yesterday. 'Would y'like a feed before you go, boys?' she asks us."

"She knew?"

"Ah, sure, she knew right enough. She was a Shinner down to her bootstraps was Mam, though t'see her at her cottage door with her silver hair an' her apron on you'd never credit it."

"Fascinating."

"She fixed us a fry that mornin'. Bacon an' fried taters an' some eggs from himself's chickens an' thick slices of bread fried crisp in the fat. We was poor as hedgehogs in them days, Bonnie, but, I'll tell you, we ate like kings all the same." Gallagher felt himself warming to the Guinness and to the familiar animal jostle of drinkers' bodies, the smell of leather and wool and tobacco, the insistent merriment of the fiddle and accordion. "Soon enough it was time to go, no mincin' words. Mam cried, of course, as mothers cry whose sons go off to war, dabbin' her eyes with the corner of her apron." This poignant detail, he could see from the sadness on Bonnie's face, was having the desired effect. "Himself had been muckin' around in his garden out back— he loved his vegetables aul Da did, and no one could grow a parsnip nor turnip to match him—but he come over at the last, just as we was leavin'. 'Keep yer fukkin' heads down, lads,' was all he could say—you'll excuse me language here, Bonnie, but that's him word for word—'keep yer fukkin' heads down, lads.'"

The girl stared at him. "And you did obviously. You didn't get hurt or anything?"

"No, no, I escaped unscathed all right," he said, and again touched his neck gingerly as a reminder of his recent beating, "but not poor Martin Michael, no."

"What happened?"

"Aye, 'tis a sad tale but true." He was embellishing Dominic's original telling somewhat, and was wondering how far he should push the thing, but the tale seemed to have taken on a life of its own and was dragging him along willy-nilly. Plus the girl was obviously entranced. He felt he needed these imaginative excesses if he was to have any chance with her at all. "We crossed into the North at County Fermanagh prepared to give John Bull his due." He paused dramatically and sipped at his pint.

"What were you planning to do? Not murder, surely, or a car bomb or anything like that?" Her distaste for violence was obvious.

"No, we'd not planned to harm anyone." He tactfully scaled back the ferocity of their intended blow against the tyrant.

"So what happened to your brother? How did he get . . ."

"Killed? I'll tell you: shot in cold blood by the squaddies, that's how." Christ almighty, he was digging himself a deep hole here, but how the hell could he stop?

"I can hardly believe what you're telling me," Bonnie said with a look on her face that Gallagher couldn't read. Was she beginning to suspect he was making it all up? He stared at her meaningfully. No way out but straight ahead.

"Aye, 'tis unbelievable when you think about it so. Like something you'd see in a movie, not in real life. But happens it does and happen it did. We drove smack into an SAS ambush that night. John Bull has an uncanny nose and somehow had sniffed out the operation. Someone must've grassed."

"Betrayed you?"

"Aye. There's no shortage a spies in this country, like that wanker this afternoon. The Brits knew we was comin' and just opened up at the car ahead of us with automatic rifles, pourin' in hundreds of rounds. The car swerved and crashed, exploding into a fireball, Whoosh!" He clapped his hands together softly and stared in stupefaction at the remembered conflagration. "Martin Michael was in that car, and that's the last I ever saw of him."

"How dreadful! But you managed to escape?"

"We did. The feller drivin' our car was brilliant. He hit the brakes straight off and got us turned around and t'hell out a there before the squaddies could get us. But I tell you, Bonnie, the bullets was flyin' around us like spit from the lips of the devil himself." His sipped his Guinness and shook his head.

"And that was the end of it?"

"Well, there was the funeral, of course. That was very hard. Held in the North, all three of the lads, the bits of bone and teeth that was left of them anyway, buried together. The caskets were draped in the Irish tricolour and on top of each casket lay a black beret and a pair of black leather gloves. Black flags was hangin' from every lamppost along the funeral route. Armoured jeeps were prowlin' everywhere and RUC men with machine guns on every corner. Gerry Adams and Martin McGuinness and all the big noises from Sinn Fein were there. An' thousands in the funeral procession with riot squads all along the route. 'Twas somethin' to behold all right."

Bonnie was gazing at him earnestly and Gallagher, recognizing the greater appeal of grief than violence, worked the funeral for all it was worth. "Aye, himself and Mam walked behind the coffin, and me with them too and none of us able t'hold back the tears for long."

Gallagher scanned the crowd for a moment, everyone shaking with jouncing movement to the insistence of fiddles and pipes. He returned his gaze to her and picked up his melancholy tale. "At the graveyard, we gathered about a big Celtic cross. Prayers were prayed and speeches were made. One of the lads read the Easter Proclamation from the Risin' of '16. I tell you, Bonnie, my heart was near to breakin' with pride and sorrow both."

"Oh, Mr. Gallagher . . ."

"Aye. Nor was it a pain easily forgotten. Just the other . . . "

Suddenly a voice boomed out, startling them both, "Patsy Gallagher! Well I'll be damned!"

Gallagher and Bonnie looked up, and there was bloody Joe Sheehy again, pint in hand, looming over them like an iceberg. "Joe!" croaked Gallagher, as though he'd just been whacked on the neck again.

"Mind if I join yis, jus' for a minute, like?" Before Gallagher could reply, Sheehy commandeered a chair from a nearby table and jammed it in alongside Gallagher. He was wearing the same battered jacket and slouch cap as before. "Forgive me intrudin' this way, miss." Sheehy turned to Bonnie with a roguish grin of yellow teeth. "Y'must think me an uncivilized bog-trotter altogether."

"Of course not," Bonnie laughed. She appeared to be delighting in the authentic Irishness of it all—the jostling pub, the reeling cei- lidh band, Gallagher's embellished accounts of the Troubles, rubbing shoulders with a genuine Irishman like Sheehy.

"Grand," said Sheehy, "I've jus' a wee bit a business with me old pal Patsy, here. Won't take but a minute, although given the present company"—he winked rakishly at Bonnie—"I might be tempted t'linger a wee while longer."

"Don't mind him," said Gallagher. "Joe's an old comrade."

"We had some good times though, didn't we, Patsy, boyo?"

"We did that. Grand times all right." Gallagher was working a fine balance here. On the one hand, Sheehy represented real danger, and was sure to raise the business of his bloody parcel. On the other hand, reckless as it might be, Gallagher was prepared to humour Sheehy for a bit, knowing that talk of the good old times would firm up his own credibility with Bonnie. In this respect, Sheehy's entrance couldn't have been timed more perfectly.

"Y'remember goin' out on the wren, do you?" Sheehy asked with that slantwise way he had of looking at a person.

"Who could forget it, eh, Joe?"

"And the old curate—what was his name? Feeney, I think it was . . ."

"Father Feeney sure."

"How he tried t'shut us wrenboys down."

"The bollocks!" Gallagher slapped the tabletop in disgust. Going along with Sheehy like this, solely in order to reinforce his authenticity in Bonnie's eyes, Gallagher felt like a man digging his own grave. But of course he remembered the old parish priest, what a tyrant he'd been in the town, and mostly how he'd betrayed Francie's confession and split the young lovers apart forever. But how Sheehy, who had lived in Kerry not West Cork, knew as much as himself about it all, remained a mystery.

"They never did approve of the wren, them priests," Sheehy said.

"Nor much of anything else."

"Y'remember how Feeney'd hide behind the hedge up there on High Street, tryin' to catch you out with a young bint?" Sheehy was grinning like a dirty-minded schoolboy and shaking his head in daft remembrance.

"Aye, them was the days." Gallagher now wanted this idiotic reminiscing finished in the worst kind of way.

"Them was the days all right." The sudden shift in Sheehy's eyes gave Gallagher a small thrill of terror. "Now, Patsy, about that little matter I raised with you the other night."

"Got it sorted then, did you, Joe?"

"I wouldn't say that precisely, no." Sheehy leaned back in his chair, surveying Gallagher. The band had gone silent for a while and the room was raucous with talk and laughter.

"No?" Gallagher tried to look mystified.

"No." Like a thrown stone. "I still need your help on that account."

"Well, I wish I could help you on that score, Joe, I truly do." It was obvious to Gallagher that Sheehy was attempting to set him up in some way.

"I'm asking this as an old pal and comrade." All trace of Paddybanter was gone from Sheehy's voice, which was now hard enough to strike sparks.

"I'd gladly help you out if I could, Joe, but I can't." Gallagher spread his hands apologetically.

"Still, y've time enough for sittin' an havin' a gargle with the bints, do y'not?"

"I've got my responsibilities." Finally a note of irritation sparked in Gallagher's response. "Surely you can appreciate that."

"Ah, the Irish, Miss," Sheehy said to Bonnie crossways, the rough-hewn rogue once again. "I tell you we're a mad lot from top to bottom. Never knowin' where bravery leaves off and foolhardiness begins."

She smiled at him uncertainly.

"'Tis a brave man you're drinkin' with tonight, miss," Sheehy said with a wink, "a brave, brave feller right enough." With that he pushed back his chair noisily and rose, pint in hand. "I'll be seein' you, Patsy, all right?"

"Aye, see you, Joe." Sheehy melted back into the crowd that was once again swaying and tapping to "John Brosnan's Reel" where the fiddles were lighting fires underfoot.

"What was that all about?" Bonnie breathed. She had the look of a bystander on the street the instant after an accident's occurred, unable for the moment to comprehend what's happened.

Gallagher was staring off into the reeling crowd. He could no longer see Sheehy but the fellow's sinister presence hung in the air long after he'd gone. "Mr. Gallagher?"

"Eh?"

"Who was that man?"

"Oh, an old comrade in arms," Gallagher said, gathering his fear-blown wits. He was shaken all right, no doubt about that, and was definitely in trouble. Sheehy, he was sure, wasn't going to drop this fukkin' parcel business. Nevertheless, the intriguing woman at his side and the Guinness in his hand gave Gallagher a wonderful courage, as the same twin elixirs have given courage to untold Irishmen before him. That balls-ache of a Sheehy wasn't going to ruin his date with Bonnie. So fuk him sideways to Sunday! Plus the git had inadvertently helped shore up the veracity of Gallagher's fanciful patriot tale.

"Was he threatening you?"

"Aye, he was."

"What for?"

"Not certain," Gallagher said grimly. "One thing's sure though: those of us fightin' for a free Ireland are not a unified group by any means. There's factions, Bonnie. Disagreements.

Feuds and vendettas. Informers an' traitors." Gallagher scanned the room as though expecting to spot a few of them in the crowd. "This Sheehy's been pressin' me hard these last few days. It's why I been distracted, like, on the tour. Forgettin' my plant names and goin' after that wanker up north today."

"Should we be doing something—calling the police or something—to protect you?"

Gallagher smiled wryly and shook his head. "There's no protection from men like Sheehy. If they decide yer time is up," he said, and here he ventured to take Bonnie's hand momentarily for just a comradely squeeze, "then yer time is up." He paused for a moment, recognizing the truth of what he'd just said. Story and reality merged. Sheehy's reappearance underscored that there was a mortal danger stalking him and he'd damned well better stop playing games and get it sorted. But still, even in the backwash of Sheehy's menace, Gallagher's spirits were lifting, because the girl was obviously putty in his hands when she saw him endangered. He could almost picture her as the Countess Markievicz to his Michael Mallin.

He'd previously thought to make use of the free afternoon tomorrow to advance his pursuit of Elyse, a cause he feared had been set back considerably by the fracas at Mount Stewart. But, really, if he were honest, his hopes and dreams resided far more with the intriguing woman beside him now than with stony Elyse, for all her money. Hoping to carry the momentum forward, he suggested that perhaps he and Bonnie might spend the afternoon together. But she declined, saying breezily that she was going shopping with Carla. Was she free in the evening? No, they planned on going to the Abbey Theatre to see *She Stoops to Conquer*.

Was it his imagination, or had she become suddenly unengaged, uninterested? Perhaps she'd been frightened off by Sheehy, whose intimation of violence was anything but romantic. The excesses in his own story now seemed to Gallagher a bad miscalculation. Whatever the cause, the bond of intimacy he'd been so carefully weaving all day was shredded. Fukkin' hell anyway!

The band was flying through a medley of jigs and reels, the crowd bouncing and convivial, but suddenly he was in a mood to go, and Bonny readily agreed. There'd been a tripwire here that he hadn't seen and still didn't understand. They walked back quietly to the hotel through near-deserted streets. He wanted for all the world to take Bonnie's hand in his, to walk like this forever, through all his remaining days, with this darling woman safely by his side. But storm clouds were gathering around him. Sheehy. Bloody Sheehy. With each homeward step he grew increasingly morose. Bonnie seemed lost inside herself as well. The last thing in the world he wanted to do was to bid her good night. He feared he might never be alone with her like this again.

Just as they entered the lobby, a man who'd been sitting on one of the couches rose and strode briskly towards them. "Excuse me, Mr. Gallagher?"

"Yeah?" He was in no mood for interruption.

"May I have a word with you, please, sir?" The fellow was dressed in suit and tie and seemed unmistakably official.

"What? Right now?"

"If you'd be so kind."

"It's completely inconvenient."

"I realize. But I'm afraid I must insist."

"Thank you for a lovely evening . . . Gallagher," Bonnie said, smiling, and touching his hand ever so lightly. "See you in the morning."

"Good night then, Bonnie." She was gone.

The fellow motioned to the couches in the corner and the two of them went over and sat down facing each other. "I'm sorry to intrude upon your evening this way," he said in a voice that had no trace of regret in it.

"What can I do for you?" Gallagher's imagination was trailing down the corridor behind disappearing Bonnie.

"My name is Givens. I'm with the National Immigration Bureau." He flashed an identity card in front of Gallagher that, for all Gallagher could make out, might have been a driver's licence. "I'm afraid I'm going to have to ask you for your passport, sir."

"My passport? Not bloody likely. What the hell you want with my passport?"

"Purely a precaution, I assure you."

"Precaution? Against what?"

"We'd like to have a little chat with you tomorrow. I believe you're free in the afternoon, are you not?"

How did he know that? What the hell was going on here? "I've nothing special on, I don't believe."

"Good. If you would please be in attendance at the address indicated here," he said, handing over a business card, "at two PM sharp, everyone's interests will be best served."

"What do you mean, everyone's interests? What's this all about anyway? Is it something to do with what happened at Mount Stewart today?"

"We'll discuss all that tomorrow, sir. I'll only say to you now that we expect your full and complete cooperation. Anything short of that will land you in far more trouble than you can possibly imagine."

"Trouble? What sort a trouble?"

"All will be explained tomorrow. In the meantime, you would be well advised not to say a word about any of this to anyone. Is that clear?"

"I hear you." The fellow was so authoritative and Gallagher so off-kilter from the events of the day he felt he had no option but to submit.

"Good. Tomorrow then, Mr. Gallagher. Two PM. Sharp."

"All right, I'll be there."

"Excellent. Now, if I might trouble you for your passport, I'll detain you no longer this evening."

Gallagher fished his passport out from one of his zippered pockets and handed it over. Givens glanced inside it briefly, pocketed it, bid Gallagher good evening, and immediately left the hotel.

SEVENTEEN

"OH, MR. GALLAGHER!" Ruth Wilburn was fluffed with enthusiasm. "You were absolutely brilliant on the telly last night!" She plopped down at his table, forever faithful in her determination not to have him eat his breakfast alone. "They did the most clever things with cutting out all the bits that didn't work so well, like when you couldn't remember Margaret Foley's name, and put the segments together so smoothly you couldn't tell anything had been taken out at all."

Gallagher stared dispiritedly at his sausages awash in grease. After the fracas at Mount Stewart and his subsequent clever scheme for spending the evening with Bonnie, he'd completely forgotten that the TV piece was scheduled to air last night. Sheehy's intimidation still hung over him. And the authorities calling him in for questioning. So it wasn't as though things could get a whole lot worse from having his mug show up on every telly from here to Tipperary. "Oh, aye, that's just grand." He didn't bother to try to disguise his sarcasm.

"Mr. Gallagher, are you all right?" Wilburn peered at him peculiarly. She was wearing a kind of khaki jumpsuit, as though preparing to leap out of a helicopter in the desert. "Oh, look," she cried, oblivious, "here comes Mr. Wickerson with Mr. van Vliet. Good morning, gentlemen!" She hailed them with a gesture for them to join the table. Michael and van Vliet sat down convivially. Gallagher pushed his plate away. "Did you see Mr. Gallagher on TV last night?" Wilburn asked them.

"No, I'm afraid we didn't make it back in time," Michael said with a small gesture of apology.

"Oh, he was marvellous, him and Margaret both."

"I'm certain he was and I'm sorry we missed it," Michael said. "Several of us went down to the Guinness Brewery after dinner. We tried to track you down," he spoke to Gallagher, "to see if you wanted to come along, but no one seemed to know where you were."

"I had some business to attend to." Gallagher realized he sounded as sour as medlars but didn't care.

"Well, I'm sorry, because I'm certain you would have enjoyed it."

"It's a very impressive exhibition, isn't it?" Wilburn put in.

"Absolutely. They had some priceless archival film clips of workers from years ago," Michael said, bending his attention more to Wilburn. "I was especially impressed with the coopers making barrels from scratch, using just a few hand tools. Right from rough planks to a watertight barrel, with nothing but a couple of blades. All by eye too. No tape measure or callipers or anything. It was quite amazing, the skill of those coopers, don't you agree, Piet?"

"Most impressive," van Vliet agreed. As always, he was impeccably groomed and attired, wearing a buff cashmere sweater and slacks.

"Well, gentlemen," Wilburn announced, "we're off this morning to visit John Sparks over at Clontarf. One of our most renowned gardeners, and particularly celebrated for his daring use of colour in the garden."

"Yes, I've read a bit about John Sparks," said Piet, adjusting his watch to the clock on the dining-room wall. "It should be a most fascinating garden to view."

"Oh, indeed. And John himself is *so* charming," Wilburn said, ducking her chin for emphasis. "Do you know his work, Mr. Gallagher?"

"Eh?" He'd been miles away. They were all looking at him. He knew he had to pull himself together, make a show of it, be a bloody Stephen Aubrey clone for another day. Charm Elyse because he needed her money to save his endangered home. But at that moment he wasn't sure he was up to any of it. He felt things slipping away from him and the lonesome melancholia peculiar to Ireland creeping like bog mist over him.

The morning itself was the opposite of Gallagher's mood, splashed with brilliant sunshine and tumbling great clouds in a blue sky. The group boarded the coach, and although Gallagher would have preferred sitting alone in order to brood, Michael Wickerson came jauntily along the aisle and sat down beside him.

"How are you this morning, Gallagher?" Michael asked in a voice that indicated he realized all was not well. "Are you recovered from that dreadful incident yesterday?"

"I'm off to a pretty rough start," Gallagher mumbled.

174

"How so?" Michael softened his voice so that they should not be overheard.

"That damn Sheehy caught up with me again last night."

"What happened?"

"Same thing. Started leaning on me to retrieve his poxy parcel for him."

"Surely you didn't agree?"

"Not on your life. But he didn't like it one bit, and I fear I haven't seen the last of him."

"Well that's a tough one." Michael bit on his lower lip, thinking.

"And on top of that," Gallagher went on in a *woe is me* voice, "when I got back to the hotel, there was a feller waiting for me in the lobby. An official of some sort. Told me to report to some office in town this afternoon. Even took my passport."

"He took your passport? This sounds serious. Did he give you any indication why they wanted to talk to you?"

"None whatsoever." Gallagher stared out at the crowded shops they were gliding past. "I have to think it has something to do with Sheehy, but I'm only guessing. It may be something else entirely. They may be back on that photo they had of me at the airport. Sheehy's with the Provos—at least he was, and he talks as though he still is, or some splinter group, the Real IRA maybe. Could be a connection. I'll find out this afternoon."

"Good grief. It sounds like twenty years ago. I'm remembering an old quote, from Conor Cruise O'Brien, I think it was." Michael closed his eyes for a moment, remembering. "Something to the effect that Irishness is not so much a matter of birth or language, but rather a condition of being involved in what he called 'the Irish situation,' and usually of being mauled by it."

"Yeah, I'm starting to have that mauled feeling," Gallagher agreed ruefully.

"You must be worried about this afternoon."

"Feckin' right I'm worried. This is a bloody minefield I'm stepping into."

"Would you like me to come along with you?"

For all his woes, Gallagher was touched by the offer. He'd harboured his suspicions about Michael, that there was more to him than he let on, but now that judgement seemed ungracious. "Thank you, Michael, it's good of you to offer, but that official last night warned me not to tell anyone about my going down there, so I don't think they'd take too kindly to you showing up with me."

"Anything else I can do?"

"Well, there is that little matter we talked about yesterday, but this isn't the time or place. When the opportunity presents itself, maybe we can have a bit of a chat."

"Of course," Michael said with his charming smile.

"NOW do let me show you what I mean by the application of colour theory in the garden," John Sparks addressed the group while standing partway along his marvellous double herbaceous borders. Wilburn had introduced Gallagher to the noted colourist, and Gallagher had roused himself sufficiently to introduce John to the assembled group with a few appropriately florid turns of phrase. Dressed in a cream-coloured linen shirt and brown cord trousers, Sparks was comfortably plump while still possessing the remnants of boyish handsomeness. "I take my inspiration," he said with the casual ease of the self-assured, "largely from the French Impressionists. I confess I rather shamelessly plunder their brilliant insights regarding colour contrasts and harmonies to explore the endless possibilities of painting landscape pictures in our gardens. That's what we are, you know, we gardeners"—his soft white hands fluttered out towards them like doves, including them graciously—"we are, as much as any painter, true artists, employing a palette far more complex and elusive than mere oils or acrylics." His large brown eyes swept the group familiarly, and no doubt the ladies melted under their affectionate gaze. "We, like the painter, are engaged in bold experiment with contrasts. Just look at those vibrant red fuchsias"—he pronounced it properly as *fewksias*—"alongside the smouldering nasturtiums and burnt-orange dahlias over there. Notice how stunningly they leap out at us against the gleaming white of the summer phlox." Everyone glanced at, and instantly appreciated, the startling contrast he'd described. The borders on either side of the wide gravel pathway on which they stood were perfect duplicates of each other.

"But close at hand here too," Sparks continued, pointing to another composition, "we're also involved with the most subtle of harmonies: see here the understated play of soft pinks, mauves, creams, and muted blues achieved by combining the nepeta and dianthus with Rosa Mundi and Rosa Glauca. Contrasts and harmonies, contrasts and harmonies. Colour, ladies and gentlemen," Sparks said with passion, while praying his plump hands together like a bishop saying grace, "is first and foremost a matter of *relationships*. Think, if you will, of Monet's fantastic colour contrasts, of that marvellous gardener Gertrude Jekyll's manipulating colours into a sinuous pattern of gradual transitions." His right hand floated in undulating mimicry of the colour transitions in the borders. "Observe how the plant colours relate one to another, how they relate to their background, to the sky and to the borrowed landscape. One could go on and on . . . "

And indeed he did go on and on, for almost another hour. Afterwards the group retired to an elegant solarium overlooking the garden where John's wife and a young woman who spoke no English served them tea and biscuits. Just beyond the solarium entrance, Michael signalled with a tilt of his head that Gallagher and he should withdraw.

"Lovely garden, lovely man," Michael said as they made their way to a secluded nook behind the greenhouses. "Just thought this might be our best opportunity for a private tête-à-tête before your appointment this afternoon."

"Yes, this is good," Gallagher agreed. They were standing on grey flagstones in a little brick alcove above which an ornamental grapevine stretched its sinuous limbs. Tentatively Gallagher asked, "I was just wondering, Michael, if by any chance you'd had an opportunity to sound Elyse out on that little matter we discussed?"

"Yes, as a matter of fact," Michael said breezily, pausing for a beat, for emphasis, "I did have a chat with her last evening."

"And?"

"Well, most interesting, actually." Michael smiled as though he was on to something. "Your instincts were spot on."

"How do you mean?"

"It just so happens that, besides her comfortable home in Shaughnessy, she also owns a penthouse condo down at Coal Harbour."

"Whew! That must be worth a penny or two." Owning nothing himself, Gallagher was always amazed to hear of people who owned two or more sumptuous homes.

"Well over a million I should think. Perhaps several million. And here's the juicy part: with the market so overheated down there, she's thinking of maybe selling the penthouse before the bubble bursts and moving the money elsewhere."

"Real estate still?"

"Don't know. Haven't got that far yet. But I'll keep you posted."

"Appreciate it, Michael. Really." Gallagher had by now pretty much given up on getting anything out of Elyse, but this news from Michael offered at least a sliver of hope, and a sliver's still a damn sight better than no hope at all.

"Oh, Mr. Gallagher, there you are at last!" Wilburn was bursting up the pathway towards them. With her ruffled air and khaki jumpsuit she might have been dodging sniper fire in Baghdad. "Excuse my interrupting, gentlemen, but there's an urgent call for you, Mr. Gallagher." She held out her cell phone to him.

"For me?" He instinctively sensed trouble.

"He said it was *most* important." She was almost trembling with urgency.

Jaysus, Gallagher thought, what now? He took the phone awkwardly from Wilburn—he'd never used a cell before and she had to show him how to hold it. "Hello?" said Gallagher tentatively. Michael and Wilburn discreetly withdrew, Wilburn whispering excitedly.

"Is that you, Patrick?" A voice he hadn't heard for years and yet recognized instantly. A voice he thought he'd never hear again. His brother, his long-lost brother.

"Bosco?" A tremendous swell of emotion shuddered through Gallagher's body, a turbulent surge of mingled guilt, anxiety, affection, fear.

"Yes," the voice said calmly, "I saw you on the television last evening. Margaret Foley's an acquaintance, and she was kind enough to discover how I might contact you."

"Ah, sure." Gallagher couldn't think of what to say. He'd known all along that he shouldn't have gone on Margaret Foley's bloody television program, but the last person he imagined the exposure might fetch out of the weeds was Bosco.

"Well, you've become quite the celebrity, it seems," Bosco said. "I hadn't realized that you were back in Ireland."

"Just over for the tour, like. Just the one week." He was in a daze, unable to grasp that this was really Bosco, or to imagine why he would be calling.

"Yes. All the way from Canada, is it?"

"That's right."

"And are you well there, Patrick?" There was a touch of solicitude, perhaps even of tenderness, in the query.

"I'm okay so far as that goes."

"Good."

"And yourself, Bosco, how are you keepin'?" Gallagher gazed up at the rope-like arms and purple-tinted leaves of the vine above his head.

"Good too."

"Grand. And whereabouts?"

"Here in Dublin."

"In Dublin?" Damn it! Every instinct in him was to run and hide, to not have Bosco near to him.

"Yes." A pause. "I'd like to meet with you, Patrick."

"Ah, well, that would be terrific, Bosco, it really would, but unfortunately the tour's got me pretty well tied up." Why would Bosco even want to meet again after all these years. Surely not some maudlin attempt at rebuilding burnt bridges.

"I think it's important that we talk." There was a kind of frigid purposefulness in how Bosco spoke.

"I'd love nothin' better but . . ."

"There's family business needs tidying up, and it would be preferable if you were privy to it."

"The old ones then?" The flagstones underfoot suddenly reminded Gallagher of tombstones.

"Yes."

"Not dead?"

"Not yet, thank God."

"Good. Still down on the old place, are they?"

"That's certainly where they want to be, but it's well beyond their capabilities now. As it was they stayed on longer than they should. You know, the usual thing, taking nasty falls, breaking bones, all the sad business of growing old and incapacitated."

Gallagher had never thought about how it might be for his parents in old age. They had existed for him only as figures from the past, as had Bosco for that matter. "So where are they now? Not here?" Please don't let them be here, Gallagher thought.

"No, they're in an assisted living facility in Skibbereen. Very modern. Very nice. And of course they loathe it."

"They would. And the farm itself?"

"It's what we need to discuss, Patrick. Its disposition. That's why I've tracked you down this way, though I imagine you'd prefer I hadn't."

"Not at all." Gallagher's disclaimer was woefully transparent.

"Plans were made in your absence, Patrick, as they needed to be. But now that you're here I feel duty-bound to include you in their final-ization."

"I see." Gallagher paused for a moment, staring into the jungle of semi-tropical vines that John Sparks had growing in one of the green-houses. Gradually, during the uncomfortable silence between them on the phone, a tiny light like that of a ship on a dark horizon blinked in and out of view in Gallagher's imagination. The farm. The old family farm. Himself as eldest son and rightful heir. Oh, boy. The faraway light rapidly waxed to something much brighter. Sure there were obstacles higher than the hills of Kerry between himself and ownership of that farm, murky complications that had precluded him from ever even considering that it might some day become his. History stood against him, and he might well never surmount its obstacles no matter how valiantly he tried. But the threat to his own home had a desperate edge to it and desperation now drove him to imagine the unimaginable. Lesser men than himself had dreamt impossible dreams and dared to make them real. What a thunderous irony it would be if, after all that had transpired, that dung-covered little farm were to be his salvation. God knows what it might be worth now with Yanks and Germans and wankers from everyplace else gobbling up choice pieces of Irish real estate. The money to be had from its sale would almost certainly total more than enough for his purposes. He could forget Elyse and all that silly shite. He could follow his heart to where it was truly leading him. The dream of freedom. Ah, yes, the ancient Irish dream of freedom.

Still he hesitated. He no more wanted to meet with his brother than to stick his head in a rats' nest. He held no grudge against Bosco, far from it, because his brother had done him no wrong. No, his reluctance lay in the prickly awareness that he himself had wronged the family, Bosco included. There must be lingering bitterness there, there'd have to be, although Bosco was showing no trace of it here on the phone. Gallagher had no desire to make an appearance as the prodigal son returning in the sackcloth and ashes of shame. Nevertheless, he realized that he must meet his brother to keep alive any hope of getting the farm. The enormity of the prize to be claimed trumped all misgivings. "Well, Bosco," he said at last, "I'm sure I can find a way to absent myself from the tour for a wee bit while we get together."

"Would dinner on Friday evening be possible for you?"

"Let's see," Gallagher said, and after a pause, "yes, I think I can manage that all right."

"Excellent. We can dine here at my residence, if you like. It will give us the privacy we need."

"Sounds good to me. You're sure it's no trouble, like?"

"None whatsoever." Bosco gave him the address and directions and they said goodbye for now. Gallagher pressed his forehead against the warm bricks of a potting shed wall and felt his heart drumming as though he'd been running for miles.

▫ EIGHTEEN ▫

STILL FOGBOUND in a type of vaporous stupor, Gallagher made his way downtown and along the Liffey towards the Garda National Immigration Bureau in Burgh Quay. Bosco's startling emergence out of the murk of family history had flattened him as forcefully as the onrush of some thick-headed lout at the hurley. That damned television program was what had got Bosco on his trail, but it was typical of this bloody little country where everybody knows everybody else's business before they know it themselves.

Still and all, Bosco's news was exhilarating, and Gallagher was now entirely mesmerized by the possibilities of profit from selling the family farm—a property that should rightfully pass to him as eldest son if the sacred and ancient precedents of inheritance were to mean anything at all. Not since he'd left Ireland had he considered this even a remote possibility, and eventually he'd so entirely disregarded the farm that it never occurred to him as a possible solution to his current money troubles. But now, with Bosco seeking him out this way, the likelihood seemed not so far-fetched after all. And were it to actually come about—and of course it was by no means a certainty yet, far from it, but were it to come about—what a grand vista of possibility might suddenly open for him. His home could be permanently secured, allowing him to pursue in peace and security the great passion of his life among his roses. What a dramatic, brilliant bloody twist of fate that would be—for it had been fate, not any of his doing, that Fanslau should die, putting everything in peril, and that he himself should return to Ireland for one purpose, only to have this other, entirely unexpected twist come to his rescue. It was brilliant beyond anything you could imagine. Completely against his firmly held convictions, he could almost believe that there was some form of divine intervention working now on his behalf. He recalled the returning pilgrims in Dublin airport, the seekers of miracles. And now here he was himself, despite his disbelief, perhaps the recipient of just such a miracle.

And there was another aspect to it, equally appealing—that

he could now abandon this ridiculous quest for a benefactor. How he'd been fool enough to ever undertake such a moronic scheme he couldn't comprehend, and he smiled to himself at the gullible simple-mindedness of it. He saw how desperation drives even the wise to foolish adventure. No longer straitjacketed by financial concerns, he could turn his full attention towards where it had been yearning so ardently in recent days, the charming person of Bonnie Raithby.

Somewhere amid the turbulence of the week, he had offered his heart to Bonnie as he'd offered it to none over the course of twenty years. Not since Francie O'Sullivan had he dared again deprive his heart of concealment the way he was moved to do now. And, unimaginable as it might seem, she had, he felt, accepted the offer. She had nursed him, encouraged him, restored him to himself. True, she'd become a bit standoffish last night, after that vile Sheehy showed up and ruined his handiwork, but he suspected that had been a temporary aberration, the kind of passing squall that all lovers temporarily experience. In truth, Bonnie Raithby was precisely what had been lacking in his life all these years. He had spent too long in solitude and secrecy. Now was the time to emerge from the dark and neurotic corner in which he'd been hiding. Now was the time for him to emerge into the sunlight, hand in hand with the woman he loved. As he stood there on the quay, transfixed amid the ebb and flow of pedestrians, love bloomed within him like a mystical rose. Within its rapture all the trivial fragments of his predicament faded into insignificance. His financial woes were already evaporating as naturally as dew on a summer morning meadow. The agents of his oppression, guards and thugs both, slunk away into the shadows. He was a free man, free to devote himself entirely to the intricate courses of love. All he required, he was confident, was the few remaining days of the tour to secure Bonnie's affection forever and his lasting happiness with it.

As he stood on the quay, oblivious to the bustle of passersby, his emancipated heart glided like a gull. How long he lingered in that exalted state he didn't know, but when at last he came to himself and glanced down at his watch, he realized with a start that he was already running late for his appointment. He hastened on. The office he was looking for was in the old Irish Press newspaper building, but he had a hell of a job sorting out what was what from the Visa Section of the Department of Foreign Affairs and the Immigration Section of the Department of Justice, Equality and Law Reform. Not being an office man at all, he became disoriented among the labyrinth of halls and doors and the purposeful striding around of polished professional people. Eventually he was shown into a meeting room and asked to take a chair and wait.

It was a windowless room, the unadorned walls painted vomity green, lit by anemic fluorescent lights. There was a large mirror on one wall, which Gallagher instantly imagined to be a one-way mirror. And who would be on the other side of it, observing him—Leary? Sheehy? The little greenish-white person looking back at Gallagher from the mirror seemed to have been deprived of sunlight for years, like a peculiar species of fish hauled up from the gloomy depths of a deep sea trough. He sat on the single chair facing a long table and four empty chairs on its far side.

Within minutes the door opened and in came Givens from last night, followed by two other men and a woman, all looking as solemn as morticians who haven't been paid yet.

"Good afternoon, Mr. Gallagher," said Givens, "thank you for being here." Gallagher nodded and said nothing. All four of them seated themselves at the opposite side of the table from him, so it looked like a court martial or something.

"Permit me to introduce my colleagues," said Givens. "On my immediate right, Mr. Francis Coyne, the Assistant Commissioner for Crime and Security." Coyne had a boiled-egg head and the air of someone who had far more important matters to attend to than this. He nodded brusquely at Gallagher. "Next to Mr. Coyne," continued Givens, who even Gallagher could see was the junior member of this formidable quartet, "Inspector Ellen Callwell from the Security and Intelligence Unit." Another of the grandmotherly type, with silver-grey hair stylishly coiffed and reading glasses suspended from a gold chain around her neck, but with eyes that could slice steel.

"And, lastly, Inspector Dominic Griefer of the International Cooperation Unit." A small man with delicate features, immaculately groomed and tailored, he smiled wistfully at Gallagher. "So, as you can see," Givens summarized, "we are representing several different branches of the Department of Justice, Equality and Law Reform."

"Yeah," said Gallagher, still not properly focused, "I see that." He'd worn his suit jacket and tie to try create an impression of respectability, but the jacket was badly creased from having been stuffed into his duffle bag and he felt both small and shabby facing this authoritarian quartet.

"I should inform you at the outset," Givens said, "that this meeting is being video recorded, so you'll be fully aware of that while answering whatever questions may be put to you." Gallagher hadn't noticed the video camera mounted up near the ceiling and aimed straight at him. "First," said Givens, opening a file on the table in front of him, "just to verify some of your particulars. Your name is Patrick Veadar Gallagher?"

"Yeah."

"Born in County Cork on October 6, 1965?"

"That's right."

"Presently resident in Vancouver, British Columbia, Canada?"

"Right."

"Became a citizen of Canada in July of 1991?"

"Correct." He couldn't really remember the date, but that seemed about right. With each question, Givens looked up from his notes and straight at Gallagher. The other three were all gravely perusing documents on the table and not looking at him at all.

"Entered the Republic of Ireland on August first of this year?"

"Yeah."

"For the purpose of acting as tour director on a one-week tour of gardens in the greater Dublin area."

"That's right." This was like playing ping-pong with a ten-year-old, but he knew from the solemnity of the other three that tougher questions lay ahead.

"Inspector Callwell?"

Granny put her reading glasses on, perched near the tip of her nose so that she could peer directly at Gallagher over top of their tortoise-shell frames. "Do you know this gentleman?" she asked, holding up a large black-and-white photograph.

Gallagher squinted across the table. He wasn't all that surprised to recognize Sheehy in the photo. "I ran into him a couple of times," he said.

"This past week?"

"Yeah."

"Where did you meet him?"

"Pubs."

"Which pubs exactly?"

"Let's see. Once at Connell and Larkin's, up there on Lower Baggot Street and another time at—where was it?—Michael Quinn's on Anne Street South."

"So over the past few days you met with Mr. Sheehy on two separate occasions in two different pubs here in Dublin?"

"That's right. Well, no, hold on here a minute. I didn't *meet* with Sheehy. I was in a pub, havin' a drink, and Sheehy approached me out of the blue. That's different." By now he was forgetting all about Bosco and Bonnie and everything else, concentrating instead on the predatory elements encircling him within this room. His hands, gripping the armrests of his chair, felt sticky with heat.

"And what was the purpose of those *approaches*?" Callwell stayed as cool as a pitcher of milk in the morning.

"Didn't have any purposes."

"Surely there must have been some purpose?"

"I'm tellin' you there wasn't." A large bluebottle had somehow got into the room and was now circling above them noisily.

"So we're to believe that you travel—what?—six or seven thousand miles and meet a man in two different pubs on two separate occasions without any purpose whatsoever?" Granny peered over her spectacles at him as though he were schoolboy caught telling outrageous lies.

"I didn't travel six or seven thousand miles to meet with Sheehy," Gallagher said firmly. "I'm here to lead a garden tour plain and simple, as I've already told you. I bumped into Sheehy by accident and there was no bloody purpose at all!" Already he was beginning to get hot under the collar with this poxy cross-examination, which was not a wise thing on his part, as his brain was never at its best when his dander was up.

186

"What did you discuss?"

"The old days, mostly, down in Ballydehob, when we were young."

"So you knew him from years ago?" The bluebottle buzzed close to Gallagher's face and he swatted at it with his hand.

"Yeah. Well, no, not really."

"What do you mean *not really*? Did you or did you not know him previously?"

"He kept carrying on like we were old pals from them days."

"Yes?"

"But I didn't remember him, couldn't place him at all." Gallagher had already decided before the interview that if Sheehy's name came up—as was likely to be the case—he would hold to the story that he did not know or remember Sheehy.

"So you don't recall him from your youth?"

"No I don't."

"But you led him to believe that you did?"

"More or less." The goddamn bluebottle buzzed him again.

"What do you mean *more or less*?" Granny put just the slightest scintilla of parody on the quotation.

"He made like we were old pals and I played along with it, even though I couldn't remember him."

"Why would you do that?"

"Dunno exactly. It was awkward, see."

"Awkward."

"Yeah. And I guess I was scared of the feller. Didn't want to cross him, like."

"Thank you for clarifying that. What else did you discuss?"

"Not much."

"Mr. Gallagher!" Egghead broke in impatiently. "You perhaps don't fully appreciate what a perilous position you are occupying at the moment. My advice to you, sir, for your own sake, is to answer the inspector's questions as fully and frankly and truthfully as you are able. Do I make myself understood?" A flush of reddish purple suffused his jowly face and his fierce dark eyes glowered.

"Yeah, all right," Gallagher said. These fukkers weren't playing games.

"What else did you discuss?" Callwell repeated her question, as composed as ever.

"He asked me to pick up a parcel and deliver it to him."

"A parcel?"

"Yeah."

"A parcel from where?"

"Dunno. He never said. It was coming in by boat was all he said."

"Did he indicate what was in the parcel?"

"No." The wooden chair on which Gallagher was sitting was becoming increasingly uncomfortable, its backrest pressing painfully against his spine, but he didn't want to begin shifting position, as it might give the impression of guilty nervousness.

"Did you have any suspicion about what might be in this parcel?"

"Plenty of suspicions, but no information."

"Did you suspect that this parcel might involve illegal activity in some way?"

"Well, I knew it wasn't somethin' they were sending through the feckin' post."

"So you suspected that illegal activity was involved?"

"I'm tellin' you plain and simple I didn't know. I couldn't make out if the feller was on the level or not, whether it was some prank or something of the sort, or he'd got me mixed up with somebody else, or what the feck it was all about. At first I thought he was just an alkie shaking down the tourists, but not for long."

"Why not?"

"Just how he was. Mean, like. An' tough as fukkin' pig iron. If he wanted a snug in the pub, never mind how crowded it was, he got it, just like that." Gallagher snapped his fingers.

"A hard man, then."

"Right."

"And you were frightened of him?"

"After a bit I was."

"Did he give any indication that he was a member of an organization?"

"Not directly. But I took it for granted he was."

"Why?" Gallagher watched in fascination as the bluebottle seemed about to land on Egghead's shiny pate, but at the last second retreated to the ceiling.

"Just his talk about messages and connections and all like that."

"Did you conclude that he belonged to any particular group?"

"I figured him for one of the IRA factions from what he said about Good Friday and such, but I was far from certain."

"Why did you meet with him a second time?"

"I went to Michael Quinn's to be clear of him, figuring Connell and Larkin's was his regular. But there he shows up at Michael Quinn's too."

"You hadn't planned to meet him again?"

"No, I was avoidin' him, I'm telling you."

"Did you have the sense that he was following you?"

"Yeah, or maybe havin' me followed."

"How's that?"

"Another feller showed up at Connell and Larkin's and I had the feelin' he was watchin' me."

"Can you describe him?"

"Not really. Ordinary-looking guy. Bald. He had a moustache. Wore a suit. Kinda typical."

"Would you recognize him if you saw him again?"

"Sure I would." At a nod from Callwell, Givens came round the table with a large portfolio and showed him several photographs of different men's faces, but the watcher wasn't among them. Gallagher considered mentioning the wanker at Mount Stewart as well, but decided against it.

"You thought perhaps this man was working for Sheehy? Keeping an eye on you?"

"He was watchin' me for sure, but whether it was for Sheehy or you bunch or for his own amusement I had no idea."

"Thank you, Mr. Gallagher." Steel Granny took her glasses off, and Gallagher thought he was home free, having held his ground quite brilliantly. But Callwell looked to Griefer on her right and said, "Inspector?"

"Mr. Gallagher." Griefer's voice was surprisingly full-bodied for such a small person, "How would you characterize your politics?"

"My politics?"

"Yes."

"I can't rightly say as I've got any politics."

"You don't, for example, belong to any political party in Canada?"

"Are you kiddin'? Them wankers are even worse than the ones here."

"Did you ever belong to a political party in Ireland?"

"No."

"Not Sein Feinn, for example?"

"No."

"Were you a member of any republican organization of any sort while living in Ireland?"

"Never, no." The pain in his back was now intolerable and he shifted as imperceptibly as possible to move the pressure off his spine.

"What about the IRA?"

"What about it?"

"Were you ever a member of that organization?"

"Not on yer life."

Griefer smiled ever so slightly. "What about the Provisionals?"

"No."

"Did you know a man named Dominic Farrell?"

Gallagher was astonished again at how much these people knew, how they commanded scraps of information out of peoples' lives from years ago. As though one's self existed more verifiably in their files than in your own memory and imagination. That they, not you, controlled who you'd been and who you were.

"Sure I knew Dominic. I worked under him when he was head gardener at an estate in West Cork."

"Did you and he belong to an IRA cell at that time?"

"We did not. At least I didn't." Gallagher wondered where Dominic might be now, what he might have told these people. No way of knowing; he would have to deny any accusation and defy them to prove him wrong. But, Jays, it was warm in this bloody room. The four of them all looked cool as cucumbers, but Gallagher could feel the heat building in his brain. And that goddamn bluebottle was still buzzing around him.

"Did you ever provide any of these groups with money or support of any kind?" Griefer asked.

"Never."

"Did you ever participate in activities sponsored by these groups?"

"I did not."

"Did you ever attend the funeral of an IRA gunman?"

"No."

"How do you explain this photograph then?" He laid on the table a black-and-white print of the same photo Leary had shown him at the airport in which a figure in the funeral crowd was unmistakably himself. He considered accusing them of doctoring the photo as Michael had suggested, but thought better of it. Hunker down was the operative strategy for dealing with these sharks.

"I can't explain it. All I can tell you is that's not me there. Never was."

"Mr. Gallagher, would you in general describe yourself as someone sympathetic to the aims and objectives of the Republican movement?"

"I might be if I lived here still."

"Of course," he said, again with a small smile, "and what about the Provisionals, say?"

"Well, they've disarmed, haven't they?"

"Indeed. And what of Continuity IRA or the Real IRA?"

"What about 'em?"

"Would you be sympathetic to the aims and objectives of these groups—*if* you still lived here?" Griefer's raised eyebrow traced a delicate irony.

He hesitated, seeing no escape route. He caught a glimpse of himself in the wall mirror, pale and shrunken.

"Mr. Gallagher?"

"I love Ireland," he said carefully, "but I'm no killer, so."

"Thank you. Inspector Callwell?"

Granny looked at Gallagher as though she were trying to decide whether or not to have him shot on the spot. "I want you to listen to me very carefully now, Mr. Gallagher," she said.

"Yeah." His bravado had deserted him entirely, swept away in the complexities of the past. The warmth of the room, the uncomfortable chair, the insistent buzzing of the bluebottle all added to his disequilibrium.

"The man you know as Joe Sheehy," Callwell continued, "is someone we have been pursuing for a considerable period of time."

"What for?"

"For crimes against the State, both here and in the North."

"I see."

"He is a dangerous man, Mr. Gallagher, and a completely ruthless individual. Your instincts in that regard were entirely correct. He is a person who will stop at nothing to attain his ends. Whether or not what you have told us, or have told him, or have told other parties, is entirely true does not concern us overly today." She was calling him a liar. A liar whose lies weren't even significant enough to be of interest. He couldn't escape her riveting gaze no matter how deliberately he looked down or away. "What does concern us very keenly is the incarceration of Mr. Sheehy. Despite authoring some truly heinous crimes, he has thus far eluded successful prosecution. But with your cooperation, we hope to put a permanent end to his unlawful activities."

Gallagher thought fast. "Sorry, I can't help you," he said. "I only bumped into the feller twice in the pub, as I've told you. I don't know the first bloody thing about him, so I can't tell you anythin' that'll help put him away." He stopped, then hastily tacked on, "If I did, if I could, I would."

"We appreciate your spirit of cooperation," Callwell said so dryly it was impossible to tell if she was being sarcastic or not. "Fortunately you are, in fact, in a perfect position to help us."

"How's that then?"

"All you need to do is simply follow our instructions exactly. If you do, we'll have our man and you'll be on your way back to Canada with our gratitude and no further questions asked. Is that clear?"

"It's clear enough all right, but I'm not gettin' myself mixed up in any of this. I'm just here to see some gardens, like. Lead my little tour group."

"Ah, but you're already mixed up in it, aren't you? Otherwise, you wouldn't be visiting here with us this afternoon, would you?" She smiled at him like a successful hostess passing out dainty petit fours.

"I'm only here because you took my passport and told me I had to be here." Gallagher was drawing the line.

"Mr. Gallagher, believe me when I tell you: you're as involved in this situation as Mr. Sheehy himself. We're not requesting your cooperation, we're requiring it."

"Require all you want. I'm not doin' any of your dirty work for you, I can tell you that."

"And I'll tell *you* this, Mr. Gallagher," said Egghead glowering at him angrily. "Either you cooperate fully with us in this matter, in every particular, in which case you'll be safely back home in Canada in no time, or you don't. However, be forewarned." He paused for a moment as the bluebottle landed on the table in front of him. He gingerly picked up a newspaper, folded it and swatted at the fly, but missed. "Be forewarned, Mr. Gallagher," he resumed without missing a beat, "that if you choose not to cooperate with us, and word of this meeting were to get back to your old pal Mr. Sheehy, he would be entirely cognizant of the threat you pose to him, in which case your safe return home, indeed your safety in general, could not be guaranteed by any means."

Gallagher hesitated, cornered. They were blackmailing him, the bastards. He licked his lips to moisten them. His stomach was churning something dreadful and a weight of heat pressed against him. "What is it you want me to do?"

"The simplest of errands," Callwell said reassuringly. "We want you to re-establish contact with Mr. Sheehy and deliver his parcel to him."

"Why?"

"We have reason to believe that the parcel contains certain materials that, if found in Sheehy's possession, will be enough to see that gentleman placed behind bars for a good long while."

"Drugs, you mean?"

"Don't concern yourself with its contents. And under no circumstances should you open the parcel. Is that understood?"

"Yeah." This was fukkin' great, that he'd be in possession of an incriminating parcel, and maybe it was himself they were setting the trap for, not Sheehy at all. The taste in the back of his mouth was like smouldering rubber.

"Good," Granny said. "Your assignment is to retrieve the parcel, let Mr. Sheehy know that you have it, and to arrange a time and a place at which you will pass it to him. It is absolutely imperative that it be Sheehy himself who receives the parcel directly from you. Don't agree to leave it for him anywhere and don't entrust it to any intermediary. Is that perfectly clear?"

"Yeah." He could see no way out of this trap.

"Excellent. Once you've made arrangements with him as to where and when the parcel will be exchanged, you will call the number on this card." She passed across a business card. "Advise us as to where and when the exchange is to take place. Our people will be there, make no mistake about that, though neither you nor Sheehy will see any sign of us. Once the parcel is in Sheehy's hands, we'll move in and that gentleman's days of terrorizing innocent people will be at an end." She paused for a moment and glanced at her notes, then looked up at him again. "Oh, and one further caution, Mr. Gallagher: say nothing about our conversation here this afternoon, about your coming here, or about this operation, not a word to anyone, anyone at all. Is that fully understood?"

"Yeah, it's understood all right, but I don't like it."

"What precisely don't you like?"

"Fukkin' around with guys like Sheehy."

"Of course. Your apprehensions are well founded. Sheehy, as we've told you, is the most ruthless of characters. Any slip-up in this operation could have the most serious consequences, particularly for yourself. That's why absolute confidentiality is essential. If no one else knows of our plan, then Sheehy cannot possibly know of it. And if we are successful, his associates will know nothing of it either, and you'll be safe from reprisals by them. So, in a very real sense, Mr. Gallagher, your fate is in your own hands."

"I still don't like it." He was remembering he'd already told Wickerson about this meeting and Christ only knows who Michael may have blabbed it to in the meantime. Again he decided to say nothing.

"I don't blame you in the least." Callwell, having successfully cornered and trapped him, now sounded like the soul of solicitude. "We don't especially like this kind of operation ourselves. The chances of mishap, of human error, can never be zero. But weigh the costs and benefits for a moment, if you will. As Assistant Commissioner Coyne has explained to you"—she nodded deferentially in Egghead's direction—"either Sheehy is behind bars and no further menace to you or to anyone else, or he's still at large and a very real threat, particularly to you, whether you were here or in Canada. There would be no escaping him. So, really, when you think about it, you don't have much of an alternative at all, now do you?"

▫ NINETEEN ▫

GALLAGHER TRUDGED despondently back towards his hotel. So, the bloody vultures of his past were gathering for a feast. This was the Ireland he'd once escaped and had known better than to return to. A landscape of ambush and treachery, that's what it was. Serves him right, the bollocks, to now find himself neatly caught in a pincer with Sheehy on the one point and the authorities on the other. He remembered that hapless hiker in the American desert, the cracker who'd got his arm caught between a boulder and a cliff and had to sever his arm to escape. Now here he was himself, trapped just as impossibly. Christ on His cross what a godforsaken pismire of a place! In the shrieks of laughter spilling from open doorways and windows as he passed along, he could hear the voices of the *Pitags* and *Buitseachs*, his mother's old witches, cackling about their mischievous business. There were malignant forces at work here, no doubt about it, malevolent elements like the fairy-winds, buffeting him this way and that, dangling a vision of bliss one minute, then rudely snatching it away the next. The heinous exhalations of evil spirits hung over the city like toxic fog.

But he must not allow these bastards to best him. He remembered one of his mother's old proverbs, "However long a road, there comes a turning." Yes, there'd be a turning in the road soon enough. He forced himself to focus on the family farm, how close he was to a breakthrough there, and to the blessed freedom it promised. By logical extension, his imaginings drifted to Bonnie, recalling how they'd stood together on the terrace at Mount Stewart, like a man and his bride. He fantasized about taking her to his home in Vancouver, now safely secured forever, and how she would glow with delight being among his roses. She'd said as much to him—that his roses were the most beautiful things she'd ever encountered, and that she wanted to devote herself to hybridization, as he had. What more would he ever want in life than that little house with its marvellous rosary and a lovely companion with whom he could share them?

No, he would not allow that filthy Sheehy or these pestiferous authorities to come between him and that wondrous vision. He was no longer the craven youth he'd been, fleeing in panic at the first whiff of trouble. There was nowhere left for him to flee. Now he'd stand and he'd fight, the way true patriots had been standing and fighting on this tortured island for centuries. They would not wear him down, the bastards, with their files and their photographs and their blackmailing bullshit. He'd outwit them, you just wait and see, he'd beat them all at their poxy scheming.

Caught up in these darkly fanciful considerations, just as he turned onto Molesworth Street, he was startled by a woman suddenly lunging from a shop doorway and blocking his path.

Muttering, "Excuse me," he went to step around her, but the woman slithered sideways like a dancer in step with him and continued to prevent him from passing. She was a peculiar-looking creature. One side of her scalp was shaved completely bald but from the other half a cockade of stiff hair dyed seaweed green swooped up and then curled downward like a scimitar, ending at a point just below her left eye. Enlarged by a heavy application of dark shadow and absurdly long black lashes, her eyes were numinous, the pupils unnaturally dilated. Her sunken cheeks were smudged with rouge and a golden ring pierced one nostril. Crimson lipstick flared across thin lips twisted in a leering grin. A cheap cotton dress scarcely hid her angular body and long bony legs. Her skinny limbs jerked in spasmodic sudden movements like those of a marionette. She wore no socks but a mismatched pair of high-topped sneakers, one red, the other black.

A brasser, Gallagher concluded, likely high on drugs, and again he made to pass her on the sidewalk but again she slid in front of him with a salacious leer. "Excuse me," he said a second time and more firmly. With a head full of conspiracies and betrayals he had no time for some crack-brained whore.

The woman cocked her bizarre head sideways with a coquettish pout. "Well, excuse me too I'm sure, Mister Pat Trick." She tittered giddily and lurched towards him.

Gallagher was stunned to hear the voice and its contemptuous distortion of his name. "Is it . . ." he began, unable even to consider the possibility.

"Is it?" she echoed maniacally, chewing a wad of gum and blow-ing a large bubble that exploded all over her lips. "Whoops!" Her thin arms flew out like broken wings, then collapsed back to clasp her list-ing torso. "Is it?" she shrieked into the street, startling several passersby. Her spastic limbs jerked uncontrollably.

"Christ almighty," he said, "don't say it's you, Francie."

"Don't say it's me, Francie!" Again her mocking echo and glassy-eyed laughter. A couple of punks deep into black Goth mode drifted past, coolly indifferent to the ridiculous tableaux of Gallagher and mad Francie.

Finally gathering his wits and realizing that Francie—and who would believe that this outlandish creature was the young beauty of long-ago Ballydehob?—was far beyond intelligent conversation, Gallagher smiled at her fondly, said how lovely it had been to run into her again after all these years, and excused himself as he had to be get-ting along to an important appointment.

"Ah, no, Pat Trick," she said, wagging a nicotine index finger in front of his face, "you wouldn't leave a girl so, would you now? Not a true-bred gentleman like yourself. And we've so much to discuss, you and I, after all these years, have we not?" A sudden illumination lit up her painted face within which Gallagher could barely detect a remnant loveliness of the girl he'd known. "Besides," she said brightly, popping another bubble with an impudent leer, "you haven't met Danno yet, I don't believe."

She swung a skinny arm towards the alcove from which she'd emerged, as though introducing a new act on stage, and out shambled Danno. He was not a large man, hardly much taller than Gallagher himself, but heavy-set and hugely muscled. He wore a black sleeveless T-shirt with *Go Ahead Make Me Day* emblazoned in blood-red letters across the chest. His small, bald head sat like a cannonball on a bullish neck. The facial features were compressed into the smallest possible configuration: narrow slits for eyes, a pug nose, and almost nonexistent lips all squeezed together, and his ears were little more than gullies on the smooth hard outcropping of skull. It was a head designed to withstand fierce battering. A sinister, low gurgling arose from somewhere deep within the barrel chest, and his enormous hands were gnarled like cypress roots into what seemed to be permanent fists. Gallagher—who'd crossed paths with a few tough nuts in his time— had never before encountered so pure an embodiment of physical intimidation.

"Danno," Francie giggled, kicking one foot high into the air, exposing the miserable flank of a skinny leg, "allow me to introduce a dear old friend from Ballydehob, Mister Pat Trick Gallagher."

"How yis," Gallagher said, nodding nervously. Danno glowered at him and seemed to tilt forward like a battering ram but said nothing. He looked to Gallagher a near-animal who couldn't wait for the next brawl to break out.

"Danno saw you on the telly the other night, didn't you, Danno?" The shining head bobbed almost imperceptibly. "He loves the garden shows especially, don't you, Danno?" Another nod. She did a sudden lurching pirouette ending in a melodramatic pose with her head lain on Danno's oxen shoulder.

"Well, that's great," Gallagher said, trying to sound enthusiastic. That goddamn TV show! Why in Christ's holy name had he ever agreed to go on it? It was that fukkin' Margaret Foley with her High Society airs had forced him into it. So then Bosco comes out of the woodwork like some goddamn termite, and now this! Oh, he'd tell that bloody Foley where to put her snooty Royal Horticultural Society horseshit if ever he had the chance.

"That's how we knew you were here," Francie said, kicking high into the air again, "and so we took the time to search out where you were staying, like. Now wasn't that thoughtful of Danno and me?" She fluttered her farcical lashes.

"It was that, and I'm delighted you did, truly I am," he said, smiling feebly. "Nice to meet you too, Danno." He almost reached to shake hands with the pug but thought better of it. "And lovely to see you again, Francie, sure it was. How you're getting on and all. But now, as sorry as I am to say it, I must be on my way."

"How very gallant of you to offer, Pat Trick." She rolled her mad moppet eyes as though bedazzled by him. "Yes, of course, I'd be delighted to accompany you." She stuck her arm through his and made as though to promenade with him up Molesworth Street.

"Ah, no, Francie," he said, trying to disentangle himself from her, "it's private business I'm after just now."

"Private, is it?" In a sudden collapse, Francie crouched down beneath him, arms and legs stuck out like isosceles triangles, and stared upward open-mouthed, as though he were a commanding figure towering above her. He could see the wad of pink gum lying on her tongue. "Oh, I see." Then slowly she slithered up his side, her bony hands sliding like reptiles across his body, until at her full height and up on her toes, she in turn looked down at him. Then she bent and whispered huskily in his ear. "I'll tell you a wee secret, Pat Trick, shall I?" Gallagher said nothing. Danno shuffled closer, as though to hear too. "Danno likes to hurt people," she whispered. "I'd hate to see him hurt you, being as you're my old sweetheart and all and a person who would never hurt a soul yourself, would you now?" He almost gagged at the stench of gum and tobacco and cheap perfume coming off her. "So why don't you and I just slip away together for a bit, just you and me, okay?"

"Sure," Gallagher said, whispering himself. Danno gurgled like a draining bathtub.

"Pat Trick and I are proceeding to his hotel," Francie announced to Danno, her raised hand pointing ahead of her as though she were Catherine the Great. "I shall summon you if I need you." Danno glowered at Gallagher like a heavyweight anxious for the bell. "Shall we?" Francie said to Gallagher grandly. Her arm clinging to his, the two of them strode up Molesworth Street, she the queen of crack and he her reluctant consort.

Gallagher's brain was a blind alley in which scraps of paper and plastic swirled this way and that with each gust of wind. What could he possibly say to Francie in her current state? Sure she was his childhood sweetheart, the lovely creature he'd lain with, naked and chaste, in the sea cave of innocence. And, yes, he'd later made love with her in the long grass of late summer a million nights ago. Hadn't he thought of that night behind the old mill, dreamt of it, never known the equal of that ecstatic tumble in all the intervening years? Though he realized this goggle-eyed strumpet on his arm was one and the same person, she wasn't at all. The real Francie, the young beauty he'd grown up with, lain with and loved, remained alive more surely in his memory than in the wreckage of this broken doll giggling beside him.

As they approached the hotel he glanced back down the street and saw that Danno had followed at a distance and taken up an outpost position leaning against a brick wall. The hotel doorman held the front door open for them, and Francie kicked her leg high again as they stepped into the lobby. There was no one about. What the hell was he going to do with her, Gallagher wondered, or what the hell was she planning to do with him. He suggested a coffee in the bar, thinking it might settle her down. "Aw, c'mon, Patsy darlin'," she cooed, batting her eyes at him, "you can do better than that. Let's go to your room."

"Ah, I don't think so." He patted her hand paternally and tried to steer her towards the bar. Just then Nuala emerged from the office behind her counter. Taking in everything with a quick glance, she gave Gallagher the faintest I've-seen-it-all smile and busied herself with paperwork.

"Let's play a game!" Francie cried out, breaking away from him and raising her arms high.

"What game would that be then?" he asked soothingly.

"Let's play: you do exactly what I tell you or Danno will rip yer fukkin' face off and stick it up yer arse!" She giggled hysterically.

"All right, all right," said Gallagher, trying to appease her, "we'll take a wee peek at my room, shall we?" He got the key from Nuala, whose neutral expression contained a lengthy catechism of moral imperatives, and guided Francie to the narrow stairwell. She bounded up the first flight of stairs with startling agility, then struck a Kate Moss skanky pose looking down at him from the landing. Just as he got there himself, he heard women's voices and a door being closed and suddenly there stood Bonnie and Carla. It was a hopeless moment. The two young women looked from crazy Francie to frantic Gallagher on the stair below her and back again, struck speechless by the absurd spectacle. Gallagher struggled to say something, anything. Then Francie asked with the authority of an abbess calling her novices to order: "And where do you two think you're going?"

Carla and Bonnie glanced at each other and burst out laughing. "We're going shopping," Carla said.

"Shopping." Francie chewed her noisy gum and considered things. "Well, that's all right then. You have fun. Pat Trick here and I are going up to his room to fuck, so you'll excuse us please."

"No, no," Gallagher said, wanting to explain.

"Come along, big boy," Francie leered, reaching down to hook him by the collar and haul him up. "Me loins are on fire for you."

"Bonnie . . ." he pleaded. But Bonnie and Carla squeezed past him and clattered down the stairs laughing uncontrollably.

"Jesus Christ!" he hissed. "Now you've fukkin' done it, haven't you?"

"Not yet we haven't," Francie teased, still holding his collar. She cocked her head sideways and trilled, "Oh, Danno boy, me pipes, me pipes are callin'."

He was at her mercy and saw no sign of her having any. The damage with Bonnie was surely irreparable. Jesus, what an afternoon from hell. He fumbled with the key and let them into his room.

"Very nice," cried Francie throwing her spindly arms wide. "Oh, Pat Trick, isn't this *sooo* romantic!" She deftly kicked the door closed behind her and pressed herself wantonly against him. He could feel the angular bones of her body articulated like a skeleton's. "Who'd have believed the fire could be so quickly rekindled, eh, after all these years." She was groping at his belt buckle. "Oh, Pat Trick, we were made for each other, you and me." She had the belt undone and the zipper down. "I knew it then and I know it now." His trousers fell around his ankles and she was on her knees, her index finger hooked on the waistband of his briefs. Gallagher stood immobilized. His brain had seized up, refusing to acknowledge that any of this was real.

"Do you remember that night at old Ballydehob, that night that shook the world?" Francie sounded like Vivien Leigh in melodrama overdrive as she slowly drew down his briefs.

"I do." He barely got the two syllables out. He felt not a dram of eroticism in the moment. Awash in fear and regret and shame and disgust, he was no more likely to achieve an erection than a stigmata. His genitals hung mushy and soft as overripe figs. Francie took his limp penis in her mouth. He could feel the wad of her gum rubbing against his nub. She worked for a bit trying to arouse him. She fondled his balls, slowly slid her hand up his arse and her finger into him. Nothing at all; he was impervious to arousal.

Suddenly she jumped to her feet and spat out her gum. "Maybe y'need to see me naked first, to get really hot, do you, darlin'?" She spun away from him in a dizzy pirouette and with a single fluid gesture hoisted the cotton dress up over her head and cast it onto a chair. She was naked but for the running shoes and a skimpy thong. She was a misery of bones, all points and sharp angles like one of Picasso's prostitutes. Her shrunken breasts hung down pathetically. "Suck me tits!" she commanded him, pulling her elbows and shoulders back. Gallagher leaned forward reluctantly. "You were mad to suck them once upon a time!" she cried, bitterness at last hissing in her tone, "so suck them now!" Gallagher bent and put his lips to a shrivelled nipple. "Suck, you asshole!" she shrieked, and Gallagher did his best. She clamped his head in both hands. "Now this one," she commanded, guiding his head to her other withered dug.

"Ah," she crooned sentimentally, "that's just how he sucked, y'know, the wee one, our little babe." Gallagher was choking on his own saliva, but she pressed his face fiercely against her bony chest. "For the first few days, that is." Her tone sharpened and hardened again. "Until they took him away." A little spasm trembled through her skeleton. "Y've lost yer touch in the tit department, darlin'," she mocked, roughly pulling his head back and glaring down at him like an avenging Madonna, "so lick my clit!" She forced his head down hard and he buckled to his knees. "Go on, lick me! Lick me like yer sorry fer what y'did to me!"

"I am sorry, Francie," he blubbered. "Jesus Christ, you know I am."

"Go on, y'sad little fuck, put me over the moon!" She jammed his face into her crotch, but Gallagher could go no further. He clasped her skinny buttocks and sobbed against her.

"Do you have any idea how they treated unwed mothers in this fukkin' country back then, eh?" Of course he knew, but really he had no idea. Him or anyone else. "Like livin', breathin' bags of shit, that's how." All mockery had fled from Francie's tone, replaced with bitter rage. "And why do y'think I was put through that, eh?" She was pressing his face against her cadaverous belly. "Because you fukked me and got me knocked up and then you just bleedin' fukked off, didn't you, y'selfish little prick? Left me there on me own."

"I tried to help you, Francie, honest to Christ I did. I got the money and everything..." He was sobbing against her wrinkled flesh, wretched and vile in his own eyes.

"Sure y'got the money. And y'fukked right off with it too." She punched the side of his head hard.

"Yer old feller was after me though." His ear was ringing painfully from her blow.

"Yea, well he didn't catch you, did he? But he sure as shit caught me and fukkin' near beat me to death. And nobody in town would as much as give me a good mornin'. All them pious Christians with their noses in the air. So off it was to the fukkin' jail for unwed mothers. Nuns on my arse mornin' noon and night. And they take my baby away from me before I know what the fuk's goin on. They took my little baby." Her voice broke, trembling, and she seemed about to cry. "My little boy." She closed her eyes and gently rocked Gallagher's head as though it were her baby. "Never told me what they'd done with him. Just suddenly he was gone. After all those months inside me, in my belly where you're pressed there now." Gallagher, needing something to cling to, clung to her. "Then they locked me up in one of them Magdalene prisons with dozens of other girls. They cut off our hair and took away our clothes, made us wear a coarse brown tunic. They fed us slop you wouldn't give to pigs and beat us if we did anything other than grovel. The Sisters of Mercy. Ha! We worked in their fukkin' laundry like slaves, twelve hours a day, six days a week. Then the fukkin' priest would show up and try to feel you up in the confessional. The Magdalenes they called us, the Penitents. Hypocritical fukkers. Christ, how I hated them! Well, I'll tell you, I put up with that shite for longer than I should and then I got the fuk outta there. Meanwhile"—she yanked his head back again and stared at him as though she'd kill him then and there—"you're off in fukkin' Canada breedin' roses and playin' Mister Big Shot, eh."

"Francie, I..."

"No, save it, will you? I don't want to hear any of your shite about how the Provies were after you so you had to run and hide, or how you were goin' to come back fer me when the coast was clear and we'd live happily ever after. I've had a lifetime of losers feedin' me that kind of shite and I won't hear any more of it from you." She pushed him back roughly and broke from his grasp. Plucking her dress up from the chair, she slid it quickly back over her upstretched arms and on.

"Well now, that was fun, wasn't it, John?" She leered at him, still down on his knees. Her mood had swung again. "Now it's time to pay the piper." She rubbed her fingers in front of his face with the universal gesture for cash.

"What?" He slowly got to his feet.

"Well surely y'don't think I'm doin' it fer free still, do you?" He couldn't think what to say or do. "Ah, no, lad, y'had yer free sample back there behind the mill. Today's a business proposition entirely. Sure, I thought we had an understandin' on that score."

Rousing himself, he pulled up his trousers awkwardly. "I'll give you what I can, Francie, of course, but I've not much." She was straightening herself in the bureau mirror, licking her fingertips to twist the tips of her ridiculous hair. He fished out his wallet, but she pirouetted suddenly and deftly snatched it from him. Examining its contents, she pulled out a thick wad of euros, what was left of the expenses money they'd given him at Berenice Travel, and rolled them into her fist.

"Traveller's cheques," she said with a snort at the rest.

"Aye, safer that way," he said, relieved he'd no more cash she could pilfer.

"You're a great feller for safety, sure you are. So why don't you and I take these safe traveller's cheques of yours down to the bank on the corner and cash them, and then we'll be square, eh?"

"But that's hundreds of euros," he protested. "That wouldn't be fair a'tall."

"Oh, fair is what we're after lookin' for, is it? Ah." She placed an index finger against her chin, her mouth hanging open. "So considerin' what you've done to me over the years and what I've done for you, what would you think would be fair, like?"

"Francie, I know you must . . ."

"You don't know the first fukkin' thing about it!" she flared at him, her face right into his. "You've no idea how you wrecked me fukkin' life, you miserable little fuck. So don't you tell me how I *must* anything." She glanced at the alarm clock on the nightstand and paused for a moment thinking. "Now I see the banks are closed already," she said, changing to a businesslike tone, "so here's what we'll do. I'll go down and tell Danno what a wonderful romp we had together, you and me, pure ecstasy and all, but that you couldn't afford my fee when all was said and done. Naturally Danno will be upset, he's very sensitive on these matters, but I'll do me best to calm him down."

"Jesus, Francie . . ."

"And what you'll do is head straight to the bank bright and early tomorrow morning and cash those traveller's cheques of yours in order to pay outstanding debts. Danno and I will be in touch very shortly. And John," she warned, ferociously focused now, not a trace of the loony addict left, "don't fuck this up or there won't be enough of you left to feed to the dogs, do you understand?"

"I do," he said again.

"Grand!" She was instantly back to her crazed marionette self. "Then I'll be on me way, so. Goodbye, John," she jeered, winking at him lewdly, "for now," and let herself out.

⬚ TWENTY ⬚

BY THE time dawn finally broke over the city, Gallagher had been lying awake for hours to meet it, assailed by voices from his past, accusing, condemning, taunting. He'd drifted in and out of bizarre dreams and half-dreams. He saw Francie, naked and pathetic, spread-eagled hopelessly beneath the bodies of grunting men, and was powerless to help her. His mother ran towards him across a misty hillside wailing that he was her lost son, stolen from her by the Unseen Ones. Gradually, horribly, her face became that of The White Lady, the *Ben-sidhe*, and he fled from her. In an unfamiliar city he was menaced by a violent man who at one minute was Sheehy and at another Danno, but in essence his father. Gallagher finally emerged from the dark world into the light, exhausted and dazed. He skipped breakfast altogether, contenting himself with a cup of tea brewed in his room. He sipped the tea indifferently, watching from his window as Dublin City shook off its slumber and prepared to begin another day.

He could barely face the group at all as he clambered, late, into the coach and made his way unsteadily down the aisle. He was invisible to them as they chattered among themselves, nobody so much as glancing in his direction as he passed. It was as though his corporality was dissolving, leaving him a wraith-like figure, all but transparent to those around him. He sat alone and disconsolate near the rear.

The coach carried them out to County Kildare, through the high-end horsey country west of Dublin, to visit the walled garden of an expansive estate. Gallagher could give a shite about any of it, the encounter with Francie had unnerved him that badly. His spirits were slumped and a nagging sense of shame oppressed him. Of course Francie was in the right, her rage entirely justified. He'd had his bit of fun with her and then deserted her. Bedevilled by self-disgust, he sought half-heartedly to justify his behaviour to himself. Really, what the hell option had been open to him back then? He couldn't possibly have married her. He'd no money. The old ones were still working the farm and there was no place there for a young wife, much less a bawling baby. He'd done his level best to try get her fixed up over in England, but that damn fool father of hers had buggered the whole business. He'd stolen the money for Francie, not for himself, and hadn't been a coward, at least not at the outset. There's many a tomcock wouldn't have had the guts to double-cross both the old man and the comrades in arms the way Gallagher had. If only Francie hadn't blabbed to that meddling priest and got that damn fool father of hers alerted. That's what had spannered the whole business, not himself. No, all things considered, he'd done what any man would do, ignoble though it might appear in hindsight. He was no better nor worse than any young fool caught in similar circumstances. And in the final analysis, he tried to reassure himself, it wasn't him who'd turned Francie into the human wreckage he'd encountered yesterday. She was who she was, not who he'd made her. He was not responsible for other people's misery. Nevertheless, despite his rationalizing, he couldn't banish her skeletal nakedness from his mind. Her insane laughter and burning rage. With all his wherewithal, he strained to eradicate the persistent accusation that his cowardly desertion had permanently smashed Francie's life.

And what of his own life? What had become of that fun-loving lad cavorting with his pals and flirting with the girls on the warm summer evenings of youth? Not a care in the world in those days, or so it seemed to him now. He was choosing not to remember his drunken and abusive father, his own rage against the man. No, from his current perspective his youth seemed sweetly innocent, the carefree simplicity of days. All of it gone, long gone, squeezed into a cramping narrowness, an elemental sourness. He wondered how that had happened, how he had been corrupted and crimped into his present stingy state.

Oh, and that look in Bonnie's eyes when she'd seen him on the stairs with Francie, her hysterics with Carla as they left. What she must have thought of him. All his painstaking groundwork smashed in a moment. Could he ever face her again? He would avoid her all morning and, he sensed, she'd be wanting to avoid him. What was she feeling? Disappointment at least. Disgust most likely. Disgust was what he was feeling himself.

By the time they'd returned to the city and poked around a fussy little rose garden in Cabinteely—even the roses had failed to interest him, and Loretta Stroude had seized the opportunity to install herself as the de facto expert rosarian of the tour—Gallagher once again nudged his concentration towards the one small balefire visible in this desolate landscape: his meeting with his brother tomorrow night to discuss the prospect of inheritance. The remote but not impossible chance that the family farm, for all its ancient byres and piggeries, might rescue him from financial ruin. If he were to inherit the farm—hypothetical, unforeseen, preposterous as that possibility was—then Sheehy and the guards and Peter Fanslau and the whole fukkin' lot of them could take a hike to Ballyhoolahan. He'd be beyond their reach. Set for life. He held to this vision like a talisman, an elf-shot, to keep from thinking about how he'd make things up with Bonnie, what he could possibly do about poor mad Francie, or his growing sense of terror around the scheme to entrap Joe Sheehy.

THAT evening the group splintered in various configurations to dine and spend the evening as they chose. Gallagher would have loved to squeeze in a few hours with Bonnie, to explain about Francie, clear the air between them, and restore that ambience of affection he had felt developing only two days ago. But Bonnie, Carla, and Amanda sauntered off somewhere together, chatting happily like carefree schoolgirls. He watched them from his hotel window, walking arm in arm down Molesworth Street. He envied their easygoing youthfulness, their sisterhood. They might have been himself with Francie twenty years ago, when the world was young and innocent.

Shortly afterwards he observed Michael and Elyse leaving the hotel together. Gesturing broadly, Michael said something that caused Elyse to laugh gaily. She reached out and touched Michael's arm for a moment, a gesture so subtle, so womanly, it made Gallagher wonder whether he hadn't misread Elyse entirely.

Left alone, grudgingly, he set about doing what he knew he must do: find Sheehy and set the devices of entrapment into motion. He decided that returning to Connell and Larkin's was his best bet, though he realized Sheehy could find him anywhere. He strode rapidly up near-deserted Kildare Street, conscious that Francie and Danno might appear any minute. He hadn't cashed his traveller's cheques and had no cash for Francie should she accost him. He could picture himself being pounded to pulp in the gutter by that psycho Danno, and Francie dancing with delight at her bitter revenge. Jays. He felt he should do something for her by way of token reparation—not to do so seemed detestable—but he had no idea what. Giving her a few hundred euros that she'd soon squander on drugs hardly seemed like doing her a favour. And if not that, what? And something else had occurred to him too—that perhaps the reason Sheehy knew so many intimate details about Gallagher's youth was that Francie had told him. For all Gallagher knew, Francie might get her drugs from Sheehy. Twisted with uncertainty and confusion, he hastened on.

When he arrived at Connell and Larkin's, slightly breathless from haste, he was greeted effusively by the feral-looking publican himself, who escorted him with great ceremony into a cozy wee snug. Gallagher could sense the hand of Sheehy behind the fellow's deference. The publican talked briefly but passionately of the stout resistance being mounted against the government's abysmally ignorant initiative to ban smoking everywhere, including within the sacred precincts of the pub. "Can you believe it?" he fumed, "in the bloody pubs!" Gallagher shook his head in requisite disbelief. After fetching him his pint and a kidney pie, the publican withdrew, leaving Gallagher sitting alone.

There he remained for an hour or so nursing his pint, then a second one delivered without his even asking. The comforting sounds and aromas of the pub offered him no comfort. Eventually, just as he'd anticipated, Joe Sheehy appeared out of nowhere.

"Well, well, well, Patsy, how are yis, an' all?" Sheehy clapped him on the shoulder and slipped into the seat beside him.

"Hi, Joe." Gallagher braced himself for a tough go. "How's tricks?"

"Couldn't be better, man, couldn't be better. Sun shinin', birds singin'. An' here we are, you an' me, a couple a fellers from aul Ballydehob sittin' in one of Dublin's finest like we owned the place. I tell you, Patsy, 'tis a grand country altogether." Sheehy's craggy face was all smiles and joviality. He was, Gallagher realized, every bit as much a psycho as Danno.

"Aye, 'tis all right."

"Speakin' a which, have y'had an opportunity to reconsider my propositon, Patsy, by chance?"

"Oh, yeah, I have that." Gallagher tried to sound nonchalant. "Turns out I've got a few hours free on Saturday afternoon. I could likely fetch your parcel then, if that suits."

"I knew it!" Sheehy slapped the tabletop hard with the palm of his hand. "I knew you'd come through for me, Patsy. That's grand, that is."

"So where's it to be found?"

"Over on the north side, like." Sheehy tilted his head in that direction. "I'll have a feller pick you up at your hotel and take you over. He'll know the spot, okay?"

"Right you are. But if you don't mind my asking, why don't you have your feller pick the parcel up—why do you need me?"

"That's a complicated situation, Patsy, really it is." Sheehy's voice was a low rumble cut with multiple scratches. "Let's just say that it's preferable that the party holdin' the parcel doesn't recognize the person who's receivin' it, if you get my meanin'. They'll not know you from Adam." Here Sheehy reached across and tapped Gallagher's arm lightly. "And so they'll have no idea where the item in question is bound."

"Won't they know your man though?"

The publican entered just then with a pint for Sheehy. "All right, then, are you?" the publican asked Gallagher, nodding to his glass.

"Fine, thanks," Gallagher said. The last thing he needed was to get blootered while dealing with Sheehy. The fellow bowed slightly and withdrew.

"No, he'll drop you off a few bocks away," Sheehy continued. "Then, once you've got the parcel, a cab will pick you up and deliver you back to your hotel."

"And you'll come fetch it there?"

"Not a bit of it. I'm too closely watched for that." Sheehy grinned slyly, as though being closely watched were a mark of honour.

"How'll I get it to you then?"

"I was thinking we could arrange a drop-off that evening."

"Let's see now," Gallagher said, rubbing his chin, "That's Saturday night. Nah, that won't work, I've got a farewell dinner with the tour group way the hell and gone out at Howth."

"A Last Supper, like? Always a grand thing to say a proper farewell when you're parting though, isn't it so?"

"It is too." Gallagher couldn't decipher Sheehy's meaning.

"So how about Sunday evening, are you still around then?"

"I am. And the group will be gone, thank Christ. I can get it to you Sunday for certain."

"That's perfect then." Sheehy grinned broadly.

"Grand." Gallagher sipped his pint.

"Out lookin' at gardens again today, were yis?"

"That's right. County Kildare to begin, then back over Cabinteely way."

"Lovely. Say, have y'met up with any of the aul gang since y'been back?" Sheehy cocked his head to one side, as though expecting something.

"Not a soul, Joe."

"None a'tall?"

"Never a one."

"Well, 'tis not the place we once knew, Patsy, I'll tell you. All manner of new influences about these days." Everything Sheehy said seemed to have some sinister second meaning.

"Appears to be that way, Joe, right enough." Gallagher sipped his pint, trying mightily to look entirely unconcerned.

"Not all of them healthy influences either."

"Suppose not."

"Some of them plain unhealthy, if y'don't mind me sayin' it to you."

"I'd believe it really."

"You want to know who you're talkin' with these days," Sheehy said, nodding grimly, "an' who they're talkin' with in turn, if y'know what I mean." Did Sheehy know he'd been talking to the guards? Surely not, but you couldn't tell. Or did he know about Francie? Sheehy was watching him closely with those venomous eyes of his that so belied his cheery countryman act. Any doubt about his viciousness—not that Gallagher had entertained much from the outset—had been banished at his meeting with the guards.

"I know exactly what you're sayin', Joe." Gallagher was applying all his effort not to be cowed by Sheehy. "Speakin' of which, how was it you came to know that I was back in Dublin in the first place?"

Sheehy grinned. "Believe it or not, I'm acquainted with a few gardeners myself, Patsy, and once word got around the gardening crowd that you were on your way, it didn't take long to get to me." Once again Gallagher was amazed at how small a world they moved in, how tiny and tightly interlaced a society Ireland was. "Now, you're off to visit more of yer grand gardens tomorrer, are yis?"

"That's right. Powerscourt Estate, down Wicklow way."

"Ah, I envy you, Patsy, the beauty an' all."

"Yeah."

"So y'll carry on as normal through tomorrer, not a care in the world, like. You'll get the package Saturday, my man will pick you up at two sharp, and we'll do the exchange Sunday night."

"Sure enough." Gallagher sipped his pint.

"Good. So at eleven thirty Sunday evening, be at the corner of Kildare Street and Saint Stephen's Green North on the far side of the street. A car will pull up. They'll ask you for the parcel. Give it to 'em. Simple as that, an you're home free, Patsy, to yer cozy bed an' nothin' more to worry yerself about a'tall. Yer conscience will be as clear as if y'd just stepped out of the confessional on a Saturday afternoon with all your sins forgiven." Sheehy spread his gnarled hands as though dispensing absolution.

"Will y'not be in the car yerself then?" Gallagher had to be careful here, to get the transfer arranged properly, but without being too obvious.

"I might an' I might not." Sheehy squinted, malignantly enigmatic.

"Jays, Joe, that's chancy though."

"How so, boyo?" He looked at Gallagher sideways, expectantly.

"Well, Joe, it's just with all the shite and corruption about these days, and not knowin' who the fuk y'can trust, I'd not rest easy unless I put the item into yer own hands meself. That way I'll know you've got it well and true and me job's done, and done proper, at last."

"I see yer way a thinkin', Patsy, all right. Y're a real pro, I'll say that much for you." Sheehy grinned his saurian smile. "A real pro. And y've not lost yer touch, even bein' hidden away there in Canada all these years. Okay, let's say I'll be in the car meself then, sure enough."

"Grand. I'll rest ever so much easier, Joe."

"Remember now: eleven thirty sharp Sunday night. The far corner there. Alone. With t'parcel. Okay?"

"Just so."

"Good man, Patsy. And oh . . ." Sheehy leaned forward ominously, "I know I don't need t'tell you, but not a word a this to a soul, right?"

"Naturally, Joe. Mum's the word."

▣ TWENTY-ONE ▣

FRIDAY MORNING dawned sublimely bright and sunny. As the group gathered on the sidewalk and boarded the coach for the ride down to County Wicklow, Gallagher felt himself floating, detached from everything tangible. Elyse Frampton's polite "Good morning, Mr. Gallagher," Amanda's shy smile, the animated conversation in which Michael and Piet were engaged, Wilburn's fussing, all their chittering and laughing—he drifted beyond them, disconnected. The risk he was running with Sheehy ticked in the back of his mind like a time bomb. And Francie, poor mad Francie. For the first time he was considering the child he had fathered with her. He'd deliberately erased its existence from his mind all those years ago. Whether it was male or female, whether it had lived or died, what might have become of it. Now the reality of the child, his child, was back, with Francie. She'd said it was a boy. He'd be in his twenties now. For a wild moment Gallagher wondered whether Danno might be his son, but drove the thought off, the way you would a mongrel dog. Huddled in his coach seat, he shivered, but not from any cold.

They'd scarcely left the sprawling Dublin suburbs when Bonnie Raithby once again made her way down the aisle and asked if she could join him. She was back to the sweater and pleated plaid skirt outfit that had so aroused him earlier in the week. He'd resigned himself to the bitter reality that she'd have nothing more to do with him after that humiliating encounter on the stairs with Francie. But, miraculously, here she was, beside him again. He felt unhinged, wobbling crazily as in a house of illusion where floors tilt in opposite directions and bowling balls appear to roll uphill. As delighted as he was to have her close by him again, nevertheless he remained wary. Badgered in every direction by deceit and treachery, he no longer trusted anything.

"Oh, I do so wish you'd been with us at the theatre last night, Gallagher." She beamed at him, and against his better judgement his spirits rose a notch at her casual use of the familiar name.

"Aye, I'm sorry to have missed it. I'd some important matters to attend to. Enjoyed it though, did you?"

"Oh yes, it was absolutely brilliant! I don't know Goldsmith really at all, do you?"

"Well, happens I do somewhat, yes," he admitted modestly. In point of fact he knew Goldsmith no better than Joyce, except for *The Deserted Village* with its sunken bowers and shapeless ruins, which had been one of his favourite poems from boyhood.

"Young Marlow was so great."

"Yes, I'd expect so." Here he could just play along, as he did with plant names, and he'd be on firm-enough ground.

"And Miss Hardcastle posing as the barmaid . . ."

"That's a juicy bit, right enough."

"And then as the poor relative."

"Very convincing altogether." The green fields and woodlands beyond the coach window shimmered in slanting sunlight.

"I just adored every minute of it! I could go back and watch the whole thing over again tonight."

"I'm delighted you enjoyed it."

"Yes. I do so wish you'd been there."

But did she really? How could she see him as anything other than contemptible after that squalid episode with Francie? Surely she recognized him as a fibber, a bungler, and a sly conniver. She'd have to be a simpleton not to, and she was no simpleton. Was she perhaps suppressing her disgust at him for other purposes? He was out of his depth, floundering in unknowns. All that seemed real to him at the moment was the deliciousness of her physical presence beside him. Her voice, her scent, the splendid curve of her knee. Despite his misgivings and his mood of self-contempt, he felt himself being pulled inexorably into her force field. Suddenly he saw an opening through which he could conceivably redeem himself in her eyes, and he leapt for it. "About that wee incident at the hotel the other day," he began tentatively. A faint shadow, as from a passing cloud, crossed the girl's face.

"Oh," she said, as though she didn't care to be reminded of it.

"I thought I should explain . . ."

"There's no need to explain," she murmured, looking away. Unsure of what she might be feeling, he knew he must seize the opportunity if he was to have any hope of her at all. But he could not tell her the truth; the truth was so repugnant, even to him, it would destroy all possibility. And so he chose to lie, and to layer this fresh lie onto others he'd already told her.

"That woman," he said, speaking *sotto voce* so as not to be overheard. Bonnie seemed to squirm in her seat, as though the reminder of Francie made her skin crawl. "It's a pitiable story, that. She was Martin Michael's girl."

"Oh! Your brother. How sad."

"Sad's not the half of it." Despising the necessity, he decided to work the fertile ground of pathos, as he had with the funeral tale that had proven so effective with Bonnie. "Yes," he said, nodding gravely, "she was carrying his baby at the time."

"When he was killed?" Could he still detect a note of incredulity in her tone, or was his own discomfort with this tissue of lies distorting what she said?

"Aye. Not only that. They took the baby away from her."

"Who did?" The gears of the coach groaned as it slowed on an incline.

"The authorities—priests, nuns, government people, all of them were in it together back in them days."

"And . . . ?"

"Well you saw the result with your own eyes, there on the stairs, didn't you?" Gallagher extended a hand, as though indicating an exhibit. "A broken spirit, that's what. She took to the drink in her despair and then to the drugs to follow the drink. She's near lost her mind entirely at this point. She thought at first—when I ran into her on the street, like—that I was Martin Michael myself. Poor thing she's that addled. It's why she spoke that way to you and Carla about . . . you know."

"Yes." She looked away out the window to where two young foals were frisking on long, slender legs in a meadow of jubilant green.

"I gave her a cup of tea, tried to settle her down, like, but I fear she's lost to herself, poor soul. I provided her with what money I could spare, maybe more than I really could spare, and saw her on her way." Gallagher felt a shudder of self-disgust at using poor Francie this way,

217

betraying the truth solely to win favour with Bonnie. He still held a vague determination to do his best by Francie, to make amends somehow, if only he could figure out a way. By its mere existence, the determination led him to judge himself a little less harshly, and he held it now as a shield against the shame of his exploiting Francie for his own selfish purposes, just as he'd used her long ago. He believed that his construction of untruths was a temporary measure, forced upon him by circumstances, and would be eventually demolished and swept away once conditions improved.

"What a dreadful situation," Bonnie sighed, "that poor, poor woman." Neither spoke for some time. The coach glided on smoothly towards Wicklow.

It was Bonnie who broke the spell at last. "You know, Gallagher, I'm feeling dreadfully guilty about something."

"What's that, then?" He was instantly wary again.

"Just that you and I have never made the time to have a real in-depth discussion about your work with roses."

"Oh." Relief gusted up, catching him off balance. Perhaps he'd survived that dreadful stumble with Francie after all. Maybe he and Bonnie could put it behind them and resume where they'd left off.

"I was so excited after I learned that you'd be replacing Stephen Aubrey on the tour," she said with an impish smile. "He'd have been fine, I'm sure, but certainly not the gold mine you are."

"A gold mine? Heh, heh."

"Yes, I was thrilled at the opportunity to really pick your brain about rose propagation. As I told you, I live in Saskatoon, which has its limitations as far as roses go. But the roses you've created I think are absolutely sensational. I've read everything I could about them, and I have to tell you"—she paused for a moment, glancing down at her hands folded in her lap, then continued, almost shyly—"I've become sort of fixated on them, you know, obsessed almost. I think they're such manifestations of absolute beauty."

"Well, well now," Gallagher chortled. She'd disarmed him entirely. Glancing at the girl, he couldn't imagine her capable of anything but sincerity. Sure there was a certain cheeky slyness about her, but overall she radiated a wholesomeness entirely incompatible with duplicity.

"Yes I think hybridization is something I'd like to get into myself."
She hesitated for a moment. "I know this is a lot to ask—because you're so in demand from the others and so forth—but I was just wondering . . ."

"Yeah?"

"Well, I noticed on the itinerary that we're free to wander around Powerscourt Gardens on our own today . . ."

"Aye." He and Wilburn had briefly discussed whether they should all tour the grounds together as a group or just let people wander where they would.

"So there's no guided tour or anything."

"No, that's right."

"So I was hoping, you know, that maybe you'd agree to just you and me going around together. So that we could talk about roses as we go. Of course, if you'd rather not . . ."

"No, no," Gallagher leapt instinctively at the opportunity as though from a burning building, "I think that would be lovely." But would it? Would it be lovely or just another miscalculation on his part in a long saga of mistakes? On the one hand he'd been aware that ever since Mount Stewart he'd been failing in his obligations as tour director. Traumatized by his encounters with Sheehy and Francie, he couldn't properly focus on the gardens or the tour-goers entrusted to his leadership. The tour was in its final days and surely he should make some effort to supply a bit of the expertise for which these people had paid top dollar. On the other hand, he'd been feeling himself isolated in an increasingly hostile environment. To now have in his extremity this clever young woman seeking his companionship—well, what man anywhere in a similar predicament would be able to resist? Duty be damned; failure and foolishness be damned; he would take his chances. "But what about Carla, like?"

"Oh, she's quite happy to be rid of me for a bit." Bonnie laughed and the answering Wicklow Hills in the distance cast rainbows across the sky. "Actually, she wants to spend some time with Loretta and Suzy because they're *sooo* knowledgeable."

"They are so, bless 'em."

"Then that's what we'll do, shall we?" Bonnie beamed.

"That's what we'll do right enough," he agreed, large with largesse.

"Thank you, Gallagher, you're so sweet." Bonnie squeezed his arm convivially and returned to her seat up front. Looking at the flounce of her pleated skirt, the poetry of her rump as she moved, the gazelle legs, Gallagher believed he'd died and gone to *Tir-na-Og*, the land of the forever young.

AS the coach wheeled into the parking lot at Powerscourt, Wilburn announced over the microphone that she and Gallagher had concurred that all should wander the estate at will, take in the beauty of the grounds at their own pace, and meet back at the coach in two hours.

Gallagher knew that his first task was to steer Bonnie clear of the rest of the group and then, within the solitude, advance his subtle courting of the girl. For courtship was now his determination. Forget all the other shite; he had come by his own peculiar path, after so many years of resistance, to recognize the great truth repeated over the centuries by poets and mystics, that the only thing that truly mattered in life was to love and be loved. All of the rest was background noise, as meaningless as the thunder of surf against headlands. After so many wasted years, he'd decided, he must finally plunge deeper than the superficial skin of things. He had to seize this chance for a life that was truly a life, with love at its core. Nor was this course as preposterous as it would have seemed mere days ago. Plainly Bonnie was taken with him—how else explain her readiness to ignore the ugly episode with Francie and her eagerness now to be alone with him on this large estate. All his misgivings were now fled like wild swans before winter. He had two hours—two precious, Godsent hours in one of the world's great gardens—in which to capture the affections of this woman and redeem his aimless life. The scale of the thing, the sheer outrageous, operatic ballsiness of it, strengthened him immensely.

The interior of the great house had been ravaged by fire some years before, and only a shell of the building remained. But stepping out onto the upper terrace of the house—with brilliant Bonnie by his side, Gallagher, like Lord Powerscourt himself, surveyed his sprawling pleasure grounds with joy.

"Oh, look at that!" Bonnie exclaimed, pointing to a plump conifer on the terrace that had been clipped into a perfect conical reflection of Sugarloaf Mountain prominent above the hills beyond. "Isn't that marvellous!"

Gallagher nodded appreciatively, as though he'd been clipping the shrub himself all these years. Seeing most of the group drift down the pebbled steps to the ornate Italian garden immediately below the house, he suggested nonchalantly that he and Bonnie follow the long and near-deserted path around through the Tower Valley. She readily agreed and off they set.

"Now, Gallagher, you must tell me everything," she said, linking his arm familiarly, causing his heart to flutter like the wings of a bat against his chest.

"Everything?" He wasn't sure what she meant.

"Yes. I want to know your secrets."

"My secrets?" Quick suspicions stirred again. Was there no final shaking off these wretched misgivings?

"About hybridization. I want to know your secrets."

"Me secrets, eh? You're a naughty girl, aren't you?" Relieved, he patted the marvellous hand clasping his forearm. "Well, as you might have guessed by now, I'm one more for doin' it than talkin' about doin' it, if y'know what I mean."

"Yes, I do." She bent her head towards him pertly. She was considerably taller than himself, but as they strolled along the gravel path she had a charming way of leaning in towards him that intimated a breezy equality. "And I'd love to be doing it too. I wish I could do it with you, really learn how it's done. But I guess I'll have to settle for you telling me, at least for now."

Gallagher thrilled to the possibility that the girl was being allegorical, that their affections were already converging, more firmly than he'd imagined possible. Oh, she's deep, this girl, deep and sweet as a soft moss rose kissed by silvery dew on a summer dawn. A thin veil of overcast had trolled across the sky so that the great lawn off to their right stretched like a sea of tarnished pewter.

"The first thing you have to understand," he began studiously, as he imagined a professor of botany might begin, "is that roses are by nature bisexual . . ."

"Really? I hadn't thought of it."

"Ah, sure, they'll pollinate themselves unless you prevent them, which is as it should be in the natural course of things, but not if you want to create a new rose entirely." They were nearing the Pepperpot Tower, a lifesized folly in the woods, built to resemble a pepperpot, but Gallagher adroitly steered them past it—there was a pack of boogering little brats up on the parapet throwing pine cones at one another and threatening to destroy the mood he was so masterfully creating. "And, of course, I stick with the old ways of doing things—I'm not one for all this genetic engineering and tissue culture and all that sort of muckin' about."

"Me neither. I hate all that." Bonnie made a grimace of disgust.

"Good girl." Again he patted her hand, as though there were just the two of them now, romantic throwbacks forever at odds with the soulless ghouls of genetic manipulation. "So," he continued, smacking his lips pedagogically, "first off, you choose what you suppose might be two suitable varieties as parents, roses with the particular qualities you're after."

"I see." The voices of the warrior brats faded behind them as they walked deeper into the wooded valley.

"Just like with people, you've got two parents. One's called the pollen parent—that's the male, like. The other's the seed parent, the female."

"And I suppose the ones you choose would have to flower at the same time in order to cross-pollinate?"

"Right you are, Bonnie. There's none of your May/September romances among roses." He squeezed her darling hand again. Was he being too blatant? The hell with it! This was his chance, perhaps his only chance. You don't win a goddess by grovelling. Young Francie aside, this was the only other time in his life when the Fates had offered him a chance at abiding ecstasy. Who but a timid fool wouldn't throw caution to the winds! He would take the act of love he knew best and lay it as an offering at the feet of this woman. "Usually I bring my selected parents into the greenhouse in autumn, so. Ideally you want them flowering around the end of May and you don't want any pollinating insects getting in there and muckin' the whole thing up on you."

"Okay." She tossed her lovely hair back with a gesture of abandon that drove him wild.

"You choose a sunny day for your actual pollinating work. First off, you take a flower from the seed parent—that's the female now, mind—and carefully pull off all its petals one by one, so." Holding an imaginary rose in his left hand, he removed its petals for her, pinched between his right thumb and forefinger. "It's critical you make sure there's not even the tiniest piece of petal left." The depetalled rose seemed entirely real as he held it before her for examination. "That done, you next have to emasculate the flower by removing all its anthers to prevent self-pollination. You're familiar with what I mean by anthers, are you, Bonnie?" He squinted at her slyly.

"Of course." By now they were deep into the valley woodlands and perfectly alone. The forest through which they walked was of massive conifers from the Pacific Northwest, but the two of them were too engrossed in their rose talk to notice. "How do you remove them?" she asked.

"Take a wee pair a scissors or tweezers or something of the sort and simply nip 'em off, like." Again he mimed the delicate snipping operation with his fingers. "This leaves just the stigma of the seed parent. By the following day, if the weather's sunny and warm, the stigma will be shiny an' sticky an' what they call *receptive*."

"Receptive?" The girl's eyebrows flirted into arches.

"Aye."

"I like that." She smiled and squeezed his arm again. Jays, paradise should be so sweet!

"Then comes the critical part of gettin' the pollen from the male parent to the stigma of the female parent."

"Oh, this is so erotic! I just love it!" Bonnie was radiant.

"Steady, girl," he teased her, "steady on now. Some people use a wee paint brush for the purpose, dabbing at the pollen and brushing it carefully onto the stigma." He dabbed and brushed with a miniature and invisible brush. "Others prefer to just hold back the petals of the male so its anthers are protruding with their pollen, and gently rub the female's sticky stigma with the male's protruding anthers." Jays, he couldn't be much more blatant than this!

"Which method do you prefer?" Oh, she was coy, this enticing Bonnie!

"Neither of them" he said, almost giddy, "I prefer to use me finger."

"Your finger?" Yeah, sure, she was leading him on now, priming his pump, no doubt about it.

"Aye." He held up the knobby small finger of his right hand. "But this method requires great delicacy of touch. You can't be too rough, if you get me meaning, Bonnie."

"I think I do." She grinned.

"Good girl. You just dab the pollen off the male plant, then, ever so carefully, you rub it on the protrudin' stigma of the female, so." He rubbed his small finger delicately against imaginary stigma. "Then, if everything goes according to Hoyle, the grains of pollen will germinate and pollen tubes will work their way down to the ovary and fertilize the ovum to form an embryo. And there's your new rose in the making, as simple as that."

"Oh, Gallagher, that's beautiful how you describe it! Pure poetry. And so sensuous. You must love doing it, do you?"

"I do, Bonnie, I'll not lie to you. 'Tis the greatest feeling in the world to get a new life of yer own creation started like so. Now, naturally, not all of them are going to survive, and most of them—even if they do survive—will not make desirable varieties, for whatever reason. You could do hundreds, maybe thousands, before one of them produces a real winner."

"But you've come up with so many already."

"Ah, well, I've been lucky, let's say."

"More than luck, I would think. More like genius."

"Or just a delicate finger, so." He held up his finger again and Bonnie laughed in little ripples like wavelets on a pebbled strand. He'd won her, he knew, won her entirely by his virtuoso description.

Just then a pair of men emerged abruptly from a hidden pathway off to their left. Gallagher flinched and stiffened, certain they were after him. But the pair moved on, jabbering in Italian or Spanish or something, and he relaxed again, freshly aware that, for all the magic of it, he was on a brief reprieve from his woes, not permanent escape from them.

As they neared the Japanese Garden, just by a little cascade that trickled and splashed down a green hillside of ferns and mosses through a series of small pools, they came upon Robert and Nicole

Long. "How're you doing?" cried Gallagher buoyantly, "enjoying the gardens, are you?"

"Fabulous!" said Robert. "What a place! We've never seen anything like it, have we, Nicole?"

"It's lovely," she said shyly.

"We just walked through the woodlands," Bonnie said. "Where have you been so far?"

"Came down through the Italian Garden," said Robert. "You wouldn't believe the stonework in those steps. And the stone orbs! Out of this world. Then we came on down around the lake over here, with the big fountain and all." He gestured back towards the lake. "I tell you, they got nothing like this back in Edmonton, not even close, except maybe the West Edmonton Mall. Right, honey?"

Nicole looked wistfully down into the Japanese Garden below them and said again, "It's lovely."

Gallagher and Bonnie moved on around the lake. "They're sweet, those two, don't you think?" Bonnie mused tenderly.

"I do. There's something very appealing altogether about a marriage that's endured over the years."

"Like your parents."

"That's right, God bless 'em. Yours too?"

"No," Bonnie said pensively, "my father died when I was quite young."

"Ah, pity that."

"Yes. I used to miss him awfully. I cried on my pillow every night for the longest time. Now I can hardly even remember him, except in photographs. Funny what the mind does over time, isn't it?"

"Hm."

"Were you ever married, Gallagher?" Unseen crows were cawing raucously in the treetops above them.

"Me? No, never."

"Why not?"

"Ah, well, never found the right girl, I suppose."

"Francie wasn't her?"

"Eh?" What the hell was she doing asking about Francie? How did she even know her name?

"The story you told me—about holidaying in the Mountains of Mourne with a girl named Francie. When the ram butted you picking strawberries."

"Ah, sure." Jays, he was getting paranoid, and all from losing track of his own stories. "No. She wasn't the one, more's the pity. Mind you, she might have been, dear Francie, if circumstances had turned out different."

"What do you mean?"

"I lost her to another."

"Oh, no!"

"Yea. Feller from Belfast. Proddie an everything." Gallagher paused. Again he felt a spasm of guilt over betraying Francie, and this time it was enough to make him realize that creating a story in which he was abandoned by Francie, victimized by her, would be altogether too vile an obscenity. "Anyway, all that was long ago, and best forgotten."

"And you never met someone else?"

"Aye, one or two more, now and then."

"But never the right one?"

"Never. Not 'til now anyways."

"Oh, look!" Bonnie exclaimed, pointing. They'd wandered into the pet cemetery where rows of gravestones marked the burial spots of various animals from the estate. "Isn't this the sweetest thing!" Bonnie cried, breaking away from him. "Look at this one." A gravestone was inscribed with the name Eugenie, a Jersey cow that had produced more than 100,000 gallons of milk in her time along with Princess, an Aberdeen Angus that had been "three times Dublin Champion."

"I'd say 100,000 gallons of milk deserves remembering, wouldn't you?" Bonnie said.

"Aye," he agreed, though his enthusiasm for the dead animals was secondary to his desire to resume discussing matters of the heart.

"Oh, look here!" she cried, farther along. A rising wind swirled her skirts about her lovely legs and tossed her hair. She was entranced by a stone commemorating a Chou named Sun Yat Sen whose epitaph read:

When the body that lived at your single will
With its whimper of welcome is still how still

When the spirit that answered your every mood
Is gone where ever it goes for good.

"Oh, Gallagher," Bonnie said suddenly, pressing her face against his shoulder, "I think I'm going to cry."

"There, there," he said, mystified, and patted her softly on the shoulder. This fukkin' pet cemetery was getting everything spannered. He moved her along gently, and gradually she regained her composure.

"Sorry," she said, trying to smile while dabbing her eyes with a handkerchief, "that sad story of yours about Francie and then seeing those grave markers, well . . . I just got overcome."

"Understandable completely." He nudged his forearm over, trying to get linked with hers again, but without success. "I was moved meself by the spectacle."

"Ever since my father died," she said, "I really haven't been able to look at death. I detest it and keep it locked outside myself. I think it's better that way."

He was touched by the girl's sincerity. Surely he'd only imagined that she harboured doubts about the truthfulness of his yarns. "Well and good, if you can," he agreed, nodding sagely, "although death walks close to your shoulder in this country."

Nearing the Dolphin Pond, Gallagher spotted Carla, Loretta, and Suzy a long way off but coming in their direction. Deftly he headed Bonnie down a side path before she could notice the other women. Soon they were walking through a hillside grove of majestic pines and firs. The corrugated bark of their enormous trunks seemed thick with ancient mysteries. The sky was rapidly darkening under inky clouds boiling in from the west.

"What did you mean back there," Bonnie asked, "when you said 'not until now.' Have you found someone finally, if you don't mind my asking?"

"How could I possibly mind?" So here they were at last. Now or never, boyo, now or never.

"Well, I don't mean to pry into your personal affairs."

"Not even if they're your own affairs too?" He was stepping off the cliff's edge, prepared to risk everything now in one wild plunge. The rising wind soughed through treetops high above them.

"What do you mean? I don't follow?"

"I mean I never thought to find another after I'd lost Francie. I sealed my heart against the hurt, I believe."

"Yes, I think that happens. Just as I did with my father."

"But now I have."

"Have what? Found somebody?"

"That I have."

"Oh, I'm so glad for you, Gallagher!" She clapped her hands in glee. "Who is she—do you mind if I ask?"

"'Course I don't mind. Sure you know who she is."

"Really? It's not somebody back home then, it's someone in the group, is it? Oh, Gallagher!" Good Lord, she was being coy, teasing it out so deliciously this way.

"'Tis." He winked, playing along with her.

"You rascal, Gallagher! I had no idea." She nudged him affectionately with her elbow. "Let me guess . . ." Her playful smile was near to breaking his heart. Raindrops were beginning to splatter down through the moaning trees.

"No, you've got me," Bonnie said, surrendering, "I can't for the life of me think who it could be."

The moment had arrived. Gallagher's life was balanced at the tipping point. He could prolong the sweet agony of disclosure no further. "'Tis yerself, girl, as you know full well."

"Me?" A look of astonishment swept across her face.

"Aye, none other." He was solemnity itself now.

"Me?" she repeated.

"I've been waitin' t'talk with you about it for days." He wiped a pendant raindrop from the tip of his nose.

"Oh, Mr. Gallagher, you musn't . . ."

"But I couldn't work up the nerve somehow, what with one thing and another." He was bashful and bold together.

"But, Mr. Gallagher, please, no I . . ." All trace of playfulness had left her. Somewhere high above a branch cracked like a gunshot in the wind.

"It's a hard thing, naturally, speakin' on matters of love."

"Mr. Gallagher, I'm so sorry, there's been an awful mistake . . ." She reached out to place a consoling hand on his arm.

"No mistake at all, Bonnie, it's the heart itself I'm speakin' from now." He stood his ground against the rising tempest.

"I know, but . . ."

"I realize I've caught you comin' sideways with this, Bonnie, but I felt I could wait no longer." He could see her resistance, her incredulity—the staring eyes, the parted lips, how her body was angled away from him as though to protect itself against his advances.

"Oh, you're such a sweet man, Mr. Gallagher, but really, there's been the most dreadful misunderstanding here."

"There's no misunderstanding true love, Bonnie, and true love's what I feel for you, girl."

He opened his arms to her in graphic demonstration that she was everything to him, that without her he had nothing. The wind died abruptly and a sudden burst of sunlight illumined the dripping hush.

"But, Mr. Gallagher, please, you must understand. I think you're a dear sweet soul and I love spending time with you, hearing your stories, learning from you . . . but not . . . not in that way."

"What way's that?" He knew really, but couldn't bear to hear her say it.

"As . . . intimates."

"Intimates?" The sky was lowering again under the weight of bruise-coloured clouds. He had his chin upturned boldly.

"No, it's impossible." She said, shaking her head.

"Impossible? Why? Y're not spoken for, are you?" His resolution was crumbling as he realized how completely he'd missed the pier on this one, but he still couldn't quite accept it. All he knew was that every bit of him had been drawn to the girl, like iron filings to a magnet. She was lovely, yes, but more than that, much more than that. He had no words for it, but what she represented to him was what he believed was meant by love. And he'd thought she felt the same; at times at least, he'd been quite certain she felt the same. A grey drizzle had now closed in around them.

"You know, I guess I'd rather not discuss it," Bonnie said. "Not like this. Not here. Oh, shit, this is a mess." She wiped the moisture from her forehead impatiently, then smiled at him ruefully. "I'm so sorry this has happened."

"But, Bonnie, I thought..."

"Oh, I know! I see that, Mr. Gallagher. And I'm really flattered. Really." Again she went to touch his arm but drew back in mid-gesture. "And you know I care for you, quite profoundly in a way." Her voice had turned artificially gooey, as though she were speaking to a troubled child. "Like today. It's been perfectly lovely talking about hybridization and everything. To me you're a mentor, don't you see? An inspiration. Someone to learn from. Someone to admire and emulate." Her hair was going limp in the drizzle.

"But nothing more than that?"

"Well, not a romance. No. I mean, it's preposterous."

"Preposterous?" The word was a slap in his face.

"No, I mean... I'm sorry," she said, stumbling over her words, trying to make amends. "It's an awful misunderstanding. If only I'd known..."

"Aye." Gallagher, once toppled, was lost. Down he went like a felled tree, down into darkness. Raindrops were splattering heavily now. He looked forlornly at the girl. She was surely slipping from his grasp. Dabbing her eyes with a handkerchief, though whether from tears or the rain he couldn't tell, Bonnie began moving slowly backwards away from him into the thickening mizzle. The wind was a cold knife stabbing at him maliciously. He wanted to cry aloud, to shriek with the dripping ache of love. He extended a hand towards her, but with a regretful smile Bonnie shook her head slowly, kissed her fingertips and held them for a moment towards him, then turned and walked away.

■ TWENTY-TWO ■

OBVIOUSLY THERE'D been some balls-up with the address
Bosco had given him over the phone because Gallagher now found
himself standing outside the presbytery of an imposing stone church.
It was just off Northumberland Road, close enough to his hotel that he
could have walked over, but he'd had no heart for walking and caught
a taxi instead. His spirit was entirely shivered from his failure to win
Bonnie. And the loss of Bonnie had been only the beginning of disasters.
Once she'd rebuffed his advances there in Powerscourt, everything had
begun to disintegrate. Mount Usher Gardens in the afternoon were
awash with gloom and heavy rain, the celebrated Robinsonian wild
garden reduced to a squelchy mess. The Vartry River flowing through
the garden was defiled with slimy green entrails of filamentous algae.
Most of the group had huddled dispiritedly in the tearoom making half-
hearted small talk and sipping tepid tea. The coach ride back to Dublin
might have been a funeral cortege. Ruth Wilburn strove against the
gloom, as though it were a failing on her part, by playing audio tapes of
corny Irish comedians at whose jokes nobody laughed. Bitter gall they
were drinking on this garden tour. Bitter gall and vile. Back at the hotel,
each of them had fled to their room alone. Gallagher was engulfed by
despondency. Bonnie was lost to him, that was certain. This was a loss
in the same order of magnitude as losing his home. Some essential part
of himself had been torn away and would not be restored. It was as
though she had been a missing element of his spirit, momentarily
rediscovered, only to have her withdraw again into the mist, leaving
him a partial being, a shell, the facade of a burnt-out building like Lord
Powerscourt's gutted mansion.

He thought of mad Francie; she, too, had lost something of herself, the husk of her left to walk the streets, emaciated and ruined. They
were a pair, he and Francie, pledged to each other all that time ago, and
ever after jointly married to misfortune. He still had the dirty work
with Sheehy to do, though the dangers of that now seemed to him less
consequential than they had. Everything was less consequential now.

His entire mission was a shambles. The family farm remained his last and only chance, although even a successful outcome there might not suffice to heal the grievous lesions to his spirit.

The cabbie had insisted that this was the correct address, snatched his fare rudely, and sped off. Grubby little pisser anyway. The afternoon's storm clouds had been blustered away by a brisk west wind and now golden evening light gloried over the domes and spires of the city. Gallagher mounted the worn sandstone steps to the presbytery with rising apprehension. He couldn't fathom what Bosco would be doing here in a rectory. He rang the doorbell and waited. A massive construction of mahogany and elaborately leaded glasswork, the door confronted him with disapproval. Although he was wearing his suit jacket and cardigan, he hadn't bothered with a tie, nor brushed his shoes, nor shaved, and felt himself too shabby for the daunting ecclesiastical formality of the place. He was a schoolboy again, in ragged short pants and scuffed boots, trembling before the visiting bishop.

The door was opened by a tall, gaunt priest in a clerical suit and Roman collar. For a split second Gallagher failed to recognize his brother. "Good evening, Patrick," Bosco said, extending a long and bony hand, "good to see you." Completely unbalanced at finding his brother in a priest's garb, Gallagher shook hands and shuffled nervously. "Do come in," Bosco said dryly, and ushered Gallagher through an entrance hall into a visitors' parlour. He was mesmerized by sunlight filtered through stained glass and the gleam of richly polished oak. Thick scents of beeswax and mortuary lilies assailed him. Somewhere a clock was ticking insistently. Sensations from the churchliness of his childhood—its commingled antiquity and mystery and fear—swathed him like a suffocating blanket. He hadn't been near a church or a priest since leaving Ireland.

He and Bosco seated themselves in facing stiff-backed parlour chairs. Gallagher was shocked at how his brother looked. There was something bloodless, almost cadaverous about him. His large ears still protruded, level with his thin lips, but where in youth this peculiarity had given his face a mischievous, impish appearance, now the pendant ears merely accentuated the face's gaunt mournfulness. As people do after a long absence, Gallagher had expected his brother would still be the youngster he'd last seen years ago, not this solemn spectre. On the wall behind Bosco a crucified Christ hung by blood-dripping nails, his head lolling to one side, the dregs of life ebbing away. The Saviour's mournful eyes stared balefully at Gallagher. Who died for our sins, was crucified, and rose again on the third day.

"Well, Patrick, and how have you been keeping?" Bosco broke the ice but with a neutral, dispassionate tone. There seemed nothing left of the laughing lad Bosco had been.

"Good enough, all things considered," Gallagher offered tentatively. He would, he knew, have to set his woes aside for the moment if he was to make any headway here.

"It's Canada you're living in then, is it?"

"That's right, Vancouver. So you're a priest then are you, Bosco?"

"I should think so, Patrick, dressed like this and living here."

"Heh, heh," Gallagher fake laughed, unsure whether Bosco was being funny or not. "I'd never have guessed you'd become a priest."

"No, I suppose not."

Gallagher had seen raw oysters floating in ale that had more life to them than this bloodless Bosco. I mean, was it not himself who should be down and out and requiring emotional support after the heart smash of Bonnie's rejection? But instead of receiving comfort, he was having to pump some life into this ecclesiastical corpse. He poked the embers of fraternal reminiscence to try warm things up a bit. "What was it you always said back then you wanted to be—an architect, wasn't it?"

"Yes, that's right."

"You were always after building something or other, weren't you? Even as a nipper you'd be putting little sticks to make a bridge across the gutter." The priest smiled slightly, but it was a smile as mirthless as the soughing of wind across a stony hillside. Gallagher pressed on. "Do you remember telling me what your great ambition in life was, Bosco?"

"I'm not sure that I do." Gallagher could see tiny galaxies of dust spinning in a diagonal shaft of sunlight that slanted down across the parlour.

"You wanted to design a skyscraper taller than the Empire State Building," Gallagher said, grinning affably. "Do you not remember that?"

The priest seemed to look inside himself for a moment, his slender fingers knitted together in his lap. Gallagher had never encountered anyone so devoid of animation. Bosco reminded him of those things in caves—was it stalagmites or stalactites, he could never keep the damn things sorted—that just hung there dripping in the dark.

"So how'd you get to be a priest and all, Bosco?" This was getting to be damned hard work, keeping the energy up, but Gallagher remained unswervingly aware of the high stakes at play here. Any miscalculation, however slight, might prove to be ruinous. Bosco was just about to reply when they were interrupted by a discreet tapping at the parlour door.

"Yes?" Bosco answered.

"Excuse me, Father," a female voice said from behind the door, "your dinner is served."

"Thank you, Veronica," Bosco replied, and turning to Gallagher with a gesture of his hand, said, "Shall we?"

The brothers rose and made their way to an adjacent dining room dominated by an enormous oval table of oak. Eight chairs ringed the table and a massive matching sideboard squatted blockily against the far wall. Above the table a brilliant crystal chandelier glittered. There was no window in the room. Instead, large Gothic paintings of biblical scenes in heavy gilt frames dominated the walls. Gallagher made out an overweight Salome holding for King Herod a platter upon which lay the severed head of John the Baptist, its teeth grinning in death. Just the thing for eating dinner by, Gallagher thought. The two men seated themselves at opposite sides of the oval. The table setting was exquisite, fine china edged in gold, oversized silver cutlery, and crystal glasses on an intricate lace tablecloth.

"My curate's away for the evening," Bosco said, unfolding a linen napkin and spreading it on his lap. "We shall dine alone."

"Fine," Gallagher said. "Just the two of you then, is there?"

"That is correct. As you can see," he said ruefully, his reedy hand indicating the empty table, "this was once home to a sizeable group of clergy. But times have changed and we are no longer what we were." A sense of hopeless resignation seemed to press down upon the priest, reinforced by the disconcerting hollowness of the room; voices resonated strangely in its cold emptiness.

Just then a portly woman bustled in carrying an enormous tray loaded with platters that she placed on the table between the two men.

"Thank you," Bosco said. "Veronica, this is my brother, Patrick."

"Ah, yes," she said, a motherly smile lighting up her florid face, "the gardener! I saw you on the telly there with Margaret Foley and weren't the two of you so clever together with the names of all the roses and whatnot."

"Are you a bit of a gardener yourself then, Veronica?" Gallagher welcomed the woman's homespun liveliness as relief from the sepulchral Bosco.

"Ah, well, not like yourself at all," Veronica flattered him, "but I muck about a bit in me own little way, don't I, Father?"

"Veronica is actually a very accomplished gardener," Bosco told Gallagher. "She does all the gardens for us here besides the housework."

"Just like women everywhere!" Veronica laughed.

"Thank you, Veronica, that will be all for now," Bosco said.

"Will you be wanting tea or coffee?" she asked, gently rebuffing his dismissal.

"Patrick?" Bosco cocked an inquiring eye.

"A cup of tea would be lovely," Gallagher said.

"A pot of tea then, please, Veronica."

"Very good, Father," she said and left the room, closing the door behind her.

Bosco joined his hands in prayer and lowered his head. "Thank you, O Lord, for the bounty You have seen fit to bestow upon us this day, poor sinners though we are. We humbly and gratefully accept these gifts from Your great goodness. We thank You for the return of our brother Patrick and pray that he may be bathed in Your redeeming grace, as may we all through Christ Our Lord, Amen."

Gallagher made a grunting noise that might have passed as an Amen.

The meal consisted of poached salmon in a cream sauce, with wild rice, fresh asparagus, and steamed baby carrots and peas. "Still eatin' fish on Fridays, I see," Gallagher observed jovially.

"Yes, it's no longer a requirement," Bosco said, "but it's one of those old practices I see no good reason to abandon."

"Farmed salmon, is it?" Gallagher wouldn't touch the stuff at home, it was that contaminated with antibiotics and sea lice.

"I suppose so, yes." Bosco seeemed indifferent to its source.

The meal was largely wasted on the brothers. Bosco took only tiny portions as befitted the ascetic he'd obviously become. Gallagher's spirits were too low to accommodate much in the way of digestion. His mind drifted back repeatedly to the heartsore scene of Bonnie retreating from him in the mizzle. They ate for a while in a silence scratched only by knives and forks against plates. Gallagher's gaze kept drifting to another of the old paintings that surrounded them, this one a grisly rendition of Jesus encountering a group of lepers with their bells. By now Gallagher was thinking that a wee drop to drink wouldn't have been amiss, but the sole decanter on the table held iced water in which slices of lemon floated like bloated minnows.

"So the old ones are in a home now, you were saying." Gallagher launched his opening gambit in what he now suspected was going to be a very challenging game.

"Yes, I got them settled at a small facility in Skibbereen." Bosco dabbed his lips with the napkin, folded it precisely, and placed it on the table.

"And they're right enough with the change, are they?"

"A fair bit of grumbling and complaining, as you'd expect. But they're content enough in their own peculiar way. Are you planning to visit them, Patrick?"

"Well I might, you know, after the tour, like. But how do you think they'd take it, me poppin' in after all these years?"

"I'm not certain," Bosco said, looking straight at him with pale grey eyes, "but it might very well be your last opportunity to see them alive."

"Are they still right in the head, like?" Gallagher glanced back at the lepers to avoid Bosco's fishy scrutiny.

"He's a bit vague nowadays. Forgetting things, mixing things up. A mild form of dementia, I suppose. But she's still sharp as a tack."

"So they'd recognize me if I were to visit?"

"Oh, yes, they'd know you all right."

"And what about the farm then?" Gallagher didn't especially want to wade into the quicksand complexities of reconciliation with his parents. The farm was more tangible and certainly more urgent. Somewhere off in the hall a clock struck sonorously.

"Yes, that's largely why I wanted to get together with you. Of course, it's a very difficult situation . . ."

Veronica re-entered the room with the tea things on a tray, placed them before Bosco, and removed the remains of dinner, sniffing to herself, presumably over how little had been eaten, but saying nothing.

"Thank you, Veronica, that will do for the evening," Bosco said.

"Very good, Father." She paused with the tray of dishes. "A great pleasure to meet you I'm sure, Mr. Gallagher," she said with a merry look, as though she were in on a joke that he hadn't understood. "Good luck to you."

"Goodbye," Gallagher said. That was his word for the day. *Slán*. Goodbye. Goodbye, Bonnie. Goodbye every fukkin' thing.

Once the housekeeper had closed the door behind her, Bosco picked up the thread. "Yes, disposition of the farm has raised some difficult considerations indeed."

"Must be worth a fair bit now I would think."

"Indeed. We had an appraiser in to look at it. The value of waterfront property in that part of the country has risen astronomically in recent years. Having the old abbey ruins on it makes it that much more valuable again."

"Who'd have thought that old heap of stones would ever be worth anything?" Gallagher remembered how as kids they'd played among the remnant stone walls and arches of the ruins, inventing ghosts and marauding raiders from the sea. Bosco would build miniature towns from the rock rubble and Francie would join them sometimes, to listen to Patrick telling stories about the fine lords and ladies, the monks and magicians, who had dwelt in castles of stone along the coast.

"It's one of the great conundrums of our times," Bosco mused, "the inordinate treasuring of antiquities while simultaneously destroying the values of which those antiquities were a manifestation."

"Eh?" Gallagher had missed his brother's meaning.

237

"No matter." Bosco waved the idea away with one hand as he poured their tea with the other. His brother seemed to Gallagher gripped by a melancholy longing for another age, another world.

"So what did the appraiser have to say?" Gallagher took up his dainty teacup. Really, a spot of whiskey was what was called for in this type of business. He wondered if he should ask; but there was something in Bosco's solemnity that made Gallagher feel insecure and just the least bit timid.

"I'd had some idea of rising real estate values," Bosco said, putting his own teacup down without having sipped from it, "but frankly I was astounded at his evaluation. One significant factor appears to be that two nearby properties of quite similar size and prospect have recently been purchased by entertainment industry people."

"Movie stars, you mean?"

"One from London, a television and movie personality. The other's a well-known musician from Dublin here."

"Big money then."

"Extravagant amounts of money." Bosco sipped his tea. "The purchase prices they paid, plus what they're now putting into their buildings, have pushed the values of nearby properties even higher. Of course," Bosco said, putting his cup neatly back on its saucer, "these wealthy outsiders work a great hardship on the old families who wish to continue living where their people have lived for generations but can no longer afford to do so."

"I know what you mean," Gallagher said warmly, thinking of his own home. "So what's the old place worth, Bosco?" He wanted firm figures upon which to base negotiations.

"The appraisal came in at just under a million and a half euros."

"A million and a half!" Gallagher spluttered, spewing a spray of tiny tea droplets that spotted the spotless tablecloth. "Euros! That's near on two million dollars!"

"Approximately." Bosco shared none of his excitement. But great Christ almighty, here was Gallagher's redemption on hand at last. Even a half of that astonishing total could see him out of the woods, securing his place and his beloved roses in perpetuity. All right then, all else might be a ruin—he may have loved and lost with Bonnie; he may have buggered everything with poor Francie; he may have been bullied by cops and thugs—but if he could emerge from his travails with a million bucks in his pocket, well, what does any of that really matter in the end? He didn't concern himself with whether or not the capital could be taken out of Ireland, gladly succumbing to the marvellous illusions that big money can conjure, about its power to make all problems disappear.

"Naturally, some portion of the estate is to be set aside to ensure that our parents are able to live out the remainder of their time in comfort and dignity," Bosco said.

"Of course." Gallagher was more than sufficiently benevolent to write off a few thousand in this way. The lepers with their bells stared down at him.

"As for the remainder," Bosco said, then paused and looked away to a far corner of the room before returning his gaze to Gallagher, "our parents have expressed to me and have specifically enshrined within their will a determination that the property be sold and the proceeds applied to the Church's missionary work in Africa."

"Eh?" Gallagher was gobsmacked. This was like being struck by fukkin' lightning on a cloudless day. "Missionary work? What?"

"As you surely remember, Patrick, Mother especially was always a deeply religious person, and extremely devoted to Holy Mother Church."

"Oh, aye." Gallagher remembered their piety well enough, their grovelling in front of the parish priest and handing over to the church more money than they could afford. Endless breast-beating and fumbling with rosary beads. Just about shitting themselves with anxiety on the day of the priest's annual visit to their miserable little hole of a cottage. Not to mention when the bishop waddled into town every few years. Same as he remembered getting regularly slapped about by the old josser as punishment for some perceived transgression on his part. His father had a habit of seizing him by the earlobe, pinching it between his horny thumb and index finger, and twisting his ear 'til he was ready to scream with the pain of it.

"Even Father became increasingly devout in his latter years," Bosco said. "A portion of that I attribute to my having entered the priesthood and then spent whatever time I could spare from my ministry in order to be with them."

"Sure enough." Gallagher could just picture Saint Bosco buttering up the old ones with an eye to inheritance. His astonishment at what his brother had just told him was quickly giving way to outrage. But for the moment he had to ignore the stinking vindictiveness of the thing because he was feverishly searching for some angle by which he could prevent this idiotic giveaway.

"As well I think their piety deepened over the years as a way of softening some of the crueller blows life had dealt them," Bosco said.

Gallagher knew Bosco was meaning him. Conveniently forgetting, of course, that this particular prodigal son had dealt his parents far fewer cruel blows than what he'd suffered from the old man's fist. Gallagher was of half a mind to say as much but held his tongue while there still remained a remnant of hope that something could be salvaged from this debacle.

"But did they have any real idea what they were doin' here with the farm?" Gallagher said warmly. "I mean, we're not talkin' about a pittance to be sent to help out some godforsaken orphanage in Uganda."

"Absolutely they did." On top of everything else, Bosco's sanctimoniousness was really beginning to grate.

"They knew how much the place could fetch?"

"They had some idea. By the time the appraisal was done Father's comprehension of it may have been a bit vague, but Mother grasped it completely."

"And they still wanted to give it all away?"

"To a worthy cause that they believed in, yes. And I completely support them in that decision."

Oh, you would, Gallagher thought to himself, but held his tongue.

"You know, Patrick, if I was a younger man," Bosco mused abstractedly, fingering the delicate handle of his teacup, "I might consider going off to labour in the African missions myself. The church there is so much more vital and dynamic than this poor hollow ruin of a ministry we're left with here. Ghosts and whispers is all we have, that and heretical new ideas designed to speed the Church's imminent collapse."

Gallagher was far more concerned with his own financial collapse, but before he could get a word in, Bosco resumed his gloomy narrative. "I so admire the African bishops. Men of purpose and integrity. None of this disgusting compromise over married priests and gay priests and women priests. They'll be wanting to ordain cats and dogs before they're through, some of these great reformers." There was almost a sneer in Bosco's expression. "Birth control and abortion and God only knows what other abominations. The African bishops are having none of it, and I admire them immensely for it. The gospel true and pure, as it came from the lips of our Saviour Himself and the insights of the evangelists. How fulfilling it would be to apply oneself to a ministry like that . . ." Bosco faded away, musing on an apostolate less desolate than his own.

Gallagher brought it back to earth. "But, Jaysus, Bosco, the whole inheritance."

"Please, Patrick."

"Aye, sure, it's all well and good for the Africans, but what about you and me?"

"Well, as you see, I have no need of money at all." Bosco spread his hands to indicate that he had everything he needed. "Whereas the Church can make very good use of those funds in places far less fortunate than this."

"I suppose so." Gallagher had to be more careful than ever not to say what he was really thinking. "But it does leave me out of the equation altogether, does it not?"

"Yes, it does." Bosco's dreary passionlessness was driving Gallagher crazy. He wanted to grab his brother by his pendant ears and give his head a good shake. "And that's a painful thing for all of us, I'm sure."

"I am the eldest son here, Bosco, and should by rights inherit the place."

"Normally, yes, but these are hardly normal circumstances, are they?"

"How not?" Gallagher sounded sharper than he'd intended.

"Oh, come along, Patrick, let's not play games." Bosco leaned forward, his elbows on the table, his buzzard face and neck all lines and stringy sinews. "You broke your mother's heart when you pilfered their life savings and then fled without so much as a fare thee well."

"It wasn't that *simple*, Bosco." Gallagher punched the word out.

"Wasn't it?"

"No it was not!" Gallagher was getting really vexed at this over-righteous arsehole, brother or not. "I was in a terrible fix. My life was in danger. I had to flee and I had to do it secretly so as not to put any of you in danger as well. It was in fact a considerable sacrifice on my part."

The priest gave him an unctuous smile. "The only danger you were in was from Tom O'Sullivan, who, as you knew, would have wrung your neck if he'd have got his hands on you after what you did to his poor daughter."

"I did my best for Francie, whether you believe it or not. It was partly for her I took the money."

"Are you trying to suggest that you gave it to her?"

"Not exactly, no, but I had her in mind for it." Gallagher knew he dare not mention anything about a planned abortion. "But circumstances turned on me and I had to flee for my life."

"Please, Patrick, spare me any of your gallant Republican nonsense. You stole from your own parents and abandoned them, just as you abandoned poor Francie after impregnating her." He paused for a moment, considering, then continued, "She lives here in the city now, you know."

"Aye, I made a point of looking her up, to see if I could give her a bit of a hand."

"So she told you, did she, that she gave the baby up for adoption?"

"Yeah." That wasn't quite how Francie had put it, but he let it go.

"She came to see me a couple of years ago, asking for my help in locating the child."

"Why would she ask you?"

"Well, he's my nephew, after all, isn't he?" The point being that holy Uncle Bosco would be far more caring and considerate than the kid's own deadbeat father.

"Did you find him?"

"I did eventually, yes."

"And?"

"Typical horrific story. Bounced from one inadequate foster home to another. Years of abuse and deprivation. Poor fellow never had a chance. He was in juvenile prison at the time and extremely hostile. I believe he's still incarcerated for several quite serious crimes. I considered that nothing would be served by reuniting Francie and him, so I made the difficult decision to deceive Francie, telling her I was unable to locate him. I'm not sure that you or anyone else could give her what she needs at this point."

"She seemed in a bad way, all right."

"Dreadful." Bosco shook his head sadly. "Such a lovely young woman reduced to that."

"Drugs was it?"

"Drugs, alcohol, prostitution. Every conceivable degradation. I have no illusions about who she is and the squalid life she lives."

"What a pity." Gallagher was working flat-out to try to beat back waves of self-recrimination.

"A pity indeed. And yourself unhappily at the heart of the tragedy. Speaking frankly, Patrick, I find both Francie and her son, your son, less to blame for their circumstances than you are." Gallagher squirmed to hear his brother say what his own heart had been whispering to him ever since he'd encountered Francie. He felt he couldn't deal with any of this just now. Himself to blame for so much misery. It was brutal, insupportably brutal, and equally inescapable. He glanced wildly around the room, but the Gothic monstrosities of the Baptist's severed head and the lepers' scabrous bodies leered at him.

"You acted shamefully," Bosco continued, obviously considering he'd gained the upper hand now, "without regard for anyone but yourself. You might at least have sought to make reparation over time, to right the wrongs you'd done." Bosco had the palms of both hands pressed on the table, shoulders back, head high, like a patriarch passing judgement. "Instead we had nothing but silence from you. We had no idea where you were, whether you were alive or dead. Apparently you had no thought at all for the anguish you'd caused. And so in time you ceased to exist for us, Patrick, except for the indelible stain you'd left behind."

"It was no million dollars I took!" Gallagher cried defensively. Undermined most thoroughly by the revelations about Francie and their child, he sought to argue the less damaging charge of theft, but he was finding it impossible to get a leg up onto any moral high ground. It was as though his foot kept sliding down some godforsaken turf bank where the dark bog water would squelch out under your boot.

"No, but it was what they'd scrimped and scraped to save over all those years," Bosco said. A red rash was rising on his scrawny neck above the Roman collar. "Mother told me later that their intention had always been to leave the farm to you and give me that money to earn a degree in architecture. You had a knack for growing things, we all knew that, and I had my heart set on architecture. But with the money gone, that put a finish to that. I ended up at the seminary at Maynooth instead, the only school we could afford." Bosco ran a finger under the chafing collar. "Due entirely to your own selfish actions, Patrick, you've forfeited any claim to the farm which otherwise would have been yours in due course. It's a bitter irony how things have unfolded, isn't it?" The way he smiled at Gallagher contained a disconcerting blend of the trenchant, the sardonic, and the triumphant.

"Bosco, I'm sorry to hear all this, I truly am." Gallagher was feeling crushed beneath an immense weight of sadness over the mess he'd made of things. He wished with all his heart he had done better, been wiser, acted more nobly. But he hadn't. He'd made a cock-up of it with the girl he loved, as well as with his mother, whom he also loved. And Bosco too, back then. He'd betrayed them all, and the stench of that betrayal lingered still, pungent and repulsive. But he couldn't afford to let himself be swamped by his past. It was over and done with; nothing could be changed. He must deal with the urgencies of the present, come hell or high water. He considered whether a touch of contrition might help in the present circumstances. "I'd no idea at the time, Bosco," he said softly, "we were only lads after all."

"Yes we were," Bosco said, nodding solemnly, "and I've forgiven you in my heart, truly I have. After being angry for far too long, there came a turning in the road, as Mother used to say. With the insight of God's grace, I eventually realized that it was actually a blessing that had been sent me, the fact that I became a priest because of your misdeeds."

"Aye, that's the positive way to look at a thing." Gallagher tapped the tabletop in approval.

"Our parents, however, never forgave you."

"Ah, no." Gallagher felt another pang of remorse entirely disconnected from the money.

"You were always Mother's favourite, you knew that, her first-born son. She was bitter at your betrayal of her love, Patrick. Far more than about the theft itself, it was your callous betrayal of her affection she could never forgive." Bosco folded his arms as though to reinforce the immovability of their mother's hurt. "Although I've counselled her repeatedly to seek forgiveness in her heart, in the true spirit of Christian charity, she cannot. She remains bitter about it to this day."

"She's not forgiven me?"

Bosco shook his head. "Neither of them has. Whether or not they'd accept you now if you went to seek reconciliation, I couldn't say. I do know, however, that they've purposively excluded you from any inheritance whatsoever."

"They have?" Gallagher's hopes were swill gurgling down a gutter.

"Both in their will and in their expressed intent to me as holder of power of attorney. They might perhaps find it in their hearts to forgive you, but I've no doubt whatsoever that they will not even consider altering the provisions they've made with respect to the estate, and if they thought you were cozying up to them now just to try alter that, you'd only be making things worse than they already are."

Gallagher sat in silence, slumped in his chair, his half cup of tea unfinished. A storm of emotions was roiling in his mind. He could feel an urgency of adrenalin roaring into his bloodstream. Bitter regret and self-recrimination assailed him. Foolish, selfish, impetuous—he'd smashed everything he held dear and ruined the lives of those he loved best. All of that was true. But long ago, long ago. When he was only a boy. When he'd known no better. When all about him were liars and connivers too. And it was also true that his home and his beloved roses were now surely lost. Needlessly lost. He was to be deprived of what he loved best in this poxbottle world merely because of long-held grievances and sanctimonious stupidity. All he could see was a mountain of lovely green money, a torrent of dosh flowing away from him into the bulging coffers of a church that had blighted his life from the moment of his conception. Wasn't it enough that they'd robbed him of his childhood, made him grovel and snivel and hate himself for years as a poor, worthless sinner. Wasn't it that ignorant priest who'd betrayed Francie's confession and triggered the awful consequences. Now here they were stealing his inheritance too. Oh, the fukkers! And fukkin' Bosco with his nose up his arse orchestratin' the whole filthy business. The eldest son cut off entirely, the sacred laws of birthright breached, his rightful inheritance stolen out from under him to provide these sanctimonious arseholes with fancy dinners provided by smiling servants. It was enough to make you vomit, really it was. Remorse and anger raged against each other like clashing storm fronts from off the Atlantic.

Bosco interrupted Gallagher's interior tirade. "Do you still attend church nowadays, Patrick?"

"Eh?"

"Are you still practising your faith?"

"Well, I'm not so much at going to church anymore—there's not one convenient where I live, like."

"I see."

"But I'm still true to the teachings and the general idea of the thing." He was holding on to his rage like a snarling dog on a leash while answering Bosco's silly questions.

"And confession?"

"Ah, no, they've done away with that, at least in Canada they have. You don't have to tell the priest anymore. You just sort of feel sorry in general and then they give everyone together the apo . . . apolos . . ."

"Absolution."

"That's it."

"And do you?"

"Not for a wee while." He was answering by rote, most of his brain still churning with a frenzy about how he could reverse his disinheritance. Not only would the money help him secure his home, he rationalized, but also he could maybe make some reparation to Francie, get her into treatment or something. That would be a far wiser use of the money than it going to some fundamentalist African bishop. Maybe a legal challenge was the thing. Go to the courts. Demand his rights under the law. But, realistically, could he afford the lawyers? And wouldn't it be a kangaroo court anyway with him, a disgraced expatriate, trying to challenge the almighty Church and his own brother, a priest? He'd as much chance of winning at that as he would an Olympic marathon.

"Would you like me to hear your confession now?"

"What?"

"To confess your sins."

Gallagher couldn't believe it. Was Bosco seriously proposing that he get down on his knees and start blubbering his mortals and venials to him? Sure, he had a few stains on his record—who doesn't?—but what the hell business was it of Bosco's. Same old story with this bunch, rob you of your self-respect then grab your money too.

"Some things are above the fashion of the moment," Bosco explained, his grey eyes as mournful as those of any repentant sinner. "The sacrament of Penance remains as relevant today as it's ever been. I could hear your confession. Give you absolution. Lift from your shoulders the dreadful weight you've been carrying all these years. It might be a beginning, Patrick."

"A beginning of what?" Was Bosco hinting that a penitential show of faith on his part was a necessary first step towards a reconciliation that might lead to his reinstatement as legitimate heir?

"Of opening your heart to the redemptive energy of Divine Love."

"Oh, I see, yeah."

"I'm thinking of your patron saint, Patrick, when he climbed the sacred mountain and spent forty days and forty nights banishing the dragons and snakes and demonic beings that assailed him."

"Aye." Gallagher hated all this old religious rubbish. Grown-up people clinging to fantastic stories no more real than Santa Claus.

"I feel you are beset by demons, brother."

"Right you are." What the hell would Bosco know about demons while cloistered in this morgue where nothing real would ever menace him? Gallagher had faced more demons in the last two days than his brother would see in a decade.

"You remember the story of your blessed namesake standing on the heights of *Croag Padraig* and being assailed by the demons that infested all of Ireland, the evil influences encouraged by vile pagan practises and filthy rites." Bosco almost spat the last words, as though

247

roving mobs of depraved Druids were running amok on the streets of Dublin. "Remember how the malignant beings accosted the saint in the form of hideous black birds, thousands of ghastly birds of prey. They filled the air around him so that the holy man could see neither earth nor sky." Bosco spoke with a rapt intensity that he'd shown no trace of all evening, staring up into the chandelier as though its glinting crystals were a flock of murderous birds. His brother's mind, Gallagher realized, was consumed with apocryphal battles between the powers of Heaven and the dark forces of Lucifer. "He prayed to God Almighty to disperse the demons, but his prayers went unanswered. He cried aloud but his tears were in vain." Gallagher was astonished at how Bosco was working himself up, like one of those oily evangelicals you see on TV. "But even in his desolation, assailed by these vile creatures from hell, Patrick did not waver in his faith in God. By the power of his faith, after much travail, he cast that heinous congregation into the waters of Clew Bay." Bosco made a violent casting motion, as though throwing the forces of darkness onto the parquet floor. "And then you know what happened, brother?" Bosco posed the question with wide-eyed urgency.

"What's that?"

"An angel appeared before him and announced that his prayers had been answered, that the Irish people would remain true to their Christian faith until the final day of Judgement." Looking at his brother's rapturous face, it occurred to Gallagher that Bosco might be not only a deluded fool but actually quite mad. Maybe the whole thing about the will was just a figment of this same fantasy world. He wondered if this might help in a legal challenge. Call into question Bosco's mental stability. But uncannily, as though reading his mind, Bosco said, "It was Patrick's disinterestedness in material things that formed the bulwark of his faith. He slept upon cold stone, went barefoot through snow and ice, wore only a rough hair shirt to mortify the flesh. Whenever wealthy converts to his preaching offered him precious gifts, he declined them. He had come to Ireland not to enrich himself"—Bosco's mad gaze was full of slimy insinuation—"but rather to bestow upon her the most precious gift of all: abiding faith in Divine Truth. To that end he persevered in fasting and prayer and penance."

Oh, sure, Gallagher was thinking, these God-fearing wankers are forever disinterested in material wealth but somehow always end up getting their hands on it. And here's bonkers Bosco eulogizing Saint Patrick sleeping on cold stone and going barefoot and all the rest of it, while Bosco's living like a medieval prince with his fine crystal and linen sheets. The accumulated vexations of the day were building towards an explosive pressure inside him and he wasn't sure how much more of Bosco's daft ranting he could tolerate.

"The demons are within us, Patrick, you know that," Bosco carried on, oblivious. "The demons are the fears we carry in our hearts." The priest pressed his hand against his own breast. "The fears we carry in our hearts. But we can banish those fears as Saint Patrick himself did on his holy mountain. Will you not do the same, brother, will you not fall on your knees, confess your wrongdoings, and be bathed in the redemptive love of our Blessed Saviour?"

Gallagher had heard enough. If there was even a smidgen of hope that he could get his hands on the money, he wasn't beneath a bit of religious malarkey beforehand, but he'd be fukked if he was going to go through all that fuss and bother and not come away with a euro to show for it. "Bosco," he said suddenly, throwing his napkin onto the table and scraping back his chair violently, "do us a favour and call me a taxi right now, will you?"

Bosco sat unmoving for a moment, his euphoric train of thought derailed. "But . . ."

"But nothing," Gallagher snapped. "You've conspired with the old ones to steal my inheritance out from under me and now you've got the gall to sit there preachin' about divine love and redemptive energy and all that shite and expectin' me to get down on my knees and confess everything to you. I tell you, Bosco, if you weren't me own brother I'd give you a kick up the arse so hard you'd never sit on it again. Now call me a taxi and shut the fuk up!"

TWENTY-THREE

STRANGELY, GALLAGHER slept more soundly that night, after the great Battle of Bosco, than he had for weeks. With the chimera of the family farm gone forever, as surely as his roses and his home were now lost, as surely as the love of Bonnie was lost, he had little left to lose. There was no goad to kick against. Drained of tension and striving, he was an empty vessel, no piss and vinegar to spill, floating in zero gravity.

Ruth Wilburn approached him again at breakfast, but her intrusion didn't detract from the simple comfort he was deriving from a bowl of creamy oatmeal. "Well, you'll never guess what, Mr. Gallagher," she said, clattering her handbag and satchel onto the table and scraping a chair back in order to join him. She was wearing her brown almost-uniform again. "I received a call late last night; luckily I hadn't tucked in just yet, although my John had toddled off long before, but I'd checked the doors and turned off the lights and everything else, and was just about to climb into bed for a good read—I love a half-hour with a good book before dozing off, and I've got a wonderful Maeve Binchy on the go just now—when the phone rang. And what do you think?"

Gallagher, staring at her as though she were a black hole, didn't think anything.

"Our visit to Anthony House this morning has been cancelled."

"Oh."

"The final garden of our tour, an absolute must-see, and here they pull the plug on us, literally at the eleventh hour." She rolled her eyes to underscore the impossibility of certain people. "All terribly mysterious about it they were too, as though it was some state secret that required their keeping the garden closed today. Of course, it's new money has taken over the estate and, between you and me, they don't have a clue." She pursed her lips in disapproval. "The place will be back on the market within a year or two, you mark my words, and her ladyship-in-waiting will be back where she belongs." Wilburn looked quite pleased about this inevitable come-uppance. Gallagher spooned his porridge, indifferent.

"But never you mind, Mr. Gallagher," she continued, head tilted sideways knowingly, "because, unlikely as it might seem on such short notice, we've been able to find a replacement that I think surpasses Anthony House in *every* respect." She waved in greeting to Amanda and Elyse at a table across the way. "And I daresay you'll share my enthusiasm once you've seen it. I'm a silver-linings person myself, Mr. Gallagher," she said, tapping the table for emphasis, "so bring on all the dark clouds you like, I say, because they, too, will pass and all will be for the best in the end." She looked as though she might break out singing "The White Cliffs of Dover."

"Aye," he said, pleased for her in her hopeless naïveté.

"But I'm not going to breathe another word about the garden we'll be seeing—I want it to be a grand surprise for you. Oh, I can't wait to see the look on your face!" She was brimming with mischievous glee. "Now I'd best go find Declan, so he'll know there's a new route to drive." She pushed back her chair, reclaimed her scattered possessions, and bustled away. Bemused, Gallagher watched her scuttle across the dining room, then poured some tea from his cup onto its saucer, blew across it, and gently sipped.

JUST as Wilburn had predicted, Ballybroggin Garden up near Trim caught Gallagher completely off guard. He'd sat quietly during the coach ride out, unmoved by Bonnie's tender smile and how she'd touched his shoulder softly with her fingertips as she passed him in the coach. Unmoved by the soft green fields and tidy farms of County Meath, by Michael Wickerson's too obvious attempts to cheer him up. But the garden undid him completely.

They were greeted at the front gate by the Kavanaghs, Niall and Sile, a handsome young couple dressed for gardening and radiant with wholesome vitality. "This is Mr. Gallagher," Wilburn introduced him to them as though he were Albert Einstein.

"I can't tell you what a thrill this is for us." Niall shook Gallagher's hand, holding it for a moment in both of his. Tall, with a mop of unruly red hair, Niall smiled down at Gallagher with undisguised admiration.

"Oh, I think I'm going to faint!" Sile mimicked a Victorian lady's swoon. She was a small and slender young woman with the sleek black hair and dark eyes of the true Celt. Her pantomime was all in good fun, everyone beaming and laughing, although Gallagher had no idea why. The way the rest of the tour group was hovering around, it was obvious everybody was expectantly in on some secret that he didn't know.

"Now you must indulge me just this once, Mr. Gallagher," Wilburn said, laying both hands on his arm, "and close your eyes."

"What for?" He was hardly seeing anything anyway he was in such a stupor, but he didn't want to close his eyes in front of them all. He'd had his fill of secrecy for the time being, and of sudden disclosures as well.

"Never you mind," Wilburn said, almost maternally. "Just do as I say: close your eyes tight and keep them closed until I tell you to open them." Mystified, Gallagher reluctantly did as he was told. "Niall and Sile will guide you along," Wilburn reassured him, "and you'll be perfectly safe, all right?"

Gallagher nodded, his eyes closed, feeling a bit of the fool, as though the butt of a childish birthday party game. He felt a pair of hands take him gently by each forearm. Together they moved forward a few feet, then around a corner, down a single shallow step, then forward again for a bit, crunching on gravel. "Are you all right, then, Mr. Gallagher?" Niall asked him as they shuffled along.

"Fine," Gallagher said, still wondering what the hell this foolery was all about.

"Just a wee bit farther," Sile said, pressing her shoulder softly against his. He could hear the group tittering and gasping behind him.

Then, with his eyes still closed, he gradually became immersed in heavenly scents. Sublime and wonderfully familiar fragrances were wafting all around him. Honeyed and spicy and musky perfumes greeted him. Traces of tender memories flickered among familiar essences in the air. He felt his spirit, his poor battered and bruised spirit, soaring like a skylark through the sweetly evocative fragrances. It was as though he floated upon a bouquet of scented dreams.

"I think you can open your eyes now," Niall said to him softly.

Gallagher resisted leaving the dark dreaminess of perfumed air, then slowly opened his eyes. He felt his heart lurch inside its cage as he beheld a rose garden not at all unlike his own. He paused for a moment, uncomprehending, and then stepped forward. Yes, unbelievably, here was Sophia's Lips radiant in all her carmine glory. He took a bloom in his hand, bent over to inhale its ineffable perfume, and then kissed its petals tenderly. Right next to her was Raunchy Rachel, so heartbreakingly lovely. And Nicole's Knickers, with her plum-coloured, sullen velvet petals. It was a miracle of sorts, dozens of his roses all blooming fulsomely. Far smaller than his specimens at home, yes, but his own dear beauties nevertheless.

Gallagher nearly collapsed beneath the impact of unexpectedly beholding his lovelies all these miles from home. Sensing his unsteadiness, Sile and Niall gently took hold of his arms again, although as much now in companionship as in support. Several of the group were taking photos of the trio. Carla was capturing the scene on video.

"How?" Gallagher asked, glancing from one to the other young gardener, amazed.

"We have a very dear friend over in Victoria," Sile said, smiling. "She's a great admirer of your introductions and insisted we must have them for our garden. Since they're not available here yet, she arranged to have a number of them shipped to us and, as you can see, they've taken to life here splendidly."

"They're tremendous," Gallagher said.

"These are the only specimens in Ireland, so far as we know," Niall said, "but everyone who's seen them is mad for them. Of course, we'd never propagate them without first discussing it with you, sir, which is another reason we were so delighted to have you visit us today."

Nodding, but still in a bewilderment, Gallagher detached himself and moved slowly from them into a bed of roses. He took a bloom of Michelle's Mischief gently in his hand, holding its full cup of glossy cerise, feeling the heartbreaking softness of her petals. He'd been working with her, he remembered, the very moment Wendy Trang came into his life and his long sojourn to this moment began. He stared intently into the deep mysteries contained within the chalice of beauty. Warm tears coursed down his cheeks and his heart was crushed between love and anguish.

▫ TWENTY-FOUR ▫

THAT AFTERNOON the group was "at leisure," leaving people free to do whatever they chose on their final day in Dublin. All would reconvene in the evening for a traditional farewell dinner. The day had turned gloomy, with a leaden grey sky lurking above the city. As arranged, Sheehy's man picked Gallagher up at the hotel. They crossed to the north side and headed along the Liffey and then through a maze of derelict buildings, parking lots, and construction sites. Gallagher sat in the back seat, staring out the window, saying nothing. The driver, pinched and dour, with a fag hanging from the corner of his mouth, didn't speak either. Within the confines of the car, each of them sat in unremitting isolation.

The car pulled over and stopped in a rundown block and the driver handed Gallagher a piece of paper with an address scrawled on it in pencilled block letters. The driver tilted his head to indicate the direction Gallagher should take, then turned away from him. The second Gallagher was out of the car, it sped away from the curb with a squeal of rubber.

He set off down the street, observed by thick-faced women at front doors and windows. A row of young toughs lined along the graffiti-smeared brick wall of a derelict factory looked him over as he passed, snorting assinine comments that Gallagher didn't bother to hear. Two drunks stood in an alley, each with an arm extended straight against a wall, pissing copiously. Farther on, by a rusty iron paling, a cluster of teenage girls, smoking cigarettes and looking for trouble, strutted their arrogant buttocks and thighs in skin-tight denim. "Hey, Popeye, lookin' fer some fun, are yer?" one of them jeered at him and the others shrieked at her brilliance. They might have been seagulls screaming on a sandbar for all the attention Gallagher paid them.

He came to the address he'd been given. An old wooden door, painted jaunty blue decades ago, the paint now chipped and peeling. The bay window in front had iron bars across it; where a pane of glass was missing, a sheet of murky plastic had been stapled in its place. The brickwork of the housefront hadn't been painted for several lifetimes

254

and the red bricks sagged as though exhausted. Gallagher twisted an old brass doorbell on the wall, but it made no sound. He rapped firmly on the door, which instantly drew a dog lunging against its inside and snarling fiercely. Somebody shouted and the dog yelped as though it had been kicked. There were shuffling noises, then a rattling at the door as bolts were withdrawn. The door opened a crack and a bloated face—whether of a man or woman Gallagher couldn't tell—eyed him suspiciously, then muttered, "Wait here."

The door banged shut and was rebolted. Gallagher stared at the blistered and peeling paint, sensing the desolation of the place, the palpable hopelessness to be found at the bottom.

After a few minutes the bolts slid back again and the door swung inwards onto a squalid hallway. An exhalation of foul odour brooded in the hallway air. A cardboard parcel, about twenty inches square, sat on a tattered rug in front of him. An obese body in grubby sweats— whether male or female he still couldn't tell—was shuffling away from him into the gloom of the hallway. The dog snarled and barked behind a door at the far end of the corridor. "Taxi's on its way," mumbled the figure. "Shut the door when you leave."

Gallagher stooped and picked up the parcel—it weighed perhaps fifteen pounds—then withdrew awkwardly through the doorway and closed the door. The instant he did so, he could hear the dog race barking down the corridor and lunge snarling against the door. As he turned to the street, a cab came speeding along and screeched to a halt where he stood.

"Hop in, mate," the driver called through his window, "quick." Gallagher pushed the parcel onto the back seat and climbed in beside it. The cab accelerated away.

"Dirty piece of town, eh?" the cabbie said, glancing back in his rearview mirror.

"Yeah."

"Don't get many calls down here. Don't want to."

"Can't blame you." They went speeding past the graffiti-covered wall where the young toughs still hung about.

"Someone should knock all this shite down and hose the vermin out into the bay," the cabbie said with a banishing gesture.

"Suppose so."

"Stanton's on the south side, is it?" Another glance in the rear-view mirror.

"That's right."

"More my cup of tea," the cabbie said. "People with a bit of decency at least, which is more than you can say about the scumbuckets in this pigsty."

Gallagher sat silent, remembering the roses from the morning.

BACK at the hotel, Nuala agreed to put the parcel in storage for him until tomorrow. "Oh, and there was an urgent phone call for you, Mr. Gallagher, not more than thirty minutes ago. I suggested the caller leave a message for you on your room phone. You might want to check it now."

"I will, thanks," said Gallagher. He wondered who the message might be from. Not likely Sheehy. Maybe the guards. Or Wilburn. No message now could be of much importance.

"Ah, Gallagher!" Michael Wickerson was descending the stairs. He was wearing blue jeans and a rust-coloured woollen sweater that show-cased his boyish good looks. "Just the person I need to see. Do you have a moment?"

"Sure I do," said Gallagher.

"Let's have a coffee, shall we?" Michael laid a hand casually on Gallagher's shoulder and steered him towards the café. They sat with their coffees at a small table by a window. "That was a lovely episode this morning, Gallagher," Michael said with obvious sincerity, "seeing you with your roses. I was very moved by it."

"Yes, it was very touching," Gallagher said.

Michael looked a trifle uncomfortable about what he had to say. "I just wanted to clear up a few small things with you, Gallagher, before our farewell gala this evening." He smiled ingratiatingly and ran a hand through his silken hair.

"What things need clearing up?"

"I wanted to tell you about Elyse and myself."

"What about you?"

"You remember asking me to see if I would break the ice a bit there on your behalf?" Despite his best effort to sound cheerily offhand, Michael was plainly uneasy.

"Sure." None of this mattered to Gallagher anymore.

"Well, I did as you asked . . ."

"Yeah?"

"Well, the long and short of it is," he said, looking away through the window at nothing. "Damn it, Gallagher, the long and short of it is that Elyse and I have grown rather fond of each other over the course of the week."

"Have you?" Gallagher had suspected as much.

"Yes we have. And, well, that investment opportunity I mentioned to you earlier . . ."

"Yes?"

"You know, the Coal Harbour condo Elyse was going to sell?" Michael was avoiding looking directly at Gallagher.

"Right." Gallagher's mind was wandering off to who the urgent call might be from and whether he should be attending to it straightaway rather than listening to Wickerson's self-justification.

"The thing is, I'm sorry to have to tell you that's not going to happen. I mean, Elyse has changed her mind and isn't going to sell it just now after all."

"No?"

"No. You see, actually, actually I'm going to move in there myself for the time being."

"Is that so?"

"Yes." Wickerson looked more sheepish by the minute.

"What about your house with the garden you promised your wife you'd keep up in her memory?"

"Yes, well, truth to tell, that was—what would we call it?—a wee bit of an exaggeration on my part."

"An exaggeration?"

"Yes. In point of fact my wife didn't die." Michael was toying nervously with an earlobe as though tuning an old transistor radio. "That is, she died in a way, for me anyhow. No, it was more that we separated. We'll be divorcing soon."

"Okay." Michael was fading into irrelevance by the minute.

"But I didn't want to air all that dirty laundry in the group, you know? Too depressing. So I thought a little white lie, about Rose-Anne dying, would be quite excusable, all things considered."

Gallagher mused over the proposition that news of death might be less unsettling than divorce. Try telling that to the old ones eking out their final years in remote and lonely cottages, listening through the long nights of winter to the wailing of the *Ben-sidhe* drawing near. Tell it to the famine victims whose restless spirits still wander the roadways by night. Your poncey little literary divorce might be too depressing in comparison. Sure. His initial instinct about Wickerson had proven sound. The truth of the matter was that Wickerson was along on the tour to improve his own prospects, by lying if necessary, just as Gallagher himself had been. But Michael had succeeded where he had failed. The old Gallagher might have been bitter, might have railed against this polished imposter who'd usurped him. But that old Gallagher was gone. His skin was here, his shell, but inside he might as well have been stuffed with straw.

He excused himself as soon as he could, on the legitimate grounds that he had an important phone message to attend to. Climbing the stairs to his room he felt a fleeting sense of satisfaction that the elegant and accomplished Michael Wickerson was at heart a schemer no better than himself, in fact worse insofar as Michael's duplicities were successful. But this was a small twig of gratification amid a forest of misery.

Gallagher pressed the message button flashing on his bedside phone. "Hello, Patrick." It was Bosco's Voice of the Living Dead, a voice that Gallagher had not thought to hear again. "I'm sorry to disturb you, and I imagine that you would prefer no further communication from me. However I felt compelled to advise you that Francie O'Sullivan has been rushed to hospital. A failed suicide attempt, I'm sorry to say. She's at the acute medical admissions ward at Saint James's. I thought you should know, Patrick. She'll be in my thoughts and prayers today. I regret that we parted last evening on such poor terms. I shall keep you in my prayers too, dear brother. Goodbye."

The message ended and, after a click, a robot woman's voice advised Gallagher that he had no new messages. He sat on the side of the bed and listened to the sounds of things falling. Everything breaking apart, collapsing to the ground in dust and rubble.

Nuala ordered a taxi for him and he set off straightaway for the hospital.

AT the nursing station Gallagher, who had identified himself as Francie's former husband, was given a brief summary of her condition by a friendly but harried nurse. Apparently Francie had suffered a bad drug experience during which she'd slashed her wrists and almost bled to death. The medics had stanched the bleeding and her stomach had been pumped, but the doctors were not optimistic that she had sufficient resources to recover. She was chronically malnourished and was suffering from severe kidney and liver damage. Whatever could be done for her they had done; she was now heavily sedated and not in pain. A man who'd accompanied her in the ambulance—probably Danno, Gallagher thought—had gone beserk and was eventually restrained and removed by the police.

A young nurse showed him into a cluttered ward and to a bed on which the wreckage of Francie was lying. Her emaciated arms lay outside the sheets, their wrists heavily bandaged. Several clear tubes fed liquids into one arm. An oxygen tube was attached to her nostrils, but she seemed scarcely to breathe at all; the sheets covering her skinny torso hardly rose or fell with her breathing. Although she was comatose, her eyes were wide open, staring blankly at the ceiling. Gallagher would have taken her for dead had a screen above the bed not indicated that her heart still beat.

He sat in a chair alongside the bed. The clatter of comings and goings in the wards and corridors faded away. He was alone with Francie, as alone as he'd been with her in the sea cave when they'd pledged undying love to each other all those years ago. Reaching out, he took her hand in his. The cold hand was all fragile bones, like the body of a small bird. He held her slender, ravaged fingers tenderly and willed that his lifeblood might flow into hers, willed that she might come back from the precipice. A plaintive longing filled his heart, that they could be children together again, angels of innocence, subsumed in the guileless discoveries of first love. Oh, Francie, he moaned to himself, oh, Francie.

How long he sat there, wrapped in memories and longings, holding Francie's hand, he didn't know. Nor did he know at what moment the screen above them ceased registering a heartbeat. No rescue team rushed in to try resuscitate her with shouting and pounding and electric jolts. Francie had slipped away as a phantom does, leaving an emaciated corpse, with Gallagher still holding its lifeless hand, awash in remembrances and regrets.

ESCAPING from the hospital, he wandered for miles through the city, restlessly, aimlessly, seeing and hearing nothing. He went over and over again in his mind that final encounter he'd had with Francie in his hotel room, trying to align that hideous creature with the girl he'd loved.

Eventually he found himself standing on Hoddington Road gazing up at the facade of a church. Although it was only yesterday that he'd denounced Bosco and his conniving fellow churchmen, the upswept lines of this building, its high bell tower and large rose window, offered a symmetry his spirit craved at the moment. Looking at the limestone walling, the granite dressings, and carved tympana in sandstone, he felt a pressing need to take sanctuary within the church. Tentatively he tried the big front door, found it unlocked, pushed it open and entered. There was a solemn hush within. All the lines of the nave surged skyward, everything light, shining, soaring. In dazed wonderment he wandered up the central aisle, then knelt for a while at the communion rail, gazing at the high altar of gleaming white stone in which twin kneeling angels were carved. He looked at the golden tabernacle and the slender golden candlesticks, at the semicircle of tall stained-glass windows that lined the rear of the apse. The pointed arches of the apse met high above his head in a Gothic Revival celebration of transcendence. He studied the magnificent rose window of Our Lady and the Four Evangelists, its dramatic cross with the sun at its centre, the evangelists each in his own circle, and the Blessed Virgin above them. Even on this dull afternoon the colours of the glass glowed brilliantly.

As he made his way along a side aisle, he glanced at the Stations of the Cross on the wall, the figures depicting various events as Christ carried His cross to the hill of crucifixion. Jesus Falls the First Time.

Jesus Meets His Mother Mary. The *Via Crucis*, the *Via Dolorosa*, the Way of Sorrows. Fairy tales he'd called it only days ago, old religious rubbish. Partway along, he paused in front of a confessional. Whether it was any longer used he didn't know, but there was neither priest nor penitent in it today. He glanced around the near-deserted church—there were only a few old women in black mumbling their rosaries in hidden corners—and then opened the confessional door and slipped inside. In the dark and confined space he had to grope to find the cushioned kneeler. There was a musty smell of old sins in the box. He knelt, staring at the dark grid in front of his face, almost expecting that at any minute the dividing screen would slide back, revealing the dim outline of a Father Confessor. But the darkness and silence held.

What would he confess? Not the silly misdemeanours of childhood—the stealings and lyings and using profanities—that he'd catalogued each Saturday afternoon at their parish church in a confessional just like this one. He'd never confessed that time of lying naked with Francie in the cave because he knew in the Church's judgement it would have been a mortal sin of the most heinous type. But for him it was never a sin, quite the opposite, it was a holy act, a sacrament, and it would have been a betrayal of himself and of Francie, and of their love, if he had degraded that sacred moment by naming it a sin. But what had followed was sinful for certain. Not the sex or the pregnancy, those were not sins either, he was sure of it. But everything after—the planned abortion, stealing from his parents, and, worst of all, the abandonment of Francie—those were surely sins, misdeeds that had blackened his soul and eventually led to poor Francie lying dead in a hospital bed. These were crimes he could confess. "Bless me, Father, for I have sinned . . ." he muttered into the disappearing darkness. "Bless me, Father, for I have sinned." Over and over again he mumbled the familiar incantation. "Bless me, Father, for I have sinned."

⬚ TWENTY-FIVE ⬚

ON SUNDAY morning Gallagher had no desire to say farewell to anyone in the group. Although he felt an unaccustomed affection towards them, sparked in part by appreciation of how generously they'd delighted with him in the visit to Niall and Sile's rose garden yesterday, there was none among them he wished ever to see again. The previous evening the coach had carried them along the north shore of Dublin Bay out to the little village of Howth where their traditional farewell dinner—what Sheehy had called their Last Supper—was held at a large pub. Half a dozen other coaches were parked alongside as they drew up. The group entered a cavernous room jammed with long tables and chairs. A large group of German tourists clustered near the front were incongruously bellowing German singalong songs. Gallagher's heart would have sunk were it not already irretrievably sunken. He was present in name only. He could not look to Bonnie, nor to Michael. He fixed a vacant smile upon his face and laughed on cue and remained a million miles away. Toasts were made, including a flowery one to him by Michael Wickerson that might have been touching had he been close enough to touch. Wilburn and Declan were saluted, photographs were taken, plates of tasteless fish were devoured, a band of accomplished but compromised musicians played schmaltzy versions of "Danny Boy" and "Raglan Road." None too soon the coach returned them to their hotel. The tour was over. Everything was over.

To avoid any maudlin farewells this morning, he unplugged his phone, drew the curtains tight, and hung the Do Not Disturb sign on his door. Then he fell back into bed and pulled the covers over his head. He lay there, prostrate with despondency. He wondered whether those addled Catholics weren't maybe right after all, that this life is nothing more than a vale of tears made bearable only by belief in a better life to come in the hereafter. Perhaps he should have confessed his sins to Bosco, been shriven, forgiven, bathed in the Blood of the Lamb. Sure. This much he knew: You're born alone and you die alone, all the rest is just distraction along the route from one aloneness to another.

Sometime in the mid-afternoon, when he was certain that everyone was gone, he stirred himself. He called Givens to reconfirm the time and place of tonight's drop-off. "We'll be there," Givens assured him. He picked up the parcel from Nuala at the front desk and took it up to his room. He put it on the floor and sat on the edge of his bed staring at it. What the hell could be in the damn thing? He was tempted to open it, see what it contained, but it was wrapped and sealed so well, there was no way he'd be able to reseal it properly. Plus he didn't really give a shite. He curled up in his bed again and drifted into the kind of sleep from which some people never awaken.

He was startled out of sleep in darkness and fumbled for the bedside clock. Ten-thirty-three. Christ, he'd better be up and on his way. But his movements were like those of someone trying to climb out of quicksand. There was no spirit in him at all, not a flicker, as he lethargically put on his clothes and straightened up his appearance a bit. He still hadn't shaved today, nor would he. He made a cup of tepid tea from the electric kettle in his room and ate a shortbread biscuit the maid had left yesterday. There's my grand Dublin dinner, he thought bitterly. He put on his rain jacket, then took his brolly and the poxy parcel and left the hotel.

The streets were deserted. Light from street lamps and occasional passing cars gleamed mercury silver on wet pavement. The rain drummed down as it's been drumming down on bogsodden Ireland forever. He had a hell of a time trying to keep the bloody parcel from getting soaked. He should have put the damn thing in a plastic bag in the first place; it would have fit into the laundry bag in his room. Better still, he should have tossed it into the trash and told them all to hell with it. Nattering away to himself, he got to the corner of Kildare Street and Saint Stephen's Green North across from the Shelbourne and there he stood. Dark and disconsolate rain sloshed down upon him as he slouched under his umbrella. Gay laughter spilling from the bright lights of the Shelbourne across the way mocked him bitterly with a brilliance he knew in his cold bones would never be his.

He stood and stood. He could see no guards anywhere. Behind its iron palings Saint Stephen's Green cowered in shadows. He thought of the Shinners in the Risin' of '16 huddled behind shrubs in the park, taking futile potshots with antique rifles while the Brits raked them with machine gun fire and crushed them as surely as Cromwell had crushed them centuries before. Still, they'd made a stand at least, which was more than he could say for himself. Believed in something passionately enough to die in its service. He thought of the Countess Markevitz, her fierce womanhood bold against the tyrant. Then, despite himself, he thought of Bonnie. Rose-soft. Gone. And Francie, lying quietly in the embrace of death. Oh, Christ, the futility of it all!

He stood some more. Lights were gradually blinking out, the city turning over to sleep. His brain was still a roiling mass of shattered possibilities. All hope was dashed and trampled. Every fukkin' thing was dashed. He wasn't even going to think about it anymore. Still he stood, but Sheehy never showed. Nobody showed. He was tempted to leave the crapulous parcel right there in the street and walk away from the whole feckin' deal. But he remembered that the Gardai had his passport still, and even in his bitter despair he knew he'd best not muck it up. After more than an hour of waiting he gave it up as a mug's game and started walking back down Kildare Street still carrying the sodden parcel. What was going on, he wondered. Was this some elaborate game the guards were playing with him? Was it him they were really after, not Sheehy at all? Was Sheehy working with the guards, and would Gallagher now be apprehended with the incriminating parcel? There was no way of knowing who the hell was who.

As he trudged along, a sudden gust of wind got under his umbrella and blew it out. Cold raindrops pelted his head and slithered down the back of his neck. He struggled one-handed with the useless brolly and then in frustration flung it violently into the street. Finally the dam burst within him and his accumulated grief and rage erupted. "You fukkers!" he shrieked into the drenching darkness. "You fukkin' useless arsehole gobshites!" He meant everyone, friends and foes, lovers and losers, the whole useless pack of them. "You moronic goddamn fuckbuckets all of yis, get the fuck away out of here before I fukkin' . . ."

Suddenly a black van screeched to a halt right beside him. All in a flash the side door flew open, two big guys leapt out, seized the parcel from him before he knew what was happening, then grabbed him roughly by either arm and threw him into the back of the van. The sliding door slammed shut and the van screeched away into the night.

"Jaysus Christ!" yelped Gallagher, sprawling in the darkness. "Y'fukkin' near broke me arm, you bastards!"

"Shut the fuck up," growled a voice close beside him.

Gallagher could hardly see anything. "What the fuk's goin' on here?" he demanded, and then everything went blank.

WHEN he came to, his head was pounding like a jackhammer and he was blind. He lay sprawled on something springy and smelly, some mouldy old chesterfield maybe. His hands were tied together in front of him. He reached towards his face and felt the blindfold across it.

"Leave it on," said a man's gravelly voice. He couldn't tell if it was the same voice from the van or not. "Go tell him," the voice said to someone else. Footsteps clattered. A door rattled open and closed with a bang. Rain was drumming on the roof overhead, pellets hitting corrugated iron. The room felt cold and draughty.

"Where am I?" Gallagher asked. His throat was raw and dry.

"In shit," the voice sneered. "Now shut the fuck up."

The door rattled open again and footsteps entered the room. More than one person it seemed like. There was a whispered conversation Gallagher couldn't make out. He felt nauseated by the stench of mould.

"How are you, Mr. Gallagher?" A different man's voice, close beside him, soft but deeply resonant, like a radio voice.

"Oh, I'm fukkin' brilliant all trussed up here like a turkey in this shitpot. Who the fuk are you?"

"Mr. Gallagher," the voice said calmly, "I think perhaps the first thing we should establish between us is the advisability of your being civil and cooperative towards me, all right?"

"Civil? You're after me bein' civil when I'm treated like this?"

"Yes, I am," the voice said reasonably. "And you know why? Because I've got a lovely big pistol in my hand. Here, I'll let you feel it." The man drew close. His warm breath on Gallagher's face smelt of peppermint. Gallagher felt a cold metal point pressed against his temple, just above the blindfold. "If I were to pull this trigger," the voice said calmly, and there was a menacing click, "your brain—small as it is—would be splattered all over the wall across there. Do I make myself perfectly clear?"

"You do," Gallagher said trembling. Suddenly he felt a warm wetness spreading across his crotch and down his thigh. Jays, he'd pissed himself.

"Good," the voice said. "Now, if you'd be so kind, I'd like you to answer a few questions for me. How you answer them will determine whether you live or whether you die. Do you understand?"

"I do." What he couldn't understand was who his captors were. They could be Sheehy's thugs, or enemies of Sheehy, or undercover guards. Maybe Special Branch wankers. No way of knowing. One thing he knew: whoever they were, he was at their mercy.

"That's more like it then," the voice said reasonably. The muzzle of the gun retreated slightly, but he could sense it barely touching his temple. "Now tell me: what were you doing out on the street at midnight with that parcel?"

"I was delivering it to someone."

"To whom?"

Gallagher hesitated and the cold metal point pressed into his temple again. "A man."

"What man?"

"Named Sheehy."

"Joe Sheehy?"

"Yes."

"He a friend of yours?"

"Not exactly."

"But you know him?"

"I met him a couple a times."

"Had you known him before?"

"No." A suddenly ferocious gust of wind buffeted the building and set loose pieces of metal roofing rattling.

"He wasn't a pal of yours back in Ballydehob?"

"No. I don't remember him from there."

"And you never encountered him in connection with any other, let's say, activities?"

"No. Never."

"But you were bringing this parcel to him?"

"Yes, I was."

"Why?"

"He asked me to."

"Do you know what was in the parcel?"

"No, I have no idea."

"He didn't tell you?"

"No." Gallagher's wrists were raw from the rough cords cinched around them, but he remained utterly focused on the lethal interview.

"Did he tell you where it was coming from?"

"He didn't."

"Where did you get it from?"

"I picked it up from a place on the north side."

"Why would you agree to do that, to put yourself at risk that way?"

Again Gallagher hesitated and again the menacing muzzle pressed into his temple. He knew this might be his final answer. His final words. The power of inventiveness that had served him so well all these years had now deserted him entirely. He had no story to tell but the truth, kill him though it might. He wet his lips and spoke.

"The guards told me to."

"The police."

"Yes. They took my passport and they threatened me."

"Into delivering this parcel for them?"

"Yes."

"Did they know about Sheehy?" Somebody nearby—Gallagher couldn't tell if it was in this room or not—began coughing hoarsely, trying to clear his throat, then spat loudly with a shouted curse.

"Yes, they knew about him, all right."

"How did they connect you and Sheehy?"

"They knew Sheehy had talked to me on two different occasions in the pubs."

"So they had someone following him?"

"Or following me."

"Why would they want to follow you?"

"Fukked if I know. But they warned me at the airport when I came in that my movements would be under observation."

"Did they?"

"Yeah."

"Did they say why?"

"They took me for a Fenian."

"A Fenian?"

"That's right."

"Do you suspect that you were being kept under surveillance?"

"I know I was."

"How so?"

"I spotted a guy keeping an eye on me."

"You're sure?"

"Positive."

"So the guards used you as a courier to get this parcel to Sheehy?"

"Yes. They told me to give the parcel to no one but him."

"And why was that?"

"They said he was a criminal and a menace to society. That they'd been after him for years."

"So they were planning an entrapment?" The interrogator's voice remained uncannily calm and purposeful.

"I guess you could call it that."

"They were going to be there when you handed over the parcel?"

"They said they would."

"But they didn't show?"

"Nobody showed. They didn't and Sheehy didn't. Finally I said to hell with it and was heading back to my hotel when you fukkers grabbed me."

The gun again clicked by Gallagher's ear and he took a sharp inwards breath, waiting for annihilation. The last drops of piss drained out of him. "Am I mistaken, or did we not agree on *civil*, Mr. Gallagher?"

"We did. Sorry." He opened his eyes again behind the blindfold. He could hear the rain still beating on the roof and the breathing of his interrogator beside him. He couldn't tell if there were others in the room or not. The stench of rot was gagging.

"Now tell me, Mr. Gallagher, what are your political affiliations?"

"None."

"None at all?"

"No. I'm not a political person."

"But you were, once upon a time?" Gallagher hesitated. "Answer the question, Mr. Gallagher. Were you, or are you, sympathetic with the objectives of any Republican group—the Thirty-two County Sovereignty Movement, for example, or the IRA, or any of its splinter groups?"

Here was the question whose answer could bring a shining bullet exploding through his skull. He picked his words with utmost caution. "I'd like to see a united Ireland. And I'd like to see an end to the violence and the hatred."

"I see. Tell me about the cell in West Cork."

Oh, Christ. They knew. Suddenly all the pieces clicked lethally into place. That's why they'd grabbed him. That's what the whole bleedin' charade with Sheehy was really about. They'd come for their pound of flesh, the fukkers.

"Mr. Gallagher?"

"Aye, well, I used to muck about with a few of the lads back there in the old days."

"Doing what?"

"Sweet fuk all, really. We'd organize a bit of a rally now and then, if there was a speaker coming in. That sort of thing."

"What else?"

"Raising money mostly, for the lads up north. We'd put the squeeze on them's could afford it."

"And Dominic Farrell was a comrade of yours back then, was he not?"

"He was one of the group, yeah."

"Now correct me if I'm mistaken, but was there not an incident back then in which a certain amount of the brigade's funds disappeared mysteriously?"

Here it comes, thought Gallagher, I'm well and truly fukked.

"Well?" the voice was insistent.

"I did myself at one point have occasion to borrow a small sum from the coffers, if that's what you're referring to."

"How small a sum?"

"A few hundred punt as I remember."

"And why would you pilfer money from your comrades?"

"It was more like a loan. I was in a fix."

"What sort of fix?"

"I'd got a girl into trouble. I took the money to get her over to England."

"For an abortion?"

"Yes."

"She went then, did she?"

"No. Word got back to her father. He was a mad bastard at the best of times and he'd have torn me to pieces if I hadn't got the hell outta there."

"So you returned the brigade's money and left?"

"Not exactly, no."

"Well what exactly?"

"I used the funds to get away."

"Over to Canada?"

"Yes."

"And never repaid the debt?"

"I'd meant to, but between one thing and another . . ."

A long silence ensued. Gallagher couldn't tell what was going on. At last the voice resumed. "How long were you planning on remaining in Ireland?"

"A few more days. I'd had half a notion that I might go down to West Cork. But now . . . well."

Another pause. Rain battered relentlessly on the roof. "Is there any good reason you can think of, Mr. Gallagher, why I shouldn't blow your brains out right now and have your corpse thrown into a bog where you'll never be seen again?"

Gallagher thought for a minute. "Not really, no."

"None at all?"

"I've got no family, no kids or anything. No friends really either. Nobody would miss me. Nobody would even notice I was gone."

"That's pretty pathetic, isn't it?"

"Yea. I'm a worthless little arsehole really." He was making the admission more to himself than to his faceless interrogator. It was a self-assessment he'd lived with all his life but never so pointedly articulated. Now he'd said it, fully acknowledging the cold hole of loneliness in which he'd always lived. No, not always. Not when he was in Francie's arms, when they lay curled together, smooth as spoons, or walked side by side laughing and teasing. Then he'd been alive and everything had mattered.

"So, tell me, would you prefer I put you out of your misery? End it all for you right now?" Again the metal point pressed against his temple.

Gallagher pondered the offer. What more was there to lose when all was already lost. What was there worth clinging to when everything had been stripped away from him. He was down to the hard, cold core of himself. A pitiful insignificance. But not an evil person, not really. He'd meant no harm to anyone. Certainly not to Francie or Bosco or his parents. The fears. What was it Bosco had told him, talking about daft Saint Patrick on his mountain: the demons are the fears we carry in our hearts. The fears we carry in our hearts. Now, strangely, all terror was gone. The prospect of death—and surely this is the root of all fear—seemed not so dreadful after all. And what was there more to be feared than death? But not here. Not like this. "Well, to tell you the truth," he said, clearing his throat and moistening his lips, "all things considered, I'd rather go back home and at least see my roses one last time and have my ashes scattered under them. Lying in a cold wet bog for the rest of eternity doesn't appeal to me all that mightily."

The voice laughed softly, cynically perhaps, and again Gallagher steeled himself against the obliterating bullet. But instead, the cold steel point of death was withdrawn from his temple.

"Mr. Gallagher, we appreciate your cooperation here tonight. The information you've provided I think will prove extremely useful to us." Gallagher still couldn't figure out who these people were or what they wanted. The man laughed again, cynically. "I don't believe you have any idea what you got yourself involved in, do you?"

"In Ireland, that's what. And I should have known better. I did know better."

"Of course. Don't we all? Well, we can set you free of that at least."

"You're letting me go?" He couldn't tell how he felt about this. He should have been exultant with relief, but he wasn't. Although he had no belief in an afterlife, the embrace of death, with its promise of liberation from the striving, was strangely hard to pull away from. To just let go, as Francie had, to be no more, had an immensely comforting allure.

"Not exactly, no. But in exchange for your cooperation tonight we will do you the service of taking you where you need to go."

"Where's that?"

His question went ignored. "And we'll keep your parcel, with thanks, if that's all right with you."

"I never want to see the fukkin' thing again."

"Now, Mr. Gallagher, listen to me very carefully, all right?"

"Yeah."

"Tonight never happened, all right? You were never picked up or taken anywhere or asked any questions by anyone. Do you understand?"

"Yeah."

"I hope you do. Don't slip up in this regard, Mr. Gallagher."

"But what about the parcel? I'll have to explain what I did with it."

"True enough. You could simply say you were mugged on the street, knocked unconscious, and when you came to, the parcel was nowhere to be seen."

"Aye, that sounds all right."

"But let me repeat myself. One thing is certain: if you breathe a word of this meeting to anyone, in any way, I promise you that I or one of my associates will hunt you down wherever you are and put a bullet through your brain without a moment's hesitation. Do I make myself perfectly clear?"

"I understand."

"Excellent. Now I want you to drink this." He placed a cool glass between Gallagher's tied hands.

"What's in it?"

"Drink it, Mr. Gallagher. Our time together is done."

Gallagher gulped the vile liquid and within seconds felt a roaring darkness swamping him, dragging him down, down and away.

◙ TWENTY-SIX ◙

FOR COUNTLESS hours he seemed to be hurtling through darkness, jolted this way and that. He might have been sprawled on a flatbed speeding through an endless tunnel, racing towards the dark heart of the earth. He slithered back and forth between being semi-conscious and unconscious. Always there was a distant roaring and sometimes a rasp of metal grating against metal. Voices echoed far away. Darkness shattered now and again into incandescent shards of light.

Eventually he was tumbled into a cold dampness. He floundered through depths of murk. He was surely drowning in a bog; he could feel the dark bog water closing over him. He fought to get free, but was relentlessly pulled down, sucked into a dank cold. He couldn't breathe, couldn't fight free. He flailed and cried out and then was awake.

"Christ All Fucking Mighty!" he exclaimed, looking up, his legs trembling, the juices of panic and terror boiling in his brain. Touching his head, he felt a cold place on his temple where the muzzle of the gun had pressed against him. It was as though a sharp steel point had pierced the bone of his skull. Where the hell was he?

Outside somewhere. He was outdoors, sprawled on damp grass in a meadow. Uncomprehending, he stared at the grass beside his face. Glazed with silvery dew, each blade glistened like spilled mercury in the aqueous light of dawn. Spiderwebs strung among tall seed stalks glimmered with beaded patterns of liquid silver. Off to the east he could see a pale blush of pink brushed across the underbelly of lowering dark clouds. The terrors of the dark withdrew, leaving him sluggish and spent. Slowly he pulled himself up to a sitting position and there, straight ahead of him, he saw the mountain. It loomed before him, perfectly conical, its summit shrouded in cloud. He sat staring at the massive bulk of it, dimly aware of what it was, though he'd never seen it before. Perhaps in pictures, perhaps in dreams. The Reek. *Croag Padraig*.

Unable to take his gaze from it, he felt the mountain call to him. His flesh, the marrow of his bones, rather than his brain, registered that the mountain was drawing him to itself. Shivering in the clammy morning air, he got unsteadily to his feet. Every part of him ached with weariness. He shook his head, trying to clear the mist from his mind. Some distance away, sheep grazed languidly on the pewter green meadow. There was no actual thought in his mind, only a dim instinctual impulse that urged him towards the mountain—an instinct towards completion that was to be found only on the stony heights ahead of him. Cold and damp as he was, clothed only in trousers and a shirt, exhausted and hungry, he would not seek shelter in any warm, safe haven. Something deeper than creature comfort drove him. He would climb the mountain, to find himself or lose himself forever.

He bent and unlaced both his shoes and then kicked them off, one and then the other. Awkwardly he raised a leg and peeled off a sock. Then the other. He was ready. His gaze fixed upon the sacred mountain, he wobbled forward on unsteady legs, leaving behind him a trail of dark footprints outlined in the silver grass.

Gradually his limbs began to loosen, his stride to lengthen. He could feel the crush of cool, damp grass beneath his bare feet. The scent of wet greenery came to him. Away off to his left, the sheep cropped their grass contentedly, paying him no attention. Abruptly, out of nowhere, a sudden swooping curlew cried a plaintive note and disappeared into the greyness of sky. The pink hint of dawn had been swallowed in brooding cloud, and daylight advanced only in grudging increments. A thin cold wind began probing his flesh for entry. He walked on, thinking of nothing, aware only of the animal sensations of his body. All words had left him.

He came to a low stone wall that was crumbling from decades of neglect. The weathered boulders were crusted with golden and ochre lichens. He ran his fingertips across their coarse, grainy surfaces. A sudden movement caught his eye a short distance along the wall. Some furtive, quick creature—a stoat, or weasel perhaps—gone instantly, more not-seen than seen. He undid his fly and relieved himself against the wall. Vaguely he remembered something—pissing himself, yes, he'd pissed himself when the death-threatening pistol had touched him. The wind buffeted him, sharp with hints of hawthorn and heather. He felt a throbbing in his brain like the insistent beating of a bodhran.

Something was arising within him, he could feel it, a thrumming expectancy.

He crossed a second meadow, larger than the first, and scrambled over another low wall. He sensed that he had arrived at the beginning of the pilgrims' way. A few steps on, a ghostly statue of white stone loomed before him at *Tobair Padraig*. He recognized his patron saint, his namesake, hand raised to the sky while clasping a tri-partite clover. For a long time he stood staring up at the spectral statue, dumbfounded by its stony power. Mad Patrick and his demons. His abiding faith in Divine Truth.

From this point a rough track led off through the heather. The path was littered with cobbles and abraded by small troughs from heavy rains. There was no pilgrim but himself to be seen on it. Was he truly a pilgrim, and, if so, what was the point of his pilgrimage? Far off, perhaps over the distant waters of Clew Bay, he heard the cries of seabirds sounding in the thin morning air.

He set off along the pilgrims' walk. The stones and rough surfaces of the path jabbed fiercely at the soles of his bare feet. His shoes and socks were left far behind in the meadow. As he continued walking, he became more accustomed to the pain. Where was it he had been, not all that long ago—oh, yes, that church, the Stations of the Cross, the *Via Dolorosa*, the Way of Sorrows. And daft Bosco somewhere in there too, rhapsodizing about angels.

As he continued along the pathway, suddenly swarms of small green flies attacked him, fiercely biting his neck and face. He swatted at that them uselessly. "Jesus Christ, give over, will you!" he shouted at the fiendish insects and hurried on.

Off to his right, he saw the deep combe known as *Log ne nDeamhan*, scratched like a scar up the mountain's northeast face. After what seemed an eternity of trudging gradually upward, he came to the end of a saddle where the path connected with the original Patrick's Causeway. From here he could see to the north the mountainside sloping downwards towards Clew Bay. Away to the south rose the dark lonely hills and mountains of the Murrisk. Still there was no pilgrim to be seen. After several deep breaths he set off up the wide causeway. Dully he noticed that along the way pilgrims had spelled out their names or initials using small stones to form the letters. He had no thought to do so himself; he might not have known what to write.

When he arrived at *Leacht Benain*, the pilgrim's first station, he didn't stop to read its plaque or perform the prescribed penitential ritual of reciting seven *Ave Marias* and seven *Paternosters* while circling the cairn seven times. He had no prayers to say. Nor a god to say them to.

A little farther on, he paused to rest before commencing the final steep push to the summit. Slowly he lowered himself to the ground and sat on the cold earth, leaning against a jagged rock. His feet were lacerated brutally from the stones and were bleeding freely. His mouth and throat were parched with thirst, but he had no water. He was no longer cold or hungry. All around him the wind combed miserably through tufts of scrub heather that clung to stony ground alongside the path. Far below, grazing sheep were tiny white dots against the grey-green fields. Sullen black clouds buffeted one another across the sky. A part of him longed not to move again, to cease the struggle there and then.

But move he must. He could feel a pressure growing inside him, ready to burst. The summit pulled at him, as oceans are drawn by the moon. Doggedly he pushed himself to his feet, finding his limbs and joints had stiffened during the rest. Taking a deep breath, he set his shoulders back and began the final climb up *Casan Padraig*, the steep and stony summit path. Again the biting flies attacked him fiercely and sharp loose shards of the scree jabbed mercilessly at his feet. Sometimes he slid on mossy or muddy patches and had to grope with his hands for purchase. His fingers too were torn and bleeding. As the bank grew steeper, he was forced to balance and probe and grapple his way forward, with a single step often taking several minutes to accomplish.

Suddenly the clouds came down around him. Within a few moments he was entirely engulfed in a grey bafflement of shifting mist. He could see nothing beyond a few feet from himself in any direction. An abyss might await his next step. But standing in the ghostly clouds, feeling their cold metallic moisture on his face, he felt no fear. He saw the clouds for what they were, portals through which he must pass. A deathly silence descended with the clouds, obliterating all sense of any world beyond. Even the wheeze of his laboured breathing and the scrape of his hands and feet scrabbling across the stones were muted. All was held in silent suspense.

He continued to claw his way upward, barely able to make out the pathway before him. He was down on his hands and knees now, an animal, instinct alone driving him forward. When the steep slope gave way to more level ground, he realized that he had arrived at the summit. The dark shapes of several small buildings huddled together, scarcely visible in the mist. Ignoring them, he found a somewhat level spot, where he collapsed and rolled over onto his back. His breath was coming in gasping pants. Blood dripping from his torn feet and hands formed small black stains on the stony ground.

Rough thoughts drifted through his mind, vaporous as the mists above him. He pictured his patron saint sleeping here on a cold bed of stone, perhaps in this very spot, exposed to the bitter elements as part of an endless penance. He saw the holy man, strengthened by mortification of the flesh, rising to do battle with his demons. The heinous black birds coming down all around him, obliterating the sun, determined to drive their enemy mad and thwart his evangelizing. And the saint's fierce resistance to them, his repeated battles with the creatures of darkness and how eventually he routed them. And how an angel appeared to him to announce a list of benefices obtained from the Almighty, one of them being that whoever recited Saint Patrick's Prayer in a penitential spirit at the moment of dying would be carried directly to heaven.

But then his thoughts drifted further back, across the many centuries during which the pagan god *Crom Dubh* dwelt in this sacred place and the harvest festival of Lughnasa was celebrated on the mountain. Centuries of pilgrimage when childless women would sleep on the summit on the night before Lughnasa in order that they might conceive. It was the pagan deity's lusty influence *Padraig* had sought to overthrow.

Lying on the earth, he thought he could see distant figures moving vaguely within the cloud mist: celebrants, believers and seekers, pilgrims by the thousands toiling up the mountain barefoot, some on their knees, sometimes by night when their massed candles made a ribbon of light all down the mountainside. Each of them maintaining faith in one god or another. He heard their muffled voices murmuring prayers.

Ancient incantations echoed through the mist. Old crones, dressed all in black, muttered their prayers or curses. He caught glimpses of familiar faces among the throng—young Francie, or perhaps it was Bonnie, the image obscured before he could make it out clearly; his mother too, surely that was her with bowed head murmuring her rosary, glimpsed, then lost in the mist. For a moment he imagined he was lying naked in the sea cave with Francie. He could feel her body pressed against his own, the warmth of it against the coldness of stone. He could hear the gentle shush of waves against pebbles and, mingled in with it, fairy music, the *Ceol-sidh*. Cold tears were running down his cheeks. Then he heard the cries of birds drawing closer, or perhaps it was the wailing of the *Ben-sidhe*. But he knew in his heart that their lamentations were not for him. It was the sorrows of the world they mourned, the sorrows of loss far greater and more painful than his own. His demons were fled; his spirit was at peace. Even as the darkness intensified and the spectral figures crowded in around him, he felt no fear. At the very moment of emergence, he had a sudden beatific vision of a parent rose, stripped of its petals and anthers, naked, awaiting the kiss of life-bearing pollen.

ACKNOWLEDGEMENTS

MY THANKS to Bord Fáilte, the Irish tourism authority, for generous assistance with accommodation. And to Donna Dawson of icangarden.com, for dispatching me to Ireland in the first place. Also to the many accomplished Irish gardeners whose fine gardens I was privileged to visit.

My late father, Tom Kennedy, a son of County Down, originally provided several of the tales retold herein.

I greatly appreciate publisher Ruth Linka and her staff at Brindle & Glass for having faith in the story and for being so entirely fine to work with throughout.

Heartfelt thanks to Jack Hodgins, who edited the work with a lovely combination of respect, enthusiasm, and profound insight. Collaborating with this eminent writer and teacher was pure pleasure.

And, as always, huge gratitude to my companion, Sandy, for her supportive affection throughout the writing.

▫ ▫ ▫

Among the many books I found useful in this writing, these were especially so:

Roses by Leonard Hollis

Rebel Hearts: Journeys within the IRA's soul by Kevin Toolis

Ireland Her Own: An Outline History of the Irish Struggle by T.A. Jackson

Inishkillane: Change and Decline in the West of Ireland by Hugh Brody

Irish Stories and Tales edited by Devin A. Garrity

Paddy & Mr. Punch: Connections in English and Irish History by R.F. Foster

Book of Ireland edited by Frank O'Connor

Whoredom in Kimmage: Irish Women Coming of Age by Rosemary Mahoney

ALSO BY DES KENNEDY

Fiction
The Garden Club
Flame of Separation

Non-Fiction
Living Things We Love to Hate
Crazy About Gardening
An Ecology of Enchantment
The Passionate Gardener

DES KENNEDY is the author of four books of essays and two other novels. His book *Crazy About Gardening* was nominated for the 1995 Stephen Leacock Memorial Medal for Humour, as was his first novel, *The Garden Club and the Kumquat Campaign* (1996), nominated for the 1997 Leacock Medal. His third Leacock nomination, in 2007, was for his most recent book, *The Passionate Gardener*. Noted as one of the most influential personalities in the Canadian gardening scene, Des writes a regular column for *GardenWise* magazine and is a celebrated speaker, having performed at numerous conferences, schools, festivals, botanical gardens, art galleries, garden shows, and wilderness gatherings in Canada and the United States. His humour, irreverence, and passion for gardening and the natural world have made him a must-see speaker in demand across the country. His work has appeared on a variety of regional and national television and radio programs that include eight years as a weekly columnist for the national CBC television program *Midday*; a broadcast on Discovery TV of his one-hour documentary of his book *Living Things We Love to Hate*; and Home & Garden TV's *Recreating Eden* series, which featured Des in a gardener's profile. Des lives with his partner, Sandy, on Denman Island, BC.